Pu Humans

Volume 1 of the Deva Chronicles

Bob Moore

All events depicted within the book are
entirely fictional and any similarity to any person
alive or dead is purely coincidental

My grateful thanks to Lois Bennett for the cover artwork

Jim Hough for cover design

And to The Kings School, Chester for information provided.

For my old mate Leo

And all cats everywhere

I

April 11th 1970

"Houston we've had a problem." Were the first words of concern Apollo thirteen's Commander, Jim Lovell was heard to utter by mission control. Prior to that, there was an exchange of panic and profanity between the three man crew.

Outside the command module, considerably more chaos was ensuing. The rupturing of an external oxygen tank had caused the *Odyssey*, still connected to the *Aquarius* to corkscrew wildly.

Careering in the opposite direction was the wreckage of a Vecigian, deep space pet food carrier. The unannounced appearance of an invisible vortex had taken the alien ship completely by surprise, drawing it toward the swirling heart

With considerably more thrust at its disposal, the Human ship was initially unaffected until the Vecigian craft slammed into it. Without power, out of control and badly misshapen, the once majestic vessel, no larger than a cigarette packet drifted into the expanding eddy, accompanied by the debris from the oxygen tank and many thousands of tons of random stellar matter. This included a top secret Soviet tracking satellite crewed entirely by mentally enhanced Moles and countless radio transmissions, one of which included the day's football result. Most notably though, was a telephone conversation from a distraught Misters Keeble, pleading with her daughter to come to Basingstoke at once because her budgie Kevin had escaped from his cage and was currently being mercilessly harassed by next doors cat.

The disabled *Apollo XIII* craft moved out of range to fulfil its place in history, while doubling in size by the second, the anomaly interrupted normal space, absorbing everything it drew in. As quickly as it had appeared it calmed, expansion slowing until seemingly content it simply sat there, a few hundred miles across, silent and invisible.

II

September 2005

Superheated air molecules, unable to escape the objects descent, glowed brilliantly as it entered the Earth's mesosphere, the outer casing heating up to produce a white hot glow. Further and further it ploughed, trailing a comet like tail until without ceremony, it cleared the atmosphere and began a rapid cool down. The resulting falling star arced across the clear September sky, unavoidably obvious.

To the planet's inhabitants it aroused little more than the odd cursory exclamation of wonder or pointed finger. Even to the trained eye; those with the know-how, armed with cutting edge technology. Searching the cosmos for just the faintest fart of a sign that extra terrestrial intelligence existed, failed to register it as anything more than your everyday meteor.

Leo hadn't seen it either. He sat in the garden, his garden, transfixed by a pair of mating frogs. The spectacle of the randy *Ranatemporaria* had entirely removed all thoughts of returning to the house, his house, where his humans resided. Not to mention the bowl of fish, they would be his, *oh yes.*

Content with his lot, Leo wanted for nothing really. Not that he demanded much from life, just sleep, lots of it and a perpetually full food bowl. The latter wasn't forthcoming, but of the former he more than made up. It was on the back of one of these marathon-slumber sessions that he now found himself. Initially, he'd dozed off as the bright, hot thing in the sky began to warm things up, and besides a couple of breaks for food, he finally awoke when the evenings cooler air began to manifest itself. That, and the bizarre nips and squeals emanating from the amorous frogs.

Now aware, his overriding concern had been to find something to eat, but the curiosity of the amphibians was just too much to ignore. Unconcerned with their audience, the frogs continued, locked within the throes of passion before suddenly freezing, becoming as still as stone. The only indication that they were alive was the regular pulse, throbbing away on the side of their heads.

Alerted to something out of the ordinary, Leo scanned beyond the frogs, toward the movement of a bush at the gardens perimeter. Squinting into the darkness and shadows, he was witness to the emergence of an object he had never seen the like of before.

He thus became the first Earthling to ever encounter such an object. The fact that Leo was a cat removed a large portion of the gravity of the situation. His point of view broke the situation down to it being an opportunity to either, eat, chase or hump it. Alas, the sexual option was just an ember of a lengthy memory, his nineteen year vintage surely unable to permit the strenuous activity.

From the depths of the bush the object emerged, a metallic sphere approximately the size of a basketball, its surface sporting a dull, weathered look with signs of scorching here and there. Upon the front was a circular transparent area, while from the rear a blue glow illuminated, every now and then clouding the plants behind with small jets of vapour and hissing noises. Most astonishing to Leo and the frogs, who had separated at the arrival of their new spectator, was that the sphere appeared to hover above the ground.

In the space of just a couple of minutes, two incidents had forced him to avert his attention from a pending meal. Not to be vexed, he refused to show it too much attention. Flashing the frogs a cursory glance, he lay his ears flat to his head, stretched out a long black paw, and began to lick.

The sphere remained motionless, levitating a couple of feet from the ground, apparently observing him. The frog's fascination now diminished, exchanged a knowing glance, before heading toward next door's pond for a refreshing post-coital swim.

Changing limb, Leo was well into his preening ritual; mouth buried deep into his fur to root out the irritating wosnames that caused the itching before flooding them in a cascade of dribble. All the time however, a beady eye was covertly trained upon the mysterious object before him.

And so the stand-off began. On one side, an ageing black cat, the gentle breeze ruffling a small furrow on his chest fur to reveal normally hidden white tufts. And a metallic sphere on the other, which for all intents and purposes occasionally let off random farts; an art of which Leo too was quite adept.

Some minutes passed before he decided to notch proceedings up a little by taking a step forward. The action was for the most part involuntary, caused by the movement of a flea around his bottom area, entering the forbidden zone and causing a reflex. The response was a slight withdrawal by the sphere.

Have that, thought Leo, initially surprised at the reaction from the interloper, yet also aware that he'd gained the moral upper ground. In addition, he was also conscious of the slight convulsions and murmurs beginning to build up at the back of his throat. Moments passed before a familiar choking and coughing sounds began to issue forth.

The sphere, although unchanged, looked as puzzled as an inanimate object could as more urgent convulsions caused Leo to change his stance. Flattening his head and aligning it to the ground, he attempted to dislodge the irritation, but to no avail. Further palpitations, coughing and gurgitation followed until, with a monumental *hoick*, he involuntarily opened his mouth, to an angle your average anaconda would be proud of, and ejected, at a fair velocity, a large saliva covered ball of fur. With a *thlop,* it hit the sphere slap bang on the transparent area. The attack caused the sphere to quickly glide back a few more inches, giving the impression that it was staring at the fur ball with an alarming cross-eyed stare. Slowly, the blob began its gravity-induced journey, leaving a wet, slimy trail down the front, until ultimately it fell with a *plop* to the floor.

Totally unabashed, Leo resumed his cleaning. His small pink tongue, flicking between splayed toes with dignity still very much intact, ultimately pleased that the obstruction was now free. Casting the corner of his eye toward the sphere once more, he just caught the branches of the bush springing back into position. Of the mysterious object there was no sign. On the ground, Leo searched for the offending fur-ball, also to no avail; it too had disappeared, leaving just a wet mark.

III

Classic Jerry Goldsmith scores boomed with necessary drama and power from the speakers within the Main hall of Chester's Northgate arena. Unfortunately the acoustics failed utterly to accommodate such magnificent melody, the majority of which rebounded back through the basketball hoops to meet the next bar in a jumble of notes. Regardless, it still sounded impressive and added greatly to the atmosphere.

This year the Cheshire sports centre was the honoured venue for the fifth, North of England Star Trek convention. In response the local populace didn't disappoint. Even at this late hour a hundred plus humanoids were still in situ as the event approached its zenith. Eager and excited Klingon's perused the hall, mixing with equally enthusiastic Vulcan's, Ferengi, Jem'Hadar and other bizarrely shaped intergalactic beings who for the vast majority only differed from each other by a uniquely patterned lumpy head.

The exception being a shuffling, shaggy thing currently getting under everybody's feet. Someone had gone to an awful lot of trouble to make this costume. Multi coloured patchwork fabric attachments were carefully layered over a large flexible plastic sheet and adorned with intricate and impressive artwork. This in turn rested on top of the unfortunate person beneath who scuttled around on all fours. It was just a shame that no one had the heart to tell the poor individual that it resembled a mobile shambling pile of Dinosaur vomit

"This," said a blue skinned man with similar coloured antennae atop his head. "Is an original Phaser." He held the weapon high for all to see, dislodging an antenna in the process. His bright white teeth managed to over emphasize the gormless grin upon his face as he did so.

"It was used by Bill Shatner during the filming of episode twenty two, season one. Which I'm sure I don't have to remind you was … The Space Seed." He seemed to take great delight in shortening William Shatner's first name as though they were great friends.

Gasps and exclamations of wonder issued forth from those observing, while one man dressed as the legendary captain himself raised both hands in the air. "Were not worthy," he exalted, his frame trembling as he bowed continuously.

On the next stall sat three men. One, dressed as a Romulan,

one a Talaxian and the third rather oddly was clad in the costume of a Cyberman. They were participating in a role playing game consisting of a large star map which completely covered the table. The map represented far distant regions of the Galaxy's quadrant, while scattered upon it were numerous model star ships and counters representing races and species along with many, many dice. Standing amongst the spectating group was a man wearing the red and black colours of a Next Generation era Star Fleet Admiral. The uniform appeared to be a perfect fit for his little under six foot frame. Deep in conversation with the Cyberman he was discussing the merits of using Star base one five seven as a forward operating area, as opposed to taking his battle fleet straight into action with the Borg. The Cyberman, although attempting to prove his strategy to be the better one was becoming irritated as he failed to make the brown haired Star Fleet Admiral see sense.

Bending over the map the Admiral extended an arm to move one of the ships.

"Don't touch that!" The Cyberman barked, rising slightly from his chair, silver gloved fists clenched.

"I'm only trying to help," replied the Admiral, his face colouring and accentuating his high forehead. Despite the objection he stayed where he was, a stupid grin fixed on his face as if attempting to indicate to those nearby that he wasn't affected by the altercation. A quick glance confirmed that everyone else's attention was in a different direction. Straightening, he meandered away in a sulk.

To look at those gathered, adorned in an array of dazzling costumes, in many cases so accurate in design that they were probably better than the ones used upon set, the majority of whom bounded from stall to stall with childish enthusiasm and happy faces. For the most part these flamboyantly dressed fanatics were simply acting out lifelong fantasies. Safe within their own community but unfortunately presenting themselves as geeks or nerds and something to be derided by the, oh so perfect and moral society we live amongst.

None of this deterred Gary Spam. Quite the opposite, he was immensely proud of his appearance. The simple fact was this. Gary ate, drank, breathed, thought, dreamt, slept and believed in everything Science fiction. Star Trek in particular.

Although he wouldn't admit it, he was in fact shrugging off the last remnants of a sulk."Wasn't interfering," he muttered to himself, relating to the incident with the Cyberman. "Well, let the Tholian fleet take star base one fifty seven, and ultimately succumbing to the Borg, see if I care."

He blurted the last statement rather louder than he'd intended, attracting a few cursory glances from a group of Cardassians returning from the overpriced bar. His thoughts

10

were suddenly drowned out as the next Goldsmith number blared from the speakers. Sulks quickly forgotten Gary was absorbed with a man with plastic pointy ears attempting to carry out a Vulcan mind meld on a green faced dwarf wearing a huge robe. As he watched, the spectacle reminded him of his younger days, when his overly ambitious father had attempted to apply destiny upon the unfortunate infant Gary.

From the moment he was born his father had treated him as though he was a seventh son of a seventh son. The fact that he was actually the first son of a second son didn't deter Norman Spam one bit. From the age of just six months he had visions of grandeur for Gary and began grooming the unfortunate child for a potential education at one of Cheshire's finest education establishments, The Kings School in Chester.

"Norman, you'll bring that child to be strange," his mother would cry. Not really an unfounded statement as on regular occasions it wouldn't be unusual for her to find Norman reading the political and world news pages from the Guardian or the Observer to him at bedtime.

On one particular day in 1975, he actually made the journey to the Kings school prior to starting his shift at Chester railway station. Parking his aged but trusty bike against the pristine railings, he trudged, head held high through the rustic gates. A short meeting with the receptionist revealed that for a full term he would have to part with something in the region of three hundred and thirty three pounds.

Norman swayed a little, sucking in his cheeks and clucking his tongue. His eyes rolled slowly to the top of his head as he conducted some simple arithmetic. His presence had attracted the attention of the deputy head, who on spying the uniformed stranger pass by his office window was under the misguided impression that some of the boys had been dodging their train fares again. He entered the reception just as realisation dawned upon Norman that there would not be much left from the nineteen pounds a week he earned from his employment as a platform assistant and cleaner.

The receptionist then spent the next ten minutes explaining to him that Scholarships were not handed out to children under five. Rather than admit defeat however, this new quandary was viewed upon as being just a minor hitch. Not to be defeated, Norman decided there and then that he would work a few rest days and promptly left with his head still above the clouds.

The receptionist, along with the deputy head, although relieved that none of the boys had been in trouble, expressed genuine feelings of sympathy, just as one would over a retarded puppy.

The eccentricity didn't end with the Kings School. For Norman had clear visions of Gary becoming a future secretary general of the United Nations or at the very least Prime Minister. In the real world this was clearly never going to materialize to anyone with a head containing a mouth, nose and two seeing eyes. Indeed anyone familiar with the Spam family would have known that Norman had less political bones in his body than your average jellyfish, except, when echoing his work colleague's sentiments by stating, "Now that nice Misters. Thatcher is just what this country needs." This would then be followed in the same sentence, rather bizarrely, by unashamedly announcing that he "never had, and never would vote bloody Tory."

If his father's eccentric behaviour helped mould his future, then Gary's mother, Felicity, would turn out to be a totally different kettle of fish altogether, she lived according to her own rules.

A partially reformed hippy with tendency's, normally during the drab winter months, to revert, temporarily, back to her wild carefree, narcotic induced days. Insisting that her name was Cosmic Juice and taking to sleeping in a tent with the large Hydrangea plant at the back of the garden because she thought it lonely. This couldn't have been further from the truth as the Hydrangea in question was very happy with its isolated spot, and had, only days before began to receive amorous attentions from a nearby fertile apple tree.

Had it been at all possible, it would have taken its revenge on Cosmic Juice with an ultra violent lash from its strongest branch. Alas this action would have taken almost two days to complete, so on these occasions it just concentrated as best it could on going to sleep, hoping to dream of apple trees budding and organic fertilizer.

At these very testing times, Gary would attempt to hang on to reality such as it was, with all the tenacity and guile of a limpet clinging to a rock when it see's Mister shell collector man armed with a shiny screwdriver. Having experienced all of that, it could be said that he never really hated his parents. Ashamed? Yes. Embarrassed, mortified, humiliated, even dislike at times but never really hate, and to be fair they never meant him any harm; they were just completely out of touch.

There was one thing however that Gary would look forward to. One salvation in his life that his parents couldn't possibly interfere with. BBC two, Thursdays at six forty five. Star Trek. Those forty five minutes following the adventures of Captain Kirk, Mister Spock, Dr McCoy and the lads, boldly going where no man had gone before was quite literally his own little sanctuary away from the bizarre stresses and strains of life, and were largely responsible for keeping him going.

He became obsessed with the show, collecting everything associated with it. The die cast metal Dinky models of the

Enterprise and a Klingon cruiser. Plastic character figures, a board game and the toys and cards found in breakfast cereals.

Whilst his peers would usually be found in the park, recreating Kenny Dalglish's latest stunner for Liverpool or Ian Botham's fabulous ten wicket haul. Gary would venture out on his purple Raleigh Chopper bike, although not a Chopper any more but the USS Enterprise. The word chopper cunningly covered by a piece of card sellotaped over the top with the serial number NCC1701 expertly stencilled in marker pen. Off he'd go to inflict large doses of moral lecturing to the Klingon Empire and other such unfortunate species, and if he wasn't doing that, Gary would more than likely be found acting out the Kirk or Spock scenes from his favourite episodes with his Trekkie friends Nigel and Keith.

They had learnt of each other's obsession purely by chance. After all, it wasn't the sort of thing you wanted made public knowledge at school. The life of a nerd was testing enough, and had the likes of Matthew Griffin or Michael Cummins, the schools vilest individuals got wind of such a thing then their pretty unbearable lives would be made almost intolerable.

The long awaited release of Star Trek the Motion Picture at the end of the seventies brought many a pining Trekkie out of an almost terminal depression. Opening night at the Odeon cinema on Northgate Street in Chester city centre was both Christmas and birthday come at once. Standing alone, just three places from the front, Gary had been queuing since three thirty that afternoon. The film wasn't due to begin for another five hours but he was more than happy to wait. So happy to wait that he very nearly wet himself thanks to his refusal to leave the line in case he lost his place.

He didn't trust the person behind him to keep his place, largely because he possessed a hairy mono-brow together with an unsightly nose, reminding Gary of a Klingon. The hard core of enthusiast were pretty much all there by five. Included in this particular group were Nigel Regis and Keith Foggarty, his classmates from school. They had never really been friends, but neither were they particularly enemies, however, the cat was now out of the bag to all parties. A short stony silence followed their mutual recognition, guilty foot shuffling and ground ward stares persisted before ignorant pretence slowly gave way to a few minutes of guarded questioning such as, "What you doin ere?" And, "Oh is it a Star Trek film? I adn't really noticed."

The ice broken, and the next two hours of queuing sped by relatively quickly as the three new found chums swapped personal experiences and stories of Trek life. From then on, Jim, Spock and Bones as they secretly liked to refer to each other, never looked back.

The intervening years passed until the September of 1990, when finally, three years after those lucky buggers in the US had experienced it, Star Trek the Next Generation was broadcast in the UK.

Big preparations were made by the three heroes in the days leading up to the twenty sixth. Things hadn't at that time reached dressing up proportions; those days were a few years away yet. Consuming large quantities of food and drink and engrossing themselves into the role playing game *Starships and Federations* well into the night for three days in a row was the main order of festivities, culminating with them taking a day off work to prepare for the big event.

This was how to have fun, this was how to celebrate and so Nigel, Keith, Gary and Sophie, Gary's girlfriend, along with her friend Kelly, sat down at Nigel's house to view the pending televisual feast with excitement, approaching obsessive proportions. Keith thought that he was in with a chance with Kelly. In reality he had more chance of taking Mister Spock himself out for a discreet lunch at a sushi restaurant followed by a stint at a lap dance club for emotionally frustrated Vulcan's

Precisely seven minutes before Captain Jean Luc Picard and the Enterprise D was launched onto our screens, the power dramatically cut off. Sheer horror etched itself upon the faces of the three lads, while the girls who had initially screamed seemed to realize rather quicker what had happened. Not so however with the Trek triplets. Nigel raced into the street, his eyes brimming with tears only to find the whole street dark, the entire electricity supply off. Keith stood up, hit the TV twice with a fist, hoping the magic thump would reinstate normal service or as close as normality had ever dared to go near them. Gary, being a lot calmer, took a more sensible and methodical approach to the whole situation.

"Bastard, bastard," he shouted over and over again, pointing at the blank screen before running round the house searching for as many batteries as he could find, in the vain belief that it would cure the problem.

It turned out that emergency gas repairs being carried out two streets down were the cause, thanks to a finely tuned expert JCB operator, delicately but effectively severing the main electricity supply. Some four hours later power was finally restored. Obviously it was far too late for the televisual viewing spectacular, but there was always good old alcohol. The consumption of which managed to quell the rising frustration in the house. But things weren't as bad as first thought; salvation was at hand, as the first couple of episodes had preceded the BBC and were already available on VHS, allowing the band of merry explorers of all things dweebish to enjoy their premiere night a couple of days later.

A shout rang out, cutting into Gary's reminiscing. The vision wavered and disappeared. Returning to the here and now he witnessed the green dwarf throttling the Vulcan. Gasps and chokes emitted from the pointy eared one, whose main form of defence seemed to be an ineffective attempt at the Vulcan nerve pinch.

Just as the Vulcan's face began to turn blue the combatants were interrupted by a huge Klingon, whence both were led away by their respective friends.

A hand rested upon Gary's shoulder. He turned to see Keith in his bright red Jersey.

"Mate," Keith enquired inquisitively.

"Err, what, dunno," spluttered Gary.

"The applications desk for Seattle is open; Nige has saved us a place."

The next year, Seattle was to host the main body of celebrations for the fortieth anniversary of Star Trek. The tickets, or rather the chance to gain tickets for this prestigious and not to be missed event were only available, in their area, by attending the North of England enthusiast convention. The pair glanced to where Nigel stood in a short queue. The Romulan Praetor, sporting the largest shoulder pads ever, turned and gave a big thumbs up with both hands, topped with a huge ridiculous grin. The pair joined him.

Sat behind the desk was an old man; the left half of his face was painted white while the other black. In front was a folded cardboard sign informing all that he was Lou Antonio, in brackets (Lokai).

A few moments passed and suddenly Gary was at the front. Excitedly he turned to Nigel, a large ear to ear grin splitting the lower part of his face, before handing his application to the man.

"Lokai accepts your application," he said in a bland American accent. "You should receive the tickets and confirmation in the next four weeks," he continued.

Nigel, with an equally gormless expression blooming upon his face, stood transfixed, application quivering in his tightly gripped hand. "Oh wow it is him, its Lokai," he blurted.

The Cyberman from earlier approached Gary, administered a prolonged stare, snorted and left the building.

"What happened with him earlier?" Keith questioned him, nodding in the direction of the departing Cyborg.

"Oh nothing," said Gary, dismissing the incident.

Keith yawned. "I'm knackered," he declared. "Think I'll go after I've put this in."

The three of them had arrived at the convention early that

afternoon. It was now fast approaching ten thirty. All the exhibits, stalls and models had been viewed a good dozen times with deep scrutiny. The many celebrity speeches listened to. Disappointment was still extent at the failure of exalted guest, none other than Jonathan Frakes aka Commander Ryker, to turn up. While they had all eventually lost out to the shambling pile of dinosaur vomit in the most convincing costume competition. The main objective however, had been achieved, as they had all succeeded in posting their applications for the fortieth anniversary bonanza. Keith snorted with disgust, "If Frakes turns up to that, I'll take him to task."

Proceedings within the hall were winding down, and so they all decided to call it a day. Armed with numerous plastic bags containing role playing add on sets, leaflets, models and posters, Gary, Nigel and Keith headed out of the centre's exit.

Outside, the cool night air was welcome, a contrast from the warm circulated air inside. Boldly they strode, still dressed in full regalia, showing not the slightest shred of embarrassment, towards Keith's car.

"Can't wait to tell Sophie," said Gary thinking of Seattle, "She'll be well made up."

"Yeh, I've got to book time off work," said Keith, "Hope I can." slightly fearful of not being allowed the time off to attend, as he had only recently started a new job.

"Can't you go unpaid Bones?" asked Gary.

Keith didn't reply to Gary's suggestion, producing the car key fob he pressed the button to remotely open the doors. With a click they released and the three men climbed in still conversing about the convention they had just attended.

With minds still full of Trek, none of them noticed the small metallic sphere with a dull weathered look to it as the Fiat Multipla slowly manoeuvred out onto the main road. The bizarre object was roughly the size a basketball, with a shiny transparent area to the front and a dull blue glow emanating from the rear. Quickly it moved out of sight after appearing to scrutinize the three men. Had the sphere continued watching them, it would surely have noticed the vehicle reversing toward it.

Despite moving slowly, it collided with the sphere, violently enough to force it against the adjacent brick wall. Slightly crushed it hung, pinned between the wall and the Multipla. Unable to move, small jets of vapour hissed from the apertures in apparent frustration.

Unaware, Keith engaged forward gear and the Fiat moved forward bringing to an end the spheres temporary forced immobility. The sudden absence of the vehicle caused it to pitch forward and downwards, hitting the ground not with the expected metallic clang, but instead with a soft cushioned *phlaff,* the transparent screen coming to a rest amongst the discarded remains of a mouldy, decaying kebab.

The drive home towards Nigel's flat was uneventful as far as genuine intergalactic occurrences were concerned, the trek talk continued all the way until he climbed out. After saying their goodbyes and conducting waves, Keith continued towards Stanney woods, his final port of call before heading home himself. Gary was still buzzing with excitement as they neared his house, ecstatic after the evening's events. He thought of the forthcoming trip to Seattle and of Sophie waiting for him at home. His mind suddenly froze, "Oh my god," he said aloud.

"You okay mate?" Keith asked, slowing down as they approached Gary's home.

"Saturday morning, I'd almost forgot, the company day."

Mostyn Oxtons had arranged a grand team building experience for Saturday, an entirely voluntary event but everyone was expected to attend. A day of tactics and of battle and strategy. A day of paintball in Delamere forest. A day of which the majority of staff regarded a total and utter waste of time, not to mention the loss of a Saturday, but they attended all the same so as to improve their career prospects and indulge in some serious bum kissing. Ultimately it was a day to which Gary was looking forward immensely. Malcolm Reynolds the company owner would be attending, whereby he would be doing his utmost to impress and hopefully set up the framework for his sought after promotion.

IV

The first evidence of the morning sun peeked over the horizon giving the promise of a glorious autumn day. Its feel good factor rays, glistening like liquid gold upon Blakemere Moss, where black sphagnum coloured water lapped towards a steep perimeter of trees, a scene rather reminiscent of a bygone prehistoric age. A small flock of birds burst from the tree tops gave rise to the image of a long reptilian neck poking through after them, eager to take a bite on the wholesome leaves and branches.

Anybody contemplating that very ideal would have had their thoughts torn apart by the sound of a car speeding into the gravelled car park, annihilating the serenity and wholly natural feel. Coming to an abrupt halt in a cloud of dust and stones, the driver glanced at the clock on the dashboard. Five, forty two, the illuminated numbers beamed back at him.

I'm a bit early, Gary thought, armed with the knowledge that they weren't supposed to meet here until six thirty, but he'd wanted to arrive before anyone else. Peering through the dusty windscreen of his new model Volkswagen Beetle, he sat, forearms folded on top of the steering wheel. Resting upon these was a preposterously smooth chin.

Mindful on how the day would unfold, he pulled a lever forward upon the steering column and Soapy water jetted forth, mostly over the roof. The small amount that did make contact with the windscreen met the wiper blades coming across as Gary attempted to clear the worst of the grime. *That's better* he thought before yawning loudly. He hadn't slept particularly well the previous night, having lain tossing and turning, wakefully dreaming of the enormous smile on the face of his boss, Mister Reynolds and the pure admiration he would have after observing him lead his team to an absolute and brilliant victory.

The strengthening sun had reached just below the tree tops, already holding the radiant power to penetrate through the glass of the windscreen, where he felt the pleasant warmth begin on his body. Closing his eyes to obtain the full appreciation, Gary was suddenly aware of a curious humming. It appeared to emanate from deep within the forest, but where? He couldn't be sure. Continuing for a good fifteen to twenty seconds, it quickly faded to leave an equally curious clunk, similar to building machinery with a bizarre artificial echo. This too ceased after a few seconds, swallowed up by the breeze and the daily dawn chorus of birdsong.

ocked his ear. Sure enough,
ned.

ne, his curiosity began to get
he car with the intention of
o too far though. He thought,

ear seat, he made his way
up the bonnet and removing a
g them on, he became aware
y along the gravelled track.
es and tyres caked in fresh
the car park, turning half a
to a stand opposite Gary.

o the interior, eager to make
the silhouetted features of

oots, and in an attempt to
s frame, patted his hair, took
rmless smile to form before
n unnecessarily exaggerated

Ine passengers, already in the process of disembarking, turned at the sound of Gary's boots crunching on the loose gravel. A chorus of disapproving sighs grunts and comments ensued, just loud enough for him to hear without giving away who uttered it.

With the arrival of the vehicle and Mister Reynolds, all thoughts of investigating the unexplained noises were put to the back of his mind. Making his way to the far side of the car Gary offered to help his boss out and on to his feet.

"Mister Reynolds sir, please allow me to assist," Gary asked, stepping backwards, appearing to almost genuflect.

Already half out, Mister Reynolds swished Gary away with his hand as if swatting a nonexistent fly. "Go away Spam, I can quite manage myself thank you."

Not wishing to show his embarrassment, Gary guffawed, breathing in with sharp intakes of air through his teeth, an action similar to when someone splashes vinegar onto a painful mouth ulcer.

Behind Mister Reynolds, others were waiting to exit the vehicle, the sight of whom caused Gary's heart to sink. *Girls!* He thought and shuddered. *They could be a problem. They're bound to slow us down. I'll try and find a use for them, cannon fodder maybe or give em a pad and pen. Yes non com observers.*

To Gary, Samantha and Chantelle were the worst kind, with makeup plastered over every inch of facial skin, wearing those bloody awful tracksuits and that ridiculous way of talking, all that, "OMG! That's sooo, like, wha-ever."

Gary felt strongly about these modern girls, brought up on a diet of Soap operas, reality shows, tabloid magazines and fruit vodka drinks, twenty at a time, the very image which according to him, would set the feminist cause back to a time when women were escorted from cave to cave by means of their hair.

From inside the vehicle, Samantha and Chantelle giggled aloud causing Gary to sigh heavily and administer a fully laden scowl of disgust.

Chantelle noticed his action and traded him a raised middle finger.

Bursting into an immediate rage, Gary sought the opinion of his boss."Sir, did you see that?" He gasped, his face reddening with rage.

Unaware of the appalling incident, Mister Reynolds was busy chatting.

The sheer anger caused an involuntary screwing of Gary's nose while his left eyeball took a downward turn, as if making a bold attempt to escape.

"Bloody chavs!" He muttered after some moments, but not loud enough for them to hear.

Just twenty minutes later and the car park was a hive of activity. The arrival of several more vehicles conveyed a whole host of chattering people. Some eagerly anticipating the event ahead, while others just looked disinterested, reflecting on a lost day in the pub or at the footy. Then there was the throng, those who clambered around Mister Reynolds, ambushing him in the hope of being noticed. As he moved toward the rear of his car they followed like Lemmings. Opening the door he stepped up on the ledge to take in the crowd before him.

"Okay everybody," he called, clapping his hands in an attempt to gain their attention. "Settle down. Now Dean and Leyton have gone to pick up the van with all the equipment we will need for today and will be here shortly," He paused. "Now," he continued, the group hypnotized by his voice. "We will, as you know, be engaging in a day of paintball." A cheer went up.

"Okay settle down, "he uttered once more. "Now, we will be engaging in three contests against our sister offices from Liverpool." A series of boo's erupted, except for a lone cheer from one individual who quickly took the hint and changed to a boo.

"Manchester." Louder boo's. "And lastly," he paused, this time for effect. "Wrexham," loud boos, fart noises and descriptive swearing joined the crescendo. The extreme response to the latter town was a throwback to Chester and Wrexham's footballing rivalry, which sometimes bordered upon hatred.

"Okay settle down please," Mister Reynolds requested, patting thin air with his hands. "Remember, this whole event is not about how much damage we can inflict upon our colleagues." A wry smile appeared upon his face. "But how well we can bond together and work as a team."

This last sentence caused some to lose interest. Gary however, stood as attentive as ever, if not more so, his face still displaying the same ridiculous look as his excitement screamed to be released.

"We also have to give a large thank you," Reynolds continued, "to Cheshire county council and the Forestry commission, who have kindly cordoned off a large chunk of the forest for our sole use today."

Another cheer went up as the group applauded a man clad in a brown boiler suit adorned with a forestry commission logo upon his back, in the process of emptying the bins. Removing his earphones, he looked at them with bewilderment and wondered why this group of idiots were clapping and cheering him.

"Our first opponents this morning will be our friends from the Liverpool Office." More booing broke out but grew noticeably weaker as the novelty began to wear off. "For this we will split into two groups, each with a leader or Captain, whichever you prefer. The captains will appoint their own sergeants as it were."

By now Mister Reynolds own enthusiasm was beginning to wane. "We will not begin our first contest until zero eight thirty hours, which will give our two captains..." He pulled up a sleeve to check the time. "It's almost seven o clock, so we will have an hour and a half to get ready and work out a strategy.

"Are you going to be one of the captain'th thir?" asked a short man nearest to him with a lisp. In his early forties, his hair hung listlessly over his forehead creating a ragged fringe. He looked very earnest. Large, blue, deep set eyes were crowned by thick bushy and equally black eyebrows. He wore desert camouflaged combat fatigues emblazoned with the word US army over the left breast pocket, which seemed to go well with his weather worn face. He gave off the appearance of tiredness and rugged experience at the same time. A similar strip of material topped the pocket on the opposite breast of his tunic, this one displayed the name Woods.

Some of those present, those who didn't know the man sniggered with amusement.

"No Woods. My goodness, no," Mister Reynolds gasped. "No I am a..." He paused as if deep in thought. "A kind of self appointed general if you like." He bellowed a short, deep, guttural laugh. "I will be here to make any final decisions and to aid and help you before you go into action and then welcome you all back at the end of each melee."

This was understood by most as, I'll be here until say eleven, then I'm off to play a round of golf with Lord Pomberry of Upper Beeston, followed by cocktails and Pimms at his hunting lodge on the edge of the forest before making a tipsy reappearance if I can be arsed.

Clapping his hands, he aimed to quieten the hushed mumbling which had broken out.

"Okay everyone quieten down. Now, the two captains will be the two most senior managers here today, so that's Chris Dobbs, and..." He took a deep breath and swallowed hard realising his mistake, wishing he'd thought more about organizing this event, "and Gary Spam."

Commotion broke out. "No bloody way." "Fix." "Not that knob," and "Oh God, We're dead," were just some of the comments.

From his jacket pocket he took a folded piece of paper and held it up. "Now, when I call out your name," he began again, addressing the uneasy crowd. "I want you to join your respective captain." Pausing again, he thumbed through the notes searching for the list. "Ah yes, here we are." Looking up he noticed that the majority had already gathered around Chris Dobbs. Just three people remained undecided, unsure as to whom to pledge their allegiance. The first was a youth in his late teens, head bowed, engrossed in playing games on a Game-Boy and utterly oblivious to the proceedings taking place. The other two were Chantelle and Samantha, defiantly chewing gum with attitude while watching Mister Reynolds through the top of their heads.

Two people however did stand with Gary. A rather confused looking man in his late twenties, his right forefinger was pressed against his lips of which formed the shape of the letter O. The other was Woods, Who, for reasons unexplained, possessed a strange admiration for Gary.

"Oh you guys," Gary chuckled through a grinning mouth. "You're such a laugh." Inhaling deeply he appeared to suck air through his teeth before emitting a ridiculous noise. For the best part of a minute he chortled dementedly while the crowd stood and stared with utter contempt. Eventually it began to dawn on him that there was a possibility that they might just be serious. The grin remained, despite feeling a little embarrassed.

The youth, who had been consumed with his Game-Boy, suddenly looked up. Aware once more of his surroundings he noticed Woods and Gary to one side while everyone else stood with Chris Dobbs. Not having the faintest idea what was going on, he felt that the safer option would be to join the rest

"Okay everybody," interjected Mister Reynolds, saving Gary's blushes further. "I'm sure Gary appreciates your little joke." He ended with an inaudible guffaw. "Now, when I call your name, can you please go to your respective captains?"

Inevitable tuts and sighs followed, but this time as the list was read out everybody did as they were bid, albeit slowly in Gary's case.

A large white van emblazoned with Mostyn Oxtons logo arrived, grinding to a halt in a cloud of dust. The door opened and a tall blonde, young man with orange skin appeared, the result of a ridiculously over the top sun tan. He was closely followed by Ian Wright, or rather the spitting image of Ian Wright. Leyton from stores was a popular member of staff whose fit and well toned form made him a hit with the ladies.

"Ah the equipment is here," chirped Mister Reynolds, glad to be able to move away from the unfortunate business with the teams.

The van was quickly surrounded by a curious crowd who began examining boxes full of face masks, visors and dark blue boiler suits, all complete with pin badges with the word Chester written in marker pen. Most popular were the large plastic crates packed with Tipman, 98, semi automatic paintball guns and ammunition cartridges.

A frustrated looking Mister Reynolds took this opportunity to grab Chris and Gary In the hope of explaining his plans for the day, while the van was systematically emptied of its contents. Before long a large jungle camouflaged marquee was erected, flanked by two large green tents; one with a plaque hung around an upright pole with the word "headquarters," crudely painted upon it. The emergence of Clingfilm covered trays of food and a large number of bottled drinks from car boots quelled the crowd's excitement somewhat. These were placed upon trestle tables set up inside the large marquee, while the smaller tents were used to store the crates and boxes containing the paintballing equipment.

An hour soon passed and most had changed into the boiler suits provided. Samantha and Chantelle were reviled by the tasteless clothing; others revelled in their new outfits. One man marched up and down like a dark blue imperial storm trooper, humming the Darth Vader theme music.

Woods sat alone, concealed within a dark corner of the marquee. His face displayed the utmost concentration as he stripped his paintball gun down to its base components. Greasing them to their maximum lubricated state before reassembling with military precision.

"Ah Mister Reynolds," said Gary, entering the marquee. He wore a very tight fitting boiler suit. His gun hung from his shoulder. "I wanted to ask you, should I not have some kind of identification?" He raised a finger pointing to the space on his shoulder.

"What are you talking about Spam?" Reynolds replied, who

had himself, most bizarrely changed into a bright red tracksuit.

"Well, I am a captain; shouldn't I have an epaulette or a badge? Or at least some stripes to show I'm in charge?"

Mister Reynolds raised a hand to his forehead and sighed deeply. "Gary, everyone knows who you are and that you are the captain." He really wished that he'd chosen someone with just a bit more popularity, such as the coffee vending machine.

"Go and grab yourself a drink will you, I have things to arrange," he said and walked out of the marquee shaking his head.

Gary stood, long after Mister Reynolds had been lost to view. Screwing up his nose, he shoved his hands in his pockets and sulked for a while before eventually taking his Boss's advice.

A loud horn cut through the air, abruptly ending all conversation. This was the pre arranged signal for the teams to muster. It was a pity that it hadn't actually been pre-arranged, which was why everyone stood in a confused state looking at each other.

Standing on a box, Mister Reynolds rose above them in front of the large marquee; Flanked by Gary and Chris.

"Okay people. Now I'll read out the list again and when your name is called you WILL go to your respective captains." Once again the list was read out and everybody went where they were supposed to.

"Now, this is the plan, I will hand you over to Chris who will explain," he said inviting Chris Dobbs to take up the mantle.

"Hello everyone," said Chris, attempting to sound super authoritative. He clearly failed, demonstrating he would never become a great orator. "Those in my team will follow the blue route into the woods." He pointed behind the groups, indicating a wooden pole with blue tape standing by a well worn track which could be seen winding its way into the densely wooded area.

"We will follow this path until we reach a large crossroads." He held up a map and pointed with a chewed pencil. "This is where we will take up our ambush positions." He paused. "Now those of you in Gary's team will follow the red route." Again, he indicated behind the group. This time to a wooden pole with red tape standing in front of another clearing fifty yards to the left of the blue one, this too had a worn track-way which disappeared out of sight in to the undergrowth.

"You will take this alternative path, which will join up with the same crossroads, however, you will continue until you make contact with the team from Liverpool."

Chattering and excitement broke out.

"Settle down," said Mister Reynolds, helping Chris to restore calm.

"Your job is to withdraw in an orderly fashion, but continue to

24

engage the enemy, hence drawing them onto our position at the crossroads," He tapped the map again. "This," he continued, "is where we will spring our ambush."

Gary scowled at Chris Dobbs with unwarranted contempt, "I could have given that speech much better, why didn't he ask me to do it?" He muttered jealously.

"Well that's the plan," said Chris, ignoring Gary's comments," simple but effective."

"Okay Gary, anything you want to add?" Mister Reynolds asked as an afterthought.

Gary sulked with his arms folded.

The teams prepared to move off when Gary decided to take his opportunity.

"Okay everybody listen up," he said putting on his Jean Luc Picard voice. Only Woods and the undecided man, whose mouth still formed the shape of the letter O, took any notice, the rest continued to disperse. Still undeterred by his team's inability to accept him, Gary strode over to the red marker post to assume his position at the front.

Mister Reynolds stepped between the two teams armed with a stopwatch, a large Yellow flag and the air horn, hanging from a leather strap from his wrist.

"Okay, at precisely nine o clock, that's in approximately three minutes, we will begin," he paused, watching the second hand creep around the clock face. "When you hear three blasts on this," he indicated the air horn. "That is the signal for recall."

Once more he observed his stopwatch while they chatted among themselves. "Ten, nine, eight, seven."

Chris Dobb's stood at the head of his team, flanked by his two sergeants'. He looked for all intents and purposes the perfect military commander, upright, attentive, waiting patiently for battle to commence

Gary stood with Woods, the latter in his US army desert combat fatigues, Boot polish and green camouflage paint hid his facial features while around his forehead, a sweaty white headband was tied. The gormless man twitched, his face briefly lighting up as his single brain cell flickered into life. The rest of his team appeared distant and uninterested. Gary viewed them differently, loyal devotees, standing to attention, hanging onto his next order as if their lives depended on it.

"Six, five, four, three, two, one." The yellow flag dropped and the two teams disappeared into the thick foliage of Delamere Forest.

Gary sprung like a cougar, bounding along, his gun at the ready leading Delta Company, Star Fleets legendary Special Forces squad on a mission to destroy a top secret Romulan installation. Looking across, he saw the last remnants of Chris

Dobbs team as they were swallowed up by the greenery. Excitedly and with all trace of ill will gone, he turned to Woods, opened his mouth to speak then closed it again. The van driver's eyes were wild, almost primal, while the appearance of an Ace of spades playing card wedged at an angle into his headband added to the warrior image. Further down he suddenly became aware of a heavy, brown leather belt strapped around his waist. At first glance it appeared to be sheathing a Gurkha Kukri knife. At second glance it still appeared to sheath a Gurkha Kukri knife.

"Arrgghh!" Gary screamed involuntarily, narrowly avoiding a small sapling. "What the hell have you got that for?" He whispered loudly between clenched teeth, pointing at the fearsome weapon.

Woods looked at Gary with a vacant stare. "I won't uthe it thir, ith juth to thcare the bathtardth away," said Woods genuinely.

Remaining silent for a few seconds, Gary was unable to remove his eyes from the lethal looking weapon. "Are you okay Woods? You do realise that we're not really hurting people don't you? it's just for fun."

"Yeth thir," Woods replied nonchalantly.

Gary became deeply concerned about what might happen when they met up with the Liverpool team. On the other hand he felt a certain amount of relief that Woods was on his team. Glancing behind, he looked beyond. His fears were allayed somewhat to see that no more additions of potential death had been added, just his team following behind in a line. He gained the impression that they were now more at ease, happier to be under his command. Smiling once more, he too felt more at ease with himself, except for Woods of course.

The sun was quite strong now, creating a strobe effect as it flickered through the trunks and branches, causing most to shade their eyes. Gary's mind began to wander again. Delamere forest transformed into Ceti Alpha IV and Gary, the dashing Starfleet Captain, tasked with a dangerous but vital away mission, exploring the virgin terrain of an alien world which as usual was unexplainably similar to Earth.

The trees and undergrowth soon receded from the track bringing them into a wide clearing, ahead was a crossroads. Gary stopped and raised a hand to halt the away team. Woods had elevated himself to a higher level of alert, managing to step aside while the rest walked into each other. After disentangling themselves they sat on various fallen tree trunks and refreshed themselves while Gary took out a map.

"I think the crossroads just ahead is the one Dobbs was on about," he said to no one in particular. Standing, he placed his hands on his hips and surveyed the nearby crossroads, *if only I had a pair of binoculars,* he thought.

If he was honest with himself, Gary had no idea whether the crossroads in front was the right one or not, blaming the inadequate quality of the map. He searched his team for answers and observed the tipping of bottles of water, wispy curls of grey cigarette smoke snaking into the sky and the youth playing on his Game-Boy again.

Who the hell is he? Gary thought, realising he had never actually seen the lad before. *He'll be the first to die,* his train of thought continued as he immersed himself into the Captain's role once more.

"Okay team. The crossroads ahead is our rendezvous," he guessed, hoping it was the correct one. "Let's move out people." More groans ensued, but slowly, the group gathered their things together and trudged off somewhat less enthusiastically than before.

Woods, who unbeknownst to Gary had veered away almost noiselessly, seamlessly blended into the undergrowth. The rest watched him go but said nothing, largely because they really couldn't have cared less. The remainder continued towards the crossroads while Gary, who had just realised that Woods was absent, looked agitatedly from side to side in search of his unstable sergeant.

Thwack!

He felt a sharp sting upon his left thigh. Glancing down, he saw a bright red splat of paint spreading as it stained his boiler suit.

"Who fired that?" He shouted, looking up.

What happened next could genuinely be described as an explosion in a paint factory. One moment Gary stood rigid with annoyance, his boiler suit a nice dark blue colour, with just the one red paintball mark on his thigh. The next, stood a man, rigid with shock, his boiler suit a bright red colour with just a couple of patches of dark blue material showing. A mere five seconds was all it took to turn him into a soggy mess.

From hidden and well camouflaged positions around the crossroads, dozens of sharp snapping sounds were heard as pellets left rifles, each ball finding its target with unerring accuracy, the splatty thudding almost congealing into one, they came so fast.

Gary's body felt as though he'd endured twelve rounds with a swarm of over excited mosquito's gripped with a zealous appetite for seconds. Finally the sheer shock of it caused him to lose his balance and topple backwards.

"Hold your fire, hold your fire, they're friendly," echoed a call.

The firing ceased, but not as quickly as Gary would have liked, his body receiving a number of hits a full thirty seconds after the ceasefire. Laying on his back and staring up at the canopy of trees above, he resembled a Dulux paint advert and he was sure the clouds were mocking him as they drifted by.

"Oh my god Gary, I'm so sorry about that," said Chris Dobbs unable to contain his mirth. "We thought you were the enemy."

Gary lifted his head, wiping paint from his face. Chris stood on the edge of a fox hole, the one he had been concealed in, his gun held up, gas residue slowly spiralling from the muzzle. Around him, bushes and parts of the ground began to rise up as more concealed people emerged. The sight of Gary forced the sniggers to break into full blown laughs from both teams.

Quickly, he jumped to his feet, took a deep breath and proudly puffed out his chest.

"Good, well done," he applauded. "Yes indeed, good to see that you're all alert."

A large red blob of paint dripped from his goggles and landed upon his lip as he spoke. *Bastard!* He thought, his face betraying no anger, *you did that on purpose.* Still smiling, he attempted to put the incident behind him, "Okay team, let's have the map," he said in a light hearted tone.

Crashing through the undergrowth, Woods suddenly reappeared.

"Reporting thir, been scouting in the woodth, he said standing to attention. The statement induced more laughter from the less serious participants.

"Ah Woods there you are, as you can see we've made our rendezvous," said Gary, indicating Chris's team. Paint flew from his hand as he swept it round in a gesture.

Most of the laughter now subsided and the two Captains huddled to peruse the map. They identified the route which Gary and his team would have to take to make contact with the Liverpool team. Happy with the plan they moved off, leaving Chris's Team to reassume their ambush positions.

In no time at all, Gary's and his troops were swallowed up by the dense undergrowth and out of site. Again, Gary took the lead with the suspiciously psychotic Woods following. His other sergeant trudged along with the others who displayed the enthusiasm of an Anteater with hay fever. More long minutes passed in relative silence, the excitement draining away to become a never-ending bore to most.

Gary slowed and turned to Woods, "Pass the word for absolute silence," he said. "We can't be far from the Liverpool team now."

"Thir," responded Woods and passed the order back. It took a minute or so to filter to the end of the line and as expected, didn't meet with wholehearted approval.

"..cking twat," was all that Gary managed to catch of the derogatory comments unleashed. Ignoring them like the utter professional he thought he was, he led them onward.

"Follow me," he whispered.

A tinny muted drum beat and suppressed music invaded his hearing. Halting again, he raised a hand to indicate to the rest of the team to follow suit. With an ear cocked he scanned toward the tree tops attempting to distinguish just where the sound was emanating from.

"Yeh, oh Mark, hi hun."

Gary stared back along the path, "Urrghh Chantelle", he muttered under his breath at the sight of the feeble girl answering her phone.

"Yeh, yeh, yeh, yeh, noooo! Like, I was, you know, like nooo," she continued, settling down for a chat.

"Yeh I know, no I can't, like I'm on this crappy paintball shit," she said. "Yeh he's ere, tosser."

"Err excuse me young lady," interrupted Gary, "can you please terminate your call and kindly switch that phone off?"

He wasn't too surprised when he received the middle finger in reply. What he really wanted was to confront the vile girl and tear a piece from her, but knowing the futility of the act he returned to the front of the line just in time to see Woods disappear into the undergrowth again.

Now where's he going? He thought.

"No mark, just leave it right, what? Oh wha-ever. knobead!" The unfortunate Mark was cut off, much to Gary's relief.

"Right, maybe we can get moving again?" He suggested. Retrieving his gun, he walked along the track again, missing another suggestive finger from Chantelle.

I bet bloody Dobb's doesn't have these problems? He thought, searching the undergrowth for any sign of the absent Woods.

They soon came into a clearing where a number of trees had fallen; their rotting, moss covered stumps all lay in the same direction, the result of a long forgotten storm. Gary took out the map once more when there was a heavy thud, as if something large had hit the ground. A violent rustling from the nearby rhododendrons followed before a number of birds, startled by the disturbance flapped skywards. The annoyed Pigeons quickly clearing the tree tops in their haste to find a more peaceful roost.

The team froze at the sound, even the girls. Gary however, to his credit was the first to recover his wits.

"It's alright everyone, it's probably just Woods coming back," he re-assured everyone.

What came crashing through the undergrowth, halting in front of them and looking equally as startled was certainly not Woods. Stood before them was a figure, easily in excess of six feet, humanoid, with exceptionally long, powerful looking legs which made up two thirds of its height. The torso was Squat, equally as powerful and well built and similar to a body builder. Arms protruded from the usual place but these also were of an exceptional length. Most bizarre was the appearance of a pair of elbows on each arm, potentially allowing for the kind of movement and suppleness your average sado masochist would pay serious money for.

Its entire body, barring the head, neck and feet was clad within in a smooth textured, loose fitting, dark red jump suit, complete with a pattern of undecipherable symbols adorning the length of both the left sleeve and leg. These in turn were rounded off by sleek brown footwear, not too dissimilar to an athlete's running shoe.

The head began where the body finished, with no evidence of a neck. Thin at the base, with a black, open, lipless mouth, tapering outwards to reveal a dark grey metallic visor, presumably covering its eyes. The top of the angled head was covered with a smooth yellow skin. This yellow cranium sported six small holes, three on either side arranged vertically.

The most striking, and by far worrying feature of the being was the large black firearm held between its multi jointed fingers, similar in appearance to a sten gun, but with smoother lines. Black in colour and connected to its owner by a black tube, leading to a kind of back pack but with no evidence of a strap to hold it in place. The barrel ended in a point which glowed yellow while the stock, designed to fit snugly under the arm pit also glowed yellow.

Gary stopped in his tracks, staring, mouth open at the whatever, as did the rest. Long muted seconds passed, before from behind somebody muttered, "Bloody hell. Liverpool have really pulled out all the stops."

The figure stood observing the group. Then, without warning, it raised the weapon and fired.

Appearing to hum for a microsecond, the rear glowing area dimmed slightly. Simultaneously the glow on the barrels point intensified before sending a bolt of light straight into the man behind Gary. Thrown violently to the ground, he emitted a shocked cry as he fell, those around instinctively jumped back, startled and fearful.

Suddenly, a wild banshee scream issued forth from the same bushes that the bizarre figure had emerged. Fearing another, the others shied away. The undergrowth rustled violently before parting to reveal a mad and wild Woods. Launching himself at the creature, the flying van driver caught it with a fantastic aerial headlock to send them both crashing violently to the ground in a tumble of arms and legs. Woods was the first to recover, quickly scrambling out of the beings reach. "Thoot it, thoot it," he screamed at the paint-ballers.

"Eh what? Woods what? Who is this person?" Gary spluttered, still unsure if this was real or part of the day's proceedings.

Rolling his wide eyes, Woods got to his feet, raised his paintball gun to his shoulder, and squeezed the trigger.

The first pellet hit the recovering figure square in the middle of its chest, its shattering causing red paint to spread over its suit. Half of the team of paint-ballers, the braver ones, attended their fallen colleague. The others, including Gary, had moved further back to give the Psychotic Woods more room to carry out his attack.

The being looked down and pressed a long smooth yellow finger into the paint upon its chest and examined it. Those watching the melee, the being in particular, witnessed tiny wisps of smoke begin to swirl up from where the paint had made contact.

"For chrith thake thoot it," yelled Woods again, this time more frantic.

His cry seemed to have the desired effect as at last a few raised their weapons and fired from very close range. Nearly every ball found its target, transforming the beings suit into something resembling a dirty protest from someone who'd moved onto tomato ketchup enemas.

The figure staggered, its mouth wide, a silent scream roaring from the black cavernous mouth. Its sinister weapon fell to the ground as greater quantities of smoke poured from every affected area. Quivering, it clawed at the paint in a desperate frenzy before emitting a loud guttural screech startling the few remaining birds into a panicked flight. Falling to the ground it writhed, contorting into impossible positions until finally, the torso arched and the agonized thrashing ceased. Relative silence reigned once more.

"Oh-my-god, like what is that? It's like, so totally gross." said Chantelle, her face pale. Rushing to the nearest bush, she reached a hand up to her face and was sick.

A smell, similar to a sickly barbecue sauce, wafted from the dead being, smoke still poured from where the paint had made contact.

"I bagged a couple of the thons of bitcheth back there in the foretht," said Woods, wiping sweat from his brow and smearing his camouflage paint in the process. Taking hold of the deadly looking Kukri, he pulled it from his belt and wiped the blade on his trousers leaving a very dark red smear on the thigh.

Gary raised his visor and swallowed hard following the movement of the evil Gurkha knife and then the smear. *That can only be one thing*, he thought grimly.

The unlucky recipient of the beings weapon fire, a man called James, was now back on his feet. A couple of shakes of his head, a long drink of water and he seemed to be none the worse for wear.

Gary turned to Woods, "What the hell is it?" He said, not able to take his eyes from the smoking corpse.

"I came acroth a group of them," said Woods, resembling a renegade GI from Vietnam. "Over there," he pointed. "I've never theen anything like it, as thoon as they thaw me they attacked." He paused, a smug look overcoming his features. "I wath quicker though. fired my gun by inthtinct," he tapped it with a reassuring nod. "Thath when I dithcovered that the paint ith deadly to them."

"Yeh right, but like, what are they right?" Samantha asked, joining the conversation.

"Okay, yes, well err, well done Woods," said Gary, deciding it was high time he regained control of the situation. "Now if you will all..."

"Thir," interrupted Woods. "I think we'd better get back, thothe things are not of thith world."

Gary thought for a moment about Wood's words. "Not of this world. Not of this world," he repeated quietly to himself. "Could that really be an alien?" He said pointing at the bubbling mess at their feet.

Woods nodded confidently.

With trepidation, Gary slung his gun over his shoulder and turned, with dismay he noted that half the team, mostly those who had attended the stricken James, had already taken good heed of Woods wise words and retreated back the way they had come. About to shout an order for them to come back, his train of thought was interrupted by a cry of alarm from Woods.

"Thir, I think thereth more of them," he said, emotion manifesting itself in his voice for the first time. Instinctively a hand reached for the kukri while with the other he raised the gun up to waist height.

"Okay everyone," called Gary, clearing drying paint from his visor, before replacing it in its protective position.

The main problem with this latest statement was that everyone now numbered just eight people, and if there were more of those things in the forest, Gary wasn't sure if it was enough. His train of thought inevitably turned to Star Trek and the various ways of dealing with aliens, all of which would ultimately be of no use whatsoever.

Cheering, accompanied by excited laughter filtered through the trees from not too far away. Click, click splat, the unmistakable sound of paintball guns firing. The next sound they heard was ominous. The dull hum and woosh of the alien energy weapon discharging. The cheering and laughter ceased. Replaced with astonished shouts, confused calling and unearthly shrieks.

Gary looked sternly at Woods; his mind's eye had a vision of a Klingon being dispatched.

"Thir?" Woods questioned.

He looked mad, much like an excited dog waiting for its lead to be taken off prior to the initial sprint. Turning from his Sergeant, his eyes rested upon the smoking remains of the first alien, when he felt a tap on his shoulder. Turning to face the shoulder tapper he saw that it was the not so clever guy.

"Hello, err, err," responded Gary. *What is his name?* He thought.

The man stood before Gary, his face screwed up with intense concentration. His mouth open in the eternal O, wide eyes matching the mouths shape. It looked as though he was building up to one of the most monumental achievements in his life. Taking a deep breath he scratched his head and calmly said, "I don't feel very well."

The sound of activity escalated, very much like the sound of battle. What they actually heard through the trees was in fact the sound of battle. The Liverpool team had engaged the main alien force mistaking them for their Chester adversaries, believing them to be wearing fancy dress. Their excitement turned quickly to awe as they realised that their opponents were something very different indeed. Stumbling into a clearing, they caught the Aliens completely by surprise. Realisation however, rapidly dawned that this wasn't the Chester team and had let fly with everything they had. They too, soon worked out that their paintball guns were very effective in giving the strange beings a serious problem. Some were deterred by the Alien weapons, running into the tree's yelling for their mothers as red and yellow bolts fizzed towards them.

Woods could hold back no longer and sprung forward. "Come on leths get the bathtards," he shouted, and plunged into the bushes.

Gary dithered, still trying to come to terms with things. Part of his mind was considering what Kirk or Picard might do. Those remaining, followed Woods into the undergrowth, albeit far more cautiously. Bringing up the rear, he saw James, understandably more reluctant than the others, guide himself through the tree's and disappear from view. A thought suddenly struck Gary, *What's his name? James was shot by the alien and he's okay.*

"Follow me everyone," he uttered, bravely coming to a decision. Regrettably there was no one left. They had all either joined the fight or fled. Gary's military instinct now took over. The fact there was no-one left was irrelevant, he was a leader, Mister Reynolds had said so. Therefore, like all good Generals he decided to lead from the rear.

The distance of a few hundred yards, where human and extra terrestrial met on the field of combat for the first time ever was covered in no time at all. Woods and the Chester team burst into the clearing, ignoring the scratching branches as they whipped back, sweat running freely down backs and necks. Gary's first sight was of Woods some way ahead, running at full speed before leaping high into the air and plunging the Kukri deep into the shoulder of the nearest alien. Instantly, it buckled backwards, issuing an awful scream. Its long arms flailed helplessly, fingers clutching at thin air before falling onto its attacker, deep dark red fluid gushing from the terrible wound.

With manic, incoherent screeches, the other Aliens responded to their fallen comrade. Brought on mostly by their own fear, they attacked the newcomers at their rear.

Gary and the rest of his team didn't have the luxury of time to decide on a strategy. A lucky stroke as he didn't have one. They simply raised their Tippman 98, semi automatic paintball rifles, shaking with visible fear. Aimed at the inhuman creatures advancing upon them and fired.

Snap, snap, snap, the guns kicked slightly as they sent their balls of deadly paint toward the unknowing aliens. The lead one screamed as it went down under a fusillade of concentrated fire, initially from the surprise as the pellets struck, quickly turning to agony as the paint began to melt into flesh. Another caught two directly in its face, it too going down heavily, hands clawing at its smoking wounds.

The air buzzed with the clicks of paintball rifles and the splatting of pellets, but now the vibrant humming of alien weapons charging and discharging came to bear. Yellow and red bolts of plasma energy fought with red paint pellets to find free air space. Despite their superior technology, the creatures advance began to falter. Caught in a deadly crossfire, pellets slammed into them from both sides. Their unearthly screams of pain echoed throughout the forest, the ferocity of fire affecting their own aim, causing it to be next to hopeless. Finally realising that to stay in this position meant certain death they backed away in as orderly a fashion as possible.

Overcome by the emotion, adrenaline pumping, Gary realised he was actually enjoying this slaughter, although not quite as much as Woods, whose personal kill tally had reached double figures. A quick pause to look around and he raised his gun once more and squeezed the trigger. Snap, snap, phut! He squeezed it again, same result.

Ooh that doesn't sound too clever, he thought. The sinister sound of compressed gas pushing against an empty chamber echoed into his mind. Anxiety surged within like a ball of pressure reaching for his throat.

Without any warning his right shoulder exploded with pain.

Like a red hot needle it penetrated deep, spreading throughout his body, dissipating as it travelled like a mild electric shock. The force of the bolt knocked him clean off his feet, his body, airborne for a split second before landing upon an unfortunate badger desperately attempting to scramble from the madness all around. Momentarily stunned, Gary stared with spinning vision at the mammal, red mist slowly clearing. The badger was slightly dazed but otherwise physically unharmed. Its credibility however had taken a bit of a knock. Shakily it faced Gary with crossed eyes, considering whether to give a bit back, but the strange glowing human looked a bit out of its league, so wisely it disappeared into the undergrowth for the safety of its set with the intention of having a good lie down.

Gary let his head drop and lay upon his back staring up, not for the first time that morning. The red tinge that had enveloped him dissolved to reveal a familiar blue sky; sunlight strobing through the tree tops forced him to shield his eyes. Sitting up, he attempted to regain his senses when his vision was darkened by a figure standing over him.

"Thir, are you okay?" The figure spoke, just audible above the ringing in his ears.

Looking up at Woods, Gary smiled, "yes Mister Spock I'm fine."

Realising his captain was okay, Woods returned to the rapidly diminishing battle.

Raising himself onto shaky legs, Gary gradually regained his strength. Scanning the clearing where the unbelievable event had occurred, the sound of battle returned to his brain, albeit much less frantic now. The Alien's rearguard action was almost complete, just a few remained. The rest had disappeared back into the forest leaving their dead and injured behind. The two teams of humans had now merged, their combined force inflicting further punishment.

Another slumped to the ground clutching its head in agony as paint splats burst all over it.

Rapidly, one by one the paintball guns phutted upon hollow chambers, their ammunition exhausted. Realising their predicament, they chose the option of staying put as the last alien attempted to follow its comrades. All fire from paintball weapons stopped. The sudden cessation of human activity seemed to act as a signal to the last one. As a final gesture, before disappearing from view, it stopped, turned to face the group, raised its weapon and fired.

This defiant last act was met by a resumption of hostility on the Humans behalf. Those still capable opened up with a hail of pellets, expending their last balls. The branches and leaves of trees and bushes whipped back and forth, becoming a red dripping mess at the exact spot the alien had stood just a moment before.

The energy bolt fired by the alien sizzled through the air frying an unfortunate bluebottle, the decision to remain on the rotting rat for those extra few seconds, ultimately sealed its fate. The bolt continued, unabated, slamming into the not too clever man. Observing proceedings, they saw him stagger backwards a couple of paces, the trademark glow enveloping his form.

Touching his chest, he inspected himself for damage. To his great surprise he found none and raised his head, mouth wide open as always. A giddy feeling overcame him as the bolts effects dissipated about his body, small electric shocks discharging upon every nerve ending. Despite this he managed to stay upright.

"Are you okay? Err, erm, err," spluttered Gary voicing the general concern, still a bit shaky from his own experiences with the alien weapon. *Christ I don't know his name either*, he thought and looked at Woods.

Woods was no help, indicating as much to Gary with a simple shrug of the shoulders.

As they watched the man with concern, a miraculous transformation appeared to take place. His facial expression changed. Gradually his mouth levelled out, the O shape disappearing. His eyes seemed to slowly emerge into a state of focus and recognition. Oddly, his ears sat flatter against his head and with a contented look spreading across his face for probably the first time in his life, he took a deep breath, turned to Gary and said, "Yes Mister Spam sir, I appear to be prodigiously acceptable thank you, and it's Peter."

Mutters of astonishment spread from those crowded around Peter, while distantly; the sound of sirens could be faintly heard.

"Peter. Err okay, Peter." Said Gary, glad at last to know his name. "Are you sure you're alright?"

The reinvented Peter ignored Gary as if the so called leader was now a full couple of levels below him on the evolutionary scale. Stepping forward ahead of everybody else, he emitted an odd puffing sound from his nose before appearing to survey the scene that lay before him, gauging it all with his thumb held out before his face.

With the sounds of battle now gone, Gary donned his responsibility coat once more and along with Dave Bishop the leader of the Liverpool team, attempted to ensure everybody was okay.

Seven paint-ballers, including Gary, had been hit by Alien fire. Happily all had suffered no lasting effects, that is, with the exception of the transformed and newly identified Peter. A couple of the more girly girls looked a little frail due to their experiences; they were being comforted by other members of the group along with one of the more girly men. Before them, lay the detritus of battle, or rather the dead and dying forms of an alien race.

Getting amongst the bodies was Woods. He was busy with the self appointed task of lining them up in neat rows. A couple showed signs of movement as they were dragged by their legs to their new position. These however, were the unfortunate benefactors of the blunt end of Woods wrath, being quickly dispatched with a swift but firm whack round the head to endure an enforced slumber.

Gary watched Woods as he worked tirelessly, a little concerned at how much he seemed to be enjoying himself. Dave Bishop joined him, grasping the limp arms of a smoking corpse; he got to work screwing up his nose, a reaction to the smell. Not wishing to be outdone in the responsibility stakes, Gary slung his hand in too, taking the opportunity to have a closer look at the aliens at the same time.

Woods looked up as Gary approached. "Twelve thir," he said wiping sweat from his brow, the camouflage paint now almost gone. "Four thtill alive, though I think they'll be athleep for a while," he chuckled as he punched a fist into his open palm.

"Thall I remove one of their vithor mathks?" He enquired eagerly.

Gary looked at Dave who simply shrugged. "Err okay Woods, why not?" He said, not sure if it was really safe, but fascinated at how an extra terrestrial would look.

The others edged closer, crowding around the line of bodies. Some curious, some simply not wishing to stay on their own. As Gary watched he couldn't rid his mind of the unmasking scene from the film Predator. Taking another look at Woods he made a comparison with Schwarzenegger as he revealed the crab featured warrior.

Woods drew the lethal kukri again, a large dark red stain on the blade catching their attention, causing gasps. The mask seemed to be attached by way of a simple strap around the beings head which blended in with its yellow skin. Not wishing to get too close, Woods inserted the point under the mask and carefully lifted. It came away easily with a click. A few took a step backwards, recoiling at the innocuous sound. Pulling the mask away, a small hiss caused more gasps. Finally free, the face was revealed. Woods carefully placed the visor upon the ground next to its head.

As suspected it had indeed covered the beings eyes. Those expecting to see a line of four or more were sadly disappointed, just the usual two. Both slightly larger with a dark green pupil upon a yellow background, but not as would be expected. Set into a depressed, moist membrane a couple of inches deep, the membrane extended from; were there any, ear to ear. Ever so slowly the left eye moved independently within its head until it could focus on the group standing over it, with the other following closely.

The eye movement brought forth more gasps as well as a muffled scream. Those still holding weapons raised them, although nearly all had neglected to reload. The aliens mouth opened, the lipless cavity streaked with its own blood and other horrible sticky substances. Dave held out a hand, an indication that more hostility would not be necessary.

"It's okay, it's not going to hurt us now," he said but kept his finger tightly on the trigger all the same.

Some distance away they all heard a curious humming. Gary raised his head, cocking an ear. He'd heard that sound before.

"That's it, that was the sound I heard back in the car park this morning," he said to Dave.

Dave looked at Gary none the wiser, the usual response he received when he spoke to anybody.

"It must be connected to these guys in some way," he continued.

"No shit Sherlock," replied Dave.

The Alien, clearly weak, began to move its eyes again, finally resting upon Gary. He stared back, mesmerised by the beings appearance and smiled. The Alien used its last remaining pulse of life to avert its gaze, dying happy that it had avoided an embarrassing end.

Human voices and undergrowth trampled by many feet invaded the silence. Gary turned towards the newcomers, making immediate eye contact with the familiar face of Mister Reynolds. Accompanying him was Chris Dobbs along with the rest of his team. Police uniforms mingled with the blue boiler suited paint-ballers. Clambering over fallen tree and forest debris, stopping dead in their tracks as they became aware, trying to understand just what had happened here.

A young man wretched, A Police officer attended him, her face, very ashen itself. Quickly, she grabbed her radio and called for immediate back up, pronouncing a serious incident.

A sergeant appeared and strode to the front, his features betraying confusion, but his rank demanded he take some responsibility. Regaining composure he looked at the dead aliens with bewilderment before slowly making his way over to Gary, Dave and the others.

"What the hell happened here?" He asked, his attention still very much upon the motionless forms on the ground.

Gary stepped forward to meet the police sergeant holding his hand out.

"Hello officer, Gary Spam, Commander of Earth forces," he

said confidently. "I'm in charge of this err," he said sweeping his hand in an arc to indicate the battlefield.

"You're in charge?" The sergeant remarked incredulously.

Dave ignored Gary's assumed leadership, spending the next twenty minutes recounting their incredible account to the sergeant. Chris Dobb's, upset that he hadn't been involved, stood with Mister Reynolds, scowling at every opportunity while his superior looked visibly upset.

The Aliens presented a fair amount of confusion for the Cheshire constabulary, who, as it turned out, had understandably, not the least experience in dealing with the aftermath of a battle with extra terrestrial beings. The survivors, now awake, were handcuffed and tied with anything that came to hand. Woods produced a large roll of masking tape from God knows where and was happily engaged in attempting to mummify them.

The Police sergeant, visibly out of his depth, agitated and with rising anxiety, was continually pestered by his blank faced officers for advice on what to do next, questions for which he didn't have the answers. Rather than being too much for a mere sergeant to deal with, it would surely prove to be a situation beyond even the capabilities of the entire Cheshire Police force. As a result it wasn't long before Westminster were informed and the whole area soon becoming infested by camouflaged and ominous looking white biological suited military personnel.

Gary and his comrades were escorted away, arriving at their original starting point which seemed so long ago. Efficiently they were ushered inside the large marquee by very serious suited men, armed with clipboards and files.

"Okay, okay," Gary chuckled, laughing in his ridiculous way. "Where's Mulder and Scully?" He said before bursting into full blown hysterics.

Nobody laughed. The men from the ministry administered deep penetrating stares. Noticing their unimpressed expressions he attempted to disguise his latest embarrassing moment with a pretend coughing fit.

Delamere forest rapidly became a no go area and was cordoned off with strict security patrols. Local residents were obliged to temporarily vacate their properties and access to the forest by civilians was prohibited. Above, the sky was regularly patrolled by army helicopters.

The paint-ballers, after being given suitable rest and refreshment, were boarded onto two coaches and taken to a nearby hospital, flanked by police outriders.

Gary sat, as did most, thinking hard as the full enormity of the day's events slowly sunk in. That is except for Woods who looked out of the window, happily humming a military marching tune while a large grin slowly spread across his face.

V

"Yes mum I'm fine. Yes I'm okay... No I won't." A deep sigh followed a long pause. "Okay yes I will... Yes I'm okay."

The blank expression upon Gary's face sagged that little bit further as his will to exist ebbed away with each tortured moment. His mother had called more than an hour previously and he was contemplating on simply putting the phone down and blaming it on a connection problem or committing suicide by the rarely used method of inserting the receiver into his brain via an ear.

Initially she'd called to ask if he could look in on his father as she was off to Glastonbury the next day to welcome the glorious alien visitors. There was also a brief enquiry as to his health after she'd heard that he'd been injured playing paintball with his chums from work. He'd long given up trying to explain that while playing paintball with his chums from work, he'd also spent the best part of that morning doing his best to wipe out her so called glorious Alien visitors.

The unprecedented situation the Country found itself faced with, namely that Delamere, as far as they knew, was the hub of an alien invasion attempt, whose intention was to use Gary's Mum and others of her species as target practice, cut absolutely no ice with her whatsoever. In truth he never thought it would, all she would say after his descriptions of laser beams and venomous evil beings from a demonic world was, "oh really, that was nice of them wasn't it? At least your okay, that's the main thing."

Nigel emerged from the kitchen holding a steaming pot noodle in one hand and a fork in the other. Glancing at Sophie leafing through the TV listings magazine, he noted that she looked thoroughly bored.

"It's his mum," she mouthed silently, catching his gaze.

"Still" Nigel remarked, not so quietly, causing the near to tears Gary to look pleadingly at them both.

The strong aroma of curry from the pot noodle reached Gary's nostrils compelling him to sniff deeply a couple of times.

"No mum I haven't got a cold. Yes I'll look after all the plants in the garden, especially the Hydrangea."

Discarding the magazine, Sophie moved across to join Gary on the sofa, picking up the remote control she flicked through the channels on the TV.

"It is now thought that the dozens of small metallic spheres seen all over the country have been linked to the incident in

Cheshire," said the news reader. "Scientist and military experts are examining the examples they have managed to capture, but stipulate to the public that there is absolutely no cause for alarm."

Nigel sat heavily with a dull thump on the worn grey armchair in the corner of the lounge, put his feet upon the plywood coffee table and began tucking into his gastronomic feast. Outside, the weather was wretched. Rain pattered against the windows of the spacious two bed roomed semi detached house on the edge of Stanney woods, while every now and then a heavy gust of wind would force the overgrown shrubs in the garden to temporarily block the light by covering the window.

"And this just in. We are receiving reports that a number of beings of a non terrestrial nature are being held in custody at an undisclosed location. These are thought to be survivors from the incident in Delamere forest last week, ministry of defence sources indicate that they will issue a further statement disclosing more information later today."

"Okay mum I'll see you when you get back. Yes okay, love you too, Yeh bye, bye."

Gary put the phone down, sunk to the floor and almost cried with relief.

"You can imagine it can't you?" Nigel chuckled. "Aliens held in custody in the local nick, did they have their shoelaces taken away ha ha?"

Sophie's mirthless face forced his laughter to quickly dissipate. Gary joined in before she turned and aimed a stare at him also. Despite the admonishment he smiled back, he often stared at Sophie. To this day he couldn't believe how lucky he was. It all happened back in 1995, the same year that Star Trek Voyager burst onto our screens. It was the second best thing to happen to him that year as he put it at the time, and his first and only serious dabble with the opposite sex.

It wasn't that he wasn't interested, more a case of when it came to girls, Gary's brain tended to pack a small suitcase and detach itself from the rest of his body. He was to women, as salt is to the general wellbeing of your average slug. However, the saying that there is someone for everyone was most accurately about to be proved right.

Back then, Sophie Redmond visited Mostyn Oxtons on a daily basis, for she was the life blood and saviour of many idle and lazy person incapable of propelling themselves to the nearby shops. More importantly to her, she made a very tidy profit providing a service as a mobile sandwich and refreshment seller.

Every day at approximately one minute past eleven, Gary would reach into his workbag, retrieve his prized Yoda lunchbox and withdraw a large shiny red apple, primed and crisp, perfect

42

for teacher, to enjoy with his cup of tea.

This day, disaster. No lunch box.

Taking deep breaths, he thought hard, *what to do, what to do.* Salvation however, was very quickly on hand as moments later the familiar sound of a car horn belting out the first few notes of *Dixie* drifted from outside.

Huh the sandwich girl. Was his original thought. *Yes the sandwich girl, she would have an apple,* he concluded, thinking a little deeper.

Quickly, removing himself from his desk he joined the queue hoping dearly that an apple would be on the menu. With just five people in front he stole his first glance into the back of the van. Not able to see a great deal he stood on tiptoes to get a better view. The view made him put apples and all things of that nature onto his minds own compost heap.

The most wonderful person ever to grace his vision had blocked his perusal of the vans contents. Closing his eyes he thought they were playing tricks on him. Opening them again, a further two people had been served and he was almost at the front.

"Oh God," he whispered.

Totally new things were happening to his mind and body, the only comparison was the throwing of three sixes and a twelve on the attack dice, allowing him to finally work out the galactic code and obtain the aged ancient Relic of Fon Harg while playing Return to Vulcan. No, this was better this was...

"Yes what would you like?" She offered. The angelic voice floated over Gary like incense. Staring, he noted her small cute nose nestled among a bed of freckles, all surrounded by magnificent Ginger, shoulder length permed hair.

"Err, err, erm hello err, have you got any err apples?" He spluttered, forcing the words from his badly constricting throat.

With a beaming smile she turned. "Certainly have. Take your pick," she said, producing a fine wicker basket containing a number of assorted red and green apples.

Taking one, he thrust some coins into her outstretched hand before using the last of his strength to propel his jellified legs in the general direction of the lavatories in order to empty a suddenly very full bladder.

Fifteen minutes and many cooling face splashes later, Gary emerged from the toilets, calmer and considerably more in control of his bodily functions. His mind however, was and would for the rest of the day, be less on this plane of existence than anything faced by Jason and his Argonauts. The only women to make him feel this way were usually green and prone to saying things like, "your Earth customs are very strange to us."

For the next two days he'd mentally beaten himself up thinking about how he could possibly get this girl to date him, deciding eventually that he would take the plunge on the next day.

Day three and he was close to cracking, not to mention suffering the first symptoms of mild malnutrition due to being unable to eat. He'd waited all morning, going over and over in his mind as to what he would say. Outside, the tune of Dixie reverberated through the building.

"Oh god this is it, this is it," he mouthed silently. Trembling, sweating, with palpitations threatening to burst through his chest, he moved stiffly with a Zombie shuffle, inching towards his target, Miss Sophie Redmond. Three from the front of the queue, his bladder began to turn traitor on him again. *Hold on, hold on,* he urged himself; almost calling out aloud. *What would Kirk do? Think, think,* and then there he was, face to face with his absolute heart's desire.

"Apple is it?" Sophie's cheerily questioned.

"Err, yes please, err erm," spluttered Gary, losing his palour.

"Are you alright?" She enquired with concern.

"Yes I'm fine," he had to force the response from his crumbling body," Yes an apple."

Mentally exhausted he paid his money, resigning himself to surrender to his feeble brain and ever expanding bladder, when from nowhere, a sudden bout of courage surged through him. With no time to consider he grabbed the opportunity with half a quivering claw.

"I was wondering if you would like to come to the cinema with me tonight."

Two girls behind began giggling, not that Gary heard. At that moment in time, a nuclear detonation would have registered as an average pop to intrude upon his resolute concentration. The last thing he remembered was Sophie smiling at him and saying, "Okay Gary I'd love to, I'm Soph..."

He awoke some twenty minutes, in the canteen drenched with sweat.

"Gary, Gary."

Back in his lounge he focused once more, Sophie's lovely face staring at him. Smiling, he took in a deep lungful of air and resumed his place among the Human race. "God that smells heavenly mate," he remarked, referring to the seductive aroma of Nigel's pot noodle.

"Did you hear that Gary?" asked Sophie. "The police have... "

"Yeh I know I heard it."

Seconds before the ungodly screech of the smoke alarm drowned out all other noise, wisps of smoke began to drift from the kitchen. Squealing, Nigel sprung from the chair, "Oh crap, me toast."

Sophie and Gary looked at each other with raised eyebrows and burst into giggles.

"What did your mum want?" She asked, knowing it would wind Gary up just repeating the conversation.

"Don't ask," he sighed. "She's completely mental. She's going to a party in Glastonbury to welcome the aliens."

The scraping of carbonised bread was heard from the kitchen before Nigel emerged for a second time, transporting two anthracite slices.

"What time have you got to go?" She asked, changing the subject.

"Around two," replied Gary, smiling. "I think they said they would send a car round."

Despite experiencing a thorough debriefing after the Delamere incident, Gary and all the other paintballers were told that they must attend the Police station in Chester to liaise further with military and ministry of defence officials. They were after all, rather unique, being the only people upon this planet to have had close contact with the invaders so far.

Gary wasn't fazed in the slightest; in fact he was in his element. All those years imagining himself as a Starfleet officer, dealing with alien threats and here it was, actually happening for real, and of course he'd given a commanding performance when questioned after the incident, at least that was how he saw it.

He'd begun by explaining how he'd taken charge of the situation, his vast knowledge of sci fi allowing him to realise just what was happening at once and adapt accordingly. The ministry man had sat. His tie loose around his neck as he plunged yet another cigarette end into an already overflowing ashtray.

"These gigantic, terrifying beings, armed to the teeth, attacked us mercilessly," explained Gary. "Bravely, we fought them to a standstill." The raised eyebrows of the interviewer would have impressed Mister Spock himself.

The TV newsreader continued, "Military experts predict the recent lull in alien activity to be of a temporary arrangement, and the worlds armed forces are on the highest state of alert...Locally the evacuation of all rural areas in the Frodsham area is now complete, with all residents being relocated to either Chester, Warrington, Runcorn, Manchester or Liverpool, Police say that the operation went smoothly and those moved should view this as a temporary measure...And now sport, David Beckham has stated that his proposed return to Manchester United as manager will not be affected by current unprecedented events."

"Were off out tonight Soph," said Gary. "First meeting of

Trekkers association since all this kicked off, you fancy coming?"

"Might do," Sophie replied, "I don't fancy staying here on my own with all those aliens buzzing around."

"It's okay," said Nigel. "It's been quiet for a good week now at least, and have you seen the amount of military activity around?"

"I know," Sophie replied anxiously, "but were so close here."

"Think I'll wear the Captains uniform tonight," said Gary, changing the subject. "Ha ha, "he mused, "Tonight, Mathew I am going to be......"

"Mate?" interrupted Nigel shaking his head.

The specially extended news bulletin eventually came to an end while outside, the dull, late morning daylight morphed into an early afternoon gloom.

"I'm going to make something to eat, do you want owt?" said Sophie, but Gary wasn't listening, he was light years away, deeply ensconced within his own over exaggerated thoughts.

"Gary," she shouted, bringing him to his senses.

"Yes please love. Can you do me one of those Pot Noodles?"

With that she disappeared into the Kitchen.

Although nobody was listening, Gary announced that he was going to put his Starfleet uniform in his bag in case he was delayed at the Police station and would go straight to the trek meeting from there. It didn't seem much more than half an hour later when there was a loud knock at the door.

"Can you get that Soph? I'm on the lav," called Gary from the confines of the toilet.

Already at the door when his plea floated down the stairs, Sophie opened it to reveal a tall strong jawed woman resplendent in an immaculate Army officers uniform, flanked by two camouflaged rifle bearing soldiers. They all looked rather miserable and wet.

"Ah Madam, sorry to disturb," the officer said, holding up an identity card, her voice crisp and easy to understand. "My name is Captain Bridger; I'm here to take Mister Gary Spam to a meeting. He is expecting us."

"Yes, of course, please come in," said Sophie ushering the Captain in.

Once inside she removed her cap, joined by one of the armed soldiers, his companion remaining outside in the rain.

"Who is it Soph?" called Gary amidst the sound of someone performing bathroom duties.

"It's a lady from the Army," she shouted back, her cheeks glowing red but fortunately hard to see in the dim afternoon light.

Captain Bridger fumbled with her cap until the sound of a toilet flushing broke the silence. A door opened and from the top of the landing a grinning face suddenly appeared around the corner.

"When you gotta go, you gotta go," he said laughing like an idiot.

Nobody else laughed; instead they just stared, aghast.

"I know. Looks good doesn't it?" He said, beaming with delight.

Three bands of gold braid glittered upon each cuff off the tight fitting yellow jersey he wore with abject pride. The black trousers, elasticated at the ankle, Navy style completed the Star ship captain look.

"I decided to wear it now," he said to Sophie, the ridiculous grin still on his face.

Captain Bridger looked more than a little concerned while her guard turned his back in an attempt to control himself.

"What?" Gary asked in innocence.

An awkward silence ensued.

"Okay I'll wear something over the top," he said, sulkily climbing back upstairs.

The army Landrover took a good forty minutes to cover the short distance from Gary's house on the edge of Ellesmere Port to Chester. The roads being ridiculously busy, thanks largely to the closure of many routes and the huge increase in military Traffic. It was only when they passed the Countess of Chester hospital when Gary, bubbling with excitement, pointed out that they were travelling in the wrong direction.

"Yes Mister Spam, indeed you are correct," responded Captain Bridger. "The law courts are now our preferred destination." Finishing with a request that he refrain from asking any further questions until they reached their destination.

"No problem," replied Gary, saluting.

Eventually they passed beneath the impressive sandstone columned entrance gates fronting the law courts, mingling well with the half a dozen other similar vehicles they parked.

Stepping down, Gary was escorted past very heavily armed security and in through the grand Roman style entrance. Once inside the four of them paused at a security desk where a photograph of Gary was taken by a tiny woman wearing a white lab coat.

"This way please Mister Spam," Captain Bridger gestured, guiding him gently by the elbow and up a grand staircase. At the summit they were confronted by a set of double doors which opened somewhat unexpectedly into a canteen. "Take a seat, and please, help yourself to refreshment, it's all free of charge," she said extending a hand in a sweeping gesture then turned and left the room, leaving his guard to oversee the canteen

Gary looked around. The rooms appearance offered the usual

unremarkable affair, clean and tidy with veneer coated tables and link together plastic chairs, offering little but the promise of a sweaty bum. Around a dozen people sat uncomfortably, shifting from side to side with ranging degree's of discomfort. The walls were adorned with numerous photo's, both black and white and colour, depicting the building through the years, while toward the window a line of serving units with clear plastic pull up lids offered various tempting foodstuffs.

Gary placed his rucksack onto a nearby table and made his way over to the food units to see what was on offer, after all it was free, that's what the Captain had said.

"Hello thir."

Gary recognised the voice. Looking across he caught sight of Woods maniacal grin beaming back at him.

"My god Woods, so they called you here as well huh?"

A further look around the room and he recognised other members of the paintball teams.

"Hey everyone," he said loudly. "Good to see you all made it in one piece."

"Yo, Leyton my main man, nuff respec innit," he said forming his hands into a rappers gesture. Despite the gesture being wildly inaccurate, Gary betrayed not the slightest flicker of embarrassment. Leyton tutted loud, shaking his head, while everybody else cringed.

"Davy boy," he continued.

Dave Bishop desperately hoped the grinning idiot would avoid him but Gary pointed a finger, firing an imaginary gun before blowing away imaginary smoke.

"Oh god, what's he doing here?" The voice was female, adding the word Tosser, disguised as a cough.

Refusing to rise, Gary chuckled, pulled out a chair and sat down next to Woods. Glancing cautiously either side of him, Woods lent forward, drawing close to Gary's face, as if he was about to disclose a top secret. Instinctively, Gary moved closer expecting Woods to pull up the large collars on a nonexistent rain coat before whispering his information.

"They hath the alienths, the ones that surthithed the dutht up in Delamere thorest, right here in the thells downthtairs," said Woods nodding.

Gary looked at him intently. "Really, how do you know that?"

"I Wath talking to thome of the chapth here, you know old comradeth and that." He suddenly straightened up, puffing his chest out and turned his head to face the ceiling.

Odd, thought Gary and looked in the same direction not sure what he was expecting to see. Returning to Woods, he saw that his face was set very clearly in reminisce mode, in fact he looked set for the duration.

"I think I'll just get myself a coffee," said Gary, largely to himself.

Sauntering casually over to the food and drink units, hands thrust deep inside his pockets, he perused the fayre on offer. "God you'd think a place like this would have a better choice," he muttered, far from impressed.

"This is the public canteen lov, all the posh lot eat elsewhere." The Liverpudlian serving lady eyed Gary lazily. Her bored face matched her tone of voice. She reminded him of a school dinner lady. She even wore a thin blue bib. He felt intimidated by her, taking him back to his days of school whereby each child would be forced to witness these fire breathing Harpy's, fiendishly disguised as caring old women who seemed to exude a magnetic effect towards the school drips at playtime. Each one super glued to her arms until a long line of gimpy kids trawled the playground under her unflinching care. That is until a fight broke out, where she would detach herself from the helpless, broken children and wade into the melee with a ferocity to which the likes of Vlad the Impaler and Beelzebub were party to.

"Err just a coffee please," said Gary.

"That's a quid kid," she said holding out a weathered claw which appeared to form scales as he stared.

Reaching into his pocket, he retrieved a whole range of loose change. "Hang on," he announced, realisation dawning. "She said it was all free, you know, the Captain."

"Don't think so lov," replied the Harpy.

"I'm not pay…" He stopped, noticing the look of resolute defiance etched onto her features.

"Up to you lov, no pay, no coffee," she barked, pulling the cup back in her direction. A quick glance behind confirmed that no-one was paying him any attention. Reluctantly, he paid the money and withdrew to his seat with the coffee. Woods was still staring at the ceiling, far from the present, reliving a military slaughter fest from days gone by.

Considerably more people had now arrived. Sat on his own in the corner was Peter. Looking in his direction Gary sought to catch his eye, with the intention of giving a quick friendly wave but Peter was alone intentionally. A different person since he had been on the receiving end of the alien weapon. He appeared to refuse to even acknowledge anyone else, choosing to sit, nose screwed, pointing upwards as if analysing air samples.

Resigned, Gary took a sip of the coffee, "Urrghh," it was appalling.

The double doors swung open and Captain Bridger reappeared, followed by her ever present guard, causing Gary to wonder if they even went home with her.

"Okay ladies and gentlemen," said Bridger in a commanding

parade ground semi shout, "If I could have your attention please."

She did, even Woods returned to this world.

"If you would all like to follow me, and please if you could hold any questions until we reach the debriefing centre I would be most grateful."

Leaving the canteen, the group descended the grand staircase, where two more soldiers joined them. Passing through a set of doors they entered a corridor before halting outside a large door locked by a keypad. Punching in the number, Bridger gained access, pausing briefly to chat to the guard positioned inside. Once through, Gary and Woods found themselves descending another less grand staircase, built for purpose and not to impress.

"I thold you didn't I?" Said a jubilant Woods.

The staircase finally ran out after another couple of levels, their way barred by a heavy set of metallic double doors. In front of that, a wooden desk guarded by two more soldiers, both armed. Here they waited while Captain Bridger sorted out the formalities.

We must be deep underground now, thought Gary, scanning the immediate vicinity, not that there was much to see, his thoughts were interrupted by a loud female voice.

"No like I'm not genna do it, no, like wha-ever hun, and I was like, oh right, oh my god, and he was like, right I'm leaving you and I was like oh my god, whaever and I said right I'm like gone."

The monotone drawl belonged to Chantelle, causing Gary to scowl involuntarily and wrinkle his nose in disgust.

"Okay ladies and gentlemen," said Captain Bridger, reinstalling quiet. "From here onwards, this whole area is strictly security restricted. I have a pass for each of you with your names and photo's on, so whilst you are in this part of the building you must wear it at all times." She held one up so everyone could see what they looked like. The example happened to be Gary's. One of the desk guards walked down the line handing the passes out. When they had all been distributed, the large doors were unlocked from the opposite side and the party allowed entry.

The security restricted area was somewhat of an anti climax to Gary. Passing through, he had expected a huge cavernous area to open up, bustling with bio suited personnel, busily working upon an array of super hi-tech machinery. The reality was just another grey concrete corridor, furnished with a plain brown veneered desk, at which sat a bored looking soldier and more plastic, sweaty bum chairs.

If Gary was dismayed, Woods was almost ecstatic. His pace quickened such was his eagerness to see ahead, which caused the guard to eventually peg him back. At last they reached yet another security check point and after showing off their new passes, were ushered into a large, comfortably furnished room, sporting a number of comfortable sofa's, armchairs all surrounding oak coffee tables. The floors were carpeted, while a low impact light gave the room the air of homely relaxation. It even had a small bar in one corner, sporting a couple of ale pumps and a bank of bottled spirits fixed to the wooden panelled wall.

Woods knew the function of this room, recognising it as a wardroom, for the exclusive use of officers to relax in. "Thith ith a wardroom," he said smugly.

"Okay, Please make yourselves comfortable," Captain Bridger offered. "A selection of beverages and snacks will be available to you momentarily," she added.

A side door opened and another army officer entered the wardroom, his uniform slightly more ornately decorated than Bridger's. He was accompanied by two men, one in a black suit. The other wore a white lab coat.

Announcing himself as Lieutenant Colonel Watkins, he proceeded to explain why they had been asked to return today.

"Due to your experiences in Delamere forest, you are to be recruited in the capacity of advisors to her majesty's armed forces," he gave a false cough as he scanned the civilian rabble before him. "I'm afraid ladies and gentlemen that you will be required to join us here in the complex until a late hour, with the possibility that a small number will be required to stay until tomorrow, I'm sure you understand, so that we can carry out our work easier." He paused, waiting for the expected moans and complaints.

Samantha and Chantelle inevitably led the chorus, but their rant about how Mark would probably get off with Ayesha if Sam didn't meet him, fell on deaf ears.

The Colonel waited patiently until the outbursts had died down. "I sympathise with your concerns, but surely I don't need to remind you that your country's national security is threatened and you must all want to do your duty?"

The argument opened up again, the objection now shifting to not wanting miss Eastenders or Big Brother.

Three new men entered the wardroom, all dressed in identical white dinner jackets.

"Now everybody let me offer you some refreshment, please allow the stewards to attend you," Watkin offered, hoping to appease them a little.

"Yeh I'll have a Yeager bomb," called Chantelle, happier now that a session seemed to be on the menu.

Gary sat, thinking of his impending contribution for his

country. *Maybe there will be a medal in it*, he fantasised, before terror gripped him. "Sir," he almost shouted, rising from his seat. "I wish to be excused from, err being, err here," resorting to a curious bow when he'd finished speaking.

The cause of his sudden panic was the realisation that staying in the complex would mean missing tonight's Star Trek meeting.

"I'm afraid not Mister, Erm," asked the Colonel.

"Mister Twat," interjected Chantelle, the hapless Samantha snorting in merriment.

"Its Spam sir," said Gary, administering a level seven death glance at the hated female.

"I'm afraid not Mister Spam, unless it is absolutely essential. Can I ask for what reason?"

"I have to go to my Star..." Gary closed his mouth. "I have to go to my... I have to start a course at night school," he concluded, thinking quickly.

The Colonel offered no reply, just a sympathetic stare, provoking Gary to enter into a sulk. To argue further would only invite more questions. The officers and suited men chatted quietly to each other for a few minutes before finally seeming to reach a decision.

"Ladies and Gentlemen." Watkin began again, bringing a hush to the room. "As I said earlier we will require a small number of you to stay with us." He paused, unsure as to whether to disclose any more information. "This is so as to accompany some patrols in Delamere, please let me assure you that you will be in no danger, are there any volunteers?"

Woods launched a full foot into the air from his armchair. "Thir I volunteer."

"Okay." said the Colonel, looking as though his thunder had been stolen from him, "I'll need another three people, anybody?" His eyes scanned the room waiting for hands to go up.

"Gary will go mate," said Chantelle, blowing a bubble.

Her lack of respect for the Colonels rank caused Captain Bridger to tut loudly.

Gary, with no intention of volunteering, paused for a brief rethink. Flashing up a mental picture of himself, he saw the returning hero, triumphant, draped with the union flag, the more he thought, the more interested he became.

"Yes sir, I shall volunteer," he said coming to a decision.

"Changed your mind have you Mister Spam? Good man. Okay, Anybody else?" The Colonel asked, his face scanning those assembled.

"My good Colonel," The voice belonged to Peter."I do declare I shall put myself at your service."

Eyes searched the room before eventually Leyton raised his hand and quietly said "Yeh."

"Okay, thank you all for your attention," said Watkin with relief. "I shall leave you all to enjoy some refreshments; telephones will be provided shortly, I shall return in about an hour." With a smile he left through the same door he had entered followed by the two suited men.

Some minutes passed before Captain Bridger beckoned the four Volunteers over and led them from the wardroom.

"This is exciting stuff isn't it?" Gary said to Leyton as they left.

Reluctant to respond, he gave Gary a look, laden to the teeth with any expletive you care to mention as long as it ended with the word off. Woods shuffled along, deep in thought. Occasionally he would punch his balled up fist into the other open palm while muttering about "Bagging thome more oth the thons of bithes."

Peter ambled along happily, analysing the walls as to their construction. Traversing another long corridor, Bridger ushered them through another checkpoint and into a new room. A makeshift sign hung upon the door. Holding Cells, with the duty officers name written underneath in black marker. An area obviously built for security, not to keep people out but rather to keep them in. A large wooden counter, fronted by a heavy wire mesh wall took up the entire width of the room. The only access was via a metal door with no handle or lock.

Gary stared, wondering how you got back in if you were the last person out. Beyond the wire mesh, another identical door was visible on the far wall. The whole room was bathed in a bright artificial light, possessing a musty smell; similar to one pervading an old museum or castle. Positioned behind the desk, conveying a look of abject tedium was a burly sergeant, dreamily filling out a Sudoku puzzle.

A discreet cough from Captain Bridger caused him to spring from his chair and snap to attention, producing a perfect salute. In the same movement his other hand deftly flung the puzzle book to the floor in a vain attempt to lose the offending item.

"Sergeant, I want you to introduce these four gentlemen to Mister Pressbond and show them what we have in our possession."

The sergeant scanned the four specimens before him, *Bloody hell*, he thought, "Err are you sure ma'am?"

"Sergeant," said Bridger, puffing out her chest, like an offended porcupine ready to strike. "I do not expect my orders to be questioned, is that clear?"

"Yes ma'am, sorry ma'am," squeaked the belittled Sergeant.

"These men took part in the incident in Delamere forest last week," Bridger continued. "They will be accompanying recon teams later; I want you to show them our finds."

"Yes ma'am," replied the sergeant, not daring to question his superior again.

"Gentlemen I shall leave you in the capable hands of Sergeant Carter here," She smiled at each in turn before scowling at the berated sergeant, turned and left the room.

Opening the outer door the soldier ushered the four bewildered men inside, closing it with a clang. Picking up a wall mounted telephone he barked out an order. Some seconds later the other door swung open. Once inside, it took a few moments for their eyes to adjust to the dull light, eventually it became apparent that they were standing in the middle of a long corridor. On both sides were a number of metal plated doors, each furnished with a small square window at head height. Twelve in total, the cells were patrolled by four guards within the corridor.

"Follow me Gentlemen."

A small grey suited man, who seemed to appear from nowhere stood at Leyton's side. His greasy, smoothed down black hair and pointy facial features gave him the appearance of a rat, while carried under his arm was a white lab coat denoting him as a scientist or similar. Smiling he put it on.

"Good afternoon gentlemen my name is Pressbond." Another smile. "I understand you took part in the incident in Delamere forest last week?" he asked rubbing his hands together.

"Why does everyone call it an incident?" Gasped Leyton, suddenly animated, "It was a battle."

"Quite," said the Rat man uninterestedly.

One of the patrolling soldiers interjected as he passed, "Sorry to interrupt sir," he said to Pressbond and then turned to Leyton, "but, it's you isn't it, your Ian Wright aint you?"

Pressbond gave a heavy cough.

"Sorry sir, I err, sorry I erm." The flustered guard resumed his previous stance looking somewhat embarrassed.

Leyton shrugged the incident off, his mood lightening, feeling happy to be associated with the ex Arsenal and England footballing legend.

"Well gentlemen, if you care to take a look in cell number one you will see one of the fellows who you were, err fighting in the inc... err battle."

"Thee I thold you, what did I thell you?" said Woods, almost bouncing with excitement.

The window in the cell door was only large enough for two people to see through at once. Gary and Peter looked first. Medical apparatus and machines were dotted around a large metal framed bed. In the corner stood the obligatory armed guard, while two white coated men, presumably doctors fussed around the bed. Securely strapped down upon it was one of the aliens.

"This fellow," said the rat man, standing behind Gary and Peter, "was wounded by your paintball guns, quite remarkable that the paint from your guns is lethal to them."

Peter turned to the ratman and puffed out his nose. "Indeed sir it is quite obvious that the chemical composition within the interjected molecular structure combined with atomic physiological strands of our unfortunate Desirion here, caused a severe chemical reaction, resulting in the paint acting upon their flesh just as an aggressive molecular acid would upon our own genetic structure."

"Quite," said Pressbond, examining Peter through narrowed eyes, "Now..." He paused and looked into Peter's face more seriously. "What did you say it was called?"

"The subject in question Is a male, I believe, example of the Desirion race, originating from the planet Shard, orbiting a solar mass known as Accropolatatis," replied Peter nonchalantly.

"Really, please explain how you know this?" Pressbond asked suspiciously.

"It's quite simple, I....I.....I don't actually know," admitted Peter.

Pressbond sighed, his mind made up that rather than being a genius or an informed person with the ability to shed some light on this alien species, he was in fact just another Lunatic.

"Man I preferred him when he was a tard," said Leyton.

The ratman raised an eyebrow, not used to such a basic level of social intercourse, "Well gentlemen if you'd like to follow me, we'll go say hello shall we?"

With a knock on the door he opened it beckoning them to enter. Once inside he closed it behind them.

"Well as you can see he doesn't look too good does he?"

"How can one be sure its primary structure is totally different to us? Who are we to say what looks good or not?" Finished, Peter leant his head back so far his chin actually jutted out further than his nose.

"As your colleague pointed out, he is physically different, therefore we have no way of attending to him medically or providing the nourishment he requires," said one of the doctors present.

"Why bother, juth wathte it," Woods snarled, eyeing the alien through narrowed slits, daring it to return his gaze.

The Being lay upon the bed, the entire torso, a mass of dark red and brown blobs, resembling severe burns. Evidence of where the paintballers pellets had made contact. Its eyes however remained resolute, trained upon the ceiling.

"At present," said Pressbond, "we are attempting to work out how to communicate with the fellow."

Gary moved closer to the being, observing its eyes all the time, they never moved. "I may be able to assist," he said, "May I?"

"Err, I'm not sure," replied Pressbond.

"He may as well," interrupted the white coated doctor, "he can't do any worse than we have."

"Oh very well proceed, but please be careful not to injure the specimen."

Positioning his head closer still, Gary extended his fingers into claws and gently rested them upon the temples, eyebrows and cheeks of the aliens yellow head.

With a sticky squelching sound its eyes slowly, pivoted, finally resting upon Gary.

"My thoughts to your thoughts, my memories to your memories, my mind to your mind," Gary preached, his eyes clamped shut, deep in concentration.

"Sir, what are you doing?" Said the doctor with a sigh, all hope of a breakthrough having since made a stealthy escape and left the building.

The alien looked annoyed with Gary, its features going through the motions until they settled upon an ultimately miserable appearance.

"It's a little trick I picked up," said Gary still brimming with hopeless optimism.

"Encountered a lot of Destrons have you Gary?" said Leyton sarcastically.

"The term is Desirions," corrected Peter.

"I think sir," interrupted the Ratman politely, "that you have been watching too much Star Trek."

Gary released the alien from the mind meld; its eyes seemed to be brimming with what appeared to be tears. "Yes well, it's an old Indian trick I learned over in the Kuala Lumpa," lied Gary.

"Yes quite, well I think we'll let Doctor Hollins continue with some genuine methods shall we?" The Ratman said, flashing Gary a smile.

Gary reciprocated quite unaware that he was being ridiculed. Shutting the door behind them Pressbond took a deep lungful of air and sighed heavily.

"Now if we move along a little, you will see another specimen in the next cell." He paused. "Now this one was found relatively unharmed and seems to have made a recovery by itself."

Peering through the small window, Gary and Leyton witnessed the alien sitting upon a bench, restrained by cuffs attached to strong nylon ropes, threaded through steel ring bolts upon the walls and floor to allow a certain amount of movement.

"We have managed to receive some speech from this fellow, but as you can imagine, it's all gobbledygook at the moment. We have our topmost linguistic experts and code breakers on it right now." Pressbond turned as if looking for something. "I say has anyone seen the other member of your group?"

"Excuse me sir I don't think you have authorization to touch that."

The voice came from the cell immediately opposite, just in time they turned to witness a bright yellow glare erupt from the small room, followed by an explosion of brick erupting from the corridor wall to leave a large jagged hole. Clouds of dust and debris billowed from the doorway covering Gary, Leyton, Peter and the ratman, who had wisely dived for cover. Woods emerged seconds later followed by the guard, both coughing and spluttering and covered in a thick layer of grey dust.

"What did you do man, for God's sake what did you do?" shouted Pressbond, rising from the debris strewn floor.

"Err nothing," Woods replied innocently, his ears whistling in e minor while yellow blobs danced before his eyes.

The rat-man entered the cell re-emerging quickly. "How did you get that to fire?" He barked with astonishment, "We've been trying to get that to work all week without success."

By now the corridor had filled with an assortment of white coated, grey suited and uniformed men, all wondering anxiously whether they were under attack. Woods who was now realising his inadvertent tampering had actually produced some positive results, swelled with pride. "I err juth pulled the trigger." he said.

Scientist types rushed from nowhere, filling the cell with the smoking alien gun while a suited man inspected the hole in the wall, giving a little wave to those inside.

The outer security door suddenly resounded with the sound of hammering accompanied by frantic shouting. Peeking through the eyehole, the guard swallowed hard and stood upright. Opening the door he slammed to such a juddering salute it threatened to dislocate his shoulder.

"What in the great thundering bloody hell is going on?" roared Colonel Watkin supported by three armed guards of his own.

"It's okay Colonel," offered Pressbond, reacting to the situation quickly. "Nothing to worry about, just a little err," he looked with furrowed brows at Woods, "accident."

Taking in the settling dust and debris, Watkins eyes eventually fell onto the hole in the brickwork and pointed. "We seem to have discovered how the alien weapon works," said the ratman.

Watkin seemed to have trouble accepting he'd got worked up for nothing.

"Okay you may stand down," he finally said to the guards, his anger slowly dissipating. "Our guests are required to attend a briefing on the reconnaissance in half an hour, please ensure they are not late," he added before turning and storming out.

The duty guard snapped to attention. Pressbond eased his mood a little while Leyton diligently issued a finger in the Colonels general direction.

"I think gentlemen we have work to do, so I'd appreciate it if you could allow us to continue," said Pressbond, reluctant for the tour to continue. With that the four so called advisors were hastily escorted from the high security area and back to the wardroom. Now empty, they sat, making themselves comfortable once more. The emergence of more military and civilian personnel cut short their relaxation. Captain Bridger and Colonel Watkin were among them, along with two similarly dressed army officers and another in RAF Blue.

"Gentlemen if I may," Bridger interjected. The room's occupants settled down to listen while Colonel Watkin took the foreground.

"Okay the situation is this; tracking stations monitoring signals from the small band of aliens hiding out in Delamere forest have picked up a huge increase in transmissions, alas we are still no nearer to deciphering them, but..." he paused to take a sip of whisky. "We believe that this may indicate a possible military response from them". There was a further delay, this time to receive a whispered message. "Right yes, where were we, oh yes, therefore we are stepping up our patrols around the evacuated area with quick response units on standby including artillery and air strikes if need be. Now you four," he continued, indicating Gary and his colleagues. "Will still be required to join our recon teams, but please don't worry you will be in no danger."

Woods thrust his hand into the air, ramrod straight. "Thir thir," he gasped, inhaling breath like an excited schoolboy desperate to answer a question.

"Yes err, Mister err?" dithered Colonel Watkin.

"Woodth Thir. Will we be armed?"

"No Mister Woodth, Woods," he corrected himself; "you most certainly will not be armed. We cannot allow members of the public to carry firearms now can we?" he finished with a sarcastic guffaw.

The rest of the room took up the laugh on a purely suck up to the senior officer basis.

"I can handle one thir, I hath therved," offered Woods, disappointment etched on his face.

"Really Mister Woods, with whom did you serve?"

Standing, Woods snapped to attention and took a very deep breath. "Thix yearth with firth battalion Royal Green Jacketh. Promoted to Corporal then Thergeant. Trantherred to Royal Marineth, three yearth in four two Commando, trantherred again to Parathutte regiment then recruited by Thpethial air thervice, promoted to Thergeant Major. Leth thervithe ath a Regimental Thergeant Major thir." He took another deep breath before continuing. "Theen thervith in Northern Ireland, the Falklands, Africa, Yugothlavia, Iraq and other clathithied thituathionth worldwide", he took a last deep breath, his body still at attention, saluted and ended with "thir."

The rooms chuckling ceased, replaced by a gaggle of dropped jaws and an all round sense of awe.

"Well Mister err, indeed, ha ha err, Sergeant Major Woods your credentials seem to be more than suitable," flustered Colonel Watkin. "Maybe we can sort you out with something after all."

A stunned Gary turned to Woods, "My god why didn't you ever tell me you had done all that?"

"Never theemed appropriate thir," said Woods still standing to attention.

"Err you may relax Mister Woods, stand easy," said Colonel Watkin.

The rest of the meeting was spent discussing possible tactics and strategies until eventually the formal discussions ended. A side door opened and the same white coated stewards emerged. Before long drinks and snacks were being served, allowing the rooms occupants to adopt a more relaxed posture. Gary however was staring into space, a Brandy hanging limply from his left hand. His mind mapping the next day's exploits, where he, Gary Spam, space adventurer, could. Just could save the planet.

VI

Prime overseer Lax's image reflected back at him through the observation port of the Desirion command vessel *Paraxatar*. Quite alone in his personal quarters, his face betrayed much of the mixed emotion which swelled within. His skin tone transformed thanks to the rooms subtle blue lighting from its natural light sandy yellow to a pale green. Ornate robes adorned with graceful calligraphy swirled at his feet, robes which, even to the untrained eye, clearly belonged to one of position or high rank.

The personal quarters, although isolated from the rest of the ship, were connected directly to the centre of operations or Hub, as it was referred to, by way of a concealed bulkhead doorway. Invisible most of the time, it only revealed itself when in use. A kind of safety device should the ship require an air tight seal and rather useful if ever boarded by a hostile invader.

The outline now glowed briefly before parting, allowing Lax to enter the Hub. Despite it being the ships nerve centre, it was a most sedate place to work. Circular in shape, smooth concave walls with an array of oval displays screens around the wall. Some depicted lines and lines of data while others offered detailed maps and diagrams. No one sat directly at these screens. The operators could be found in a circle of luxurious recliners in the centre, resembling the petals of a flower. From these positions, multi layered retractable touch panels elongated themselves on stalks from the floor to form a seamless circle around them.

Most evident was the absence of taut nerves among those present, all appeared happy, content and relaxed. The workstations themselves emitted a similar calmness, lacking all of the bright flashing in your face lights or large red buttons with the word alarm in a big font, designed to send the heart leaping. All of this of course was no accident.

The current era of Desirion imperial expansion was surpassing any previous level, and they saw no reason to do it upon an uncomfortable chair. The evidence was there to see in all of their vessels, vehicles, buildings and even clothes. All built or made to offer the most comfort possible.

Despite this all of this, Lax was not calm, far from it. His mind weigh heavy with the responsibility for the investigation of this planet and its dominant species.

"Hooomanns." His lipless mouth was not quite able to Say the alien word, but even in its pigeon pronunciation, it caused severe irritation. With a sigh he pictured the images he'd seen, their ridiculous ugly heads, feebly balanced upon equally feeble shoulders. The pressure placed by the Minister Lords upon Shard of his need to succeed hadn't seemed so daunting back on launch day. Maybe the glitz and fanfare and the promised riches and titles when he became the Prime Overseer of the planet Basingstoke, had concealed the real responsibility. So far however, this adventure hadn't got off to a great success.

The Hooomanns should have been powerless against us, why was our intelligence so inaccurate? These and other thoughts hammered hourly throughout his mind, culminating with the once calm and authoritative leader to frequently doubt his own mind. *And what on Shard was wrong with our equipment?*

The approach of someone interrupted his train of thought. Turning, Lax observed the newcomer. He was bent forward and in the process of conducting one of the most impressive bows made by anyone, anywhere, ever.

"Exulted majestic overseer," he purred, the words muffled due to his position. "Commander Pox gives you joy of the age and wishes to inform you that the particle dispersal interphasers have passed test level three, and are ready for final assembly, once we gain a purchase upon the surface."

"Ah Pix," replied Lax, his mood lifting a couple of notches already. "That is indeed good news at last, be so good as to inform the commander that as soon as we reach the surface he will arrange their assembly and commence operations."

"As you wish most exulted majestic overseer sire," gushed Pix, scraping himself up before genuflecting with practiced ease toward the door.

Lax watched with growing annoyance, almost pity; He didn't connect well with all this exulted majestic overseer grovelling rubbish. Having proven himself worthy of his position by merit, he preferred to connect with those working below him on their own level, probably because he too had once been a grovelling menial like Pix. Sure he understood the concept of respect and honouring a superior rank, even agreeing that such should be duly remarked upon. However, a short, "Sire," or, "Overseer," would suffice.

Having followed all the traditional protocols on their departure from Shard, he'd accepted the lavish decorations bestowed upon the assumed successful overseer and his armada, but as soon as they had left the Accropolatatian system, Lax intended to ensure that things were carried out on a more casual basis. This however, had been met with only partial success and he now accepted that that was probably about as far as it would go.

Pix finally disappeared from sight and returning once more to his previous train of thought, Lax's heart sank again. Not a single success worthy of mention, recon probe, those that returned covered in filth and the fight in the trees with the pathfinder team. Defeat was certainly not an option. A return to Shard empty handed was unthinkable, his name would be shamed forever. More than two centuries had passed since the Desirion race had failed to obtain an acquisition and he had no intention of changing history.

The sight of a dimly illuminated ship, The *Garefex,* similar to his own command vessel but somehow meaner looking, hove into view, drawing his attention from his oh so draining inner workings. Swelling with pride, a feeling of invincibility enveloped him as the forward sphere of the brand new Capital vessel came about to reveal her full extent.

"Magnificent," he mouthed. The most up to date technology had been crammed into these new ships. Antiprototonic propulsion, self generating gravity emitters, thermal transfer plasma weaponry, not to mention electro magnetic resonance shielding and he was in command of a whole fleet of them. As he watched, more emerged from the gloom, the need for visual concealment now dispensed with as very soon the whole area around the outcrop of rock the humans called Beeston castle would be swarming with the entire armada.

His mouth rose at each corner as images of impending success manifested themselves subconsciously. The more ships which came into sight the more excited he became. *The Hooomanns will be no match for us,* he thought. *Prime Overseer Lax would go down in history as the Desirion who conquered the Hooomann species.* He liked the sound of that.

Light rain caused the many hulls to glisten, the bulbous outlines broken only by the soft silhouettes of other ships making the same descent just metres away. Dull, almost invisible blue sparks crackled as the electromagnetic resonance from the defensive shields interacted with water droplets. Covering the last few metres the lead vessels descended not altogether smoothly, the slightly heavier gravity forcing the engines to work hard until extra positioning thrusters emitted loud whooshes and huge landing stanchions unfolded allowing them to touch down in the dark and eerie fields beneath the dominating shadow of the ruins of Beeston castle.

The old fort, virtually destroyed by Oliver Cromwell's forces, as the civil wars of the seventeenth century came to an end, was positioned high upon a rocky outcrop. A superb commanding location providing dominating views of the Cheshire countryside mid way between Chester and Crewe.

Positioning himself closer to the Hubs front viewing port, Lax felt a great power course through his body as he observed the landings against the backdrop of the crumbling masonry, the dizzying feeling of immortality banishing all previous thoughts of defeat as if they had never existed. Unfolding his curious double elbowed arm he extended an elongated finger, gently making contact with the inner surface of the view port. Behind, a doorway fizzed and he was soon joined by two more figures. Both dressed in a similar style to their overseer but with less ornate markings upon their differently coloured robes.

Commander Pox and senior physician Dix flanked Lax and quietly observed the proceedings outside. As one, they both focused upon Lax. Unhampered by an anxious disposition, they were ultimately confident of success while possessing the utmost faith in their overseer.

On the outside surface, large drops of rainwater began to run down the smooth surface. Joining others en route they made even larger ones, causing them to gather momentum. With his outstretched finger Lax traced their journey, transfixed with its descent until inevitably disappearing from sight. His eyes remained still, motionless within their transparent membrane, a look of puzzlement, almost wonder filling the nose-less face. Bending his head sideways, he focused upon the trail of the raindrop. "Told you we'd need windscreen wipers," he uttered

VII

RAF Sealand, Located on the Welsh border near to Chester was one of those old airbases which had managed to cling onto existence. Hidden away, it was a relic of the cold and second World Wars. These days it was past its prime. The old parade ground had long since passed into disuse, having succumbed to the inevitable onslaught of dandelions and various strains of grass breaking through the tarmac and concrete. The runway, although still in its full extent was reduced very much to the same state. Never again would it hear the powerful roar of a piston engine thrumming the air, or the ear splitting thunder of jet aircraft preparing for take-off.

Recently erected units offset the decay to some extent. Built to house private business enterprises, with one even dedicated to military defence, but the days of a bustling air base whether it be under the flag of the RAF or the USAF as was the case in the 1950s, were now long resigned to the history books.

The image which seemed to finalise the end was the base's football pitch. Two goals standing proudly amidst grass reaching to two thirds their height. The playing surface had more in common with a large colony of adders, a family of foxes and the odd roaming Badger or amphibian than a slick one, two, followed by a half volley into the top right hand corner..

Inevitably, time and budget restrictions had caught up with Sealand and gradually it had been run down by successive caring governments until finally the decision for almost total closure was announced. Almost that is, apart from the sophisticatedly advanced, secret and very much active surveillance and communication centre. Not just secret, it was most totally top secret and no one in the area should have even had the slightest idea of its existence.

It was however, just about the worst kept secret around. Not only was it common knowledge that there was a base still operating there, but the base Commander enjoyed semi skimmed milk on his morning wheat flakes, and Snoogs his cat ate Rabbit and Hamster flavoured gourmet food.

It existed or didn't exist, rather in the same way that Area 51 doesn't exist, the Loch Ness monster is just a floating tree with sticky out bits and UFO's are just weird shaped clouds. Although given current circumstances the latter anomaly may be just a trifle hard to defend now.

The run down look was not quite purpose made but the gradual crumbling served the MOD's purpose nicely and so was allowed to quietly continue, all adding to the perfect disguise.

Should the unsuspecting visitor look a little closer however, it would become apparent that all was not quite as it seemed. Housed inside the run down aircraft maintenance hangers, complete with big red DANGER UNSAFE BUILDING signs, was a whole array of state of the art radar and surveillance instrumentation, cunningly hidden behind false wooden walls. Looking beyond the decay, an eagle eyed sleuth may just notice the well oiled hinges on run down and apparently un-openable doors fronting the wooden barrack blocks. The most unexpected sight had one managed to ignore the broken windows and black out curtains, would be the fully functional lift, which had been installed with adjacent spiral staircase, leading deep into the bowels of the earth.

Approximately seventy feet beneath the decay and neglect, the contrast was remarkable. Smooth white plastered walls with brand new fittings furnished the redundant nuclear shelter. The size of a small village, the complex had, after the end of the threat from the Soviet bloc, been reduced in size, use and population. It was however, retained by successive Governments as its usefulness could be essential at any moment. With the commencement of hostilities in the Persian Gulf and the potential for a new era of terrorism upon British soil, it was decided to upgrade the facilities at Sealand to enable it to operate as a major covert surveillance centre.

Deep inside the grey concrete complex, one room in particular buzzed with an air of anxious excitement. High ranking military officers dressed in brown, blue and black mingled with dark suited official types from the ministry, while lower ranks manned various devices and pieces of equipment. Those not employed in the daily operation of apparatus tended to walk around a lot. Quicker still were those who clung to seemingly blank pieces of paper, massively important and essential in the making you look busy without actually doing anything stakes.

The whole labyrinth smelt strongly of garlic. Thanks to a fault with the air conditioning which was drawing in air from the kitchens. Not great if you don't like garlic.

"Sir, I'm picking up interference." squealed an RAF operative, excitedly checking and re-checking his findings. "It appears to be exactly the same distortion wave that was picked up by that Yankee sub last week."

The console was indeed displaying the same distorted mess of a signal received by the U.S.S Wyatt Earp during its encounter with one of the alien vessels the previous week. Sliding practiced fingers over the touch screen the operator was greeted a second or two later with the response he'd hoped for.

"Yes sir it's an exact match," he exclaimed, indicating the

screen now running the current distortion alongside a projection of the one received by the Wyatt Earp.

After the encounter the United States authorities had reacted promptly and positively. Realising the seriousness of the situation and dispensing with the usual secrecy associated with an incident of this nature, they shared their findings with the rest of the world, including the French.

A tall, overweight and balding officer displaying the insignia of an Air Marshall of the Royal Air Force fought to gain control of himself as he entered the control room. His uniform sported enough coloured medal ribbon to be successfully mistaken as an artist's pallet. Bulging alarmingly in places it was clearly a size too small while beneath a sweaty arm-pit he clamped his cap. Removing a red handkerchief from a trouser pocket, he mopped beads of perspiration from his brow as he spoke.

"Do you have a location Barret?" He quizzed the operator.

Barret was quiet while he entered various commands into the computer, "I have a fix, fifty three degrees and two minutes latitude by minus two degrees and sixty eight minutes longitude and approximately twenty three miles south, East, East of our current position." He paused to look up the reference. "It's Beeston Castle sir."

A quick glance at the large clock on the wall revealed one thirty five am.

"I don't think there's any doubt about it do you?" The Air Marshall asked of his staff.

His staff comprised three officers, all sporting rather less finery, each one bent double behind their superior watching the recording of the signal.

"Oh yes absolutely sir," the reply came in triplicate.

Turning quickly on his heels the Air Marshall almost caught the three officers a glancing blow. Striding into his office, he picked up one of the three telephones neatly positioned upon his immaculately tidy desk. After only a couple of minutes, he replaced the receiver and took a deep breath. Orders had been issued and within seconds two of the most important phone calls ever made were being relayed at the speed of light towards London, Washington, Moscow and Beijing to inform the relative governments of their findings and to seek the relative responses.

VIII

The rain continued to fall that morning bringing a thin mist with it. Forming initially over the nearby Shropshire Union canal it had spread slowly in large pockets. Hugging the ground as it crept, appearing to lap gently against the tree trunks that grew at the base of the outcrop of Beeston Castle like waves on a lake.

Lax, Dix, and Pox, having exited the stationary *Paraxatar* were joined by an entourage of high ranking military personnel and dignitaries, some willing others not so. Walking, they reached the heights of the inner bailey and were treated to a spectacular sight. Spread out below on the flat ground around the rocky outcrop were the many ships bearing an array of cargo's ranging from food and clothing to ground assault vehicles and weapons.

Beaming with smug satisfaction, Lax observed his fleet; illuminated by huge powerful flood lights they emptied their payloads. Beyond the armada, in the distance, the glow from the human dwelling of Chester could just be made out while in the other direction those of Manchester shone brighter still.

A slight gurgle, not too dissimilar to a chuckle escaped his mouth. This was no coincidence as his mood was on the upward curve of his minds eternal roller coaster. From the larger transport ships an array of equipment was being carefully unloaded, some of it stowed inside the abandoned farm buildings nearby. From other vessels issued forth a continuous exodus of well armed and rather efficient looking foot soldiers. Resplendent in red and orange loose fitting body suits with helmets with eye covers. Each clutched a weapon, similar in design to a sten gun but with smoother, more graceful lines. Rendezvousing at a pre arranged area they routinely began the procedure of checking their personal equipment.

The surviving Desirions from the skirmish in Delamere had reported that their weapons had had little effect upon their human adversaries. Armourers and weapons experts therefore carried out diagnostic tests upon the plasma rifles. After necessary adjustments, Lax and the relevant department commanders had been assured that they were now operating at maximum efficiency. No particular reason had been discovered for the malfunction, possibly the dreary damp conditions down on the planet's surface. Shard enjoyed a considerably dryer climate than Earth. That same damp atmosphere was thought to be the primary cause of the current failure to install a defence grid around the landing site. Beacons had been placed at regular intervals with the intention of linking them together via a simple wall of laser beams. All that was generated however was the odd fizz of sparks. While the area's which did operate properly were continually activated by the local wildlife who hadn't been briefed on the use of a perimeter alarm.

Beyond the mass of troops a large grey container was moved clear of the main bulk of activity and opened to reveal a number of long metal racks. Each one held a dozen metallic sphere's, approximately the size of basketballs. One by one they were attended to by an operative before being sent to scout the way ahead.

From large access doors located on the underside of the rear fuselage, the largest Vessels now bore their fruit. Emerging, one after the other, bulky, green and brown camouflaged vehicles trundled off. Moving upon linked tracks, similar to a tank they measured a good forty feet from end to end. Dropping from their mother ship onto the contoured ground, the caterpillar tracks of the lead vehicle absorbed the dips and bumps with only the slightest disturbance or distortion to its motion.

The look in Lax's eye was magnificent. He was only a stage away from steepling his fingers and mouthing "excellent," in slow and deliberate tones. "This, my friends," he said, a hint of maniacal excitement creeping into his speech. "Is where our tidings will change."

His entire manner had changed again. Gone was the dejected leader of just a couple of hour's previous, optimism coursed through him, even developing a small twitch in the left corner of his mouth. His attention and of those around him was suddenly drawn to the unloading of a very different container, the sight of which sent further waves of excitement pulsing through those who were aware of what it contained. Unlike the other square or rectangular grey boxes, this one was of a highly polished metallic affair. Covered in glyphs and of no particular shape, the container was clearly built to fit its contents. Large numbers of black uniformed figures attended the container, clambering over it like ants. The panels were quickly removed, revealing, albeit briefly, a number of prefabricated transparent partitions and an array of large dull metal tubes each the size of a post box. Metres of silver cabling and other tech were also removed before a huge pre assembled shiny gazebo was brought over to conceal the device from prying Eyes. As far as they could see, at least another three gazebo's had been erected close by.

Finally, unable to help himself, Lax's fingertips joined to form a steeple. "Excellent!" he exclaimed. "Indeed, now we shall see what these Hooomanns are made of."

"Excellent!" Emulated Commander Pox, also caught up in the euphoria,

"Excellent indeed Pox my old friend," beamed Lax, "the Hooomanns will have no defence against the Interphaser, and soon, very soon...."

In all, five Particle dispersal interphasers stood hidden under their respective coverings. Thick cables snaked underneath tethered to nearby ships causing them to resemble bloated insects. Outside, Desirions milled about curiously, hoping to gain a quick peek at the contents inside. To no avail, their black clad comrades stood firm, blocking the entrances.

It wasn't long however, before through the slight gaps in the covering, a warm orange glow could be seen, accompanied by a gentle but noticeable hum, gaining in intensity as each one was energised. Lax, along with his senior advisors and commanders and content with all they had seen, uttered another three excellents before finally leaving the inner bailey to join proceedings below.

"I am most surprised with the Hooomanns," he stated, "I was expecting some kind of limited resistance, but they have been very quiet."

No one commented as they followed the route towards the castles ruined gatehouse, having decided to take the scenic walk. Beyond that, a very steep, sloping bridge confronted them. A nearby small stone structure, circular in shape was surrounded by a number of Desirion soldiers, all appearing to look down into it. Turning suddenly at the appearance of the entourage, one of them drew a sharp breath. With grunts and shoves he informed his colleagues. At the sight of their overseer they all straightened, looking for all the universe like a group of guilty alien schoolchildren. One however, seemed to be struggling to hold something within the well. Far from wishing to appear disrespectful, he attempted a kind of strained bent over sideways attention stance. As if pre empting his leaders next question, another broke away from the group and bowed majestically, his double elbowed arm scraping away dust and small stones as it swept before him.

"Exulted lord overseer, I must report that one of my Cadre is..." His words were suddenly cut short by a loud scream from within the well, the echoed cry quickly cut short by a thud.

Lax gave the cadre leader a stern look.

"Has fallen down this large hole." continued the leader with one eye swivelled anxiously towards the well.

With a sigh, Lax continued as if nothing had occurred. Following the Overseer, Commander Pox reached out an extended arm and grabbed the grovelling subaltern by the material of his suit. "Get him out and never bother his majestic Overseer with such trivial news again."

With the sound of frantic scuttling behind them, Lax and his party made their way over the bridge and down the well worn path towards the outer gatehouse.

"What design of building is this place Pox?" Lax asked looking around with fascination.

"I believe it is what the Hooomanns call a fort," replied Pox, struggling slightly with the pronunciation. "Constructed many of their earth years ago, it is a stronghold or defensive structure, similar to the Arga Vaster back on Shard."

Had he been inclined, Pox might have continued to state that the building was in fact constructed to house two hundred, foot high, half human Gerbils, bred for the purpose of submarine cable laying, such was Lax's attention span.

"They cannot penetrate our shielding, majestic overseer," stated Chief physician Dix, guessing Lax's train of thought. "The perimeter screen will soon be operational and scramble beams have rendered their detection systems useless. The Hooomanns really have no idea we are here." he continued, confident in his knowledge.

"Indeed Dix," Lax replied loosely before falling silent.

Another quarter of an hour passed before they rounded the rocky outcrop and stood amongst the vast array of forces at their disposal. The majority now either unloaded or in the advanced stages of preparation. As far as the eye could see, impressive ships of all sizes blocked the horizon. Buzzing around like irritating flies were spherical drones, policing the embarkation areas perimeter. Most notable were the uniformed lines of infantry. Illuminated under immense floodlights, large numbers of some of the best trained soldiers Shard had to offer, all fully equipped. Elsewhere many hundreds of others were already climbing aboard other bulky caterpillar tracked and other smaller vehicles.

This new vehicle could fit four or five Desirions at a time. It too had caterpillar tracks with a kind of cab at the front. Access was via a roof opening at the front. Mounted towards the rear was the vehicles primary purpose, a large double barrelled weapon, very similar to a bofors gun but with sleeker lines, a fearsome looking weapon and easily capable of inducing fear into any adversary.

Behind all of this activity were a number of larger craft of a totally different design altogether. Hovering above the ground, they simply bristled with weaponry, long, flat and not too dissimilar to a hovercraft. With a distinct area at the front for the crew, it carried two thermal transfer plasma bolt guns, each barrel some six inches across. As if that wasn't enough, Mounted upon a long trestle and running down the centre was a huge cavernous black tube, twenty feet in length and capable of rotating three hundred and sixty degree's. It was obviously also a gun of some design and terrible looking with it.

So awesome was it, had the words DEATH RAY been printed upon it in big red panicky letters it would have been the perfect accompaniment.

Lax and his colleagues admired the rigid impressive rows of soldiers, committed to fight and possibly die for him and the Desirion cause.

"Excellent," he said for the final time that day, rubbing his hands together. "After they have been interphased, they will be untouchable and impervious to all Hooomann weapons."

Staring at his Overseer, Pox grinned. "Exce..." He stopped. Maybe the word had been used too often of late. "Fantastic," he substituted, casting an eye toward Lax, but the Overseer was now deep within a world of his own.

IX

The ten soldiers of the first battalion of the Parachute regiment had been observing the alien invaders for a couple of hours, ever since the first ship had landed. One of many patrols sent out to reccee the evacuated areas, initially to deter looters and report on any residents who had been missed or possibly overlooked by the evacuation.

Tasked with checking out the area along the banks of the Shropshire union Canal, Charlie Section were caught rather unawares as they proceeded towards a pub called The Shady oak.

A pilot of the Army air corps, passing over the previous evening had spotted what he described as Human activity upon the premises. Chances were some of the local villagers, having avoided the exodus, had taken advantage of the deserted environment and decided to enjoy the mother of all lock-ins.

The Initial response, when their orders were passed down had been groans, but it soon turned to eager curiosity when it dawned upon the patrol that their search area was a deserted pub in an evacuated area. Sergeant Dave Doberman was to command, a seasoned soldier with eighteen years service within the regiment and the medals to show for it too. Tall and shaven headed, the west countryman was possibly not the best choice for a mission to a pub, given his past experiences with alcohol. Although to be fair, that was exactly where those experiences were, in the past. Still particularly partial to the odd pint or seventeen, but he believed he had it under control now. Regardless, he felt his mouth moisten at the prospect.

Simple job, he thought. *Go in, couple of beers and then back to report nothing out of the ordinary, what could be simpler?*

A nice thought if you could guarantee the outcome, however, nothing out of the ordinary, was probably the least applicable quote any of them could apply to the situation they now found themselves in.

Each man was currently spread out in a large ditch next to the canal. Some were soaked, having rapidly taken cover in a flanking marsh bed. The more agile and possibly quicker thinkers had avoided this area, concealing themselves within undergrowth and bushes that made up the canals bank. They were relatively comfortable compared to their damper colleagues and just fifty, short, agonising yards from their quarry, The Shady Oak.

Private Croft was convinced he could smell the beer from where they were. Just a tad more alarming however, was the vast alien armada which had, and still was, in the process of landing and disembarking in the fields around Beeston Castle just a few hundred yards away.

Carefully, Doberman raised his night vision binoculars for the umpteenth time in the last ten minutes; the view was no better, worse in fact. Splayed out before them, easily outflanking the range of the binoculars, was a vast panorama of unusual shaped vessels, vehicles, craft, equipment and many, many odd looking humanoid figures. Even more alarming was that this force seemed to be growing larger with every passing minute.

The first craft had descended from the early morning darkness as the patrol were merrily walking and chatting somewhat inattentively along the towpath. Beginning with a low hiss, the sound grew with intensity as the craft descended, accompanied by clanks and mechanical noises as it neared the ground. At the sight of the unearthly visitors, Doberman and his men had instinctively flung themselves into the ditch running parallel with the canal, making best use of the undergrowth and had remained there ever since. Before the interference from the ships blocked all radio transmissions they had managed to relay as much relevant information as possible to HQ. No more attempts were made for fear of giving themselves away.

Fortunately, the information they had managed to transmit was enough to prompt the Government to put the whole country on a full scale invasion footing, consequently sending the complex beneath RAF Sealand into spasm, and raising the level of garlic even further.

Since the loss of communication, Sergeant Doberman had been furiously scribbling down information on enemy description, numbers etc, in the hope of sending one of his team back to headquarters when it was safe. On more than one occasion the possibility of trying to make it to the pub had crossed his mind. They would be concealed and the pub would certainly be safer than the position they were now in. Being the professional soldier however, his trained mind soon took over and against his better judgment, dismissed the idea, knowing that he would be expected to return to his unit at the first opportunity. Had he put the idea to a vote he would undoubtedly have received a unanimous vote in favour of the pub.

So they sat and watched, absorbing as much as possible of the fantastic illuminated scene before them. Doberman, along with two others continued writing feverishly. Private Simmonds, who was generally accepted as being artistically gifted, was adding the finishing touches to a masterpiece pencil sketch of an alien ship.

"Just a basic drawing will do Simmonds. It's not going in the bloody Tate is it?" Doberman chided.

"Sarge." Simmonds objected, gesturing with open hands and looking dejected.

The initial shock of being one of the first Human beings to witness a massed alien invasion, together with the bizarre and unearthly goings on attached to such an event had begun to wear off, and the squad now settled down as best they could under the circumstances. A watch system was organised with five observing for two hour shifts while the others relaxed as best they could, Doberman being the sole writer now.

In an attempt to make things a little more homely, Croft produced a pack of cards while keeping an eye on the Sergeant for any objection. Doberman looked up from his novel sized report, which was at last nearing conclusion, but with no objection forthcoming the cards were dealt

It was a little before three o'clock before they witnessed the strangest thing so far.

"Sarge something's happening. Those figures seem to be massing by the canopy thing they put up," remarked Corporal Casey.

Grabbing their weapons, those not on watch, quickly joined their comrades at the brow of the ditch. Indeed something was happening; groups of twenty to thirty of the alien were seen to enter the gazebos. Once a certain number were inside the entrances were sealed, remaining so for a few minutes until the same figures re-emerged. Proceeding towards another area, they took up positions in neat ranks as before. All however was not as it was previously.

"Those aliens, who have been through that tent thing look different to the others," observed Private Dawson, indicating them with a pointed finger.

Doberman peered closer through his binoculars, "Eh? What you on about Dawson?"

"Well look, they look sort of see through don't they?"

Doberman sighed and took another look, this time at a new group just emerging from the canopy. "Hello, I think you may have something there Dawson."

Glancing at his comrades, Dawson rather expected a well done wink or admiring nod. Smugness coated his grinning face, quickly evaporating when no one even looked up. Something indeed was very different with these new beings and as the squad peered ever more closely at the shapes emerging from the gazebo like coverings, it became apparent that they were slightly transparent. Not so as you could see right through them, but rather fuzzy and distorted, not solid.

Doberman reached for his paper pad and resumed scribbling. He had a nagging feeling that this new twist was more sinister and couldn't help thinking that these findings along with the whole host of information they had recorded, should be seen by headquarters, but without reliable communication the only way to do that was to send one of the men back, which at the moment was far too risky.

X

Those Desirions who had been subjected to the particle dispersal Interphaser now numbered in the thousands. Having broken rank they filed one by one, quickly filling the large bulky caterpillar tracked transporters. Each one was phase adapted and capable of carrying up to seventy five persons. These were in turn flanked by the mobile guns, again tracked, similar in design to the transports but much smaller. Each with a wicked quad of guns mounted upon the rear. Humming, the tips of the barrels glowed a menacing yellow.

In next to no time the transports were full, with external doors closing to leave many more Desirions to wait their turn. Lax had been in favour of conveying the whole force in one swoop using the huge cargo transporter ships they had landed with, but as the commanders pointed out, Although capable, they were not designed to operate for extended periods within an atmosphere, particularly one with stronger Gravity which exuded immense pressure upon the structures. Not to mention their non aerodynamical design, which were and to quote. "A right shit to control," with any manoeuvre other than straight up or down.

Another point of concern was their vulnerability. Although possessing an adequate defensive shield, their effectiveness would be greatly reduced whilst in flight, again due to power requirements, and so it was unanimously decided that the far more economical and equally capable overland vehicles would be used.

Standing with a contingent of his commanders, Lax gave off the bravery and confidence of a resolute leader, many miles from where all the nasty stuff was going to happen. Within the cavernous space of one of the troop transport ships their discussion echoed back at them. To the front, a large thin rectangular transparent screen, similar to a sheet of Perspex, generated a three dimensional map of the area in amazingly fine detail. The large forested outcrop of Beeston castle, their own ships, outlined with pulsing blue lights. The recently filled troop transports, and even individual soldiers, all flashing in a similar vein. Next to that, another screen displayed another map. This one depicted a much larger scale, clearly showing human dwellings, roads and rivers etc. The highlight was a glowing red line beginning at their current location, crossing the fields until it reached the main Crewe to Chester railway line. It then snaked north-west, following the rail line until it reached the outskirts of the city of Chester.

"My friends," said Lax unfolding an arm to gesture at the screens. "Our intended destination today is the large area known to the inhabitants as Kester."

"That's Chester," corrected a commander at his side.

"Che-ster," Lax repeated, subjecting his commander to a dirty look.

As he uttered the city's name a three dimensional image of it sprang into view on the screen. Where Lax's finger touched, it changed, showing a different part of the city along with landmarks, looking for all the world like a tourism promotional film.

"Majestic sentinel," Began a figure standing by Lax's side, his outline undefined and fuzzy. "What level of resistance should we expect?" Bex finished.

Commander Bex was one of a number of field commanders present at the final briefing. Once complete they would re-join their comrades in the transports and make the first glorious step in conquering this island and ultimately the planet.

Lax studied the group of almost see through commanders but had to look away after a few moments as their constantly changing and fuzzy outlines began to make him feel giddy. "Urrghh," He Spluttered, feelings of nausea subsiding. "Bex my old comrade." He rallied, extending an arm in an attempt to pat the commander on the head like an obedient dog. Diligently, he showed no embarrassment when his hand made contact with thin air. "We expect none, but." There was a long pause and a sloppy grin followed the but. "Should we encounter any, let me promise you they will be annihilated, remember now you are interfaced, we are invincible."

Lax and Bex were old comrades, almost kin, having grown up together as infants. They shared their education, even joining the military together. That however, was where their paths split. Lax, always the more ambitious, sought his learning among the military's political wing, while Bex chose to find his path amongst the rank and file, albeit senior ones. Right now the protocol of Lax's position prohibited the more junior Bex from addressing his old friend in a more casual manner. All he really wanted was to share a glass of Glook with his lifelong friend.

Glandular Lubricant of the Old Kalafrax distillery, or Glook, produced the same effect as strong alcohol upon Humans, with the added bonus of causing body hair to fall out after the first glass. Not a problem for Desirions as they possess very little, possibly a genetic defect caused by countless generations consuming copious amounts of Glook.

"All transport controllers have been issued with the coordinates for their destination," Lax informed those present.

He felt a sigh escape from his mouth as his commanders bowed in response to the confirmation.

"Majestic sentinel, will there be aerial cover?" Commander Sex asked hopefully.

"No Sex you will not, to operate the command capital ships in this atmosphere and provide simultaneous shield cover will cause too much of an energy drain. Adequate cover will be provided by ground armour and mobile artillery." He paused for a thought before starting again. "I'm afraid aerial combat cover is not available at the moment either."

This last statement caused nervous glances to be exchanged. Noticing the sudden change, Lax sought to quell their concern. "Please don't burden yourselves; you have nothing to worry about. All Cohorts report optimal strength and vehicle and ground operating systems are running at full efficiency and," he paused for effect. "Need I remind you again, in our interphased state, we are indeed untouchable."

The rousing speech had hit the mark, with Lax himself feeling quite the speaker. A few more questions were asked of the high command before, slowly the semi-transparent commanders, seemingly happy with the responses returned to their respective vehicles.

Watching them go, Lax swelled with pride. He very nearly uttered "I wish I were going with them," but knowing the statement to be crap, stopped himself just in time.

A screen fizzed into life. "Majestic sentinel?" The face looked nervous. "The perimeter defence shield is operational but..."

"Splendid news" Lax exclaimed, not hearing the but.

"I'm afraid; due to the huge amount of indigenous, wild creatures in this area the alarms are being continuously triggered." The face on the screen delivered its news and waited for the inevitable response.

"Well can't you kill them?" Lax replied, not really thinking.

"Overseer?" said the face.

A commander stepped forward, "I shall deal with this overseer, please don't trouble yourself any further."

"Ah yes, thank you Box," Lax said then walked away to watch the transports depart.

Fully crewed and loaded they began to move away, slowly at first, in order to group together before finding their pre determined route. The bulky vehicles seemed to glide above the ground, their intricate tracks absorbing the lumps, bumps and contours to give a beautifully smooth transit. These in turn were flanked by the attack vehicles, armaments fully manned and poised they kept an exact pace with the transports.

The whole untidy group of haphazardly placed vehicles quickly sorted itself out into a neat and efficient convoy. To the rear, an array of supply vehicles followed. Behind these, half a dozen much smaller machines. These were lesser versions of the heavily armed hovercraft styled vehicles but with no visible weapons. Gliding a few inches above the ground, they conveyed the brave and fearless high commanders, safe from all harm, giving them the perfect vantage point to reap the glory once the action had died down.

XI

"This is Alpha Charlie, two, two seven, are you receiving me Smoking bandit? Over."

Static crackled through Sergeant Dave Doberman's headset.

"This is Alpha Charlie, two, two seven, please respond Smoking Bandit over," he repeated, his sharp West Country twang becoming more evident as his frustration rose.

More static. He sighed, on the verge of giving up when his headphone burst into sound.

"Go ahead Alpha Charlie, two, two seven. This is Smoking bandit; please state your message, over."

A look of relief passed over his face as he gave the rest of his team the thumbs up to indicate he had at last managed to get through to headquarters at RAF Sealand.

The departure of the alien force had prompted Doberman and two of his patrol to break cover and move a sufficient distance from the unearthly proceedings in an attempt to contact their superiors. All radio communication at the contact site had been rendered impossible the minute the first of the Desirion ships had landed. Now in a position near the village of Tiverton they had finally moved clear. For twenty five minutes he had been attempting to contact headquarters, but to no avail. No blocked signal just a lack of response forcing him to eventually expand his search to just about anyone who would listen. Initial success was made with a local amateur radio enthusiast by the name of Hairy Helen. Needless to say that line of communication had been quickly severed.

"This is Alpha, Charlie, two, two seven, multiple targets are on the move, I repeat multiple targets are on the move, currently heading north-west from Beeston castle." He paused to take a deep breath, perspiration trickling down his forehead. A quick cursory glance at his two companions revealed equally anxious, if not somewhat gormless faces hanging on his every word.

"The enemy are in large numbers forming a convoy of err." He paused again searching for the right words. "A sort of a mix of floating and tracked vehicles, troop transporters I believe with accompanying firepower over."

The airways became silent.

"What's happening Sarge?" The nearest man asked. He was hushed with a wave of Doberman's hand.

"Alpha Charlie, Two, Two, seven, acknowledged. We are in aerial contact, your orders are to follow at a discreet distance, avoid contact and report back, over."

Dave sighed, careful not to rub a sweaty hand over his face for fear of removing the camouflage paint generously coating it. "Smoking Bandit, this is Alpha Charlie, Two, two, seven, acknowledged and out." Pulling up the earpiece so that it assumed a vertical position he looked once again at his two colleagues. "Okay boys we are moving. Lloyd, get back to the rest of the squad and bring them here."

Without a murmur Private Lloyd disappeared in the direction of Beeston.

Observe, thought Doberman. *Ten paratroopers armed with various semi automatic rifles and hand weapons, a radio and a couple of paper pads. Against an alien army of thousands of well armed, well equipped whatever's, as if we could do anything else.*

The familiar chopping of helicopter rotor blades could be faintly heard from high above. Doberman and the remaining man, Private Casey, glanced up instinctively, despite knowing they wouldn't be able to see it through the low cloud and darkness.

"Where we going Sarge?" Casey asked, sorting through his backpack.

"Well son," responded Doberman. "We are to follow that little convoy of ugly bastards and watch what they are up to so, same as before really."

The Sergeant wasn't best pleased, he'd had enough of observing and was eager to dish some violence out, but what really irked him was that he'd spent the best part of a night just yards from an abandoned pub, potentially full of booty only to have to leave it all untouched.

The two men sat silently for the next twenty minutes, broken eventually by the sound of footsteps. In response they both sat perfectly still, invisible in the dark undergrowth, watching intently for the arrival of the newcomers. Only when they were convinced of their identity did they break cover. Immediately, Doberman was bombarded by questions from his reunited men.

"When we genna get a crack at the bastards Sarge?" asked Private Campbell eagerly.

"When we are given permission to do so," Doberman replied calmly, in quick response, "Now less of your crap and let's move it, we have to follow that convoy and observe."

"Sarge?" asked Saunders, the shortest soldier amongst them.

Doberman sighed, "Yes Saunders what is it?" He snapped.

"Sarge, I need a dump."

XII

Colonel General Sydenham Poyntz was bored beyond all imagination. Not a new phenomenon. The unstoppable fronds of time had slowly crept upon him these past three hundred and fifty nine years, resulting in the mind numbing tediousness that repeating the same event again and again was sure to bring. Now however, the thought was very much dawning upon him, and the other three thousand members of his horse troop that on the Day of Judgment, they may have possibly, just possibly, made the wrong decision.

That August morning in the year of our lord, sixteen hundred and fifty one, and the sun broke through the pine trees bathing the landscape with a brilliant incandescence, illuminating a large idyllic wooden house situated deep in rolling countryside within the colony of Virginia. All however, was not shiny within.

Upon a bed in the largest and most comfortably furnished bedroom lay poor Sydenham. His health, It would be fair to say, wasn't the most promising thing going for him at that moment, in fact he was just minutes from death.

The room, filled with close family, reverberated with the wails of melancholy sobbing, vying for supremacy with the chanting of a Minister, whose prayers grew ever louder so as to be heard over the distraught relatives waiting with sorrow for his final breath. Outside, in the parlour were the equally anxious but not so devoted kin. Their anxiety pointed in a totally different direction. Not a mark of sorrow etched upon their faces as they rubbed subconscious greedy mitts together in expected financial anticipation.

Drifting in and out of consciousness, Sydenham was only just capable of looking about his withered body. Feeling joints begin to stiffen as his body approached its journey's end, he was slowly overcome by a euphoric inner peace spreading blissfully throughout his entire being. Looking forward to meeting his maker, Sydenham was somewhat alarmed to be confronted by a tall faceless figure draped in a dark cowl and grasping a scythe in a skeletal claw. With a splutter he gave off a loud gasp.

Assuming the final moments were near, the sobbing escalated. This in turn encouraged the Minister to increase the speed and volume of his preaching.

Obviously invisible to the others present the intruder leaned upon his farm tool and bent closer to the mortified Sydenham before speaking.

The tone of voice wasn't what he unexpected, more akin to

that of a buffet steward announcing that today's money saver special was a free pastry when purchasing more than one hot drink.

"Sydenham Poyntz," said Death. "It's almost time to go, but before you do I must tell you that you qualify for one of our special offers."

"Eh?" was all Sydenham could muster, Death continued regardless.

"This is the deal. After your err, passing," he uttered in hushed tones. "You can either choose to settle down to enjoy the everlasting life eternal amongst the crème of the deceased elite." This basically meant hob knobbing around heaven with anyone famous or notable who hadn't led too selfish or nasty a life.

With a quick glance either side to ensure there were no eavesdroppers, the Grim reaper felt it his duty to inform the incumbent Sydenham that all this wasn't actually all it was cracked up to be, and if he were totally honest, once the first thirty years or so had passed it actually became really rather boring.

His conscience now clear, Death continued. "You could spend your time in the everlasting just bumming around, however, this option would allow you to return to the world of mortals and relive just once a year a particular event, a notable moment from your life on that anniversary."

Death drew closer and eyed him with a harsh stare, quite a talent for somebody without eyes.

"It must be understood," his voice suddenly boomed.

Sydenham stared, wide eyed, still getting over the shock of being spoken to by a skeleton. "Only those who have led a thoroughly productive and worthwhile life get this opportunity," he continued with a grin.

As if actually dying wasn't enough to cope with, this latest turn of events had really blown Sydenham away. His belief in almighty God and the Lord Jesus Christ had never wavered but his perception regarding death and dying was always along the lines of it looked like a good opportunity to at long last have a really good lie down. This proposition however, had automatically turned his thoughts of just a few years previous. Of days, braving it with his fellow Roundheads during the bloody years of civil wars back in the old country.

Having fought many actions, major and minor throughout those largely enjoyable times, Sydenham had always harboured affection for one battle in particular. A broad smile of satisfaction planted itself upon his face as he reminisced about Rowton Moor. Turning his face he stared vacantly toward the room's corner as his psyche played out that deciding event back in 1645. The gathered looked tentatively towards the corner expecting to see an imp or something as unearthly but were only met by a spider spinning its web. Shyly, it sought the nearest crack to hide from the sudden attention.

Minutes passed before the very frail Sydenham brought their attention back to him. Raising his head from the pillow he looked intently at each member of his family. "Yes I do declare I rather like the sound of that," he said in a croaky faltering voice, gave of a slow thunderous fart and died.

This year would be the three hundred and fiftieth anniversary of the battle of Rowton Moor and boredom was neither here nor there, that particular pleasure had been surpassed many years previous. This year as per usual the defending Royalists led by Sir Marmaduke Langdale, out upon the field, and ultimately King Charles himself upon the walls of Chester, needed their posterior paddled once again in the name of tradition.

Colonel Michael Jones perched himself upon the edge of a strangely unreal wooden barrel. Like himself it appeared slightly transparent, the outline fuzzy and distorted. This however, took nothing away from his totally effeminate close cropped permed wig. Hanging immaculately, it's perfectly parallel centre parting cascaded all the way down to his neck, only partially hiding the ornately frilled white collar of his white silk shirt.

Irritatingly, he twiddled with one side of a neatly manicured and waxed moustache in apparent thought while inhaling deeply on a long white clay pipe. Large ghostly smoke rings increasing in size as they rose from his mouth.

"I fear that dawn has caught upon us Sydenham." A pause. "Think you that damned Blackheart Langdale has had a change of heart regarding proceedings this past year?" he asked more in hope.

"Tis a capital notion Michael my fine friend, but alas I fear it ought not to be," guffawed Sydenham, his spectral features actually appearing to age as he gave his ghostly steed its final brush before the days duty.

Not to be outdone in the dashing stakes of ponciness, he too was adorned in an outfit of almost pure flamboyance with the addition of a huge red sash. Delicately embroidered with all manner of patterns and family crests it gave him the air of a commander of a military regiment, albeit a seventeenth century one.

"Suffice to announce, but I fear the days fayre shall be the same dashing bore of a routine of past summer tides," Poyntz continued unhappily.

"I spy a few more of what the folk of this unimaginable age refer to as buildings, appear to have sprouted these last few years hence," said Jones with dismay as he sat looking out onto the old battlefield, from the edge of the picturesque village of

Waverton. A puzzled look suddenly crossed his face, "Grant this Sydenham if you may, but it's rather strange wouldn't you agree? I don't recall seeing any fellows from this age this morning, by chance have you encountered such?"

Poyntz ceased his grooming and turned to survey the ground around him. A Very different one from the one he first fought upon all those years ago. It's much changed skyline and terrain silhouetted darker against the light glare from the nearby city. Light autumn drizzle continued unabated and sure enough as Colonel Jones had pointed out there was a complete lack of present day people.

Behind the two officers, spread out across the village and surrounding fields, quite unseen at that moment, were some three thousand troopers and mounts of Poyntz regiment and proud members of Cromwell's new model army.

Some rested or chatted, others played card or dice games. Most however busily engaged themselves with the everyday but essential procedures of preparing a horse troop for a so well rehearsed battle.

"Are your men steadfast sir?" Jones asked, tapping his pipe on the edge of the barrel, the remnants of burnt supernatural tobacco tumbling to the floor.

"Oh I think it fair to say so wouldn't you my good fellow? They know of the routine or at least they should do by now," joked Poyntz, a wry smile etched across his features.

Jones once more looked towards the horizon, his face not the enthusiastic picture of excitement it had been those many years ago. Standing, he tucked his pipe safely in one of the pockets of his bright baggy tunic, "Time pursues us General sir, I'd better head my position, scarce wish to miss all the merriment now would I?" his tone was thick with sarcasm.

"Indeed Michael my old friend," said Poyntz equally unenthusiastically.

"Well good fortune to you sir, we shall congratulate on the eve, hence poor old Langdale has fled north again."

The two senior officers bade farewell to each other with a majestic waving of hats followed by a mutual deep bow. Poyntz turned to join his regiment of horse but couldn't help thinking about what Jones had said about the lack of people from the present, *where were they? Not even any of those dirty graceless, horseless carriages that they travel in.*

Jones turned towards the lights of the city of Chester, mounted his spectral horse and proceeded to join his musketeers loitering in their battle positions just to the north of the village of Handbridge.

XIII

The Desirion convoy continued unopposed. The few humans left in the area, those who had *simply refused* to be evacuated gave the convoy a wide berth. There were however, as always, one or two exceptions. Maintaining that good old Dunkirk spirit, never bowing down to anything and simply refusing to be affected by events no matter how extraordinary.

One old soldier fitted this bill perfectly, mounting a lone offensive as the convoy passed his house. Standing to attention upon his driveway he wore an ill fitting and threadbare woollen battledress of a regimental sergeant major of the Irish Guards. Proudly, he displayed numerous campaign medals while his main form of attack appeared to be a pace stick, tucked firmly beneath his armpit. Defiantly he glared as they passed.

The Desirions, aware of his presence, chose to ignore him as they considered the elderly human of no consequence. Eventually he was coaxed back inside by his wife ranting. "You've left that bloody door open again, letting all the cold in and your breakfast is on the table and your tea is getting cold too, I don't do this for fun you know."

Her Majesty's armed forces response was swift, mobilising army units into position with the utmost speed. RAF squadrons were put on high alert, while the Royal Navy, whom the Government had deemed necessary to massacre in recent years, was stretched to contribute anything. However, with its own government as much the enemy, the senior service maintained their proud tradition by just getting on with the job in hand. By pooling all available recourses they offered the use of a patrol vessel. It was of very little use, and alas all they could muster, but everyone thought it was a very nice gesture.

A squadron of Army air corps Lynx helicopters monitored the convoy as it made progress, unaltered along the Railway line towards Chester. The pilots ensured they kept their aircraft at a safe distance, although to be certain nobody actually knew what that safe distance was. Any obstacle in the convoy's way, such as a bridge or a building considered too close was simply blown to pieces by a couple of discharges from the large plasma weapons mounted on the backs of the hovering attack vehicles.

Milners Heath and Waverton received the Aliens with abandoned silence, where inexplicably it detoured from the railway line and began to spread out in a fan shape.

Two elderly ladies on an early morning trip to the village newsagents and grocers witnessed their approach. Somehow, they hadn't the slightest idea regarding evacuations and had certainly not heard anything about any alien invasion. Wondering just where everybody was, they caught sight of the unearthly vehicles passing right in front of them, causing their reliable Austin Allegro to swerve violently and mount the curb before coming to rest in a muddy ditch. Both unharmed and undaunted, the dotty old dears departed their defunct vehicle waving angry fists in the Desirions direction while remarking in very shrill tones that Lady Burrows Harkness and the Women's social guild would have very strong words to say about this.

The new terrain posed little problem for the newcomers. Gliding and rumbling forward, the convoy reached the southern fringes of Waverton where the front troop carriers found themselves in the midst of an ambush.

A rush of bullets fizzed from nowhere, tracer rounds marking their route. Each one found its target with unnerving accuracy but failed to penetrate fully functioning shielding. The spent projectiles clanging against the transports casing with no more force than that of a pinged elastic band before harmlessly dropping to the floor.

Larger, more powerful thumps, the sound of mortars, joined the constant crackle of infantry fire. The lead two transports becoming almost obscured in an incandescent frenzy of blue and yellow light pulses as the shells detonated against the shields. Despite the impressive attack, every bullet strike and shell impact was harmlessly absorbed.

Halting immediately, the convoy allowed the nearest two flanking attack vehicles to come into their own. Poised, their crews sprang into action, both firing in unison upon the general direction of the rifle and mortar fire. Orange bolts of intense localised energy burst from the guns with a crackle, discharging into the ground some four hundred feet away, throwing up large clouds of dust and earth and showering nearby buildings and roadways.

Not waiting to feel the full force of a super heated plasma blast, the soldiers of the ambush squad hastily vacated their position, each one wisely knowing when it was brown trousers time.

The two guns opened up again in the same direction, this time making a direct hit upon a small empty bungalow, which only moments before had concealed half a dozen men. The resulting explosion spread quickly, an intense ball of orange and red fire lighting up the early morning sky and reducing the building to nothing more than jagged ruins.

Muffled by the sound of battle was the sound of the incoming missile. A Lynx pilot, unable to idly stand by and watch the imminent destruction of his countrymen, disobeyed his standing order of observing until given an attack order and let forth an anti tank missile. The attack, a direct hit on the front of the vehicle, exploded with a huge fireball with a red orange plume, quickly dissipating to reveal an untouched troop transport. Undaunted, the pilot fired a second missile before quickly wheeling away to survey his handiwork. His observing however was distracted by a thunderous roar as three Tornado bombers screamed past at low level, almost unbalancing the Lynx in their slipstream.

The aircraft broke formation and began to dive, one after the other towards the impossible to miss target of the sprawling mass of vehicles. The Desirions craned their heads to follow the attack jets. Despite being tracked, the surprise didn't allow the gun operators to pivot their weapons quickly enough.

Three large bombs jettisoned directly onto the leading vehicles. The first two, again accurate, found their target to an inch, but as with the Lynx's missiles the dazzling explosions dissipated to reveal absolutely no damage to the invaders.

The third however, failed to make a direct hit. Impacting upon the ground a couple of feet broadside of the flanking attack vehicle, it exploded with a shattering din. The detonation dislodged earth from beneath the vehicle and lifted it to such an extent that its protective shield, which acted as an enveloping umbrella gave it next to no protection at ground level. Unable to absorb the impact, the vehicle, along with its terrified crew were elevated upwards and sideways, causing it to collide with a troop transport. This brought about a domino effect as the collision forced the transport to slew across into the opposite flanking attack vehicle.

The gun commander, at the instant of opening fire, suddenly witnessed a fantastic blue and red pyrotechnic display erupt around him as the colliding vehicles shields intermixed. In spite of their interphased state, those inside were thrown violently sideways as inertia took over, luckily for them their injuries were very light thanks largely to their unnatural state.

The momentum of the first mobile gun forced it to leave the ground and roll right over the top of the transport, eventually landing upside down in an adjacent field. Making a dazed but hasty exit from the badly damaged vehicle, were the crew. A wise move as it quickly began to belch smoke in an alarming way.

The second attack vehicle, its discharge now in a state of no return, fired. The plasma bolt impacting directly into the control area of the transport, the resultant light show dazzling those closest. This time it was accompanied by a huge fireball completely engulfing both itself and the transport. The crew, who were not interphased, was vapourised. The already bruised interphased troops were about to learn that although their state would protect them from the physical effects of the explosion, the mental effects of experiencing a cataclysmic inferno from within would leave physiological scars for some time to come.

The whole convoy had now come to a standstill. More attack and heavy weapons vehicles attempted to move forward but found an impenetrable jam already building. Most Desirion's witnessing the scene unfolding ahead of them were somewhat shocked at these events, they had been assured that the humans were incapable of causing harm.

The three Tornadoes completed their turn and were coming in fast for a second run. As before, at extreme low level they descended one after the other, but this time instead of waiting to close on their target to release their ordinance, the tell tale white hot flash of an air to ground missile launching appeared from beneath each wing. The first two Storm Shadows slammed home past the remains of the burning transport and attack vehicle, making a direct hit upon the nearest transport with lethal accuracy. So accurate was it that, had the shield not been up to the job, the transports operator would have had to deal with a missile protruding from the middle of his head. Exploding in a fireball of such ferocity, the transport was rocked from side to side despite its protection.

Levelling with the head of the spread out convoy, the lead aircraft met with fire from at least half a dozen alien vehicles. The mobile guns crews had recovered quickly from the initial attack, managing to elevate their menacing looking weapons and open up upon the Tornadoes. Red and yellow bolts of energy sizzled into the damp cloud laden sky, illuminating it as the heat tore holes in the rain filled clouds with a dazzling light, reminiscent of the Blitz, fortunately though they missed their targets.

Another huge explosion mushroomed into the sky, momentarily blotting out the jets as another storm shadow detonated upon the alien shielding, again causing no damage.

The second Tornado now ran out luck, the aft fuselage took a direct hit from a plasma bolt. Lancing through the metal, it separated the tail plane from the main body as easily as a hot knife through butter. Realising his hopeless predicament, the pilot, along with his navigator ejected. The aircraft completely out of control, corkscrewed helplessly, until it crashed into a footbridge crossing the nearby canal.

The missiles from the unfortunate second aircraft, still in flight, exploded harmlessly upon the convoy in much the same way as its predecessors, while the separated tail section thudded directly onto the roof of a transport before ending up burying itself into the soft earth. The pilot of the rear aircraft, rattled, after witnessing the destruction of his comrade, released his payload early, without obtaining a proper lock. The two projectiles exploding upon the railway cutting bank before he made a hasty exit, pursued by many energy bolts.

The helicopters wisely stayed their distance, reporting the attack by the Tornadoes. One aircraft was dispatched to rescue the downed crew who had floated safely to Earth but dangerously close to the convoy. Despite the entire rescue operation being carried out within full view of the Desirions, no hostile reaction was offered.

The quick firing, renegade helicopter pilot, sheepishly reassumed his station amongst the rest of his squadron after receiving a most severe dressing down over the airwaves, one which intonated that his next interview would probably not involve tea and biscuits. It was one of his fellow pilots who had in fact noticed the effects of the bomb exploding near to the troop transport and thus reported his findings.

Using the time given by the air attack, the infantry units who had attempted the ambush at Waverton were now clear, managing to pull back to pre prepared positions near to Chester.

Sergeant Dave Doberman sat, concealed with his squad, observing the action unfolding far ahead of them. "This is Alpha Charlie, two, two, seven come in Smoking Bandit over," he whispered into the radio in case any alien stragglers were nearby.

The Paratroopers were beginning to wear a little, having gone the whole night without a break from the tension and very little in the way of refreshment.

"This is smoking bandit receiving you alpha, Charlie, two, two, seven, over," came the reply.

"The enemy appears to have halted; multiple heavy explosions ahead, post air attack, stand by." Doberman raised his binoculars to his eyes and carefully re adjusted the focus, with one hand still holding onto them he spoke into the radio once more. "Smoking Bandit, the enemy has spread out and broken formation, they appear to be disembarking from their vehicles due south of the village of Waverton, I repeat, Waverton, over."

"Alpha Charlie, two, two, seven, you are to hold your position and await the arrival of friendly units arriving from a north westerly direction, we have given them your position, out." The line went dead, returning to a soft static.

Doberman snapped his mouthpiece to the vertical position. "Well lads," he said, grinning but not finding the situation in any way, shape or form amusing. "We are to sit tight; the cavalry are on their way."

XIV

The Desirion's emptied the troop transports in a quick and orderly fashion. Those disembarking towards the front of the convoy could not fail to see the twisted burning wreckage of the leading transport and its escort's vehicles. More unnerving were the still, blackened forms silhouetted upon the ground by the orange flames. The mobile gun crews had adopted a different attitude too. Flagrant casualness was gone, replaced by wary watchfulness. The first empty vehicles now began to move away toward the rear of the convoy in order to return to Beeston and re-load with the next wave. The flanking escorts stayed, quickly manoeuvring to form a vanguard while the foot commanders assembled their respective groups into order.

Lax was still in debate with his senior advisors regarding the decision to commence operations without adequate aerial cover, when news of the destruction of the transports was relayed to him by a sombre looking senior advisor Pix. The Overseer's features visibly drooped at the news, allowing a squeal along with a small blob of dribble to escape from his lipless mouth.

"Inform Commander Fax he is to launch, aerial, first group," ordered Lax.

Those clustered around exuded an enthusiastic optimism with the launching of air attack, confident that this small setback and that was all it was, would not alter the eventual outcome.

Lax turned to the incumbent Pix, "Relay to my trusted commanders in the field," he paused. *What shall I relay to my trusted commanders?* He desperately pondered.

Commanders Bex and Pox watched their Overseer waiting on his next words of wisdom.

"I expect nothing but absolute success," exclaimed Lax, in the best traditions of all good honourable leaders, safe in the sanctuary of their headquarters.

Pix rose from the floor and bowed majestically before genuflecting all the way to the exit until safely out of sight of his overseer. For the next half an hour, news filtered from the front in dribs and drabs. Firstly, injured crews from the destroyed mobile guns were expected back at the landing zone at Beeston at any moment. Conveyed in the returning, empty transports, the casualties shared a ride with those beyond medical attention.

The assault had begun badly. Despite the assurances, the Desirion's were now nervous and they had good reason to be.

XV

The underground base at RAF Sealand resembled an Ants nest. Had one been able to lift up the lid for a little peek it would have been possible to witness sheer pandemonium. Those inside were now beginning to get an idea of the scale of things, thanks largely to the numerous and thankfully, undetected observation squads in the field around Chester and the invasion point.

Quickly, Sealand became the hub of operations, its population swelling with the influx of many high ranking military personnel, not just British, but from the USA, most European countries and even a Russian contingent, complete with massive hats and stern looks down their noses at anyone not from a working class background.

The numbers of suited and collared men from various Government ministries swelled too, forcing an emergency order for A4 paper and clipboards to be made at a moment's notice.

Thanks to the intelligence, it was ascertained that a very large invasion force was on the move. Initial numbers were estimated at around twenty to twenty five thousand. From their direction of travel the destination was most definitely the city of Chester. Fortunately the army's high command had reacted quickly. Concentrating their forces within the nearest and most obvious large built up area was priority. Obviously this was all anticipation and they desperately hoped that the enemy would not swing away from Beeston in a Northerly direction and head for Runcorn and Liverpool.

Thankfully they hadn't and over the course of the evening of the twenty third and the morning of the twenty fourth, at least thirty six thousand regular and territorial soldiers of varying regiments of the British army, not to mention visiting units of the US Marines and Australian and British special forces were in place with many more en route.

Every single RAF strike squadron in the UK was at a moment's notice, each one respectively equipped with Tornado, Harrier or Typhoon fighters, with the added promise of the use of British based American squadrons.

On the river Dee, HMS Brockenhurst, a Royal Navy patrol vessel was currently giving everything she had, her Commander eager to do his bit to defend Cheshire's principal city and ultimately his country.

XVI

The dial of Sergeant Dobermans watch read 08.58 when the bright red glow reflected from the glass face. The discharge of the thermal transfer plasma bolt from the escort vehicle was primarily for display purposes as no real viable targets were in sight. It also acted as an unofficial marker for the Desirion column to resume its advance.

As one, a large number of escort vehicles, mounting twin guns, moved in front of the foot soldiers to form an impenetrable wall, many of them carelessly discharging their weapons at will, destroying houses and buildings in great explosions and dust clouds. Had anybody been in the village of Waverton at precisely 08.57 on the morning of September the twenty fourth, it's just possible that they would have seen an even more remarkable spectacle.

If the arrival of a force of thousands of extra terrestrial invaders, equipped with a menacing array of fantastical weaponry wasn't remarkable enough. Then the graceful materialisation from the cool autumn morning of some three thousand human soldiers, adorned in seventeenth century clothing, mounted on fine, strong horses led by ridiculously flamboyantly dressed leaders, would surely turn the most ardent tea totaller to sample all of the benefits that alcohol had to offer.

The lines of Roundhead Cavalry stood in casual rows. Some half materialized within the walls of houses, some buried up to their saddles in earthworks that hadn't existed all those years ago. Nevertheless they were all ready for battle just as they had been every year since 1645.

Colonel General Sydenham Poyntz sat on his horse watching, fascinated at the scene unfolding before him, his men, poised upon their saddles, spectral breath condensing from their ghostly steeds.

For the past three and a half centuries he and his comrades in arms had witnessed many bizarre and strange things relating to the changing modern world and its ever altering landscape and technology. What they saw in front of them this day was something taken from the most depraved imaginations the Catholic Church had to offer.

"Well I do declare," Poyntz remarked to the three mounted officers standing with him. "Colonel Jones's heart yearned for a change in the offering this tide. It would appear as though his desire has come become reality."

"What on Gods Earth are they?" asked Captain Charles Snittersly, a young dashing fellow, always eager to please his General.

"They, Charles, my dear fellow are not of God's Earth. They are the Devils incarnation." Poyntz replied, indicating the Desirion's with his riding crop. He sat quiet in his saddle for a moment, the officers around him picking up on the obvious anger, not sure if it was appropriate to address him. They decided not to.

They needn't have concerned themselves, for just moments later he expertly wheeled his mount to face his regiment. With a smooth hiss his sword was drawn clear of its ornately decorated scabbard and flourished high above his spectral head. The almost opaque manifestation was nearly complete as the blade shone. Standing tall in ghostly stirrups, Poyntz took a deep breath.

"My old comrades, accomplices and brothers in arms. Many years have we vanquished the old foe but," he paused for effect. "It appears Sir Marmaduke must tarry, for it seems that on this day the Devil himself has come forth, bringing with him a despicable unsightly horde. Today my brave, glorious horseman, we shall fight for parliament, for General Cromwell, for England, but most of all for God."

XVII

After all the fantastic thing Dave Doberman had witnessed over the last eight hours, he should have reacted with some surprise by now, but the sight unfolding, before his eyes may have been the final straw. Putting the binoculars to one side he rubbed his eyes, "No, no, no, oh no, no," he remarked, shaking his head.

"What is it Sarge? What have you seen?" He was asked with concern.

"Buggered if I know Green," replied Doberman, his voice very distant. *Maybe I haven't got the focus right, maybe I should get some sleep,* he thought, *or maybe I'd have been better checking out the Pub after all.*

Picking them up again he looked, this time making sure he focused them correctly. Coming into view at the fore of the new group was a very grand figure, dressed in very old style clothing. Mounted on horseback, he suddenly turned and appeared to address the many hundreds of horsemen spread out in ranks behind him.

The Para's, observing, crouched in silence. Doberman and Corporal Casey peered through their binoculars with the rest hanging with anticipation on every uttered word. Casey had said nothing except, "ooh," while Doberman's sporadic rants were becoming almost incoherent.

"Sarge you okay?" Enquired a concerned Dawson.

They never even noticed the shadowy figure creep up behind them.

"Which one of you chaps is Doberman?" Asked the camouflaged figure with the nasally voice.

XVIII

Any British ground forces between Waverton and Chester had now withdrawn past Christleton and into suburban Chester to join with the mass of infantry taking up positions in the area. Those operating outside the defensive zone were all confirmed, located safely towards the rear of the alien force. The leafy avenues and streets of Chester were not yet in range of the alien energy weapons or at least appeared not to be, but it wouldn't take long unless they were stopped and stopped they would be.

Units of artillery, comprising huge mobile guns and rapier missile batteries were accompanied by lighter artillery pieces to repel the invaders, while units of the first Royal Tank Regiment were fast approaching from the south of the alien position after a long and hurried journey from Dorset.

As soon as high command became aware that the aliens had begun to move towards Chester, the order had been given for air strikes to commence. From the observation teams, came a deluge of reports informing of the whereabouts of the Desirions. However, from the first Tornado strike it became apparent that the aliens were protected by a form of invisible shielding. Two plans of possibly combating this had been put forward. The first was the already proven theory reported by the Lynx pilot, where a very near miss would actually undermine the shield. The other and this was only a theory, depended on the arrival of the Challengers tank squadrons. Armed with depleted uranium armour piercing rounds, concentrated attacks may be enough to penetrate the shields.

Woods and Gary leant against the parapet of the medieval wall surrounding Chester waiting to accompany the recon patrol. Looking out towards the alien invaders they attempted to spot the attacking Jets that were so obviously audible. With heads craned skywards they almost jumped out of their skin as huge artillery pieces opened up. Situated in the city park, three monstrous AS90 weapons fired, each piece belching a one hundred and fifty five millimetre shell. Very soon they were accompanied by smaller field artillery pieces opening up not too far away

96

XIX

The Desirions had finally begun moving again. Advancing upon the outskirts of Christleton all seemed quiet when the escort vehicles locked onto a fast approaching target. Opening up a plasma barrage the immediate sky glowed orange mere seconds before a deafening roar filled the sky. Turning their heads, the Commanders attempted to locate this latest attack.

"The Humans come in their puny flying machines again, stand your ground and remember their weapons cannot harm us," called a Commander trying to steady his jittery soldiers, words which he knew only too well were not strictly true.

Along the column, other commanders issued similar words of encouragement, but their men were no longer as confident as they had been.

Firing randomly at the Tornado's above them, every single gun kept up a magnificent rate of fire. Miraculously, no targets were found despite the sky being filled by hundreds of glowing plasma bolts. Unabated, the marching ranks of Desirion infantry continued towards Chester when suddenly, without warning, the ground dead centre erupted in a yellow and orange fireball, expunging huge amounts of earth and debris. Another Storm shadow missile hit just a few yards ahead, creating a similar effect while a third struck on the left flank with terrifying brilliance.

Three of the Tornado's showed themselves again, screaming overhead at a height of no more than a thousand feet, firstly to inspect the aftermath of their first attack before concentrating upon the columns escorts. Unleashing missile after missile at the hovering craft, they were soon lost from view, blotted out by the chain reaction of fiery explosions.

Clearing their enemy, the aircraft veered away almost vertically, still avoiding the intense returning alien fire.

As the dust and debris settled from the attacks, the pilots, expecting to see ragged holes amongst the ranks were dismayed to see that not one gap had been made. Leaving three huge smoking craters behind, the foot soldiers continued completely unscathed.

Commander Tax marched at the very rear of the column; he was feeling extremely smug as the last vestiges of the human assault faded. He'd seen the full force of the explosion ahead of him, ferocious and violent, it should have killed and wounded many; it had not. Not a single scratch. Not one injury, although those close to the blasts were somewhat mentally shaken. The

Particle dispersal interphasers had done their job; the entire attack force was immune from these humans and any weaponry they could bring.

Barely had he paused for thought when three more missiles struck home with awesome precision, once again causing damage only to the ground and surrounding buildings.

Crude noisy things, Tax thought to himself as the Tornado's revealed their presence again. This time one of them paid the ultimate price. A direct hit from a plasma bolt met the aircraft amidships. One second it was there, the very next, it wasn't. The explosion split the sky apart as the war machine was reduced to matchbox sized pieces of wreckage which rained down like white hot metal confetti over Christleton, the pilot and navigator fortunately knowing nothing of their fate.

Suddenly, four Desirion aircraft appeared, on the tails of the Tornado's. Elongated egg shapes to look at they showed a curving lip at the front which swung back and opened out to form stubby delta wings on either side. Although fast, they appeared to labour somewhat and were certainly not up to matching the jets speed.

The bright glare from the explosion forced Tax to quickly look away. With the action, his feelings of overwhelming joyful satisfaction were strangely cut short. Unable to figure out why, he continued to march forward. knowing only that he suddenly felt very uneasy, a feeling which made him feel as though there was something behind which really was worthy of his attention. So strong was it that he hadn't noticed artillery shells begin to fall amongst the foremost lines.

One fell close to Tax. Instinctively he shielded his face from the explosion, and there it was. Allowing a second tentative glimpse he confirmed just what was bothering him. Despite enjoying panoramic vision, he was initially unable to take it all in. Another four of their own aircraft flew high above but he barely noticed them. For filling his eye line was a continuous line of humans sat upon large quadruped creatures. These looked very different from those he had seen so far. Their attire, their general look, but most of all the glint of the sharp metallic weapons, held aloft or straight forward in menacing pointing gestures. Their difference unnerved him, and that caused instant concern.

Alerting the rest of the column, it rapidly came to a stop. The very rear line, numbering some nine hundred Desirions were ordered to turn and face the newcomers, while the rest, concerned as to why their rear were turning to face, were tasked with resuming their forward momentum.

XX

Poyntz horse regiment came on at full gallop, Parliaments colours intertwined with his own as they streamed magnificently within the speed induced ethereal wind. The distance between them and the spawn of Satan was already down to a mere five hundred yards and closing when those at the fore witnessed the line of Devils who had turned to face them raise their peculiar muskets to waist height in one swift movement. At the same time their comrades drew away, enveloped in smoke and debris from artillery bursts as they advanced with the main body.

Four hundred yards and each Desirion weapon displayed a defiant glow, made more so by a collective hum.

Three hundred yards and they glowed brighter still, when with a resounding zap, an unheard order unleashed nigh on a thousand separate bolts of red and orange sizzling, thermally transferred plasma to lance through the damp air towards the magnificent charging horsemen.

The vast majority of the discharges found a target. With grim satisfaction Tax looked at his unit with pride, taking delight at its well drilled machine like efficiency. Glancing along the line, the faint clicks and hums indicated that they were ready again.

Smiling, he was about to give the order to fire for a second time. Momentarily he glanced back to the horsemen. They were very close now, a mere hundred yards, and his face crumbled into panic and his alien bowels turned to mush at the sight of the totally unmolested humans still in full charge. Immediately gathering his wits, Tax was at a loss as to why they hadn't even been injured. Some of his equally concerned soldiers were staring at their weapons as if something obvious was up with them, there was. It was however, far, far too late.

As one, the Desirion line unleashed a second discharge into the horsemen, more from fear than by being ordered. As before, each shot, despite their deathly accuracy, passed right through the horsemen, continuing to sizzle through the air until as with most, simply running out of momentum and energy.

It was then that Tax realised with absolute horror just what was so irregular with these humans. They were all, to a man, giving off a solid non distorted outline. In his phased state he had not yet got used to viewing the outside world properly, but now he'd figured it out. *It was impossible*, his thoughts screamed, but somehow they were interphased.

Recharged plasma rifles hummed ready for use. Already knowing the situation hopeless, Tax turned frantically and screamed at his units to draw personal weapons. The rear lines of the main body of the Desirion force upon Rowton Heath turned their heads, unnerved at the desperate shriek behind them, not knowing whether to flee or fire. To fire would have no effect as the weapons were modified to fire interdimensional and were only effective upon material items, as many were now realising.

What they then witnessed and ultimately became part of was nothing short of a complete massacre.

Sydenham Poyntz rode ten feet in front of the main body of his regiment when they thundered into the confused ranks of Desirion's.

"Kill them," he screamed, urging his men forward and thrusting his sabre at the undefended back of the Demon nearest to him. The blade removed the yellow head in one go, its limp body collapsing to the ground. Less than a second later the rest of the regiment hit the aliens like a tidal wave.

As it struck, retreating and panicking aliens staggered from the blow. Carried along, those unfortunate not to be killed by the initial thrusts of the rider's swords, were trampled under pounding hooves, their unusual frames bending and breaking into even more unnatural and distorted shapes.

Tax, knocked square in the abdomen by a flurry of horse legs was sent sprawling, causing painful internal injuries. Rolling over in agony he attempted to crawl to safety. Realising this to be hopeless he instinctively stretched out a long arm, grabbing at the nearest human in range. The horse tumbled, its restrained legs buckling beneath it and throwing the rider into the morass of activity. Two more mounts went down, felled by the momentum of Tax's act.

Despite the frantic scrambling, chaos and pain, he found himself able to kneel. His first instinct was to reach for the concealed blade he kept beneath his suit. Wincing, his fingers sought the weapon. Below him, the Human rider lay sprawled at Tax's knees, slightly dazed. The two species stared into each other eyes.

Tax was quicker as the human made a grab for his own blade; his reflexes, although slowed by injury still gave him the greater dexterity. Raising the wicked two pronged knife above the incumbent ghost rider he began to plunge and...It never found its mark.

Tax died instantly as the sword from the thrusting rider to his right almost rent him in two.

XXI

Major General Anthony Alistair Gregory Fartlington, assistant Commander of the North West defence force, stood at the top of King Charles tower. Situated upon the south eastern quarter of the medieval wall, it famously offered surrounding views of the city of Chester. The General was real old school, a proper Victorian officer, even resembling Kitchener himself, Pointing at the patriotic British public and insisting that they come and get slaughtered in the name of king and country.

He stood, immaculately uniformed, impressive handlebar moustache, trimmed to the nearest thousandth of an inch with thinning grey hair combed neatly over his head. He'd adopted the facial expression, not of a man in the throes of commanding a modern army, but more attune to that of someone about to suggest a spot of croquet followed by tea on the lawn with his dogs at his feet.

Accompanying him were his chiefs of staff. They were currently attempting to view the events unfolding the three miles distance between themselves and Rowton Moor. The explosions and alien weapon fire visible in the sky over Christleton and Rowton were impossible to ignore and had caused considerable worry around the city.

"Its complete bloody nonsense you know, that fool Charles couldn't possibly have been able to see the battle from here," Fartlington stated to no one in particular. "You can't even see the bloody battlefield," he continued, straining to see anything in the general direction of Rowton through his binoculars.

"I do believe you are right sir," agreed his chief Aide de Campe, Lieutenant Colonel Bamford Watkin.

Popular local legend has it that His majesty King Charles I stood in this very tower, viewing the original Battle at Rowton Moor on that fateful day back in 1645. However, even with the clearer view he undoubtedly enjoyed due to the lesser built up landscape between there and the battlefield, it would still not be possible to view things due to contours of the land. What he undoubtedly saw on that day was lots of smoke and detritus of battle rising into the air followed by the broken remnants of his army as they sought the sanctuary of the city. This and many other things were confusing Fartlington most of all.

"Watkin are you sure the reports from the observation and air teams are correct?"

"As far as I know sir yes," Watkin replied confidently, although in reality he was as confused as the rest.

"Well where on earth is all that smoke coming from?"

Before anyone could answer, there was a loud knock on the large wooden door at the tower entrance two floors below. Voices were heard before a guard climbed the stairs and informed those assembled that observation team Alpha, Charlie, two, two, seven, were reporting.

"Yes, yes burrows show him in," said Fartlington.

Shortly, a dirty sweating soldier stood before the gaggle of immaculate officers and snapped to attention with perfect efficiency. "Sir, Lance Corporal Stokes, second battalion, parachute regiment, observation squad alpha char,"

"Yes. Yes Stokes I think we can dispense with the formalities," said the General cutting him short.

"Sir," spluttered Stokes, searching for the right words. "Sir the aliens are being engaged by err ground troops."

"Well man lets have it, which unit is engaging the buggers?" Fartlington demanded.

"Well sir it's a little confusing, I err," said the unfortunate messenger.

"Stokes for God's sake man," interrupted Watkin, "tell the General what he asks."

"Yes of course sir," said Stokes, turning to the General again. "Our forces are not engaging the enemy sir. They are being engaged by a regiment of seventeenth century cavalry... sir." He snapped to attention again and saluted as if the action would make his message all the more believable.

The officers glared at Stokes as if he were himself an alien. Fartlington's face screwed slightly. "Are you trying to be funny Corporal?" Watkin retorted.

"No sir," replied Stokes feeling very uneasy.

There was another loud knock on the outer wooden door. Presently, Corporal Burrows face appeared again. "Sir, report from observation team alpha, Charlie, two, two, zero."

"Yes Burrows send him in," snapped Fartlington, his patience beginning to wear thin.

A heavily built private strode into the tower breathing heavily and sweating. He snapped to attention next to Stokes and delivered a salute so precise it would have cut his head had it made contact. "Private Edgington reporting sir. Observation squad alpha, Charlie, two, two, zero, reporting."

"Okay private," said Fartlington soundly. "I don't want to hear anything about seventeenth century soldiers attacking these damn aliens."

Edgington suddenly looked uncomfortable.

"Well, out with it man," ordered Watkin.

"Sir," struggled Edgington, "it's err rather difficult. Sir, the aliens sir, they are, erm sort off."

"For Christ sake, what is the matter with everybody today?" Fartlington gasped. "Private, give me your report. Now," he said, his patience finally exhausted.

"Sir," responded Edgington, taking a deep breath. "The aliens have been engaged to the south east of Christleton on Rowton moor by what I can only describe as a regiment of musketeers."

A pregnant pause consumed the room; Edgington stared straight ahead not daring to goad the General anymore. Stokes, who was still stood to attention, looked a little more relaxed as Edgington made his report.

Fartlington exploded with rage. "That's it get out, both of you," he shouted. With utmost speed, the messengers vacated the tower as quick as possible, glad to have the excuse to leave.

"Christ Watkin what the bloody hell is going on?" Fartlington cursed.

A telephone rang. The radio operator who had wisely stayed quiet until this moment picked it up. After a short conversation he was compelled to break his silence. "Sir if I may, I have RAF Sealand on the line, General Fisher wishes to speak with you."

Fartlington wiped a hand across his forehead and strode towards the radio operator and relieved him. "Ah Christopher, at last, some sensible conversation, yes-aha-yes-okay... okay yes... I'll see what I can do okay."

He handed the telephone receiver back to the radio operator and stood looking at the other officers in the room, his face paling, with a blank expression spreading.

"Sir?" Watkin questioned.

Fartlington smiled. "General Fisher says that a battle is taking place precisely as we have been told, it's been confirmed by aerial reconnaissance." He walked over to the towers window and looked out towards Rowton once again. The sky over the battlefield was thick with smoke. "Our orders are," he said quietly. "We are to give every assistance to the Cromwellian, parliamentarian force currently engaging the aliens."

XXII

The Desirion front ranks at Rowton Moor were too busy taking notice of the ensuing slaughter at their rear to notice the new threat unfolding in front of them. Unit commanders were as shocked and confused as the rest, their minds fogged and dangerously slow to make decisions. They had been assured that there was no danger.

The first sign of anything being amiss to their front was when a deafening crash was followed by the front line literally quivering as the shock of a close range volley of musketry thudded into them. Plasma weapon discharges flew in all directions from those still standing as order at the front quickly disintegrated, the shots harmlessly penetrating the ghostly musketeers before disappearing in the dense smoke and slamming into objects.

Despite their protection, the escort vehicle crews were as bewildered as the rest, but at least they were in control of their senses and along with attack from the air were firing into the attackers for all they were worth. Red hot glowing bolts fizzed through the air, one after the other, hoping to find a target, the only targets found being inanimate.

The crews of the Alien aircraft had the ultimate view; pleased to eventually be in action they attacked Poyntz and Jones regiments with vigour, but were as dismayed as the rest as their concentrated attacks were completely ineffective.

The sound of thunder echoed across the battlefield as another volley of musket fire was poured into the unfortunate alien attackers and that was how it continued for the next fifteen minutes as Colonel Michael Jones musketeers fired and reloaded, fired and reloaded.

The unfortunate Desirion's, unable to even defend themselves and trapped by their own confused, panicked and closely packed ranks, were simply butchered as each volley of deadly, spectral lead slammed into their miserable numbers. One or two unit commanders had the sense or bravery to mount some kind of counter attack. Quickly realising that firearms were of no use, they managed to muster as many units as possible for close combat. Forming up, they managed to advance, but even they were unable to stand up to the withering musketry.

As with all things there is only so much anyone or anything can endure and suddenly, as a whole, the entire Desirion column decided this really was about as much as they could stand. Panic spread like fire, with the surviving soldiers realising that as their weapons were next to useless, hanging around in this killing field would only guarantee an unpleasant end. The idea of running away suddenly had some rather appealing qualities, not least of all, possible survival.

The front ranks of the alien army broke. Hundreds of scared, disillusioned and panicked beings dispersed in any direction they could to escape the lethal fusillade. With the sudden exodus of infantry, the vehicles crews rapidly realised that the only soldiers of their own kind around them were the large numbers of dead and dying which littered the field as far as the eye could see. Full daylight enhanced the scene to show the full extent of the horror before them.

Some attempted a structured withdrawal while continuing to lay down an orderly but ineffectual fire against Poyntz horse and Jones musket. The only damage caused was to the smoking ruins of Christleton and Rowton's buildings which now numbered few.

Recently arrived Lynx pilots, mesmerised by the scene watched from high, a great swathe of destruction in a near perfect circle upon the human habitat was visible, caused by the powerful energy weapons as they reached the extent of their range.

Left alone at the front, the crews of the escort vehicles now began to evacuate and run for safety. Some decided to flee the field in their craft but still had to run the gauntlet of the close range volleys of musketry. The panic spread further as transports and larger weaponed vehicles powered away. Few escaped however, as the musket balls found these new Targets, causing more carnage.

The massed retreat of the Desirion force was in full flow. In many places it was large scale blind pandemonium as leaderless, terrified beings perished on an alien planet far from their own lands and homes. Despite this, other valiant attempt to bring some order to the panicked ranks was made by a number of commanders, but with the attack now being pressed from two fronts it proved too much. The impenetrable line of horse refused to allow a single alien soldier through, each being was systematically cut down by the keen, bloodied swords with no quarter being given. The demoralized and decimated front ranks that had initially fled from Colonel Jones musketeers now ran blindly into the horse troop and their numbers were reduced even further by Sydenham Poyntz and his bloodthirsty men. Instinctively recoiling from the mounted attack, the Desirion's turned about once again only to be met by the closing Musketeers of Colonel Jones.

Inevitably, the ground occupied by the invaders slowly reduced, as did their numbers as the Parliamentarian infantry and horse hacked, slashed and fired their way towards each other. Jones musketeers were eventually forced to cease their fire for fear of hitting the riders in Poyntz ranks. This gave Sydenham the chance to mop up on his own and with blinding skill and devastating efficiency they despatched every single Devil they could.

Those which had managed to flee the main area of fighting were not to find their desperately sought escape. A shouted order from Jones and the whole line of a few hundred Parliamentarians were soon on the chase with swords drawn ready for the kill, with Poyntz horse ready to follow

XXIII

"Exalted majestic sentinel," said Pix, Lax's chief advisor.

Lax swung round at the voice. "Ah Pix, what news do you bring?"Along with his entourage he had returned to the summit of Beeston Castle to view the battle from the inner bailey. Once there it became apparent that the fighting was far too distant, but he rather liked it up here, his good mood had returned dismissing the earlier setback as a minor one. "Are those ridiculous tiresome Hooomanns destroyed yet?" He asked, his face one of smug confidence.

Pix did not share his overseer's optimism. In fact his features betrayed those of someone bearing devastating news. "Majestic sentinel, I..." Pix paused long and hard, gathering himself before trying again. "Majestic sentinel, reports suggest things have not gone as planned," he said and bowed so far that his face almost buried itself in a bush beneath him on the ground.

Even though he didn't know the facts, Lax felt his heart sink for the umpteenth time since arriving on Earth. Standing up straight, obeying protocol he steeled himself. "Pix give me your news," he said, knowing he didn't really want to hear, but asked anyway.

"Majestic Sentinel, I...I..." A look from Lax informed him that should he wish to keep his safe advisors position then he'd best relay his news right now. "Majestic sentinel," said Pix, his voice wavering again. "It is reported that Number one group, is no more." On completion he shielded his face from his Sentinels eyesight.

Lax opened his mouth but nothing came out. Gulping, he took a deep breath. His previously sandy coloured face now took on a colour easily able to blend in with a snow drift.

"They were attacked overseer by a strangely clad, unidentified force travelling on the backs of large quadruped creatures." Pix paused, plucking up the courage to continue. "Majestic sentinel, reports suggest they were interphased."

Lax laughed briefly. Not a happy chortle, but a disbelieving guffaw before simply staring at Pix in disbelief, his accompanying commanders equally unable to express themselves.

"All of them?" Lax asked, breaking the silence.

"Reports are not complete majestic sentinel," added Pix, still talking to the bush.

After some moments he said, "thank you Pix that is all."

"Majestic Sentinel there is more," said Pix.

Lax's face seemed to ease strangely at this.

"The transports are on their way with the second wave," said Pix without being prompted.

Initially Lax was pleased with this new slant, the reinforcements will restore the balance, but his face soon fell again as he recalled Pix's words, "They were interphased, they were interphased," over and over again. He turned with a look of sheer horror in the direction of Chester despite knowing he wouldn't be able to see proceedings. Desperately he hoped the news to be false, however the plumes of smoke and general confusion was clear to see and spoke far more than mere words ever could. "Bring them back at once," he said calmly, turning once again to face the rising smoke in the distance towards Chester.

"We have attempted to Majestic sentinel, but we cannot make contact. We will of course continue to try," Pix turned and genuflected with the utmost precision.

"And Pix send me my Physician; I feel one of my faces coming on."

XXIV

The reinforcements from the reloaded transports arrived upon Rowton Moor before receiving the order to return. Unloading their cargo almost on the move, they disembarked amidst flashing plasma discharges and explosions. An awesome sight as the combined ranks of a vastly superior technological force gave a display of magnificent firepower, creating a pyrotechnic display the like of which Guy Fawkes Night could never hope to better in a million years.

Sadly for them that was all it turned out be.

The villages of Waverton and Christleton were reduced to a scene reminiscent of a First World War battlefield, just ruined brick walls where buildings once stood. Smoking, shattered tree stumps, cratered roads and fields. While the canal with its prestigious buildings standing pretty over the ornately painted narrow boats now filled that waterway with their rubble and masonry, the narrow boats more resembling flat boats.

Despite the hellish destruction the battle continued to rage, although the term battle may have been a little generous when regarding the Desirion's participation in proceedings. No more than a couple of dozen soldiers of General Sydenham Poyntz horse or Colonel Michael Jones musketeers were anything more than injured.

"Pray tell, this is but a mere afternoon hunt," Poyntz was heard to boast as he skewered another alien blocking the way to his next kill.

Despite their all guns blazing strategy, the reinforcements met the same fate as their predecessors as intense well drilled musketry and massed ranks of impenetrable cavalry went to work on them with the same ruthless efficiency.

XXV

After much organising and assembling of men, a brigade of Infantry was formed. The first Cheshire defence, as it was termed. Supported by light tanks and air cover, it was sent, cautiously, onto Rowton Moor soon after midday. Nervously, they wound down the streets on the outskirts of Chester towards the rising smoke, the sounds of chaos growing ever closer.

Above, a squadron of Harriers flew over making for the battle scene, the deafening roar from the six aircraft drowning out all other sounds.

"I heard that missile strikes earlier done nothing, didn't even hurt em," said a soldier, nervously to his neighbour, his eyes darting all over the place. His shoulder flashes read Royal Anglian Regiment and the name Taylor could be read on his breast pocket.

"I heard that they got some secret weapon that turns you into fizzing, bubbling shit," said Baader, his companion.

"I heard," Sounded an authoritative voice behind them, "that if you don't shut your bloody mouth you will be saying hello to em on your own, now keep quiet. That goes for the rest of you." Their moustached sergeant barked.

The brigade moved into the remains of Christleton. At first the buildings were more or less intact, just a few scorch marks or a small crater to betray any activity having taken place. However, a hundred yards further on and the signs of damage and destruction were there for all to see. Scorch marks dotted the area; the ground churned and blackened, while buildings became less intact. The closer they moved towards the sound of battle the more devastating the destruction became.

Orders were suddenly issued and the whole brigade spread out, using all available cover. Many took refuge within ruined buildings and other obstructions still standing. A wise move as the odd, stray plasma bolt caused them to scatter and take cover. Thankfully, these became less and less as the minutes ticked by.

The battle seemed very close now, smoke drifted about them bringing familiar smells, others not so. The Warrior tanks now took the foreground, advancing beyond the remains of Christleton and onto Rowton Heath itself which was still obscured by hedgerows and other obstacles but this proved little difficulty for the armoured vehicles. Welcomed by the nervous infantry, they made good progress into the remains of

Waverton, but were soon enveloped by smoke, the steady mechanical clanking purr of the warrior's engines the only thing to discern that they were there.

With no warning, the smoke cleared and all around, on the ground, lay many hundreds of dead and dying bodies of an alien design. Here and there were abandoned vehicles, many covered with large amounts of mud, dirt and dust, the debris from explosions, probably of their own making. A number of injured Desirion's were moving across the field of destruction. On sighting their human counter-parts they attempted to flee, the fight in them gone. Some, a small number, sought to recover lost weapons but such were the extent of their injuries, even this was clearly beyond them.

"Okay steady boys," said the big moustached Sergeant, "keep calm and stay alert."

Small pockets of swirling mist cleared from hollows and dips to reveal more alien bodies as the Brigade advanced.

"You notice there's none of our dead, only theirs," said Taylor to no one in particular. Nobody replied. Most had already questioned as to how these poor beings had basically been hacked to death, their bodies covered in deep slices, cuts or worse. Then there were those with huge holes blasted in them, the results of crude but lethal musket balls.

The sound of a rifle fire echoed behind them, causing everyone to ready themselves for any eventuality.

An officer, a Captain, came rushing to the front, "Sergeant tell the men not to worry about the shooting, were just attempting to do a spot of mopping up," he said, his face not altogether clear.

"Understood sir," the sergeant acknowledged, knowing well that wounded aliens were being dispatched accordingly. What he didn't realise, nor the Captain, that because of their interphased state, this would have no effect.

With most of the smoke at last cleared, it revealed the whole scene for the first time. For the soldiers of the first Cheshire defence Brigade it was one to behold.

A few hundred men dressed in what appeared to be seventeenth century clothing, many adorned with orange sashes and armed with old fashioned guns, were shooting at desperate aliens attempting to escape the slaughter. On the opposite side of the alien lines were at least a couple of thousand similarly dressed men on horseback. They were currently making kebabs out of the ugly bizarre shaped invaders. Even to the most inexperienced soldier it was quite obvious that the alien's position was pretty hopeless.

On the left flank a similar scene was taking place with yet more mounted soldiers while here and there red flashes still pierced the sky and explosions erupted as unearthly weapons were discharged.

Senior officers were quickly summoned to assess the situation and determine their next move. Lieutenant Colonel Slater, a member of General Fartlington staff, had accompanied the brigade onto Rowton Moor and was in the process of convincing his commanding officer that, strange as it may seem, the Parliamentarian army seemed to be doing a grand job on their own and rather than risk the safety of his men, shouldn't they just sit tight and observe.

"What's the matter with you man? Where's your vigour," accused Fartlington, almost pulling the headset and radio from the wall in his anger. He and his dwindling staff still occupied the safety of King Charles tower upon the walls in Chester. The strategic pointlessness of being there had still not been grasped by those present, even more so as most of the chiefs of staff had made camp at RAF Sealand along with the Prime Minister, who had, along with his defence ministers arrived at the communications base.

"I am giving you a direct order colonel Slater...." General Fartlington stopped abruptly, his mouth agape, the radio mouthpiece still in situ at his mouth.

A new person stood in the tower with them. Tall and thin, he wore long, black, knee length boots with black britches. A similar coloured coat covered his upper body, with a gold stripe running the length of each arm, while a deep red and gold sash adorned his waist with matching gloves. An ornate frilly white collar emerged from the coat while an immaculately trimmed goatee beard grew on the chin of his regal face. This was topped off by beautiful long shining black hair, which tumbled down to his shoulders, crowned with a wide black brimmed hat flourishing a huge black feather.

Looking out of one of the towers windows, he stared directly towards Rowton Heath, slapping the gloves in an irritated fashion into the palm of his hand.

Abruptly he turned towards the startled Fartlington and said in a diluted Scots accent, "You know, you can't see a bloody thing from here after all."

"Sir, are you there, what are your orders?" Asked the waiting Colonel Slater, over the radio.

"Err, yes, err stand by Slater," said a much calmer General Fartlington, who then meekly handed the radio headset back to the equally wary radio operator.

The battle began to fizzle out by the early afternoon for one simple reason; Sydenham and Jone's army were running out of enemies to kill. Rowton Moor was littered with thousands of dead and nearly dead Aliens; this was indeed a massacre without parallel.

Approximately eighteen thousand well armed and well equipped soldiers had left their base below Beeston castle. Just three hundred and twelve had made it back by the end of that day.

The British army had eventually managed to send four brigades to the heath, but as with the first, they simply stood by.

At just after one o clock that afternoon the violence ended, with both Cavalry and musketeers regrouping away from the main area of fighting. It was at this point, in the centre of Rowton Heath that a new army appeared.

They manifested in a similar manner to Poyntz and Jones and as with the former, were adorned in the flamboyant garb of seventeenth century soldiers. The only difference with these chaps was that the officers, if at all possible, were dressed even more ridiculously than their Parliamentarian counterparts. In excess of a thousand cavalrymen lined up just four hundred yards from Poyntz and his own regiment of horse. From the sight of the transparent banners and standards flapping in the breeze, a breeze which was strangely nonexistent, it was clear that these lads were here in favour of the king. At the sight of the other opposing army Sydenham and his force lined up as if poised to throw themselves once more into melee.

Sir Marmaduke Langdale, the Royalist commander broke away from his men and trotted his horse towards his Roundhead counterpart. Immediately Poyntz went to meet him. Sitting astride their mounts the two commanders were close enough to shake hands.

"Sir Marmaduke," Poyntz greeted, tipping his hat.

"General," nodded Langdale.

"Sir Marmaduke, my men have had their fill of the fight for one day," remarked Poyntz gesturing the piles of dead devils heaped around them in all directions. Sir Marmaduke looked around him and nodded his head as if in appreciation of his adversaries work then turned once again to Poyntz and nodded.

"How say you Sydenham, this day of the new year?" he offered, extending an arm.

With that, the two commanders grinned, shook hands and with a majestic sweep of hats returned to their respective sides. On reaching their own lines the two armies of the British civil wars faced each other before very slowly fading until all that could be seen were the remains of Waverton and the many, many dead Desirions.

XXVI

The second battle of Rowton Moor, as it had affectionately become known, had in a world already turned upside down, opened another huge can of worms. In just a few short weeks humanity had been forced to come to terms with the existence of extra terrestrial beings, stirring up all of the so called alien experts to a point of frenzy. But now the domain of the psychic medium and paranormal investigator threatened to eclipse that excitement as the planet now had to accept that the phenomena of ghosts actually existed as well.

A poor attempt to cover up this new sensation had predictably been made, *rare solar activity exacerbated by contagious mass hysteria,* had been the official Downing Street statement.

This was more or less the starting gun for just about anybody with a connection to the paranormal to descend upon the once relatively quiet area of Cheshire. The serious investigators arrived with an array of finely tuned motion detecting and listening devices, while for the less financially fortunate but equally enthusiastic; the prospect of living in small tent villages had sprung up. A throwback to the peace camps outside the Berkshire air base of Greenham Common in the nineteen eighties.

The heavy military presence cordoning the area prohibited any of these fanatics and mud dwellers from even gaining the slightest glimpse of the battle site and its absurd and incredible horrors. What was more disturbing however, was the fact that the vast majority of the unwashed, "Friends of Sydenham," as they had come to be known. (Not to be confused with the neighbourhood group, whose intention was to make the South London borough of Sydenham a nicer place to live), seemed totally oblivious of the fact that a military struggle, albeit a highly unorthodox one, had occurred and could potentially resume at any moment.

The authorities were unhappy with the increase of civilian activity in the area, with tensions finally coming to a head when the crew and cast of the popular digital TV show *Totally Paranormal,* appeared one morning hoping to carry out a live broadcast. Things were calm until the resident psychic medium descended into one of his many trances, claimed to be inhabited by the spirit of a dead alien and upset Zaphod, a small yappy Yorkshire terrier, by stepping upon it. The objecting campers sided with Zaphod and the ensuing argument soon escalated into a near riot, ending only with the intervention of a nearby company of soldiers. When this news reached General Fartlington, he ordered the removal, forcibly if necessary, of all civilians within a five mile radius of Rowton.

The newspapers had a field day, with the broadsheets demanding answers to challenging questions such as, *what are the ramifications to this country and its people, should we not be able to contain this quite frankly unprecedented and worrying threat?* And *should we seriously consider the use of a nuclear strike if we cannot contain them conventionally?*

The tabloids angle was slightly more general, with expected headlines such as *how do these Aliens have sex?* And *My Extra Terrestrial three in a bed nightmare,* while the problem pages contained an allegedly genuine letter by Claire from Frodsham, claiming to have been visited in the night by a horny Civil war soldier showing her just how to use a musket.

Questions also began to be asked among the more respected world of paranormal literary researchers and writers, chiefly those who specialised on hulking great hard back books often sold in discount book shops specialising upon The mysterious and the unexplained. Their subject matter had just been greatly reduced.

One thing was certain. The remarkable events which had occurred upon Rowton Heath a week ago had given Great Britain and indeed the whole world, a wake-up call, surely allaying any doubts about the reality of what was really happening while at the same time enquiring as to what the hell will happen next.

When news filtered through to Downing Street, that a battle had taken place, the Government debated long and hard into the night, finally coming to the conclusion that although the invasion seemed at the moment to have been contained to just one small area of Cheshire, the country's armed forces would have to be put on a war footing. A good decision expressed by much nodding of heads by various military chiefs of staff. This state included all Territorial and reservists being called up for possible activation. Many servicemen serving on foreign stations were recalled back to Britain, which in turn caused another major headache. Those currently serving in the Middle East were still very much required to ensure insurgents were kept at bay.

Some would argue that there were the Americans. They could always send reinforcements to replace the departing British troops. However, that statement in itself presented more problems than it solved. Sure your average US soldier was every bit as competently trained and equipped as his British counterpart, the major fault was that the Americans tended, as always to behave in a manner that best suits them.

The very private telephone call from the White house to Downing Street, when the president himself heroically stated in the kindest possible way that, should these aliens sons of bitches break out of their current area, wherever they are near to London and look like posing a threat, then the use of a strategic strike would have to be considered. The pregnant pause was finally broken by an unconditional offering of any assistance that was in their power to do so.

The British Army and Royal Air force were swift in their deployment, while the senior service responded equally magnificently to the challenge. The Admiralty immediately ordered the reactivation of a number of Mothballed warships, bringing the fleet's total strength back up to somewhere near double figures. This marvellous news included the reactivation of the recently decommissioned aircraft carrier, HMS Invincible, which could, if all possible stops were pulled out and the ship worked upon with the utmost alacrity, be ready to leave Portsmouth Naval Base in around ten months. A brilliant move which left the Admiralty with just one further tiny problem, where to find some aircraft to operate from it? The vast majority had gone the same way as the surface fleet with one or two even suffering the ultimate ignominy of being used as climbing apparatus within children's play areas.

Other help of a more humane nature was also forthcoming from the Governments of the European union, Australia, Canada and bizarrely Macedonia, who offered immediate military and humanitarian assistance, the bulk of which seemed to consist in being able lend a large number of donkeys. Her Majesties Government had politely thanked their Macedonian counterparts for the offer, but informed them that they would be gracefully declining.

Casualties however, had up until now been virtually non-existent, just the one unfortunate Tornado crew had been killed and therefore they held fire on the offers, desperately hoping that this would be the extent of casualties. The Prime Minister himself had been on the verge of conducting a visit to Chester, the intention being a kind of good will visit. It was inspired by grainy black and white footage depicting a resolute Winston Churchill stumbling through the ruined, bombed out shells of Britain's cities, giving hope to the beleaguered residents.

In reality the Government, as had the entire country, been caught completely off guard with most now coming to terms with these remarkable events, none more so than when news trickled in regarding the battle upon Rowton Moor. His aides had been at best reluctant to inform the Prime Minister of the news, not because he was afraid but because he didn't have the slightest idea where to begin or how to deliver it. Which to be fair was never going to be the easiest of announcements to make.

"Err excuse me Prime Minister," the nervous aid would address him. "The alien army has been destroyed upon Rowton Moor."

"Excellent news," A concerned Prime Minister would enquire. "Are there many casualties?"

"Err no prime minister, none. The aliens were destroyed by a ghost army of civil war cavalry and musketeers."

Regardless of the difficulties of the task these were essentially the facts. The brigade of infantry and light armour which had warily made its way onto Rowton moor had witnessed the final moments of the overwhelming destruction of the Desirion attack force. Its existence being practically impossible to deny as the soldiers of Sydenham Poyntz and Marmaduke Langdale greeted and dematerialized right in front of the disbelieving eyes of the British troops slowly advancing from Chester.

Once the spectral army had left the field, the villages of Waverton, Christleton, Rowton and other small gatherings of buildings and farms were, with just a few lucky exceptions, now just smoking piles of charred and jagged bricks and piles of rubble. Fortunately the human cost was nil thanks to the timely evacuation of the entire area.

This was far from the case where the Desirions were concerned. As far as the eye could see, the battlefield of Rowton Moor was strewn with the twitching, crawling, staggering, dead and dying of a race totally alien to this planet, which caused another problem.

The battlefield needed to be cleared of its detritus, however, due to the Desirion's interphased state, they could not be touched. Every attempt to remove the unfortunate beings was met by a hand grasping soil or thin air. Oddly, this did not apply to their weapons, each one was gathered up, completely solid, leaving many baffled as it was quite evident that the transparent untouchable aliens were also quite capable of grasping these same weapons.

The dead were less of a problem than the survivors. These unfortunate beings wandered in their almost transparent state, some descending upon Chester itself. All attempts to stop them were met with frustration, with many a surprised sentry being confronted by a gaunt looking Desirion.

"Halt or I'll fire," would come the warning. Then surprise when the unflinching figure not only ignored the demanding squaddie, but walked straight through him. The result would be the loosing off of a round or two. Completely oblivious of the ensuing fire, the Desirion would continue, with the bullets ending up safely imbedded within the upholstery of the sentries, commanding officers car.

Realising there was no way to stop these wandering aliens the authorities instructed radio and television stations to frequently broadcast bulletins stating that *although alarming, the aliens were in fact harmless and should a member of the public come across one, they were to report it to the authorities keeping well clear.* After another day or two, suffering from starvation and dehydration, they simply collapsed and died.

General Fartlington, still unbelieving of the existence of a seventeenth century army in the field reluctantly visited the scene himself. "Can't see any damn Cromwellian bloody army," he was heard to utter, still in defiance, his aides dutifully nodding in agreement. But the sight before his very eyes, albeit with the absence of historic soldiers, forced him to finally accept most of the facts.

Regardless of the Generals ignorance, it still left thousands of dead aliens littering the area. Many ideas were put forward, but the most innovative and probably only really practicable suggestion was to simply cover them with earth, or rather heap earth over the area they existed. This of course would involve an enormous effort, with an area some four square miles, not to mention the almost wiping from the map of what was left of the villages of Christleton, Waverton and Rowton.

Fartlington, not wanting to make any decisions for the time being, very firmly put the ball in the court of the Westminster. Their response was to deal with the matter in hand first, primarily the wandering alien problem. And so with no other alternative than to relieve Rowton of the Desirion's they were, for the time being just left where they fell, with the whole area cordoned off to allow the men in white coats to do their stuff.

The alien casualties were not the only things left behind. Large numbers of caterpillar tracked escort vehicles, troop transports and heavy mounted mobile weapons were abandoned when the unstoppable hoards of Jones and Poyntz horse and foot had hammered them to oblivion. Not affected by the unearthly state handicapping their operators, they were hauled away one by one. Attempts were made to move the vehicles under their own power, but the endeavours of the numerous military and civilian scientists were repeatedly foiled by nothing more than a complete lack of understanding of the technology. Finally admitting defeat, each one was attached to large heavy duty cables and carefully loaded onto commandeered farm trailers and transported towards the nearby A41. Here they were labouriously unloaded and reloaded onto the waiting trailers of the few low loader articulated lorries that could be found at short notice, before being finally ending up at RAF Sealand.

XXVII

Gary, Leyton, Wood's and Peter, arrived upon Rowton Moor in the late afternoon, in a small convoy of Landrover's accompanied by Captain Bridger, Colonel Watkin and half a dozen armed soldiers. The Colonel had taken the decision to rid himself of his passengers. However, having left in order to drop them off at a prearranged point in Chester, they had been intercepted, informing the Colonel of his immediate need to attend the battle site. An inconvenient communication breakdown followed, leaving his angered protest unheard and with little alternative he drove straight to Rowton Moor with his unwanted quartet.

Gary thought this all a good idea; on the flimsy basis of the more information they could gather, the more assistance they could offer. Colonel Watkin thought this a load of rubbish and would hear none of it. Captain Bridger agreed with her superior, but pressed him into relenting as time really was of the essence. Grudgingly, Watkin went along with it on the proviso they were kept at a safe distance and offloaded at the first opportunity.

The Landover's emptied their human cargo at the edge of the range of destruction. Peter with his newly acquired brilliant mind approached the ruins of a nearby building. Once a respectable detached mock, Tudor house with a well tended walled garden, now resembles a blackened burnt out shell, the roof having collapsed after the interior had become gutted by fire.

The vehicles other occupants watched bewildered as he rubbed a forefinger over what appeared to be a blast mark upon a Limestone gatepost, held it up to his nose and sniffed.

"Just as I suspected," he remarked, his voice imitating that of a clever pig. "It's clearly the work of a high intensity thermal transfer plasma weapon, charged by a fluctuating positron arc of extreme magnitude."

"Really?" The soldier closest to him responded. His genuine interest causing him to pause from twisting a finger inserted into his ear.

Peter glanced at him, quickly concluding that his intellectual capacity was not worthy of further attention. Watkin and Bridger in turn, ignored the irritating intellectual and wandered among the devastation shaking their heads and sighing rather more than was really necessary. A Sergeant who had observed their arrival scurried over before snapping to attention and delivering a crisp salute.

"Sir, Ma'am," he offered in his best parade ground voice. "Sergeant Pepper, B company, first battalion, Royal Engineers," he continued, ending with another salute.

Gary burst out laughing, grunting like a bear before sucking air in through clenched teeth. "He said sergeant Pepper, did you hear him? Pepper...Sergeant."

Leyton, used to Gary being a prat, simply rolled his eyes while attempting to ignore him.

Not wanting the hilarious gag to be wasted, he turned to the normally faithful Woods. "Pepper, sergeant, do you get it Woods?"

"Yeth thir, very funny thir," Woods replied, his attention consumed by the scene before him.

Captain Bridger turned and administered a devastating stare.

Unable to shake off the hilarity of his joke, Gary took a few steps back in order to laugh it off. The two officers and Sergeant Pepper could be heard chatting, the NCO filling them in on developments at the battle site while in the background the gently degrading insidious laughter of a complete idiot could still just about be heard.

"If you'd like to accompany me sir, I'll introduce you to Captain Pendleberry," continued Pepper.

Without another word the colonel held his hand out gesturing the Sergeant to lead the way. Captain Bridger turned and motioned to the four civilians to follow. "Stay with me, do not. I repeat, do not leave my sight."

Still chortling, Gary followed his companions. Before long, the military men came to a halt. Something resembling a body lay at their feet. Catching up with the Sergeant and officers, they too halted; rapidly realising they had reached the extremity of alien dead.

A tall, thin and gaunt looking officer dressed in camouflage battle dress complete with epaulettes greeted Watkin. "Captain Pendleberry sir," he offered, his tone high and shrill.

"Thank you Sergeant, please return to Lieutenant Shaw and help him with the Gun vehicles," Pendleberry said to Pepper, who saluted in return.

"Well sir, as you can see this is it," he said turning to Watkin, indicating the battle site with a sweep of his arm.

Taking a moment, the group stared aghast at the utter devastation. Dead beings from another world lay in all manner of contorted positions. Although a percentage of the grotesque distortion could be put down to extra terrestrial physiology. In the distance a number of soldiers, mainly engineers could be seen struggling with a large vehicle similar in appearance to a hovercraft with a large tube mounted on the back.

"That sir," said Pendleberry, noticing the Colonels gaze. "Is one of the alien war machines, a sort of tank if you like, nasty brute! They abandoned them all when the err cavalry and musket chappies attacked them."

Gary and his colleagues hadn't allowed their vision to extend this far yet. Their attention was very firmly fixed upon the ugly forms which lay about their feet, forms which they recognised only too well. He had stopped laughing now. Each of their faces revealing a mask of revulsion directed at the creatures, the same ugly beings who had suffered at their hands back in Delamere forest.

XXVIII

The inner bulkhead of Lax's personal quarters had suffered mild impact damage from a severely disturbed Overseer for the best part of the day now. Fortunately this did not affect the smooth running of the ship, the crew tirelessly maintained their stations within the hub and elsewhere, oblivious to the devastation being meted out not twenty yards away.

Chief Advisor Pix paced up and down the centre of the command area, his long robes swaying according to the direction of motion. His overriding duty was to keep his overseer updated on events as they unfolded, no matter how unwelcome, right now he was muttering to himself nervously.

Lax had taken the news of the disaster which had befallen the Desirion force sent to occupy the human city of Chester extremely badly.

Just over eight hundred demoralised Desirions had returned to Beeston, with all but six of them having gone through the interphase process. Initial treatment of the returnee's showed that the longer the interphased state was administered, the more difficult the process to return them to normal proved. The last few to appear had been interphased for three days by then and it was touch and go as to whether or not it would actually be possible to return them to normal. The Desirion medical and science experts were of the opinion that any more interphased soldiers returning from this point on would probably be beyond help. Alas, no more survivors appeared over the next twenty four period and as a result they were unable to prove their daunting theory.

Pix darted furtive glances designed to provoke glimpses from the Hubs operatives, largely in the hope of receiving an expression of sympathy. The basis being it would boost his waning confidence. None paid him any attention and inevitably he accepted he must carry out his duty. Braced for the expected onslaught he swept up his robes and strode purposefully towards his destination. He was within feet of the bulkhead exit when suddenly the outline appeared before him and with a smooth hiss, opened to reveal the interior of Lax's personal quarters.

Pix had very little opportunity to take notice of the interior as the concerned face of Medic Commander Dix appeared, his frame completely blocking the doorway as he toyed with a piece of apparatus. Lax emerged behind the medic and strode roughly onto the Hub like the proverbial bull in an antique shop for exquisitely delicate china. Reacting with supreme dexterity to his overseer's sudden emergence, Pix flung himself to one side.

"Pix," roared Lax, searching for his advisor, albeit not very thoroughly. "Pix," he cursed again, the frustration mounting. "Must I tolerate this continuous incompetence? Must I do everything myself?"

"I am here majestic, exulted, overseer," Pix grovelled, performing one of his most elegant bows.

"What are you doing down there you snivelling cretin?" Bawled Lax.

"Majestic..." Pix managed before he was abruptly cut short.

"Bring me more Glook."

"Majestic overseer forgive me but haven't you?" spluttered Pix before stopping short on purpose this time. He stared straight at the floor which was barely an inch from his face not daring to move. He couldn't remember ever seeing his overseer in such a foul mood.

Lax stared at the back of his grovelling advisor. "Do you dare to question me?"

Now it was Lax's turn to be interrupted. Commander, Physician Dix had appeared at the doorway and was addressing his overseer, albeit in a less formal way. "Lax you must calm down, and," he added, "I have already instructed you that you cannot continue to consume Glook after taking your medication."

Since learning the full extent of the massacre, a mortified Lax had withdrawn to his personal quarters for the rest of that day and the next. When access was finally given to Dix, the overseer was immediately administered a severe dose of what was commonly known upon Shard as a calm spreader.

Although it wasn't common knowledge yet, except of course to the Hubs occupants who couldn't fail to notice, it was now unofficially official that the Desirion majestic overseer for the vanquishment and initial colonisation of the planet Earth had become seriously depressed. Not a major problem in itself as Dix was more than qualified in dealing with and administering medications regarding the mind. The main sticking point was that Lax was consuming vast quantities of Glook, the Desirion version of neat alcohol with a twist of hot chilli and Worcester sauce, and as with all pills they do not mix well with intoxicating drinks.

It wasn't common knowledge yet, not even to those in the Hub that the Desirion majestic overseer for the vanquishment and initial colonisation of the planet Earth was officially becoming a piss head too.

Lax turned until he faced Dix. Then raising himself rather like a cat makes itself large when threatened, he breathed deeply, about to deliver another verbal attack. Dix visibly shrunk back, realising he may be close to overstepping the mark. He made to speak again but Lax stopped him, his arm unfolding before patting him on the shoulder.

"Pix," He said to the cowering advisor, still scraping the floor. "Inform the council of Commanders that I wish their company immediately to discuss new strategies."

"Yes exulted majestic overseer," said Pix, brilliantly managing to shuffle away while still at the full extent of his bow, resembling a crab trying to escape a predator.

"And Pix."

Pix stopped and attempted to bow even lower which would mean physically merging with the floor.

"Majestic overseer."

"Do not forget the Glook," Lax said vehemently.

Dix gave a resigned sigh.

"At once exulted majestic overseer," said Pix and scuttled away with relief.

XXIX

"Thith ith good ithn't it thir?" Said Woods. The look on his face was one of absolute contentment. His posture however, looked rather uncomfortable wedged up against a wooden crate in the back of an eight ton Bedford army truck. Of course the act of sitting in the back of an army truck, even in an array of even more uncomfortable and uncompromising positions was certainly not a new thing to him.

During his distinguished days of military service, Woods had sat, stood, knelt, hung, lay curled up in a ball; this one normally from the effects of alcohol. Or flat out and spread eagle, also from the effects of alcohol. On one occasion they had even managed to play football in the rear of just such a vehicle. This particular sporting spectacle had come to an abrupt end when Woods, in goal, or rather defending a piece of webbing erected upon the trucks bulkhead, had over launched a goal kick, which flew from the back of the truck without bouncing, and was right now slowly biodegrading in a dark leafy forest somewhere in the Rhine area of Germany.

On this day Woods shared the truck with Gary. A Captain of the Royal Logistics Corps trailing three eager Privates, together with a Lieutenant, a sergeant and six infantrymen of the Royal Marine Commando's. The civilians were in the truck fiercely against Colonel Watkins wishes, but the decision to have them accompany the squads was made by suited know all's in Whitehall, on the basis that they were the only living Humans to have experienced close quarter combat with the invaders, and their experience could prove crucial. An exasperated Watkin obeyed the order, quickly washing his hands of the responsibility and assigning them accordingly.

Each soldier was busily engaged in the process of checking his personal equipment, whether that consisted of cleaning weapons with time honoured efficiency. Checking and rechecking maps and navigation devices or simply sorting out his small backpack so that everything fitted inside.

Gary's personal responsibility was a Tippman, ninety eight, semi automatic paintball carbide. His particular firearm required no cleaning nor maintenance as it had been given a thorough check just the day before. This however, didn't deter the excited office worker from methodically breaking the paintball gun down, piece by piece.

The weapon, the absolute limit, he, along with Leyton and

Peter had been permitted to carry, due to their experience with it during the incident in Delamere was a modified version, boasting a larger ammunition chamber and fitted with slightly enhanced firepower too. As he pointlessly worked on it, Gary's face was a picture of pride, excitement and wonder all rolled into one. It was also totally apparent that he was just copying the others in the truck while looking a complete berk in the process. Woods on the other hand, because of his previous service had been eventually given permission to carry a firearm. His initial request of a Forty four Magnum complete with laser sights and automatic recoil loading had been turned down. He rattled off another dozen hand weapons of mass destruction before being given the choice of either an SA80 rifle or a standard nine millimetre pistol, finally settling for the latter. In the end he seemed well pleased with his acquisition and in addition to his small arsenal of otherwise unknown hidden firearms he also carried, concealed somewhere about his person, his trusty Kukri knife.

Leyton and Peter, the other two paint-ballers travelled behind in an identical truck. These, together with two Landrover's, both equipped with General purpose machine guns mounted on the back, made up the small convoy which was moving with utmost caution in the late evening darkness along the deserted road between the villages of Tarvin and Tarporley.

Their progress along the debris strewn roads slowed considerably until finally coming to a complete halt. Gary could hear the driver chatting with someone outside whose voice was soon drowned out by another. The Scottish accent identified him as Lieutenant Havelock, the Marine detachment commanding officer. His voice rose in apparent frustration with that of the stranger until with the exception of the clunk of the truck door opening, silence reigned.

Multiple footsteps were soon distinguished moving toward the rear before the tarpaulin was suddenly raised to reveal an unknown, thick moustached Sergeant. Stood by him, a fierce looking officer while next to him stood a very uptight Lieutenant Havelock. He opened his mouth to speak but before he could utter a word he was interrupted by the more senior officer at his side.

The Major wore a flawless dress uniform which made him stand out like a sore thumb among the other more suitably dressed soldiers. Thin eye slits burned into the men as if he was scrutinizing them for a clue to an unsolved crime.

"Okay men," he said, his voice deep and booming with just a touch of the aristocratic plumb showing through. "This is a checkpoint and I need to see all identification."

Without another word he took a step back, happy to let his Sergeant take over.

The Marines in the Bedford broke into a fit of patting pockets and frantic searches in backpacks, looking for their up until now un-needed paperwork. Feeling as though his authority was being undermined, Havelock turned to speak with the Major once more. While the two officers discussed protocol the Sergeant climbed aboard the Bedford and inspected the soldier's identifications one by one. Eventually he reached Gary who held up a card for the Sergeant to see.

"Oh, ha ha," he laughed falsely for all to hear. "We appear to have among us a joker." There was a pause while everybody looked. "And what may I say sir, is that?" he said referring to Gary's ID.

Gary looked confused, if not a little insulted, *my picture's not that bad,* he thought.

"Who do we think we are, Dr bleedin Spock?" The sergeant said with mirthless humour.

Gary turned the card over and glimpsed at the picture and information instantly realising his error. Held proudly in his hand was a shining plastic card, selflessly denoting that Gary Spam was a member of the United Federation of Planets, complete with a gold, Star Fleet hologram emblem and photo of him adorned in the uniform of a Starship Captain. Far from feeling embarrassed as any normal person would and should have been, he actually felt rather offended. "For your information Sergeant," he bravely uttered, "It's not Dr Spock, its Mister Spock. It's a common mistake of which the uneducated often fall foul of."

The Sergeant really couldn't have cared less. Raising himself to as high a position as he dare without banging his head on the overhead beam, he gave a huge sigh, mainly for effect before demanding Gary's real identification, threatening that if he didn't produce it, he would be forcefully removed from the truck or possibly even shot. This produced a cheer from the Marines. Now rightly embarrassed Gary produced the asked for document. Finally satisfied, the Sergeant left the truck.

The Major and Havelock had also finished, not mutually but by a minor rebuke from the Major reminding Havelock just who it was he was addressing and with a salute and a, "yes sir," uttered as sarcastically as he dare, the marine officer climbed back into the Bedford, closing the door with a slam and the trucks were allowed to proceed.

To the north, the distant sound of a helicopter could be heard. The Lynx, was surveying the area ahead, ensuring that no hostile forces barred their way, while all the time making sure it stayed safely out of range of the Desirion encampment at Beeston, the glow of which could clearly be seen emanating in that direction.

"If only I had a phaser," said Gary to the Marine next to him. The huge camouflaged soldier, even though sat down, still appeared to reach six foot, ceased the cleaning of his rifle and barked out an assertive, "What?" as if replying to a stupid child.

"A phaser. You must know what a phaser is." Gary replied, emitting a giggle while sucking air in through the gaps between his teeth which created a whistling sound.

"Ah you mean the guns they used in star trek." Said the marine smugly, realising just what Gary was talking about.

"Yes that's it, just think of the damage I could do with one of those?" Gary replied, his face beaming with interest and joy at having a co trekker to converse with.

"Of course it would have to be one from Sisko, Janaway and Picard's era. The phasers from Kirk or Archer's particular time, which although good and I must point out my favourite, did not seem to have the firepower or the flexible phase settings that the newer models possessed, although..." He droned on, his mind moving into the next gear and rapidly closing on warp speed. "To have a newer generation one with Kirks experience and attitude would be truly awesome. Which genre do you prefer, Picard, Kirk, Sisko or even Janaway? Or do you prefer Enterprise? Do you know I've got a full sized replica, season two, next generation phaser rifle at home?"

Gary's co-conspirator had left the gist of the conversation a good few minutes and couple of miles back down the road. He looked listlessly at his tormentor with a blank expression, his eyes glazed over with the onslaught of tears only a matter of time.

"Where do you think we are going thir?" interjected Woods, saving the Marines mental health and sanity.

"I err, I don't know Woods," said Gary experiencing a little trouble adjusting back to the present.

"Haven't you got anything to do O'Brian?" The short, tough looking sergeant Hornby scolded. The non commissioned officer appeared to be composed entirely of sinewy muscle. His uniform looked fit to split, threatening to outdo the hulk himself while his deep set blue eyed face topped with short black hair and stubby nose gave the impression that he could take on the whole alien force single handed. The softly spoken but forceful voice didn't quite match its owner. The accent, clearly that of a Londoner, gave a false air to his heavy, hard looking face. It could be said that he bore a vague resemblance to a Desirion, but no one had the guts to say that to his face.

"Yes Sarge, I have, sorry Sarge," O'Brian replied, bursting back into reality.

"Then I suggest you get on with it," replied Hornby.

"Sarge," said O'Brian and returned to cleaning his rifle.

"Captain," enquired Gary, addressing the tall, thin Logistics officer." Could you inform us as to where we are going?"

Captain Stanton looked up and removed his cap, vaguely aware that someone had spoken his name. He seemed to poke his nose out similar to a mouse sniffing for a piece of cheese before running a hand through his light brown hair, replaced his cap and returned to his work.

Unwilling to disturb the Captain again, Gary returned his attention to his own weapon but looked somewhat uncertain. After a moment he turned to Woods. "Err Woods, I err seem to err," he fumbled, holding a number of pieces of paintball gun feebly in his unskilled hands. Woods happily took the pieces and without a word had the weapon reassembled in a matter of minutes.

"There you are thir, good ath new," he announced, smiling.

"Thank you Woods," said Gary, gratefully taking the gun back and giving it a rub with a rag.

The small convoy trundled slowly onwards, quickly enveloped by the darkness. The occupants, largely silent were wrapped up within their own thoughts. The only sounds that of the rhythmic rattle of the engine and the distant sound of the Lynx, which gave them a somewhat reassuring feeling.

Every now and then Gary would whimper, followed by a sound similar to a young girls giggle. Those close enough saw that his face was one of a dozing idiot emblazoned with a curious smile.

"I remember when we were in Germany back in..." Woods tale was cut short as the truck turned a particularly tight corner, almost throwing those on the right hand side from their seats before coming to an unexpected halt. Captain Stanton looked up from his paperwork, slid the glass hatch connecting to the cab and conducted a brief conversation with the driver. Quick chat over, he stood and addressed the vehicles occupants.

"Okay Chaps," he said in a nasally voice, "We have arrived at the village of Tarporley; we shall be taking a short break to assess the situation."

Woods gently pushed back the corner of the tarpaulin flap and peered outside to confirm as to whether the Logistics officer was indeed correct. His initial thought was how unnaturally dark it was, only just being able to make out the dusky silhouettes of houses, roads and the unlit streetlights.

"Ooh," he relayed," ith really dark out there."

Lieutenant Havelock had been relatively quiet since the checkpoint incident, he now spoke up with an order for the men to disembark and stretch their legs. "And remember no lights at all, that includes cigarettes as well." This particular order, he regretted himself, as right at that moment he was dying for a smoke. Predicted groans and curses flowed from the men who were counting on this stop being good for a fag break.

Gary stepped from the truck and onto the road surface. Stretching his stiff limbs, he yawned before following Woods, who had perched himself on a low stone wall, where he was happily picking his nose.

"Hello Woods," he said, jumping up so as he could perch himself next to the indulging ex soldier and promptly positioned his left bum cheek straight onto a jagged piece of stone sticking out from the surface. His shout of "Oh bloody hell," echoed around the desolate roadway, bouncing from each building in turn. Fortunately for Gary, the darkness concealed the looks of certain death aimed in his direction.

"Sir, could you keep your voice down please, we don't want to attract the attention of our friends over there do we?" berated Havelock, trying his utmost to chastise Gary whilst still being polite and pointing in the general direction of Beeston and the Alien camp.

A tense silence broke out. No one seemed to want to say anything and if they did it was in a hushed whisper. The tension was finally broken when an overweight dog appeared, trotting from the darkness it headed towards the soldiers.

"The poor little mite, it's probably hungry," said Private McCormack.

"Yeh right, judging by the look of that thing it, look at it, it's bloody huge." replied his companion.

The dog, a Jack Russell, was indeed overweight and by a considerable amount. This didn't deter it and soon, despite the derisory comments from the soldiers it was chomping on biscuits from ration packs and happily receiving a heavy dose of petting. However, once it had realised there was no more food to be had, it lost interest in the soldiers and went to move off. Wondering what all the fuss was about Gary walked towards the Marines and saw the dog as it walked away.

"Wow!" He exclaimed with genuine surprise. "Look at the size of that dog," before breaking into mock football chant. "Who ate all the pies? Who ate all the pies," he sang before realising that not for the first time everybody was staring at him. "You fat bastard, you...fat...bas...tar...d," his voice trailed off into silence.

The rotund Jack Russell offered Gary a dirty look before disappearing back amongst the abandoned buildings whence it came. With the flurry of excitement regarding the dog now over, the marines turned to witness the officers and NCOs piling into the back of the truck Gary and Woods had been travelling in. Once they were all in, the tarpaulin flap was pulled down. The rest of the marines along with Gary, Woods, Leyton and Peter were left to quietly mill around and take in the chilly night air. Hushed conversation could be heard while the faint aroma of pipe tobacco smoke mingled with that of cigar, wafted from the truck currently occupied by the officers and NCOs.

The tarpaulin at the back of the second Bedford suddenly lifted to reveal two grinning faces. "Brew up lads," said one, his features heavily boot polished while revealing a perfectly white set of teeth. A small whispered cheer went up and as one the whole group descended upon the truck, the disappointment of not being able to smoke temporarily diminished.

"I say Gentlemen," interjected Peter. "If we all form an orderly queue, I'm sure that there will be more than enough hot beverage to satiate all of our liquid requirements." His comments, inevitably were ignored as he was buffeted to the rear of the mob, leaving him a little upset that his logic was wasted.

Leyton wasn't happy either. He was utterly fed up, and now, long since wished he hadn't volunteered. A couple of his friends had headed westwards to Holyhead and caught the Ferry to Dublin when all this Alien stuff had broken out. Right now he wished he'd gone with them. At last he reached the front of the unorganized mass and extended a hand to take hold of the cup of steaming hot tea offered. With one hand firmly around it he turned to depart when the soldier serving said, "Hey, you're Ian Wright aren't you?"

Leyton showed very little emotion, except to roll his eyes.

"You are aint yer? Christ, can I have your autograph?" The Marine continued without giving him the chance to explain.

The outburst caused other faces to turn upon him and scrutinize the unfortunate lad in an attempt to make out if it was indeed the footballing legend.

"I say, who is this Ian Wright fellow?" A blissfully ignorant Peter asked.

Leyton, now extremely embarrassed, not to mention exasperated with the constant mistaken identity, wanted only to escape from the crowd. Looking for an exit, he spotted Gary who had returned to the wall and headed towards him, this itself being a true measure of how stupid he felt.

Gary spotted him. "Yo Leyton," he called out, still rubbing his bottom cheek and inspecting his fingers for any sign of blood.

"Jesus man," mouthed Leyton, changing direction again, this time towards Woods, who hadn't moved and still sat on the wall. It was noticeable that Woods appeared a little odd, on the verge of asking what the matter was he thought better of it and instead just leaned against the wall and sipped his tea.

The marines were still huddled around the back of the truck drinking and discussing Ian Wright, every now and then one would shoot a furtive glance towards Leyton.

"Got anything to eat Parksy?" Parvetti called those in the back of the truck.

"No mate, only some biccies, oh and some rat packs."

A dozen or so foil wrapped packets of biscuits from ration boxes were handed down before being quickly devoured by the hungry marines, the rest of the contents were left untouched.

Gary began to feel a little lonely and wandered over to Woods and Leyton.

"Are you okay Woods?" he enquired, "Did you not get a drink of tea?"

There was No response.

"Woods, Woods, Woods, Woods, Woods, Woods, Woods, Woods,"

"Oh for Christ's sake!" Leyton interrupted Gary's repetition. "Can't you see he's in one of his weird trances, meditating or something?"

"No he's not," Gary replied, displaying his ignorance of all things he didn't understand.

"And how do you know you annoying little shit?" Leyton spat, his patience finally exhausted.

"Because," said Gary taking on an authoritative air again. "Meditation is sitting with your legs crossed in a funny way with your arms in the air and forefinger and thumb joined at the tip while chanting, Om, with your eyes closed."

Gary's further blushes, not to mention more potential physical injury was saved when the flap of the truck containing the officers opened up again. Lieutenant Havelock was the first to disembark, attempting to disperse a cloud of cigarette smoke while quietly calling everyone to his attention.

"Okay gentlemen," he continued in a loud whisper. "If you would like to gather around as close as you can, I shall explain our plans for this evening's entertainment."

The men, still clutching hot drinks and biscuits nudged forward. At the trucks rear Captain Stanton and his men could be seen busily scrutinizing various maps and documents while the Sergeant and Corporals stood back to allow their officer to speak.

"We are approximately one and a quarter miles from Beeston Castle and the enemy's base in that direction." Havelock pointed in a south westerly direction with a large stick he had picked up from the floor.

Gary looked in that direction expecting to see as much but was inevitably met by darkness. Turning back to face the Lieutenant he thought he caught a faint and curiously familiar humming sound coming from the direction he had looked in.

"Now, we will be leaving all transport here in the village," continued Havelock. "We will be on foot carrying all our gear with us, so I want you packed and ready to go." A pause. "As it's nice and dark we'll keep to the roads, this way we should make the bank of the canal in approximately fifteen minutes, we aren't in any particular rush."

The hum was still audible and gradually increasing. Gary still couldn't put a name to the sound but was convinced he had heard it before.

"We are to hold a concealed position and gain as much Intel from that point, however, if we can get closer then we shall, but I must make it clear, no risks must be taken remember we have non coms with us."

The reference to the four civilians was quite clear, with most wondering why the hell they were with them in the first place, all wishing that they would disappear. Lieutenant Havelock continued to relay relevant information to his squad, finishing off by giving two map references.

"Those with Sergeant Hornby will proceed to the first map reference while those with me will proceed to the latter." He paused and scratched the inside of his ear before inspecting his finger. "Are there any questions?"

"Yes Sir," said Parvetti. "What is that noise?"

A hush descended upon everyone while heads poised at an angle and ears turned skywards. The sound was now audible to the whole group and unmistakably growing louder. Havelock peered into the sky as if trying to decide how much of a threat this was, if any.

"Sir it's coming from the direction of Beeston," said Sergeant Hornby.

Suddenly the time for contemplation was over. "Okay lads, defensive positions, find cover now," barked Havelock, the need for quiet also apparently over.

Marines suddenly ran in all directions, but not in a disorderly way. Those with equipment and weapons quickly concealed themselves behind walls and buildings or among the dense undergrowth at the side of the road, while those without rushed towards the trucks to collect theirs. Woods, now out of his meditative state had fallen backwards over the wall in a controlled way, landing feet first in a crouching position in the midst of a large clump of stinging nettles. His pistol Cocked and loaded in one hand, a wicked looking keen edged kukri in the other. Leyton had followed the nearest group of men to a place of safety while Peter ran back and forwards, flapping his arms like a panicked chicken.

Gary was unsure as to what action he should take. Refusing to reveal his confusion he vaulted the wall Woods had fallen back over and promptly pierced his right bum cheek on the same piece of stone sticking out from the top. Landing hands first among the same pile of nettles that Woods currently nestled in, he let out a scream as the plants took to their task.

"Are you okay thir?" asked Woods calmly, still peering at the sky, his concentration resolute.

Gary slowly rose onto his knee's nursing multiple stings upon his palms but making sure he kept his head below the level of the wall.

"No Wood's I'm bloody not," he replied, the pain in his bottom currently superseding that of his hands.

The humming was now very loud, almost an intense vibration and now accompanied by a low whistle. Despite the pain and obvious discomfort he was in, it was at that moment that Gary remembered where he had heard the sound before. In the car park, prior to everybody arriving for the paintball event in Delamere forest.

"Woods I know what that sound is," he said excitedly.

"Yeth thir ith one of thothe alien thonth of bitcheth," replied Woods.

"That's right," said Gary, following Woods line of vision into the night sky.

Hovering directly above the parked trucks in the dark night sky was a moving darkness, its outline only visible due to a lack of stars, which were blotted out by its shape. Small jets of vapour vented, appearing almost phosphorescent. The size of the craft was difficult to gauge but looked to be not much larger than one of the Bedford trucks over which it hovered.

Lieutenant Havelock stood with Sergeant Hornby and two other men in the porch of a deserted house. Looking around he ascertained to make sure the rest were well hidden when he noticed the vacant general purpose machine guns on the two Landrover's concealed beneath the dense canopy of a large tree.

"Sergeant, get two crews onto those GPMGs right away."

"Sir," replied Hornby, immediately breaking cover and skirting the perimeter of the house's garden with a series of impressive shoulder rolls and dives that Bodie and Doyle would have been proud of. This was followed by a dash onto the edge of the road. A quick glance at the craft in the sky and he was crossing it before being temporarily winded by a spectacular dive which resulted in him bouncing onto the soft verge on the other side. A few seconds to get his breath back and gather his composure and the previous acrobatics were followed up by a crawl through some dense undergrowth where he knew a number of the men had sought refuge. The startled marines raised their weapons towards the violent disturbance of the bush in front of them hoping it was a curious Fox or Badger, their relief was evident when they were suddenly confronted by the sweating black and green smeared face of their Sergeant.

"Murray, Chapman get your arses moving to the Landrover and man that GPMG. O Brian, Langhorne you get on the other, Move."

The four reluctant volunteers scuttled from their concealed

position, leaving just three of their comrades behind. Sergeant Hornby retraced his steps taking the same route back to the porch. As the team on the ground observed from their positions the dark shape in the sky continued to hover as if itself watching.

"The bastards know we are here sir," said Hornby arriving back at the porch barely out of breath.

Havelock was quiet for a moment as if contemplating. "No sergeant, I don't think so, I'm sure they could easily just blast us if they knew we were here," he said more in hope than judgment.

A powerful white beam of light suddenly snapped into life, originating from the underside of the crafts hull and illuminated the scene below, causing those who thought their place of concealment adequate, to look very quickly for alternatives.

"Hold your fire, wait for my orders," stressed Havelock loudly, hoping his message had reached all of the men.

Gary was nervous but felt every part an equal member of this elite squad. Holding his Tipman98 in an upright position, he aimed it directly at the hovering alien craft.

"You okay Woods?" he attempted to reassure the dead calm van driver. Unfortunately, due to his shaking the words came out as a nervous cackle.

Woods had applied new camouflage paint to his face, and together with a new bandana tight around his cranium, looked terrifying. Poised, leaning over the wall, his body bent to accommodate his position, expressly that of holding a paintball gun in one hand, the nine millimetre pistol in the other, and the Kukri, now safely positioned in the waistband of his trousers ready for immediate use. "Yeth thir I'm okay, juth wanna get at the bathtardth again," he rasped through gritted teeth.

Those disturbed by the light had barely settled in their new found hiding places when just as suddenly as it had come on, it went out. No one moved. All stood or lay as before, ready for immediate action.

Again the light burst into life, illuminating the road and vehicles before going out again.

Peter had managed to find his way into the porch harbouring Lieutenant Havelock and company. He was trying to convince the officer that the best course of action would surely be to try to talk with them.

"Hornby," said Havelock turning to the Sergeant. "How the hell did we end up bringing these Pricks with us, what bloody use are they anyway?"

"Err direct order from Colonel Watkin on General Fartlington's staff sir," replied Hornby sympathetically.

"Yes I know that, I was speaking rhetorically," said the

exasperated officer.

Peter began to walk quite brazenly away from the porch but was hastily pulled back by Hornby. "I think we are going to stay here where we are told don't you sir?"

Peter stared at the tough looking Marine with the same look as a scientist would a blob of mould festering on a Petri dish.

The crafts light came on for a third time, stayed on for thirty seconds before once again going out. With this third extinguishing, the humming vibration changed pitch, sounding more like an old record player turntable when the drive belt begins to slip. On the flanks, large jets of vapour spewed in great puffs, much larger than before.

The marines, fearing the craft was coming in for a landing prepared themselves for an engagement, most anxiety and fear now gone, replaced by an eagerness to get stuck in.

Descending to twenty feet it hovered rather shakily, the bright light underneath illuminating once again. This time the glare reflected from the windows of houses and road vehicles allowing the men to gain their first glimpse of the craft in its entirety.

Roughly the length of a railway carriage, its fore end was shaped with a beak or lip, tapering to form a rounded bulbous section. This then curved gently away towards the rear to reveal a flatter shape, before spreading outwards on either side of the main body to form what appeared to be a pair of delta wings. Various apertures and objects were positioned over the ship at infrequent intervals, some emitting jets. At the front a transparency was visible, whereby, thanks to the interior illumination a remarkable sight revealed itself.

Fleeting glimpses of the crafts occupants could be seen, engaged in what appeared to be melee. The light went out once again plunging all into darkness before bursting into brilliant candescence for the umpteenth time. This time more or less every single light aboard illuminated, giving the whole village a luminescence only experienced on a long summers day and causing the night vision of those watching from the ground to vanish.

More jets exhausted, much louder and more urgent, before without warning, the craft simply dropped out of the air.

With a large crunch it caught the side of the nearest Bedford causing serious damage to the driving cab before slamming heavily into the ground. Large clouds of dust and dirt spewed from beneath as thruster jets powered hopelessly in an attempt to avoid the inevitable. The oddest thing was that when it did make contact, the expected sound of a metallic surface striking the ground failed to materialize. Instead, a not altogether correct sound of impacting plastic colliding with asphalt spoilt the drama of it all.

The humming now reached an ear splitting crescendo. The

marines continued to watch, frozen to the spot, holding their positions and waiting for either an order or the need to defend themselves. Neither came just yet.

All of a sudden all noise ceased. The thruster jets cut out while the lights which had illuminated everything so brilliantly, died plunging the village into complete darkness as before. Apart from the sound of small pieces of debris falling to earth, complete silence reigned.

Still they watched. Still nothing happened. The view through the windscreen was now quiet; no sign of the brawling occupants, all was silent and dark. Some ten minutes passed when unexpectedly the overweight Jack Russell returned, appearing nonchalantly behind Gary. Noticing the dog from the corner of his eye he bent towards it rubbing his fingers together in the hope of attracting its attention. The dog stopped to contemplate the person before it. Having made its conclusion it growled, showing Gary a fine set of teeth before turning back and heading straight for the silent, alien craft, curiosity and the prospect of more food its only avenue of interest.

"This may be a blessing Sergeant," said Havelock, noticing the return of the rotund canine. "Watch the beastie, see if anything happens to it."

The dog cautiously approached the silent craft, slowing as it neared. Head down it sniffed the ground in front before finally braving up and giving the craft a damn good snort.

"We can't stay here all night," remarked Havelock, deep in thought, his hand massaging his chin, "Take three men and approach cautiously, and for Christ sake get some men on those GPMGs."

"Sir," replied Hornby, already on his way, this time without the acrobatics of before. Quickly he stood facing the alien craft; looking to both flanks he made hand gestures to the Landrover's mounting the machine guns to ensure they were in position and ready. Signals from the gunners indicated they were.

Turning once again to the still silent craft, he briefly studied the Jack Russell, which was still enjoying a good sniff. "Okay lads follow me and spread out," he ordered, hoping his taught nerves were not obvious.

The dog's nose seemed to be rooted to the craft, the unfamiliar alien smells sending its nasal senses into overdrive. Slowly the four men advanced, spreading out to cover it from all angles. Every other weapon was trained ahead including the three paintballing guns, Woods primary weapon now being his pistol.

Gary watched mesmerised, sweat running down his face despite the chilly clear evening. His hands stung painfully from the nettle stings as did both his bottom cheeks, the right slightly more so. Now was the time for his mind to catch up and adjust to all that was happening and if he was honest with himself he was feeling afraid. He looked at Woods hoping a friendly face would reassure him a bit. Woods wore the same maniacal look he had when he was on his killing spree back in Delamere forest. It didn't really help, if anything it made him feel worse. Looking about he couldn't see anyone else he recognised, only the Sergeant and the three marines approaching the craft and the Landrover's with their crews covering their approach.

The dog, its investigation concluded, was on the verge of abandoning the search for food when its bloated face took on a confused look. Cocking its head to one side it looked as if it was deep in thought, it returned to the craft again. Once there it casually squatted in order to relieve itself against the outer hull.

A dull yellow glow gently fizzed into view directly above where the dog nonchalantly continued its toiletries. The shape of a doorway clearly visible, intensified until a loud hiss caused the dog to jump and make a bolt still in mid flow. The door shape, now very defined, detached from the craft and lowered, quickly but smoothly in a drawbridge fashion. This alas was the downfall of the dog. Due to its size and encumbered position, namely that of still peeing, it wasn't quick enough to escape the unannounced opening of the aperture. Connecting with its head, the poor canine was laid out flat with one back leg momentarily twitching before becoming still.

Hornby and his accompanying men, realising the need for urgency, broke into a sprint, running at full speed to cover the short distance between them and the craft. Slamming onto the surface they simultaneously straddled the open doorway. Marines Rainsborough, Starley and Corporal Clarkson stared at the opening, Hornby stared at the dog.

"Poor little bugger," he remarked genuinely, his low, deep voice just about reaching the Marines.

"I think it's still alive Sarge," replied Rainsborough. "It's still breathing."

Indeed the dog was still breathing and enjoying a good doggy dream.

The sound of movement from within the craft wrenched their attention back to the job in hand. Each man, rifle held chest height and ready. Drawing a deep breath, Hornby plucked up the courage. Edging slowly, inch by inch towards the entrance he ever so cautiously took a peek inside. *Jesus,* he thought, his heart beating triple time, a sheen of sweat covering his face.

All he saw was a wall, approximately five feet away reflecting a dull blue light. A quick glance at the others revealed their eyes keenly trained upon him. Silently and with bated breath they averted them to concentrate on the entrance. Each of them expected a slobbering, squidging monster of varying descriptions to burst forth at any moment and do what monsters do best.

Hornby edged closer still. On the verge of lifting a foot onto the open doorway, his tension reached new limits, the men with him following suit. Then, out it came. A yellow skinned being clad in a loose fitting red, track suit garment. Upright on two legs, a similar number of long arms each equipped with two elbows, while in one hand a large container resembling a bottle. The bizarre eye arrangement moved quickly from side to side in a wide membrane as if searching, each eye operating independently like a Chameleon. No nose was visible on the gently sloping head, the lipless mouth opening and closing, emitting short croaks.

It became aware of the four soldiers at more or less the same instant that they clapped eyes on it.

"Naaargghh," came the cry from the Marines.

"Eeeaaarrrkk," replied the alien.

Mutual, cautionary backward steps were taken until with enormous self control the soldiers held the alien at gun point.

Havelock decided as senior combat officer that he would take charge of the situation. Standing fully erect he felt his collar and patted himself. Taking a deep breath he purposefully strode over towards the standoff.

The alien stood still, looking scared. Recognising the rifles held against it for what they were, it held its arms out wide. The container in its grasp tipped slightly so that a small amount of liquid leaked on to the road.

"Hands where I can see em you bastard," ordered Hornby raising his gun higher.

The alien eyed Hornby. The sergeant returned its gaze feeling slightly repulsed but resisted the urge to look away.

"Hands in the air and drop that," he repeated, this time with more authority.

The Desirion slowly began to move its arms up towards its face, the container falling to the ground as it released its grip.

"That's good, there's a nice little Martian."

"Okay sergeant, well done, I'll take it from here," said Havelock, arriving on the scene. Surprisingly he felt no fear, just a wild tingling sensation running down his spine.

"Sergeant, did you notice that creature did as it was told," Havelock enquired.

"Err yes sir," replied Hornby obediently.

"That must mean it understands what we are saying."

"Err yes sir, it would appear so sir," said Hornby again. His personal opinion was that if you had several guns trained on

139

you then you would very quickly tend to grasp the meaning of any situation.

"Erkatum trrunnh errekin." Said the Alien tentatively

"There you go Sergeant what did I tell you," said Havelock, clearly hearing something other than the incoherent gobbledygook that the alien had just uttered.

Maybe it was a form of Scottish or Gaelic, thought Hornby.

It was at this point that three things happened at once. The first was the dog woke up. Slowly, its head moved, almost shaking as if trying to clear a fog. It was however, unable to rouse its overweight bloated body, largely due to a heavy door of extra terrestrial origin resting upon it, which in turn had a confused and disorientated alien standing upon it.

The next thing was for a second alien to emerge behind the first. This one similar in appearance but empty handed, stopped dead as it took in the scene. Witnessing its colleague stood with arms out wide, it deemed it wise follow suit.

The third and by far momentous thing to happen was when Woods appeared from nowhere, rushing towards the alien and roaring a kind of Banshee's scream with a lisp. Leaping a full ten feet into the air, the wicked looking Kukri loomed in both hands above his head. Woods action seemed to be the catalyst for all kinds of mayhem to break loose. The Desirion, fully realising the look of the rapidly approaching lunatic was by far more menacing than the other armed Humans, wisely made a dive for safety. This in turn meant that as the door was freed of the aliens weight, the dog was at last able to free itself, successfully accomplishing as such with a couple of twists and turns of its large body.

The tensions of those soldiers closest to the goings on reached crisis point finally bubbling into overload. Before anyone knew what was happening, the air was full of rifle shots. This in turn caused those not involved in following leaping aliens, escaping dogs and soldiers opening fire, to dive for cover, not knowing from where the shooting was coming from. All the noise and chaos upset the already confused dog which promptly ran round in circles, chasing its tail before making itself sick with dizziness. The feeling of nausea angered it further, causing it to run in a corkscrew motion desperate to escape the madness. Making its way through the crowd it saw Gary; a sight which for reasons unexplained brought on a rabid rage and when close enough it deftly jumped at him.

Watching the approach of the dog, Gary turned in an attempt to find an escape route. Not quick enough, the dog managed to snap its front teeth together piercing the flesh on Gary's left bottom cheek.

"Yeeeooowww," he screamed, landing spread eagle and face down on the road side.

The dog, regretting everything since it blundered onto the scene seemed a lot calmer now and slowly staggered back into the darkness. Woods spectacular leap had brought about mixed results. Completely missing the nearest alien, it was alerted to the approaching Human and had dived for safety. His arc through the air lasted for a few more feet before landing awkwardly. With acrobatic precision he almost managed to right himself but caught the very tip of his foot underneath the open door panel and in an uncontrolled dive, flew through the doorway of the craft, cannoning into the second alien and taking it down like a skittle struck by a bowling ball. Both landed in a tangled heap against the inner wall with a thud followed by groans, both human and Desirion.

The gunfire had now ceased and men were quickly peeling themselves from the floor. The corner of the tarpaulin from the undamaged Bedford truck peeled back to reveal a red face with a peaked cap above it.

"My god chaps what was that all about, Lieutenant?" A shaken Captain Stanton called from the safety of the vehicle.

"It's okay sir, everything is under control, just a little excitement, it's being dealt with I can assure you," said Havelock dusting himself down, his face red with fury and anger. "Sergeant Hornby, get those bloody creatures under some sort of control," he barked in a parade ground voice to match that of his sergeant.

"You mean the dog sir?" Hornby asked.

"No, I don't mean the bloody dog man, those, those err things," he raged, pointing toward the two aliens.

"Yes sir, right away," replied the Sergeant.

The first alien still lay on the ground not daring to move, unsure if the mad human or the vicious quadruped were still on the loose. Hornby instructed a guard to stand over it while he detailed others to search the craft. Woods and the other alien had managed to disentangle themselves. Two marines stood between them, preventing the psychotic van driver from attacking the terrified extra terrestrial even further, Woods mood however had subsided and he gave them no resistance.

Havelock marched over to the alien on the ground and deliberately placed a boot a couple of inches from its head. "Okay you, how many are there on your craft?" he asked slowly as if explaining to a foreign tourist the way to the beach. The Desirion scrabbled on the ground emitting nothing but a grunt.

Havelock was not a happy bunny; this whole venture was rapidly becoming a farce. Turning to the ship he looked through the open door. "Sergeant get a squad together, we are going to check that out,"

"Sir," replied the Sergeant, as obedient as ever.

Once again Hornby gathered half a dozen men together to form a squad, one by one with the utmost caution they disappeared into the craft.

Feeling satisfied that the two aliens were securely guarded in the Bedford and the dog now gone; Havelock strode over to Woods who sat on the ground quietly humming to himself. "Mister Woods," he said, controlling his voice and temper somewhat. "Exactly what the bloody hell was that all about?"

"I'm thorry thir I jutht thaw red. Having flathbackth about Delamere and thtuff, I hate the bathtardth," replied Woods sounding and looking genuinely apologetic.

"Well I'm afraid if you're going to act like that I will have to take your firearm from you. Civilian you may be but I assure you, you will take orders from me." Havelock held out his hand beckoning Woods to give him the pistol.

The two men spent the next five minutes in debate, with Havelock listening to Woods objections at having to relinquish his weapon. Wanting to press on with other things the officer relented and allowed Woods to keep it providing there were no repeats of unauthorised activity.

Sergeant Hornby and his squad emerged from the Craft some minutes later. "Sir there is another one in there but it looks dead or unconscious, it's lying on the floor." He paused, "There's also a large amount of containers with a weird liquid in, similar to what that thing had." Hornby indicated where the prone figure of the alien had lain.

The situation gradually returned to normality. Although it was difficult to determine just what normality was in a situation such as this. The third alien was slung over the shoulder of the huge six foot, seven Langhorne and deposited to the Bedford to join its comrades prior to a spot of interrogation.

The logistics team entered the alien craft with Woods, largely to keep him out of the way while the aliens were questioned. Gary followed his colleague, quietly slipping into line behind. His right bottom cheek ached severely, his left screamed with pain; an involuntary hand regularly crept to the regions of soreness to check that the flow of blood had finally ceased. *Bloody dog,* he thought as he entered the ship.

Once inside, the first thing that struck them was the calm relaxed atmosphere, a soft blue light illuminating the interior. Turning the corner the passageway opened up into a circular shape. Along each curved wall were screens with a viewing window at the front. Centrally located was what must be considered a long control panel with two seats which simply oozed comfort. The panels hummed gently as did the screens.

Gary stepped up onto a raised area in front of the viewing window, looked out and waved but no-one took any notice. Jumping down he strolled over to the control panels and gingerly sat down. Immediately the seat began to move. It's very form changing to accommodate the posture of the individual using it. "Oh wow! Check this out, it's brilliant," said Gary, his face a picture of wonderment.

The others hadn't noticed as they too were discovering the unknown wonders of exploring a craft of completely different technology. Gary sat, in awe of the comfort of the chair. Every now and then he prodded the soft fabric smiling like an idiot as he did so. Taking notice of the operations panel before him, he was intrigued by the unexplainable and unpronounceable symbols and markings which gently glowed. Despite knowing there wasn't the slightest chance of understanding, he wasn't deterred from attempting to decipher them. "Now let me see," he said, perusing over some symbols at random. Immersing himself in the crafts surroundings, his mind drifted away to the bridge of the USS Awesome, Star fleets finest and most powerful vessel, where he, Gary Spam, proudly sat in the Captains chair while his unswervingly loyal and efficient crew manned their stations with ruthless dedication.

Without realising, his finger inadvertently traced the alien symbols as he daydreamed.

"Mister Sulu, I need warp speed, now," He ordered, still far, far away from reality. "Mister Scott, full power, on my mark if you please," he continued, a ridiculous grin across his face with just the tip of his tongue poking through closed teeth.

The finger tapped the same symbol it had traced. Without warning it changed from a deep blue to a bright red and began to flash. Even more concerning was the change of overall lighting, flooding the entire ship with a deeply worrying orange.

Captain Stanton ceased his investigations and looked about in alarm. Rising, he attempted to locate the assumed problem. Sensing danger, the other three soldiers hastily exited the craft. Woods noticed first the gormless look upon Gary's face and then the flashing panel reflecting a similar orange with Gary's finger still resting upon it.

"Thir, thir," he said shaking Gary by the shoulder. "I think we thould leave. Thir can you hear me?"

"Yes Mister Spock, I suppose I am rather brilliant aren't I? Eh what, err Woods," Gary, spluttered, abruptly wrenched from his fantasy.

"Mister Spam, didn't I say touch nothing? I expressly said touch nothing, did I not Mister Woods?" Captain Stanton shouted while hastily making for the exit.

At that very moment it began to close. Regardless the three men still inside gathered pace and made for the rapidly closing gap. With a soft hiss and a click it closed, followed by a sucking noise and an organic splat as Woods launched himself at it, his failure apparent as he sickeningly slammed into its inner side.

"I say Mister Woods are you okay?" Captain Stanton asked as he bent over his twisted form upon the floor.

"Yeth thir I'm fine," Woods croaked, untangling himself, this time from his own body while nursing a painful shoulder.

Satisfied that Woods wasn't dead or seriously injured, Gary returned to the control room and the panel. "It's okay, don't panic, I'm sure I can work this out," he said as he returned to the scene of his crime. The symbol which he had caressed was still flashing in unison while orange light bathed the ships interior.

"Now let me see, if I press the same symbol," Gary mouthed to himself.

"Mister Spam, I suggest you don't press anything," urged Captain Stanton, helping the recovering Woods to his feet.

"It's okay Captain, I think I understand how this works," said Gary and tapped the symbol again.

Stanton and Woods, who were already recovering from one shock, were not ready for the next. Instinctively, both flung themselves to the floor before placing their hands over their heads. Even Gary, who was sure of his abilities, braced himself. The three remained poised in a state of self protected bracedness until precisely nothing happened. Two minutes later, nothing was still happening.

Woods was the first person to compose himself. Standing upright, Gary and Stanton soon realised that nothing had exploded and both got to their feet.

Nothing wasn't quite what happened as the red flashing light had extinguished, replaced instead by the original light blue. The exit door hadn't reopened, which to the three of them was a bit of a poser, but as problems go when you're stuck inside an alien craft that was about the extent of it.

"How are we going to get out thir?" Asked Woods, analysing the invisible area where the exit had been. "There ithn't even a door frame or anything."

"Don't panic, I'm sure one of these symbols will release it," said Gary scanning the panels once more.

"Mister Spam," shouted Captain Stanton, "I order you to leave that panel alone."

The severity of the officers retort caused Gary to jump back.

"From now on I will make the decisions," said Stanton, less severely but still authoritatively. "May I remind you that this is a military operation and in here I am the only military representative, so you will now take orders from me; is that clear?"

Gary backed away from the panel. Bowing his head he looked sheepish. Thrusting both hands in his pockets, his foot kicked at the floor. "Yes okay," he muttered in a barely audible voice.

"Right, now, let's see how we can get out of here," continued Stanton. "I'll have a look at these consoles and try to get us out of this bloody mess," he said, throwing Gary a stony glance. Gary hadn't noticed as he was still sulking.

"Mister Woods, would you be so good as to go to that window and try to attract somebody's attention?"

"Err yeth thir right away thir," snapped Woods, reverting automatically to his army discipline.

"Mister Spam I suggest you sit down and TOUCH NOTHING,"

Gary turned and trudged sulkily towards the other chair and sat down. The seats make up once again conformed to suit his body shape, partially helping to forget the ticking off he'd just received. Wiggling his still very painful bottom he revelled once more in the astounding comfort of the seat when his eyes fell upon a plastic container on the floor at the foot of the panel. It was similar to the one held by the alien who initially emerged from the craft. Taking hold, he realised it was half full of liquid. Inquisitive, he put it to his nose and took an experimental sniff. It smelt not unlike cider, its colour a deep red. *Maybe it's a kind of wine,* he thought. Taking a deeper sniff, curiosity took hold. Shaking the cup he swirled the liquid and sniffed for a third time, *wouldn't hurt I suppose, just a little taste.*

Putting the container to his lips he quickly removed it, his nerve gone. He carried this out a number of times before finally, enough courage built up, he allowed the tiniest amount of liquid to touch the tip of his tongue and the outside of his lips. Putting the cup down he swallowed and ran his tongue over his lips a number of times mulling over the taste experience.

Captain Stanton was enjoying partial success as he laboured with deciphering the alien symbols on the console, while Woods joy in attracting the sentry, who was in the vicinity of the damaged Bedford, was minimal, minimal in this case meaning nil.

"Right," said Stanton, tapping the relevant symbol a few times. "I think this should do the trick," he looked up to see if anything happened.

Gary's tongue and lips tingled at first. After another thirty seconds the feeling was replaced by a mild burning sensation before moving onto strong then severe. Finally, all sensation disappeared, similar to the effects of a dental aesthetic. Most worrying were the small hairs and couple of day's worth of facial growth vacating his chin, cheeks and eyebrows in an alarming manner. The unfortunate hairs gathered in little piles upon his lap.

"Arrgghh," he screamed, standing up in alarm. Coinciding with his squeal of anguish was the disappearance of the blue lighting again, replaced once more by orange.

Captain Stanton stood up, anxious that he'd made matters worse. Removing his cap, a feeling of dread slowly flushed through him. A hiss from the area of the exit only just preceded the outline of the doorway illuminating. With a pop, a panel detached itself from the surface and lowered like a drawbridge, culminating in a final hiss. Relief spread throughout him.

"Well done thir, well done," expressed Woods, who was only too happy to see their escape route beckoning.

Making his way from the alien craft, Stanton turned to inform Gary to follow them. "Mister Spam we should lea... My God are you okay?" He asked, noticing Gary with one hand up to his mouth and another on his chin, his eyes a look of pure terror. Slowly, alarm evident in his features, and hands still covering the lower half of his face, he followed Woods and Stanton from the craft.

The Captain was waiting outside for Gary. "Mister Spam, are you alright?" He asked again.

"Thhhrrgghh," blurted Gary, eyes wide.

"I can't hear what you're saying, damn it man, take your hand away from your face."

"Mmmmnnngghh," was the best Gary could muster.

"Thir what's happened tho your eyebrowths?" asked Woods, his face etched with concern as he too attempted to coax Gary into lowering his hands.

Soon, the burning sensation began to subside and he did indeed lower his hands.

"Oh my god thir, whath happened to your thace?" Woods remarked, seeing the full extent of the liquids effects.

Gary looked meek and simply nodded.

"Good god Mister Spam, what on earth has happened to your face!" the equally astonished Captain Stanton exclaimed.

Just the tiniest amount of the Desirion intoxicating beverage known as Glook had passed Gary's lips. The tipple, renowned back on Shard for removing body hair on consumption, and a sure bet to put the manufacturers of female waxing products rapidly out of business. Gary's face, apart from displaying a post box red colour, was totally devoid of any hair from the nose down. His eyebrows had suffered only mild plumage deficiency while his hair was unaffected. His chin however was as smooth as a baby's bottom; Gary nodded again, his mouth wide open.

While the two escapees were discussing the lack of Gary's facial hair, the rear of the truck where the officers, NCOs and aliens had been having a chat was lifted. Emerging were Lieutenant Havelock and Sergeant Hornby, both with disconcerting looks upon their faces.

"Ah, Captain Stanton," said Havelock. "There you are sir, we were looking for you."

"Yes Lieutenant, we were having, err, a bit of an episode in the craft," replied Stanton, looking once more at Gary.

"I'm afraid we haven't managed to discover any information from our alien friends. We were hoping that you may be able to get through to them." said Havelock. "Would you join us in the truck please sir?" Havelock noticed Gary's face. "Are you okay Mister Spam you look a bit red, are you ill?"

Slowly, sensation began to return to Gary's mouth and face. "Err yeth I'm thine," he replied, sounding more like Woods.

"Our friends," continued Havelock, filling the senior officer in on proceedings. "As far as we can gather, appear to be in a state not unlike being, well, drunk for want of a better description. Or at least close to it. Must be that liquid, the same stuff our alien had in his hand when he first came out."

A knocking on the back of the truck interrupted them followed by, "sir."

Hornby lifted the flap to see Corporal Clarkson standing with Woods and Peter next to him. "Yes Corporal?" Hornby asked.

"Sorry Sarge, it's these guys here, they wish to speak with the Lieutenant. Reckon they have vital information on the enemy.

Hornby eyed Woods and Peter dubiously, the latter, who up until now had been quiet, but still seemed like a bit of a dick.

"What is it Sergeant?" Asked Havelock.

"Thir, if you're having no luck with the bathtardth I'm thure I can prithe thome inthormathion from them," offered Woods, holding up his Kukri.

Havelock didn't need to say anything to Woods, the look said it all. Peter pushed himself forward. "I believe I can shed some light upon our extra terrestrial friends here Lieutenant."

Havelock looked enquiringly at Hornby and Stanton in turn.

"Sir," replied Stanton, "with all due respect of course but what could you possibly have to offer?"

Taking a deep breath, Peter puffed himself up. "They are a race known as the Desirions," he blurted, assuming a face of ultimate smugness. "Originating from a planet known as Shard. They are indeed, as you care to put it, drunk. The beverage you refer to is known as Glandular Lubricant of old Kalafrax or Glook for short. It is prodigiously famous upon Shard for removing body hair..." He paused abruptly.

Everyone stood looking aghast. "How do you know this?" Havelock questioned him suspiciously.

Peter paused and thought for a moment, "I'm afraid I'm not at liberty to divulge that information, I have no recollection of the gathering my information. It simply exists and therefore I offer it," he replied.

Stanton had a thought and put two and two together, coming up with a possible four. His train of thought rested with the alien Glook and the state of Gary just before they had left the craft. A broad smile spread across the Captains face.

"They are a race called the Desi... Desh...Dersh... oh bugger," said Havelock, obviously struggling with names.

"Desirion," interjected Sergeant Hornby.

Havelock administered the thousand yard stare, "Yes thank you Sergeant," he said, his tone thick with scorn. "The err, what he said."

"Lieutenant, some of what the gentleman here says actually matches up, believe it or not?" said Stanton, eyeing Peter.

Havelock and Hornby stared at the senior officer.

"Sir, surely you're not actually suggesting....."

Stanton interrupted. "Lieutenant, I agree it sounds rather fantastic, but let's face it, three weeks ago if I'd mentioned any of the events of the previous few days you would have thought me mad, but here we are."

Havelock paused to think things over.

"Can we afford to ignore it? We have no way of knowing if it's true. We have nothing to lose. Besides I really don't think we have any choice." Stanton continued.

"Mister err?" asked Havelock.

"Peter," replied Peter.

"Mister Peter, assum...."

"Simply, Peter," corrected Peter.

Havelock started again. "Assuming, Peter, what you say is correct," he paused. "If we took you into that craft," he pointed. "Would you be able to maybe identify anything?" Havelock offered, an idea forming in his mind.

Peter shrugged, "I cannot give a definitive, however I am by a long margin the most qualified among us to make those deductions."

"Lieutenant," offered Stanton, suggesting Havelock explain what he had in mind.

The two stepped from the truck to allow Havelock to inform his superior that he was willing to go along with his theory.

"If this is so, then maybe he would be able to identify some equipment within the craft, with the possibility of even getting it to operate or," he paused here knowing it was a long shot. "Even being able to communicate with our captive friends."

Stanton was obviously in agreement with his subordinate and Peter was immediately escorted inside the silent craft.

"Anything?" Stanton asked as the civilian surveyed the ships interior. Peter shook his head and simply puffed air from his nose.

XXX

The truck containing the aliens was guarded by two Marines, positioned at the vehicles tail gate. Woods had been watching the two soldiers for the last ten minutes. He was waiting for them to leave which he now realised was never going to happen.

"Come on thir," He said, gesturing for Gary to follow.

"Where are we going Woods?" Gary asked. His voice now back to normal but not sure if he should follow. He felt like he needed a rest, but Woods ventured away all the same and Gary soon followed.

"Woods, what are you doing?" he repeated but with no reply.

The pair sidled along the undamaged Bedford until they entered the trees just beyond its cab; crouching down Woods beckoned Gary to do the similar.

"Woods what the hell are you up to? It'll only upset that bloody Havelock, he's not keen on us already," said Gary looking about with concern.

Woods pointed at the truck. "In there," he said. "I want to have a chat with thothe alient."

Gary looked Woods in the eye, "are you serious? What have you got against them?" His words however, were wasted. Woods had already found his feet and was moving towards the lorry.

He took a quick look into the cab, "Good ith empty," he whispered. Moving round he quietly unfastened the straps securing the tarpaulin to the frame of the lorry.

Gary now realised what Woods was planning, horrified at first he slowly calmed to the idea. Another two straps were covertly undone before, with care, he lifted the tarpaulin. Initially he poked his head in. Then with a quick leap, the rest of his body followed. Gary quickly followed in the same vein, first his head then the torso, until with a jump he launched the rest of himself into the interior of the Bedford.

Woods watched from inside as the unguided Gary first collided with a half full teapot, spilling the still warm remnants over his tunic. The teapot clattered noisily to the floor, while his left shoulder thudded against a rucksack full of enamelled metal cups.

"I've told you already, shut your bloody noise," the shout came from the tailgate.

"They can't bloody understand, you twat," his colleague replied.

"It bloody well will when I stick a bayonet up its arse." A quick

149

chuckle followed and all was quiet again.

Gary looked up trying not to disturb anything else. The first thing he saw was Woods, his mouth silently moving up and down while extending an arm either side of him. Upon the benches were the aliens, all three of them. Two sat with their arms and legs tied with heavy nylon rope, both looked awkward but not uncomfortable. It was their facial expressions which said the most. While Woods looked sympathetic with maybe a hint of pity; the two extra terrestrials stared at Gary, sending him the subconscious message that they thought he was a total and utter gimp. The third offered no opinion whatsoever as it was still as it had been when carried from the craft, unconscious.

Assured that the guards outside were not going to come into the truck, Woods turned upon the alien nearest to him. "Right you bathtard thon of a bitch, I want thome anthwerth out of you," he said, all traces of sympathy ejected.

Gary was nervous of being interrupted from outside, his mind still not convinced that Woods was doing the right thing. The alien looked at Woods much the same as a teenager looks at a nice healthy salad when put in front of it as a pleasant change from all those horrid burgers and chips. Gary wondered whether he should have a go, maybe the alien couldn't understand Woods due to his speech impediment?

"Where are you from?" Woods asked quietly for the fifth time.

XXXI

"I say Captain take a look at this," said Peter looking at a particular screen.

The officers joined Peter. In front of them was a panel displaying a three dimensional map. Peter pressed his thumb upon a symbol and the map expanded to show the whole area between Beeston castle and Chester.

"Oh my," uttered Peter, his face showing concern.

"Yes, yes what is it?" Stanton said impatiently.

"I'm not sure, I err," Peter stammered.

"Can you read what it says? Do you understand it," asked Havelock.

"Certain parts pertain to a level of understanding, yes, but as such I am unable to be proficient to read or understand what it says, I simply know what some of the words mean." Peter replied. He reached out and tapped a different symbol. The map dimmed before red marks appeared upon it showing a route from the alien camp at Beeston Castle. This red mark or line extended out as the crow flies towards Chester where it broke into several different routes ending with a large circle at various equi-distant points over Cheshire's principal city. Underneath the points were alien symbols. Adjusting the control further, the screen expanded again, this time to show a map of England and Wales

"What does it say Peter?" asked Stanton.

The colour quickly drained from Peter's face, "We must stop them Captain," he said.

"Stop them, stop them, from what?" Havelock questioned, taking over the questioning.

"Please desist from asking me how I conclude my results, when I view this screen I assure you it makes no more sense to me than it does to you. Please just accept I just know what some of these markings depict." Peter explained, his attitude less condescending now the seriousness of the situation had ramped up a couple of notches

Havelock was becoming irritated with the intellectual. "Just tell us what they bloody well mean will you?" He screeched.

Peter sighed. "If you insist. From what I can gather they intend to send ships to attack Chester in retaliation for what happened upon Rowton Moor. These red lines indicate the ships route." He adjusted the panel display again. "These red circles over Chester, I suspect are targets," he stopped and sat in the chair, its contours immediately stretching to his body shape. Adjusting the display further until it displayed a map of England and Wales again but with red blobs at various points across the country. "This shows that after Chester their targets are the areas principal cities," He paused. Liverpool, Manchester...." Looking at the officers, his face regained just a little composure.

"When are these supposed attacks going to happen?" Asked Stanton.

"I cannot say, what I have divulged is the extent of my knowledge," said Peter, indicating an unpronounceable squiggle with his finger. "Except this, it just says pending."

"Sir?" Interjected Sergeant Hornby. "Are you sure we can take what he says as gospel? I mean, look at him he's a total idiot."

Havelock seemed to consider Hornby's opinion before speaking. "Under normal circumstances I would sympathise with you Sergeant, but these are not normal circumstances," he paused. "As the Captain pointed out, I don't believe we have much of a choice, we have to believe him."

XXXII

"Thith will get you talking," said Woods.

The alien hadn't moved in the five minutes Woods had been interrogating it. Gary was on the verge of taking a more subtle approach with the other conscious being when he saw Woods pull out the curved bladed Kukri.

"Woods stop, no! You can't," Gary mouthed anxiously. Woods ignored him and thrust the Gurkha weapon in front of the alien's squelchy eyes, causing an instant reaction.

"Yeh you bathtard, not tho quiet now are you?"

The Desirion looked worried, more so the nearer Woods put the knife to its face.

"Woods," Gary tried to put force and sternness into his voice. Rather difficult when whispering.

Woods turned. "Ith okay thir I'm not going to hurt it."

"What are your planth? Where are you from?" he hissed running the flat of the blade down the aliens face and making a shallow dent in its yellow skin, while drawing his own up close. "What are your planth?" He repeated, a maniacal smile on his face.

The alien looked very scared. Its skin had paled considerably and droplets of liquid were excreting from the holes on top of its skull and running down its head. Despite this it still made no noise.

Movement from outside suddenly forced Gary and Woods to look towards the rear of the truck.

"We'd better go Woods," said Gary, already heading towards the opening in the tarpaulin.

Woods had other ideas. "I'm going to dithect you, you horrible ugly little thon of a bitch." he said and tapped the flat of the blade upon its face.

Without warning, the other conscious alien shouted at the top of its voice in the unintelligible dialect of its own race over and over again. The last two words however, sounded for all the world to be in English, a very broken form but almost certainly English.

"Cheesdar, Leepal diiisstroy," it screeched.

At that very moment the tarpaulin was lifted, revealing the grim faces of Lieutenant Havelock, Captain Stanton and Sergeant Hornby. Gary was already half way out of the truck, his legs waggling like a stranded fish out of water as he tried to wriggle free.

"What the bloody hell, Christ, Mister Woods what the hell are you doing, shit! Who let you in?" Turning, he caught the eye of a red faced guard.

"Chapman, what do you know about this, did you give them permission."

"Err, no sir we had no idea," spluttered the shame faced guard.

Woods spun around, his face beaming with elation, "did you hear it? It thaid Chethter, Liverpool and dethtroy."

The uttering of these two words forced the furious Havelock to pause and reconsider his decision to have the two civilians arrested and hung drawn and quartered before being sent immediately back to Chester.

"That sort of ties in with what we found out in the craft sir," said Hornby.

"Aye Sergeant, I'm well aware of that thank you."

"Mister Woods," said Havelock, steeling himself before taking yet another deep breath. "Put that damn knife away and who is that?" he continued, indicating the pair of legs still in situ emerging from the side of the lorry. Woods grabbed hold of Gary's legs and pulled him back into the Bedford with a tumble.

"I might have known. The other half of Laurel and Hardy," said Havelock.

"Ah Lieutenant," said Gary, desperately improvising. "It's not what it seems."

"Don't even attempt it Mister Spam, just shut up, right now."

Outside, sergeant Hornby could be heard grilling the two guards for their failure to prevent Woods and Gary from gaining entry into the lorry.

"We shall have to contact brigade HQ and inform them immediately, we could have reinforcements here within the hour," said Stanton.

"Sir," Havelock interjected. "Radio's tend not to work around the alien base area and even if they did surely it's not a good idea to transmit, we may give our position away. Remember these guys didn't know we were here, May I suggest we keep it that way. I also believe sir that we must act immediately."

"Lieutenant, we are a reconnaissance squad made up of twenty seven infantrymen, four logistic and four civilians. How are we supposed to take on a highly advanced and well equipped force of invading aliens?"

Havelock looked the Captain once more in the eye and sympathised to a certain extent. "Captain," he paused, giving the situation more thought before continuing. "Sir if you and your men take one of the Landover's back to Chester with the civilians and alien captives and inform headquarters, requesting everything they can spare, I will take my men on towards the alien encampment at Beeston and do as much damage as possible."

Stanton went to open his mouth then closed it again, he knew in his heart of hearts that Havelock was speaking out of a sense of duty and realism. He also knew that his plan made military sense and was really the only plausible one.

"Sir I will hold out for as long as possible, you must reach brigade and send reinforcements."

The whole episode was beginning to take on the air of a classic World War two movie. Impossible long goodbyes would surely follow, as the fearless patrol bade their last farewells before embarking on a mission of certain death. Those present may have found some amusement from all of this had that not been just the case. This reality was very much upper most in the thoughts of the two officers as they exchanged relevant information, of which Captain Stanton would take to headquarters back in Chester.

My god, thought Stanton, *there are no guarantees that even I am going to be believed when I relay all this, but as Havelock said there didn't really seem to be any other alternative, this information had to be acted upon.*

The task to load as much supplies as possible onto the one remaining, drivable truck and Land Rover began, making sure that there was enough room for the twenty seven marines as well as all their equipment. Lieutenant Havelock delighted in the duty of informing Gary, Woods, Peter and Leyton that they would be going back to Chester on the Land Rover with the captain and his men. The latter pair looked rather pleased with the announcement, but Woods and Gary were far from happy.

"Thir I mutht come with you, thurly you need ath many men ath you can get," complained Woods.

"Mister Woods I'm sor..."

"Thir," interrupted Woods, snapping to attention and pulling off just about the most perfect salute ever given. "You know my thervice hithtory, I will be uthefull. Thir you need me."

Despite his better judgment, Havelock considered Woods passionate plea. After a moment he spoke again. "Okay Mister Woods, in light of your previous service you will be allowed to accompany the squad, but I must stress this is a very dangerous mission, I don't have to tell..."

"Thir I underthtand, I am prepared, ith what we thigned on for," replied an elated Woods still at attention.

"Okay Mister Woods join the truck," said Havelock before turning to Gary. "Mister Spam you must join the Land Rover and return to Chester."

Gary's gaze flitted between the Bedford and the Land Rover with scorn.

"Thir," he said turning back to the officer, his mouth suddenly experiencing a relapse of Glook induced face droop.

"Lieutenant you need me thoo, you need all the men you can uthe.

"Mister Spam you are a civilian. You are also a massive pain in my arse. You have no military experience, you must return to Chester," ordered Havelock.

The Bedford was now fully loaded and ready to proceed. The longing faces watching from the tailgate, expectant that their officer would be joining them.

"Mister Spam, I don't have time for this, I'm not arguing with you, you will climb aboard the Land Rover with the others and return to Chester and that is the end of it," said Havelock, already backing away towards the idling lorry.

Realising he really had no choice, Gary sulkily slumped towards the Landrover, its occupants watching and waiting for him. Climbing aboard he gave the Bedford a last forlorn look. As he stared, it suddenly hit him that he would never see these men again. Sitting down, the vehicle began to move away. Giving the truck one last glance as it too moved away in the opposite direction, he just caught a glimpse of the grinning face of Woods as it disappeared from view into the darkness.

XXXIII

The gentle resonating, melodious note changed its pitch. As it changed, so did the colour of the lighting, subtly bringing a whole new atmosphere to the room. Soft lime greens slowly transformed to blend into a light orange while tranquil, relaxing sounds conformed to the change in colour giving the impression to the ear of bouncing from each wall only to cascade back to the centre of the room to form a new note.

This was relaxation at its finest, and of course a healthy container of Glook just to top it off. The seat changed its contours along with the changing position of its occupant. The figure stretched out even further in order to make himself as comfortable as possible.

Bex had been longing for this moment for many of these Earth days now. The endless meetings, discussions with Lax, taking the flak for the continuous disasters and setbacks ever since they had touched down on this miserable planet had taken their toll. As one of the senior military commanders he had been in the thick of it from day one, but now the Overseer had ordered the attack to commence the next evening Earth time and he was snatching a rare chance to relax. Forcing all thoughts of responsibility and the job in hand from his tired mind, his thoughts blended with the music and the ever changing colours before inevitably diverting to home, his partner and offspring.

Behind a defocused membrane his mind's eye pictured the five younger versions of himself; this made him feel more cheerful. His arm unfolded and stretched out to take hold of the Glook when his down time was interrupted by a different sound, similar to a lift bell chiming when it reaches the desired floor.

Bex ignored it forcing his happier thoughts to return again, using the soothing notes and colours to aid the recurrence of those memories.

Bing, the sound repeated a moment later, resignedly he refocused his eyes. Desirion eyes don't close when they rest; they simply stop focusing or switch off. Swivelling the left one he concentrated on a small panel positioned upon the small unit next to his drink, the screen snapped into life to reveal the face of Pix, Lax's chief advisor.

"Yes Pix, is it important?" asked Bex Uninterestedly.

"Commander it is imperative that I see you, now and in

private," Pix replied, concern evident in his tone while he could be seen glancing worriedly from side to side as he spoke.

"Can't it wait? Or just tell me now," Bex replied, clinging desperately to the last vestiges of his moment of relaxation.

"I'm afraid not commander, I must see you now, it is of the utmost urgency."

Bex shuddered, "Okay Pix but make it quick." he said, now irritated. Rising from his chair he hoped very much to return to it soon. The screen went blank and Bex stood up. Immediately the music ceased and the lighting returned to that of the more functional light blue. Grabbing an ornately decorated robe he strode to the door way and waved an arm in front, to allow Pix access.

The door outline illuminated from the blank bulkhead, glowing bright white to reveal a large double door silhouette before both sides gently swung open to reveal the Advisor. On seeing the commander Pix gave a superb bow, not as ornate as one he would give to the prime overseer but a very good one none the less.

"Yes Pix what is it? I'm very busy." said Bex, the container of Glook once more filling his left hand.

"Commander, it appears," said Pix, looking behind him while still prostrate to ensure that the door had closed behind him. "That a scout and recon craft has either been destroyed or taken without authorisation."

Bex was still uninterested. "Is that it, is that the important message you had that couldn't wait?"

"Commander, three members of Commander Tax's force are also missing."

Bex's look rapidly changed to one of anger, "Pix, I..."

"Commander," Pix interrupted, running the risk of Bex's wrath. "The three missing are the crafts operator and Cax and Lix."

Bex sighed deeply, still looking deeply unexcited. "And your point, advisor is?"

"The latter two," Pix Continued before the commander could butt in. "Are, or rather were being held on suspicion of being members of the Basingstoke movement."

Bex's expression changed once again, this time to one of confusion. He'd heard rumours of a growing number of discontented Desirion's opposed to the continuing conquest of this planet, due mainly to the huge losses and continuing disasters. There had even been talk of the formation of a breakaway faction called the Basingstoke Movement, so called because the Desirions believed that Earth was originally called Basingstoke after receiving the initial telephone message some forty years ago. Their supposed intention was to oppose the current command structure, however due to a complete lack of any evidence of a concrete nature having come to light it was conjectured that it was simply that, rumour!

Now it was Pix's turn to be irritated, but of course he didn't show it, he daren't. "Commander, it is alleged that the two in question have openly stated that they oppose the retaliation against the Earth cities." Pix paused to allow it to sink in so far. "It is also feared that they are not by any means alone and are in fact part of a growing number of..."

Bex held up a hand to hush the advisor, quickly adding a deep and hearty "Silence." knowing the prostrate Pix wouldn't be able to see him.

"We believe," continued Pix on a different tack, "that they have absconded with the craft and taken the operator against his will."

Now Bex looked worried. "Are you sure? Do you have any proof?

The first few aircraft had only just been passed out on efficiency test flights after their useless showing Thus far. "Something may have gone wrong, there were problems with them coping with this atmosphere, and these two err..." He paused, realisation dawning that, although what Pix was saying was extremely distressing, it was probably just the next event in this total disaster of a campaign. His facial features took on a new slant, one of unwanted rising stress levels finally culminating with a verbal outburst of, "oh bollocks!"

Pix stayed silent.

"Pix why are you telling this to me and not Lax? I mean his exalted majestic sentinel." asked Bex, correcting himself. "And Pix pick yourself up from the floor will you?"

"Thank you Commander," said Pix. With relief he straightened himself to stand vertical once more. "Commander," He continued, once more on the back foot. "I thought it best if you were with me to inform his exalted, majestic, sentinel to, err break the news gently, as it were."

Bex turned his back on the advisor and thought for a moment. "Are you absolutely sure about this?" He asked, administering a sneaky drag of Glook.

"No, but it seems to be the only logical course," answered Pix, more at ease.

Logic, thought Bex, *when did that ever play a part in all this?* He turned back to the advisor, his face showing yet another different expression. Pix couldn't help but be impressed with the range of different facial expressions the Commander was capable of displaying in such a short time.

"Where is the craft now?" asked Bex.

"Commander, it was last traced in area V-six, the vicinity of the human dwelling known as Tarporley, not a great distance from here, but its registration pulse hasn't transmitted for some time now, we believe it may be damaged."

"I see." responded Bex, appearing to come to an inner decision. "I will gather some things, you will meet me outside Lax, I mean his exalted majestic sentinels chambers. Oh and summon Commander Pox, I wish him to accompany us."

"As you wish Commander." finished Pix and bowed again, his arm sweeping below him magnificently, the double elbow allowing perfect curvature.

Arriving in the corridor, Pix and Bex Loitered just down from Lax's chambers waiting for Commander Pox. They stood, or rather Pix stood while Bex paced up and down like an expectant father. The next person to appear wasn't the expected Commander but the serious looking figure of Dix, Lax's Physician. Dix eyed the pair suspiciously, not expecting them to be here and judging by their guilty stance, he immediately assumed that there was a problem.

"Ah Dix," Bex gushed, greeting the Medic a little too overenthusiastically before diplomatically prompting Pix to relay his unfortunate allegations. After he had finished, Dix looked grave.

"Are you sure?" He asked.

They both nodded.

"The Overseer will not take kindly to this. His mind at the moment is..." He paused to consider his words. "At best unpredictable and I've already had to up the dose of his calm spreaders three times." He paused. "And he continues to consume alarming levels of Glook... against my wishes."

"Lax is on calm spreaders?" Bex blurted.

Dix stared gravely while an uncomfortable silence descended on the small group, each one knowing that regardless of the Overseers condition or how he was likely to react, Lax had to be told.

The silence didn't last for long as Commander Pox soon arrived adding to the three figures loitering outside the Overseers chambers, he too was told the same news. A short discussion ensued before it was decided that the four of them would face their Overseer together. On entering Lax's chamber the three senior Desirion's deliberately stood back, allowing the unaware and terrified Pix to take the foreground.

"Lax," gestured Dix warmly. "And how are you feeling?"

"I feel considerably better, thank you," replied Lax. Just by looking at him, it was obvious to the eye that he was indeed, in better spirits.

"Our friend Dix here has a wonderful supply of sweets, don't you Dix?" He said cheerfully. "And they work wonders," he continued. "I feel our luck will change now, we need it to, don't we?"

The three commanders exchanged looks of varying degrees of questionability.

"If I can get through just one of these Earth days without any kind of disaster, I will feel much the happier, now my friends what can I do for you?"

Bex, Pox and Dix backed away another step. "I believe Pix has some information you must hear." Pox offered bravely.

Dix glanced at the commander, implying that it may have been better left unsaid after all. Pix spluttered before regaining his composure and slowly explained his news for the fourth time that morning.

Lax, who had been sat on the edge of his most comfortable relaxer, now lay down. He reached out and grasped a huge beaker, presumably containing Glook and took several large gulps. Turning his head, he faced the small group who had unconsciously taken yet more steps back towards the exit leaving the poor Pix to receive anything that should result from the Overseer flying into a rage. Contrary to their expectations he appeared to remain calm. The advisor was almost flat on the floor in the midst of his best bow ever, resembling a reversed limbo dancer. This scene remained for the next five minutes. The three seniors looking sheepish with stupid grins on their faces and Pix sprawled upon the floor, appearing to settle like an ever advancing runny cow turd.

The sudden movement of Lax springing from his relaxer made them jump. Thanks to his position, Pix was only aware of a sudden movement by the noise Lax made. Striding over, he scrutinised each of them with a stony glare. Dix, Pox and Bex gave it everything they had not to return the stare, knowing what the outcome could be with one whose mind was so imbalanced. The overseer circled them twice more, almost trampling Pix on one perambulation before quite unexpectedly bursting into cackled laughter. Dix and his co-confused stole nervous glances at each other, simultaneously deciding it a good idea to share their Overseers joke whatever. So that's what they did. They laughed long and loud, except for Pix who was suffering from the onset of severe aches, not to mention it being rather warm down on the floor. Some moments later the laughter stopped, first Lax then the others.

"You fools, you fools," Lax gasped, sounding and looking quite mental again. "I know all of this. Shall I tell you why? Because I ordered them to do it." He plopped into his relaxer once more looking quite exhausted.

Dix, Pox and Bex were now utterly confused.

"I decided to send out a ruse. A fake, call it what you like." said Lax, his tone sounding more normal now." I took it upon myself along with Commander Pox here, to venture among our numbers and seek out these so called unbelievers, Picking out those known sympathisers and telling them they would be carrying out a mission to infiltrate the humans and plant the idea that we would be changing our plans, thus lulling them into a false sense of security. Then when the Hooomanns." He almost spat the word Humans out. "Move their forces away to defend the other cities and think that everything is nice and easy and peaceful here, we hit them hard and fast. Those against us would be detained, while I sent out two who were true to the cause, to spread the ruse amongst the Hooomanns, which my foolish friend is what I have done."

Lax's grin disappeared, his eyes rotating independently, practically protruding on the end of their short stalks.

Bex wasn't the first to feel that, far from being a good plan, it could just be one of the worst pieces of news that they could have heard. He was first alerted to this fact by the sharp intake of breath as Pox's face showed a pale orange and his hands slowly went up to his face."

"Lax, you bloody idiot, what have you done?" Pox spluttered, all respect of rank and protocol dissolving quicker than the plan in question. "The two so called loyalists you set free to spread the plan were real sympathisers of The Basingstoke Movement, known to have anti occupation tendencies. They were not in agreement with you or your plans. All you have done is given a couple of traitors a craft to get away and possibly warn the humans of our real plans, you have set the wrong ones free."

Bex face was aghast. "Are you sure?" he said to a slowly recomposing Pox.

Pox said nothing but walked over to a communication screen set on a unit; its screen flickered into life at his approach. "Secure holding area, Commander Pox." he said to the face appearing. The screen changed to that of a different face. "Controller Fix," said Pox to the face on the screen. "Can you confirm the whereabouts of detainees four, zero, two and four, zero, three, the two who were to undertake the operation decoy."

Controller fix momentarily turned away to operate another piece of apparatus.

"Yes Commander they are taking refreshment as we speak, in the social area."

"Thank you and can you give me a full inventory of detainees please?"

Controllers Fix's face looked down. A minute passed when he faced the commander once more, this time with a puzzled look. "Commander, Detainees one, seven, six and two, three were released this very morning on the expressed orders of his exulted majestic sentinel to undertake a classified mission..." He stopped realising the error.

"Thank you Fix, that will be all," said Pox calmly, the screen blanked out.

Dix strode over to a large storage unit, opened it and took out a very large dosage of maintaining calm spreader drug in anticipation of using it. Commander Bex had his hands on top of his head, his mouth wide open.

A low, barely audible, "oh dear," came from a seriously cramp afflicted Pix which just left Lax himself.

His Exulted Majestic Sentinels smile, which had been so confidently planted upon his face crumbled muscle by muscle, fading to eventually form a flat line for a mouth. It peaked again as he enquired with a squeak, "Are you sure?"

Pox nodded.

The smile dissolved once more to be replaced by a bizarre ripple effect, moving along the length of his mouth. His eyes had ceased their almost uncontrolled wanderings, replaced instead by large black orbs staring into empty space. He didn't even notice as Dix administered the drug through his robe.

"Exulted Majestic Sentinel, may I be permitted to rise?" Came a desperate muffled plea from the agonised Pix.

"Get up Pix," replied Bex, knowing the Overseer had other things on his mind right now.

Dix looked at the two Commanders questioningly. "What are we to do?" He said, returning his medical instruments back into their unit.

The two commanders were deep in thought for a moment before Pox broke the uneasy silence." I don't really think we have much choice, we must either bring the attack forward or cancel it altogether."

Another silence descended upon the chamber. He turned to Bex in the hope of some sort of acknowledgment, Bex nodded.

"It would appear to be the only course open to us," stated Bex. "If the two escaped detainees have disclosed any information then the Humans, will as we speak be assembling a force to either attack us here or strengthen their defences both here and at the target cities. And as has been seen we are not impervious to their weapons. We must bring the fight to them."

"Might I just add a little something?" Asked Dix.

No reply was forthcoming, so he said it anyway. "Has it occurred to anyone that the two in question are highly unlikely to be able to speak human."

This was in fact a true statement. The Desirion's top language experts had managed to decipher English, French, Chinese and oddly Welsh, but had by no means managed to teach these to many, not even Lax. What was even more ironic was the two detainees who had been set free and given the use of the flying craft, had about as much sympathy with a rebellious movement as your average Ant has with the maintenance and well being of your best patio paving. The facts were simple, Cax and Lix were merely what you would term as a couple of jokers, not really interested in anything but because of their disruptive influence, had automatically been banded with the fifth column tag and detained.

Their sudden freedom coupled with the added bonus of being given their own personal runabout was too good an opportunity to refuse, and so as with all good hell raisers, they took their opportunity, got pissed and went on a joyride. The fact that they managed to pass on the Desirion plan to attack to Lieutenant Havelock, was the simple act of operating the crafts data system, which was linked up to the fleets mainframe. Wood's Kukri had simply prised what information they possessed. These facts were understandably lost on Lax and the Commanders.

"Okay, I want all commanders ready for orders by mid earth day," said Pox turning to Pix, who was still attempting to bend his almost fused frame back to normal. "And the attacks to commence as soon as the ships are ready and prepared. I want them moving by star down, this Earth evening." Pox then approached his Overseer and repeated his plan. "Do I have your authority to carry out this attack Lax?" He said finally.

Lax lay sprawled on his recliner, once more oblivious. Gently, he hummed to himself interrupted only by the occasional whimper. The room took on a light blue hue as Dix adjusted the comfort controls. As the gentle musical notes softly echoed about the chamber, Lax's eyes continued to stare at nothing as a small line of dribble escaped from his mouth and slowly made its way down his chin.

"Pix, continue." Ordered Pox.

"At once commander," replied Pix and waddled from Lax's chamber like an invalid crab while the three remaining Commanders stayed with their overseer in an attempt to obtain his seal of approval.

XXXIV

"Given the exceptional circumstances, I can assure you this is the most appropriate course of action." Peter stated to no one in particular. His darkened silhouetted frame bounced around, jostled from side to side as the Landrover's not so comfortable suspension made steady progress over the debris strewn tarmac as they sought the main A51 road. Taking the corner outward bound from Tarporley the occupants took a last glimpse of the Bedford truck they had left behind. Most of those on board were relieved to be leaving a very dangerous area. Leyton for one was glad to get away from the Marines. The constant comparisons to Ian Wright were really starting to grate on his nerves. Captain Stanton was eager to report his findings and to deliver the three alien captives unceremoniously bundled onto the floor.

Gary however, was not happy. He was convinced he had something to contribute to the team left behind. An agitated hand reached up and twiddled with the thick cloth of his battledress collar, bending it between thumb and forefinger he was suddenly conscious of the change of material. A quick glance revealed he had grasped the soft flexible feel of the synthetic fabric of his Starfleet uniform. A sudden pride burst into his chest, quickly rising to his head and filling it with a feeling of invulnerability and superiority, only equalled after six pints of premium strength ye olde country ale.

This, coupled with the image of the Bedford receding from view was all that was needed to inspire him to undertake the bravest and most reckless thing he had ever done in his life.

"Leyton can you grab hold of this for me for a moment please?" Gary asked, offering the heavy camouflaged backpack to the Arsenal and England star look alike. With a heavy sigh he relented and held out his arms. The moment he took hold, quick as a flash, Gary raised himself to a standing position, luckily missing his head upon one of the rigid stanchions. He then vaulted over a stunned Leyton and Captain Stanton with all the grace of a concrete girder and out the back of the Land Rover.

Whether it was luck or judgment was irrelevant as Gary landed on the roadway with both feet before falling to the ground with a roll any parachutist would be proud of. Another three more of these and his momentum came to a halt, with no more injury than a few sharp stone cuts to his legs and a tear, as a stick pierced his Starfleet tunic ripping a diagonal line at chest height and enhancing the Kirk effect further. What rather ruined the moment, although unbeknownst to Gary was a large brown smear which had appeared upon his backside, the result of a concealed dog turd he had inadvertently rolled over. Had he been paying attention to his surroundings he may just have been able to make out a faint Mutly style snigger from an overweight Jack Russell.

All this however, was irrelevant as Gary returned to stand on two feet, a moment's pause to gather his composure before breaking into a sprint in the direction of Tarporley and the Bedford truck. In the short time it took him to accomplish this unprecedented act of athleticism, the Landrover had come to an abrupt halt. A few hushed calls aimed at the disappearing hero had been offered before Captain Stanton gave the order to continue without him.

"He knows what he's doing and we cannot commit anybody else to any more danger just for the sake of one reckless individual," he said to no-one in general.

Turning the corner Gary realised he was in luck, the Bedford hadn't left yet. This was good news indeed, but that was where his fortune abruptly ran out. The insane adrenalin fuelled burst of furious physical exertion suddenly took its toll on his unused to sporting exertion body. His chest began to fill with fire while involuntary gulps racked his body just to make sure there wasn't a loose lung in his throat waiting to be violently coughed up. His legs turned to concrete at the same time as his brain fogged with the fug of someone suffering from a bout of terminal shagged out syndrome.

In the space of just thirteen seconds Gary had transformed from a figure resembling the Bionic Man on chilli steroids to that of a dehydrated sheepdog on its last legs prior to facing the proverbial shotgun. By pure luck the Bedford had not yet left thanks to Lieutenant Havelock insisting upon a last look inside the flying craft in case anything relevant could be found. The Royal Marine officer was in the process of climbing up the tailboard when a smiling Woods tugged at his battledress.

"Thir look, ith mithter Thpam," he said excitedly, rising to his feet. Havelock spun round and peered into the darkness. His focus upon the approaching form of Gary was wrenched away as the unmistakable boom of heavy artillery came from the direction of Chester. A few seconds later the equally unmistakable roar of the shell as it screamed through the air above them towards the alien encampment at Beeston.

Havelock turned to his sergeant, "one, five, fives," they both mouthed in unison, not really paying attention to each other, concentrating more on the sound with an ear cocked to the sky. The booms were soon occurring at regular intervals of roughly ten to fifteen seconds. Sergeant Hornby leant forward over the tailgate of the Bedford and reached down to grab the ancient looking shrivelled up figure that was almost on all fours. Wheezing heavily, he made a sound rather like a novelty party balloon being let off.

"Mister Spam," remarked Havelock, sternly and loud enough to be heard over the shriek of the artillery overhead. "What the bloody hell are you doing? I thought I gave you strict orders to return with Captain Stanton and the others." He left the question open, not really caring for an answer, assuming that the Landrover had gone without him and also partly because the wasted form at his feet would need at least an hour to recover before any speech was capable.

Unceremoniously, Gary was bundled into the truck with at least two heavy boots crashing into his already mortally wounded backside, causing him to croak feebly, his throat unable to carry out any function other than to aid his breathing.

The sound of shells detonating, from a distance of just over a mile away sounded very close, the violent explosions echoing around the deserted village. Gary instinctively covered his head with his hands with the expectation of flying shrapnel to enter the vehicle at any minute.

"Bloody hell that was quick, how the hell did they get to Chester so fast?" Said Chapman, referring to the speed at which Captain Stanton and his men had managed to relay their information to Command headquarters.

"I think Chapman," said Havelock, applying a little logic to the situation. "That they were intending to attack regardless, this would have been planned and ordered some time previous, unless Landover's are suddenly capable of travelling at the speed of sound."

"Sir," asked Corporal Barnet at the wheel. Havelock had to wrench his mind from the bombardment that was continuing over their heads.

"Yes Corporal," he replied in a raised voice, barely audible over the noise.

"Are we to proceed to the drop off point? You know, what with the err." He pointed to the sky as if to indicate the activity overhead.

Havelock paused to think for a moment then turned to his sergeant and quietly consulted with him.

"Dogs, aliens, bombs, Arrgghh, mummy," gibbered Gary, rapidly hushed by a few more kicks.

Woods, feeling sorry for his work colleague, moved to the front of the truck." Ith okay," he offered compassionately. "I'll look after him. Come on thir leth have you thitting comfortably thall we?" Woods continued, putting a friendly arm around his

167

shoulder.

Havelock, his brief conflab over, returned to the attention of the driver, "Corporal, we shall continue to..." He stopped and in unison with most others, glanced upwards. The air was split apart by the shriek of a shell, moments later the resulting explosion, then silence. Havelock continued his voice perfectly calm and natural as if ordering a burger and fries. "Continue towards our drop off point. We'll make a reccee from there."

The truck eventually moved off one man heavier than expected towards whatever fate awaited them. It hadn't travelled more than twenty yards before the sound of its engine was drowned out by another thunderous roar, this one vastly different. This was the ear splitting sound of a number of aircraft screaming overhead in the general direction of Beeston. The sound hadn't faded when a second wave was heard approaching, the unidentified type and number of planes just a faint flash of a silhouette, punctuated by red hot afterburners.

Gary rose on to all fours, groaned then coughed, managing to keep his internal organs internal, before looking up. The first face he saw was that of Corporal Clarkson who had been one of the main deliverers of boot when he had returned to the truck. Staring at his face Gary attempted to smile. He managed only to grimace, giving an impression of mockery. Fortunately Clarkson was pre-occupied with the arrival of the jets.

The aircraft flying over Tarporley and the Bedford containing Gary, Woods and the marines were Harriers and Tornado's. The Landrover taking Captain Stanton and his men had not even reached the outskirts of Chester. The order for this strike had been taken the night before, having been cleared by the ministry. The only objection came from English Heritage who were keen to stress that the thirteenth century castle was actually a scheduled monument and had protected status, therefore it would be a good idea if one of their field engineers was present to give advice about how not to damage it. The reply came as no surprise. "Due to the fact that your thirteenth century building is currently occupied by an alien force determined to turn us into organic waste, could you politely bugger off," won the day.

The eventual plan of attack was for a brief artillery bombardment to bring about confusion with hopefully a few lucky shots hitting home too, this would be promptly followed up with an air attack. The British Military were only too aware of the defensive capabilities of the aliens with their penetrative shielding device. However, thanks to the Lynx pilot who had witnessed the air strike on the initial break out from Beeston prior to the massacre on Rowton Moor. They saw that as the shield worked like a large umbrella; a ground strike would force the surface under the vehicle upwards, propelling it into the air too and hopefully toward untold damage.

XXXV

The artillery bombardment had not caused considerable damage to the equipment assembled at the Desirion camp, with just one transport disabled and one mobile gun destroyed. Another two suffered slight damage while a total of eight Desirion's had been killed, unluckily blown into the air by an upward blast which flung them against the rocky outcrop of the castle.

Commander Pox stood upon the hub of the fleet command vessel, *Paraxatar.* His long fingered hands clenching and unclenching, his gaze fixed angrily upon the debris and pandemonium on the field below. The longed for spell of peace and relaxation he had craved was now a light year distant. Half a dozen small fires glowed, illuminating running figures and the odd moving vehicle while the upturned transport was attended to.

The sound of a door frame materializing fizzed behind him, he didn't turn.

"Commander Pox?" Lax asked in a clear and booming voice. Pox did turn this time, the unexpected voice jarring him from the view outside while the sight of his overseer forced him to take a deep breath. Lax stood flanked by a concerned looking medic Dix and commander Bex who looked just plain worried.

"Lax," Pox gasped questionably.

The Overseer held up an arm to quell any questions. "I am fine," he answered. "Now, what is happening here?" He continued, leading the other two towards the viewing area. Pox glanced sideways and caught Dix's worried eye. The medic returned the look, accompanying it with a hand gesture indicating that he had no part in these proceedings.

"Pix where is commander Bex, find him immediately," Lax barked, not waiting for an answer.

Pox opened his mouth, but nothing came out, he couldn't even see the advisor and as for Bex...

"Err, he is with you majestic sentinel," came a disjointed reply from the rear of the hub.

"Don't try to make a fool of me Pix," Lax said turning. As he did so he caught a glance of Bex. "Ah Bex there you are," he said, as if the commander had just entered the room. Lax took a few steps forward until he stood with his face almost pressed against the viewing port. Reaching out, he leaned upon the bar beneath the window.

"Excellent," he remarked, his hands coming together in a

maniacal rub gesture. "Things seem to be going according to plan for once. Soon, very soon my friends we shall vanquish these irritating Hooomanns."

Now the three senior staff with Lax looked seriously worried, could he not see for himself what had happened?

"Commander, we have a number of Hooomann aircraft approaching our position." No sooner had the words left the console operator's mouth than the night sky was lit by red glowing pulses as bolts were unleashed to counter the oncoming threat. The alien barrage was intense, and this time deadly.

The first wave of Harriers approached the Desirion camp. Before any of the jets weapons had been deployed an aircraft erupted into flame, caught broadside on. It slew downwards out of formation before exploding into an uncontrollable ball of fire to shower the Desirion's upon the ground with red hot pieces of debris. The other pilots pressed on with their attack, forcing their early loss temporarily from their minds, their targets, the smaller vehicles strewn about the fields below them. At a height of barely a thousand feet and a distance of fifteen hundred yards the targeting computers locked on and the pilots made no delay.

Almost as one, seven Maverick Missiles parted company from their host craft and sped at incredible velocity towards their impossible to miss targets, four making direct hits slap bang in the middle of their victims. The resultant fireball cleared to reveal as expected, no damage. The other three also found their target but with absolute pinpoint precision. One moment the crew of the Desirion transport were attempting to manoeuvre their vehicle to somewhere out of harm's way, when the ground beneath them simply erupted.

The first Maverick impacted a mere fifteen inches outside the shields umbrella, the explosion reaching deep into the ground and causing the transport to elevate a good ten feet into the air, turn upside down and slam into the rear supporting stanchion of a nearby capital ship. The electromagnetic shielding of the transport was forced to intermix with that of the ships much more powerful one, thus igniting a fantastic light show of blue, green sparks and static. The grounded ships shield attempted to absorb the unwanted object, but the size of the transport and the speed at which it was travelling was just too great. The force of recoil from the ships defensive shield held, only just, but something, somewhere had to give.

That something somewhere was the transport vehicle itself. Trapped in between two strong opposing forces it was literally crushed, the ultra strong plastic polymer offering little resistance, eventually coming to rest at the foot of the capital ship. Fizzing with sparks its battered and agonisingly twisted and mutilated shape now measured a mere thirteen inches thick. This wasn't the end of matters however, as the ship gave an alarming lurch. Its starboard side dropping at the rear as the stanchion which had received the impact with the transport partially gave way.

The remaining Maverick Missiles, although successful were not as effective, causing the partial destruction of another transport and a mobile gun which was flung so high into the air it eventually landed in the Shropshire Union canal some five hundred yards away.

Now came the turn of the Tornado bombers which were following the Harriers who had run the range of the alien weapons and were circling to enable them to come in for a second run. The Tornado pilots had no difficulty in identifying their target area as great swathes of it were lit up like a Kuwaiti oil field in the Gulf war. The most alarming prospect for the aircrews was the curtain like stream of bolts relentlessly rising into the night sky toward them, including a variant not seen before. More intense it deviated from its upward course and appeared to follow the aircraft. Regardless, the job had to be done and they sped toward the maelstrom. The lead Tornado received a glancing blow upon its port wing from one of the new weapons but through brilliant skill, the pilot managed to keep the aircraft on course.

Whilst manoeuvring a turn a second Tornado was hit slap bang on the cockpit canopy. Fortunately the crew knew nothing of what had hit them, the windshield and the cockpit area melting away before instantaneously bursting apart with a thunderous detonation. The resulting explosion caused an adjacent aircraft to receive a piece of fuselage into its tail plane. Once again the skill of the pilot kept the aircraft from disaster but the damage meant he would play no further part in this attack, forcing him to break formation in an attempt to reach safety.

The remaining eight aircraft pressed on and released their payloads. These general purpose bombs were not laser or computer guided, merely a modern version of the classic world war two weapon; reliant for the most part on the expertise of the pilots and the sheer power of their explosive force to create as much damage as possible. The sight that unfolded beneath Beeston castle could only be described as similar to that of a Napalm attack during the Vietnam War, only larger, and one surely enough to give any English Heritage inspector serious palpitations.

Eight huge explosions erupted from the ground amidst the already much contorted terrain. The damage was immense, causing craters of fifty feet in diameter while debris was flung high into the air. Again, compared to the firepower used, the damage to the Desirion's was not comparative. Just two more transports damaged. One beyond repair along with the caterpillar tracks of another, visibly seen flying through the air like a pinged elastic band. The attacks effects were however felt elsewhere.

The damaged capital ship now suffered further. The mangled stanchion, unable to take the strain from the new shockwaves spreading through the ground promptly collapsed. The rear starboard side dropped fifteen feet, crushing those desperately attempting to prevent that very thing from happening. The shield was unable to protect it from this further impact. As it hit the ground the weight caused the casing to crumple while the opposing port side reared into the air like an angry horse. Precariously, it teetered, wobbling for a few seconds before settling in that position, emitting pyrotechnics as the shield fizzed and crackled in an attempt to maintain polarity.

Pox watched all this unfold through a mist of anger, he had already given the order to prepare the fleet for immediate departure to destroy Chester but was informed that the vessels were not yet ready and wouldn't be for some time yet. It was then that his attention was brought to the stricken ship. Not being able to see from his position he rushed to a panel. The screen immediately illuminating to reveal the horrendous sight of one of the most up to date vessels laying in a prone position with an alarming amount of smoke billowing from the damage area.

Lax had refused to leave the *Paraxatar*'s Hub, "My place is here to guide the glorious victory," he shouted insanely. His rantings quickly ceased by Dix administering more calm spreaders before being coaxed into a nice comfy seat. It was in fact his command chair in which he sat, where he proceeded to create an unidentifiable scribble upon a hand held screen.

"He seems restful now," stated Dix returning to Pox, who remained at the console. "Oh dear, that doesn't look good does it?" He said catching sight of the disabled vessel.

XXXVI

The Bedford slowed as it passed the sign indicating the small hamlet of Alpraham."Sir, we're here," called Corporal Barton from the driver's seat, bringing the truck to a halt.

"Okay lads listen up," said Lieutenant Havelock in a raised voice. "This is the plan." He reached into his tunic and pulled out a well used map. "Right," he added unfolding it and took a moment to find their position. "We are here in Al-pr-a-ham" he tapped the map pronouncing the villages name in syllables. "This is our drop off..." Barton cut the engine and the lack of sound plunged the surroundings into silence making Havelock's voice that much louder."...Point," he continued at a quieter level. "Shortly we will split into two groups, one, under my command, the other will be under the care of the sergeant here." A pause. "Now, we will set off down this road here." Once more he indicated as such on the map. "The sergeants group ten minutes after us towards the canal. Upon reaching it we will move along the towpath using whatever cover is available which could well mean getting wet Hooper." The truck burst into muted laughter, Hooper being the butt of a private joke.

Strangely, the person who laughed loudest was Gary, who, apart from his throbbing backside had almost completely recovered.

"When we reach a point near to the enemy base we will stop and observe, with a bit of luck we can obtain an idea of what is going on and reappraise the situation." He looked up, "Are there any questions?"

Anxious and eager faces searched their comrades in anticipation of any enquiry.

"Yes I have one." stated Gary standing up.

Groans erupted but with superb willpower Gary ignored them.

"I'd like a weapon please," he said more in hope than expectation.

All eyes turned to the Lieutenant, Sergeant Hornby's most of all. "Sir I strongly advise against it," he pleaded.

"You have your, err paintball gun do you Mister Spam?" Havelock asked.

Gary thought for a moment. "No I lost it," he admitted. This wasn't actually a lie but his ego not to mention his backside was bruised enough and he was hardly going to reveal he had lost it tussling with an obese, overweight dog.

"Thir," interjected Woods. "Mithter Thpam can have mine, I won't need it now," he said affectionately caressing an SA80 rifle.

Havelock stared at Woods wondering where he'd got the weapon from especially as all his men were still equipped with theirs. Woods handed Gary the Tipman semi automatic paintball gun. Grudgingly Gary took it. "Thanks," he said, his voice thick with scorn.

"You'll be okay thir, juth thtick with me," Woods replied, appearing to take the unfortunate Gary under his wing.

"That, Mister Spam is a very good idea," Said Havelock with a stern tone. "Stick with Mister Woods and don't give me any trouble."

Sergeant Hornby quickly rattled off eight names, "the rest of you are with me," he finished with a grin, wedging an unlit cigar into the corner of his mouth. It gave him the appearance of Clint Eastwood. All it lacked was a "Punk," reference.

Further orders were issued before the final instruction to move was given and the truck burst into a flurry of activity, taking only a matter of a few minutes for the Marines to gather their necessary equipment and disembark. Standing on the roadside, almost invisible in the darkness, they divided into their pre determined squads. Gary and Woods were tagged onto Lieutenant Havelock's team. He was happy enough to have an old soldier such as Woods along. He could even come in useful, but he insisted on Gary, partly because he could keep an eye on him and also because Woods seemed happy to do the same.

Minutes later Havelock and his men were moving at a steady pace along the short road that led from Alpraham to the canals bank, keeping as much as possible to the darker areas. Gary however, was soon trailing behind just like the fat kids on a school cross country run.

The road began to rise quite steeply before a bridge came into view. This forced the strange unexplainable pull that compels people to look over the edge no matter what it spanned to come into play; in this case the shimmering still water of the Shropshire union canal. In daytime its murky brown water remained largely unremarkable. By night the smooth dark surface emitted a different air. The glare of the crescent moon reflected while every now and then faint traces of red, yellow and orange would violate it, the glare from not too distant dancing flames beneath Beeston.

The sound of more aircraft could be made out again but very distant and soon replaced by the sound of more Alien flying machines which seemed to be patrolling the skies around the base area.

Gary crossed the bridge a full five minutes behind the rest of his squad. As he did so the sky lit up in a brilliant show of red raw energy as alien firepower once more reached toward the heavens. The aircraft, Harriers, were a third wave which had been sent to compound the destruction further. Havelock and his team peered towards the cacophony of activity. They couldn't see the target area due to high ground blocking the way but were certainly able to appreciate the display in the sky.

Their speed and cover of darkness rendered them almost invisible, the Harriers let fly an array of missiles. Screaming almost directly overhead they were closely followed by a number of other aircraft. Quick though they were their faint silhouettes and blue exhaust were clearly not of human origin.

Woods thought he could make out eight jets before he lost his night vision to another brilliant explosion, the result of a collision between an aircraft and a plasma bolt fired from behind. Instantly the Harrier disintegrated into small parts. "Jethuth Chritht!" he said aloud and dived for cover as wreckage rained down, most of it harmlessly slamming into the ground or into the canal to sizzle as the superheated metal rapidly cooled.

Gary, who was still on the bridge, took cover too, ducking behind the brick parapets. He considered this a shrewd move, especially as seconds later the sound of hundreds of small particles of metal could be heard pinging against it.

Sergeant Hornby's squad had also reached the canal bridge. After witnessing the Harriers destruction they had wisely also taken to ground seeking cover where they were. The sound of the surviving jets had vanished and could no longer be heard when Havelock and his squad emerged from their hastily sought positions of safety. Dusting himself down he turned as O'Brien alerted them of the approach of a figure; it was Gary. Looking beyond him, just a few paces away he noticed Hornby and his men approach.

"Good to see you are you okay," said Havelock, completely ignoring the wheezing figure bent almost double in front of him.

"Yes well, I'm fine thank you," Gary replied, the words struggling to come out. *I knew they would accept me sooner or later,* he thought, pride swelling within.

The response from the Sergeant behind caused his heart to sink once again, *Bugger,* he thought realising his error.

"Mister Woods," called Havelock.

"Thir." Woods snapped to attention.

"Do something with this, err person will you?" He said, causing more injury to Gary's feelings. Woods put an arm out to console Gary but was rebuked. Regardless, they both walked away towards the nearby canal; Gary sat on the bank and sulked.

"I'm fed up with this Woods," exclaimed Gary, his faltering voice betraying slowly crumbling emotions. "I could help here. I could be a useful part of this team."

176

Woods listened. Although he liked Gary for reasons unfathomable, he tended to feel the same hopeless sense of futility when it came to his work colleague. Unlike the Marines though, he would never say it, not aloud anyway.

"Well if they won't appreciate me I'll leave, then they'll be sorry," Gary continued, only pausing to breathe.

"Thath the thpirit," encouraged Woods, holding his tongue.

"This is getting hairy sir," said Hornby to his commanding officer.

"You're not wrong sergeant." Havelock looked about him not liking what he saw and paused to think for a moment, "time to go I think."

They moved a lot slower this time, keeping to cover so as not to silhouette themselves against the flames from the burning vehicles under the castles outcrop. This new pace suited Gary a lot better. His chest still felt as if it would explode and his mouth salivated with a distinct taste of iron but all the same he kept up, just. Every now and then Havelock would hold up a hand and the squad would go to ground. He welcomed these pauses very much. Despite that, on a couple of occasions he missed the officers hand gesture and cannoned into a not very gracious Hooper, his expletives and threats causing Gary to frown.

Eventually they cleared the artificial hilly area between the canal and the Castle and the whole scene opened up before them like a diorama. The most prominent feature by far was that of Beeston Castle itself, beautifully illuminated by the raging fires on the field below. The orange, red and yellow tongues of flame appeared to give the image of a mock medieval pageant, the imagination easily able to conjure jousting, archery and feasting taking place. A closer examination however and all would be betrayed. Instead, unfamiliar hell unfolded before them.

Huge caterpillar tracked vehicles silhouetted in the glow were followed by a number of not quite human looking figures, making their way through twisted and distorted shapes that were once equally unfamiliar alien vehicles of transportation and war.

Gary stopped, this time without collision and crouched behind Hooper. His wheezing and coughing, very much like a consumptive walrus continued, earning further niggled looks and hushed threats of unconditional violence. Havelock produced a small pair of binoculars from his tunic. Adjusting the focus he swept them across the field obtaining much the same view but this time with clarity. Surveying the scene once more he took in the whole spectrum before suddenly darting back to an object he had initially ignored. Fine tuning the focus again he adjusted the view. "My god!" he exclaimed aloud. "Those planes have done some considerable damage."

His reference was to a large ship with three interlocked spheres which was tilting over at an alarming angle, its front portion high in the air. The damaged section where the rear stanchion had given way was obscured by flames and masses of dense smoke. Dozens of alien figures could be seen racing around, attempting to put the flames out. He lowered the binoculars and faced his men.

"Hooper, go back and find Sergeant Hornby, ask him to join us here immediately."

With a quick, "sir," Hooper disappeared, "The rest of you find some cover," he added.

No sooner had he finished speaking when the distant boom of artillery opened up again from the direction of Chester. "Shit," said Havelock. He knew that the artillery would be trained more or less on their very position. As if to confirm his theory the tell tale sound of shells screaming through the air could be heard, followed, after a much shorter time by the inevitable explosion. The artillery was more accurate than expected, the vast majority of projectiles raining down exactly onto the alien base with nothing coming dangerously close to them. The very jittery squad of Royal Marines were alerted by approaching footsteps, each weapon immediately trained upon empty darkness. Out of the night air, moving in a low crouched position appeared the familiar faces of Hooper and Sergeant Hornby.

"Sir," said Hornby, squatting down.

"No need to tell you what's going on here Sergeant, I think we'll lay low until this barrage has stopped," suggested Havelock, the right side of his face illuminating in a red glow as each shell detonated. "It seems one of their large ships is out of action thanks to all this activity," added the officer, shouting now in order to be heard above the din.

"How many are left sir?" The Sergeant enquired, his facial expression not changing with the good news.

"I could only see another two from here, but I haven't got a good view and I think there are more around the other side of the castle." Hornby nodded as if in agreement.

The barrage continued for another ten minutes before as suddenly as it had started, it ceased, the abrupt silence almost as intense on the ears as the barrage.

Gary had at last recovered his wits, his body however was a different story. His heart beat was as normal as could be expected in a situation such as this but his chest still rippled with pain after every breath and to make matters worse he was beginning to regret his decision to jump from the Land Rover back in Tarporley. *I could be safe at home now, but if I don't deal with this, Chester will be destroyed and then what?* Rather philosophically his train of thought assumed that the responsibility was solely his. Cringing at the possible outcome and consequences, he shut his mind, forcing himself not to think any deeper. Looking up he was dismayed to see his squad gathering their equipment once more and preparing to move.

Once again he was mobile, albeit more slowly this time. They kept to the canal towpath, ducking and crouching as they crept closer to the castle, the glow illuminating it now much dimmer.

Havelock's squad were more or less parallel with the ancient ruin when the officer's hand was raised with all immediately going to ground. Some lay flat, others took to the undergrowth for better concealment; the Lieutenant, leading by example just crouched on the towpath peering through his binoculars. Shortly Hornby's squad appeared again, this time the Sergeant and Havelock moved away to discuss the situation in private.

"Alright lads it's simple," said Havelock returning after a couple of minutes. "There are four ships that have to be destroyed; you can't miss them, they are the big buggers, look like giant rubber dog toys".

A few blank looks were exchanged between the marines.

"Do you mean the ones that squeak when a dog chews upon it?" A voice asked from the darkness.

The Sergeant returned a stare in its direction.

More footsteps could be heard on the towpath, this time from the opposite direction. The Marine officer ceased his chatter and froze, all men already at ground level quickly sought places of further concealment. Long seconds passed, eyes straining along the sights of rifles anxious to make out any movement in the darkness before finally a camouflaged form slowly emerged. Equally as alert, his weapon held before him, the blackened face moving from side to side searching. He was followed by others.

"Hold it right where you are." The command was whispered from the bushes. "Identify yourselves."

To a man the newcomers spun in the direction of the challenge, each weapon trained similarly. The figure at the front revealed three stripes upon the front of his battledress as he turned.

"Doberman, second battalion Parachute Regiment." replied the Sergeant unemotionally.

A marine emerged from the bushes "Sorry Sarge can't be too careful."

"No, good work," replied Doberman genuinely pleased.

Sergeant Doberman had been sent back to the area with a platoon of Paratroopers, an attachment of Royal engineers and others, at present impossible to make out. The Sappers and the unseen men, who were in fact civilian's had been engaged in work upon captured alien vehicles retrieved from the battlefield at Rowton. Command was of the opinion that their varied success at understanding them could prove invaluable. Doberman had requested to be platoon commander. That honour went to an officer, but he was accepted onto the squad due to his previous experiences with the invaders. The purpose of his team's mission was really a delaying one. As yet, no long term answers as to how to deal with the invaders had been offered, other than to harass them with guerrilla tactics and to simply pound them into submission.

As more hardware and units became available this was carried out, however thanks to the aliens shield system only very minor success had been achieved. They had indeed suffered horrendous losses in manpower, but this had all been at the hands of a supernatural army which had now disappeared. Grateful though the nation was they were not expected to return. Human casualties were beginning to mount, the one air raid that had taken place that very night had returned three aircraft plus their crews down and one seriously damaged and they had been chased a considerable distance by the alien aircraft, who's use seemed to be intensifying as time went on. So attention was turned to covert operations, working under cover of darkness and using the land.

Three platoons were sent into the very heart of proceedings with their own respective engineers and civilians. They had made considerable progress upon the alien technology, the weaponry proving relatively easy to operate once understood. The propulsion system control was not giving its secrets away too lightly though and these were central to the any plan, albeit a rather rushed one, but one worth trying.

The captured vehicles in the possession of the British forces were slowly being assembled into a usable force with the intention of towing them and using them upon the invaders; this was however taking some time, slow really being the operative word in this case. In the mean time the combined platoons were to take to the field under Beeston and capture, where possible, working, tracked mobile guns.

"Okay Sergeant," interjected Havelock, automatically taking command of the situation. "We had no idea you or anyone else was about."

"Nor I you err sir," replied Doberman peering at the Lieutenant in the gloom and realising his officer status.

"Well I for one am glad you're here, we could do with some extra hands."

"Right Sergeant I'll take over from here." The new voice came from a small group of newcomers.

Havelock, a little shaken by the abrupt brazenness of the man approaching, looked up. "And you are?" He demanded, leaving the question in the air.

"My name is Lieutenant Parkin." said the officer brashly, his large eyes bored into Havelock which, set against his darkened face looked as though there was a light shining inside his head and using his eyeballs as torches, "Are you in command here?" He added.

"Indeed I am," replied Havelock, ignoring the attitude of the Parachute officer and offered his hand.

The two men shook hands and sought safer, more protected ground where Sergeant Doberman and Lieutenant Parkin were brought up to speed on events and vice versa.

"Well Havelock," said Parkin, in a more friendly tone this time. "It seems our objectives more or less lie along the same path."

Some thirty minutes had now passed since the most recent barrage had ceased. Aircraft activity appeared to have stopped too and Havelock was eager to get some sort of plan going even if it was just to get his agitated men doing something. The fires on the field beneath the castle were now all out and the whole area plunged into darkness once more apart from the odd light here and there while the only sounds belonged to those of alien movements and a low mumble as the hidden soldiers chatted.

The two officers accompanied by their Sergeants spent the next twenty minutes agreeing on a mutual plan of action. It was recognised by all that their options were rather limited, due largely to low numbers and their relatively nonexistent knowledge regarding the enemy they were dealing with, although the accompaniment of the team of engineers and civvies had been a boost in that department. It was determined that the force would be split into their respective regiments pretty much as before with the engineers and civilians also divided. Ten men would accompany each squad while Woods and Gary would remain with Havelock also as before. Using the cover of darkness they would penetrate the alien encampment and attempt to disable the remaining four ships with whatever means they had at their disposal.

"Well Ross," said Havelock with a grin as he addressed the Parachute officer by his first name. "Should be an easy job, can't see too many problems can you?"

"Walk in the park," Parkin replied with an equal amount of optimistic sarcasm.

Fortunately, the darkness revealed no visual sign of the obvious apprehension that they were feeling. Internally, all were sure that there was no coming back from this one. Except that is for Woods who was utterly confident he could complete the entire mission on his own, and Gary, who although now a reluctant bystander, his brains heroic side refused to let him admit defeat.

Havelock glanced at his watch. "Okay, I make it one, fifty five; shall we rendezvous at the canal bridge just down there?" He pointed in the direction of the bridge, "At zero, eight hundred?"

Watches were synchronised while the necessary stiff upper lips were maintained. "I'll shout you a wee dram in the mess tonight," offered Parkin mimicking Havelock's accent, albeit very badly. Havelock grinned, "arl hold ye ter that Jimmy," replied a grinning Havelock, thickening it somewhat. With that the two squads parted and went their ways.

Havelock led his men back past the man made hills, once a huge underground oil storage facility. Then eastwards along the canal which blocked off the view of the castle once more. Skirting along this they soon came to a bridge which took them away from the canal and under the railway line before opening up into the car park of Beeston cattle market. Not surprisingly Gary was having considerable trouble keeping up with the super fit soldiers. Even the Engineers and civilian's who were not as trim, trailed Gary in their wake. His chest wheezed again while his legs ached, not to mention his backside which still throbbed, but stalwartly he carried on regardless. Onward they continued through the car park before Gary noticed a not so subtle change, the ground under foot was softer, the reason being they had broken into open countryside. Soon the terrain changed again as they came under the protection of a canopy of tall trees, the perimeter of a small but dense copse.

Havelock stopped here to survey the area. On reaching the group of soldiers Gary dropped to the floor with a thump. It was difficult to make much out in the darkness but Havelock looked through his binoculars towards the castle which was now lying in a south westerly direction.

"Okay lads, we'll take five here," he said and consulted Hornby who stood shoulder to shoulder with him.

Gary dragged himself up and sat upon on a tree stump, jumping back up as pain seared through his wounded rump. *Bloody dog*, he thought and fingered his paintball gun menacingly while picturing the despised rotund Jack Russell, wiped from existence with many well aimed paintball pellets. *Bloody Havelock, bloody aliens in fact bloody everything,* he'd had enough of being pushed around, now it was time for..."

"Okay kiddiewinks let's move it," commanded Sergeant Hornby.

Groans erupted. "Oh come on Sarge I was just getting comfy," Starley whinged.

The group moved off but at a more sedate pace, crouching and keeping to cover.

"Are you okay thir?" asked Woods, slowing considerably to keep pace with him.

"Not really, no I'm not," remarked Gary, his bad mood evident between heavy cough laden breaths. "I'm fed up with the attitude of certain people around here; I don't have to be here you know."

"Good, well piss off!" came a quick reply from in front.

"Don't worry thir we'll thoon do thethe bathtardth, then we can go home," said woods hoping to divert a confrontation.

The trees eventually gave way to reveal a small country road, wide enough for just a single vehicle travelling from east to west. Havelock stopped and consulted his map with the aid of a tiny shielded torch light. "Okay lads, listen up," he whispered. "We are not far from the castle now, stealth is the name of the game, mustn't compromise ourselves."

Gary was sure all eyes were trained on him when Havelock had finished talking, the words, mustn't compromise, burning into his consciousness. Tucking the map into his tunic pocket, Havelock turned right onto the road, travelling at a dead slow pace to ensure a very cautious approach to the castle. Almost invisible, they blended superbly with the darkened undergrowth.

Barely had they covered thirty yards when one of the patrol stopped and eagerly sought his Sergeant. His face, muted and wide eyed was followed by a little hopping dance, rather like an excited child on Christmas morning. The two could be seen looking at something through the hedge in the field to their left. Havelock, aware that something was amiss, returned. Crouching in the bushes he produced his binoculars and had a look.

"You know McCormack I think your right," he said still holding the binoculars up, a wide grin spreading across his taught face.

"What ith it thir?" whispered Woods.

"It's one of their ships," replied Hornby, not taking his eyes from it.

"We have to be quick now," said Havelock looking at his watch, the dial reading two, twenty six. "We have to complete this by daybreak."

"Not going to be easy, I count six of those mobile guns and lots of movement, could be any amount of ground troops, err soldiers, err whatever you call em," said Hornby, still peering through the binoculars.

Havelock called for the Engineer Sergeant.

"Sir," came the prompt reply as a female N.C.O appeared from the darkness.

"Sergeant?" Havelock prompted.

"Telford sir."

"Well Sergeant Telford, this is where you make a name for yourself, you see that hulking great item in that field?"

Telford pulled back some of the thick hedgerow, pricking her finger. Using Havelock's binoculars she took her turn at peering through.

"That," said Havelock.

She adjusted the focus further until she could make out the three huge spheres of the alien ship. As her eyes adjusted she could make out all kinds of activity going on around the ship including the presence of a number of caterpillar tracked guns. Pulling herself from the hedge, the binocular strap became caught in the thicket and half choked her in the process.

"If you can get us there safely sir, then my men can get to work on those guns," she said, the threat of suffocation eased.

"If we go back down the road and turn right at the fork," offered Havelock, consulting the map again, "there is a farmhouse which will allow us to get closer and provide us with more cover."

Keeping as ever to the shadows, close in to the edges of the hedge they sought the farmhouse. After the considerable rest Gary had found his second wind and now felt that he was coping admirably under the circumstances, considering he'd almost died from exhaustion not half an hour previous. The fork in the road was indeed where it had been predicted, as was the farmhouse just a few yards further on. Skirting around the empty darkened building the marines carried out a quick reccee to ensure the area was secure before moving into a large open yard. It was littered with various forms of machinery ranging from Tractors, large spiked trailers down to the mandatory caravan slowly deteriorating in the corner. It also provided a surrounding low brick wall which offered excellent cover.

Gary paused close to the house in order to get his breath back. "God I need a drink," he said, his voice a strained whisper as flecks of uncontrollable dribble left his mouth. Reaching into his backpack he pulled out his bottle and drained the last drops, "bugger!" Looking at the building he was aware that he was standing next to what appeared to be a back door. Peering through the glass he thought he caught sight of a sink, cupboards and other regalia usually associated with a kitchen. "Jackpot," he said softly to himself.

Gently, he tried the handle, it turned.

"What are you doing thir?" asked Woods, who appeared behind him.

"I need a drink Woods, my bottle is empty, I'm just going to see if the tap in this kitchen works."

Woods didn't reply, instead he remained where he was and waited for Gary to re-emerge from the house.

The door opened easily enough and into the kitchen he went, spotting a light switch on the wall he automatically reached for it and pressed the switch. All too late realising his error he switched it off again. Stricken with panic he missed the switch five times before realising with audible curses that the light hadn't in fact illuminated. "Oh Jesus, thank god for that," he said with a huge sigh of relief. Gathering his wits for about the three hundredth time that night he strode over to the sink, opened a cupboard and took out a cup which he luckily found first time. Hoping that it was still working he turned the tap and was relieved when it spluttered a couple of times before filling his cup with water. Draining it instantly, he held the cup out to refill it when from behind a door on the other side of the kitchen he heard a clicking noise. Carefully putting his cup down he turned towards the door. The burning in his chest and lungs replaced with a heightened feeling of frozen anxiousness.

"Woods?" he called, silently, knowing that the Psychotic van driver would not hear him.

Click! There it went again accompanied by a grinding similar to a heavy piece of furniture being dragged across a floor. Swinging the Tipman from his back in one movement he held the paintball gun level with his stomach and then strangely, against all reasoning and certainly his own will, found himself slowly walking towards the door. He knew it would have been easier to just leave the house and get Havelock or Hornby to deal with it but he felt he had something to prove and prove it he would.

XXXVII

Lieutenant Havelock, Sergeant Hornby and Sergeant Telford squatted behind the brick wall. The view of the Alien ship couldn't have been better. Its entire length in full view, clearly visible in the darkness without binoculars, in fact it seemed that as they drew closer a kind of luminous hue appeared to emanate from it. The new position also revealed that instead of the previously counted six mobile guns, there were in fact at least ten and many more figures moving around the vehicles.

"We really need some kind of a diversion sir," said Hornby optimistically.

Now some believe in God, others are superstitious while some actually believe that British Leyland produced truly remarkable cars, but, even the most devoted believer could not have predicted what happened next. No sooner had Hornby verbally sought intervention when the sky in front of the north side of the castle was illuminated by a huge fireball which split the darkness apart. Less than a second later the sound of the explosion hit their shocked faces. Once the din had died it was replaced by alarms and sirens, all sounding as though they had the expressed intention of informing someone that all was not well. Activity around the ship near to them became frantic. Alien figures rushing this way and that like a colony of ants.

As Havelock continued to observe, it became apparent that the number of aliens around their target was actually reducing, evidently being drawn from the area to investigate and aid at the explosion area.

"Holy shit. Well done Parkin," whispered Havelock to no one in particular, assuming that the Parachute Regiment Officer and his team were responsible for the explosion. Even if it wasn't them, it was still the diversion that they required.

XXXVIII

Gary reached for the door handle. On the verge of investigating the clicking sound when his attention was jerked towards the sudden explosion. The door opened violently, pushed from the opposite side and causing his head to swivel back again. In the receding orange glare of the fading fireball, Gary easily recognised the unmistakable features of one of the Desirion invaders. At the unexpected sight of each other both species appeared equally as shocked at each other's presence, however, the alien's reactions were quicker, its weapon levelled and poised to pull the trigger. Strange, unknown forces now took hold of Gary. Completely ignoring his own aching body he dropped to the floor as if he'd passed out, lashing out with a leg at the same time. His outstretched limb caught the extra terrestrial a hefty blow on its own limb and with a squeal it went down, its weapon clipping the back of a chair as it fell, wrenching it from its grasp to clatter harmlessly to the floor.

Within seconds both were in a kneeling position, again the alien was quickest, pouncing with alarming speed and knocking Gary onto his back in a sprawl of arms and legs. Gary responded by shouting the word, "bastard," over and over again as the two figures grappled, no coordinated effort, just flailing limbs producing continual wild kicks and punches.

Woods, who was keen to re-join the marines before they advanced, looked into the kitchen window expecting to see Gary at the sink. At first he couldn't see him, and then the frantic tumble on the floor caught his attention. Bursting through the door he raised his pistol but daren't fire for the risk of shooting his comrade, he couldn't even join the melee because of the kitchen table and chairs which took up most of the floor space. So with no option open, he calmly jumped onto the table and crouched above the grappling figures, his pistol levelled, waiting for an opening.

His opening arrived at that moment in another form. A second alien burst through the door from the room beyond and made straight for the fighting pair on the ground. It hadn't even seen Woods, who, although startled, was still able to keep control. Firing off two shots in quick succession, the retort of the gun sounded impossibly loud in the small room.

The first round grazed the door frame before ricocheting into the darkness of the room beyond. The second struck the Desirion plumb on the side of its head, the violent impact throwing it backwards without a sound, never to move again. This extra commotion was the first alien's downfall, the sound of Wood's gun discharging causing it to look up, giving Gary the perfect opportunity. He didn't however take it. What he did do was to continue to flail at the alien, most of which was carried out with his eyes closed. A balled up undirected fist hit his adversary straight in the eye membrane, a purely lucky shot. As he made contact there was a yucky squelch. The Desirion screamed as it was forced sideways by the blow, landing right next to its fallen weapon and it wasted no time in recovering and grabbing the gun before quickly moving it upwards to bring the muzzle to bear. Gary already had his Tipman poised and Woods the nine millimetre. Without a moment's pause, both pulled their triggers simultaneously. Pellet after Pellet poured from the semi automatic paintball gun, rapidly emptying its magazine, although beaten to its target by the pistols rounds.

The alien initially looked shocked as if expecting something worse than the sharp stings it received as the pellets hit, but whatever it didn't feel from the paintball gun it certainly did from the pistol, both rounds striking home, one in its left arm the other in its left shoulder area. Gary could have sworn that it actually gave him a momentary grin before its expression suddenly changed. With mouth clamped shut its eyes appeared to strain within their membrane. Opening its mouth wide, a blood curdling scream issued forth, building as it went on. Throwing its own weapon aside the Desirion's overlong arms frantically scratched and tore at the points of impact as the paint slowly spread out and burnt inwards, much of it into the open wounds caused by Woods shots.

A wretched Smoke filled the room as the unfortunate creature writhed on the floor in agony, it's screaming ceased but still it thrashed around before eventually with a jerk and a final squeal it was still.

Within the house all was quiet again. "Are you okay thir?" Asked Woods, who had moved to stand above the alien he had downed giving it a hefty kick to make sure it was dead.

"Yes Woods I'm fine," said Gary, feeling himself all over, inspecting for any cuts or other damage. "What's happening? I heard the explosion," he continued, now satisfied he was intact.

Woods automatically changed the magazine in his gun before wandering into the room the two aliens had emerged from, only to re-appear seconds later. "Not thure," said Woods, seemingly pre occupied. "Think it wath the Parath, you know Lieutenant Parkin."

"You think there are any more in here?" Asked Gary.

Woods never answered, instead he bent over the still forms of the two dead aliens, the one Gary had killed still bubbled in places. Grabbing their guns he offered one to Gary. "Thethe will come in handy," he said.

Gary glanced at his smiling face before taking the weapon. It felt surprisingly light in his grasp but when he held it in a waist high position it felt awkward, uncomfortable.

"Ith becauth of their phythiology, the gun ith made to fit their body thape," said Woods Recognising Gary's discomfort. He actually looked rather comfortable holding his. "Come on we'd better go," and off he went through the back door.

Gary looked around quickly, "Hmmm," he uttered before securing the Tipman around his neck with the strap. He held the alien weapon in an attempt to feel more comfortable with it and followed Woods out into the night.

XXXIX

Lax's brain or rather the parts of it still operating had sagged even further towards jellification. Currently he was responding to soothing sounds, colourful pictures and the wonderful effects of yet another large dose of calm spreaders within his chambers on board the *Paraxatar*. Commander Pox had reluctantly assumed the role of Overseer, "Temporarily!" he had vehemently stated, "until Lax regains control of his mind."

The other senior commanders, high grade statesman and those holding noted positions agreed, in fact it was one of these who suggested the very simple plan that Pox was currently in the process of executing. Commander Bex had mentioned it at the first meeting, shortly after Lax's temporary incarceration.

"Commander wouldn't it be a prudent move if instead of attacking this Chesdar, Libepool and Me...Ma...The other one. We move our ships to another area away from the human build up of armed forces here?"

Those present looked at each other, Pox built himself up ready to reject the plan immediately but he couldn't think of a reason. "So simple, so very simple," he said softly to himself and upsetting Bex a little who thought the reference was aimed at him.

"Yes Bex, we don't have to stay here hammering the Hooomanns." He paused a moment for thought, *Not that there had actually been a great deal of that going on.* He immediately pushed the negativity from his thought processes." It has taken the Hooomanns a considerable time to assemble the forces they have deployed against us so far, almost as long as we have been here," he added.

"Except for their air vehicles," interjected Commander Max.

"Yes Max thank-you," replied Pox.

"And it's highly unlikely this is the extent of the human opposition. They would surely have equally adequate defence's planet wide." Max continued.

"Yes Max, point taken."

"Not forgetting also, acting overseer, the capital ships will not operate anything like maximum efficiency in this atmosphere."

"Yes thank-you, Commander Max, your comments are noted," the exasperation in pox's reply evident. He wasn't entirely sure that his use of the term acting overseer wasn't a rebuke either.

"I thought also," Bex said, knowing that he was on a roll, "that the islands commercial capital and seat of Government would be the ideal target."

Instantly the screens upon the panels they were sat around illuminated, depicting a three dimensional map of the British Isles. Pox spoke the words of the city, or a close approximation and the map transformed to an overall view of London. "It's the centre of trade and Government, not to mention being the largest gathering of Humans on the entire Island."

"They would defend it," offered Max sticking to his guns.

"Not if we made an immediate strike," replied Bex. "When we landed here we stalled, we gave them time and plenty of warning, if we strike this Llorndorrn then we do it with absolute surprise. Our remaining ships in orbit around the fourth planet are fully powered up and can attack immediately and besides if the two detainees have informed the Hooomanns of our plans to attack nearby dwellings they cannot possibly know that we now intend to strike elsewhere."

"An area of that importance would be heavily defended, all the time," offered Pox as an afterthought...

"Not so," Bex replied as he brought up image after image of London, "It is an area of habitation and commerce, not military, I would imagine there were some defences but remember, the Humans are geared up to fight other humans, our capabilities far outreach theirs."

A hush descended as they all searched each other's faces. Not one Desirion within the room could find a reason to object, even those who secretly thought that the best plan of action would be to count their losses and leave the Earth, still with so some credibility.

"Okay, I want preparations for the entire fleet to move," Pox said suddenly. He turned to a screen and uttered a few words.

A face appeared, "Commander," it said.

"How soon before we will be able to leave?"

"Leave, Commander?" The operative looked confused.

"Yes leave, get away from this miserable place, how soon?"

"Err, err," came the stuttering reply. "By the time we recall all forces and load vehicles and units, probably not until the end of this Earth day at the earliest. That doesn't take into account the damaged ships, vehicles and unaccounted troops, and there are thousands of them...."

Pox looked uninterested in the inventory being rolled out by the operative. "Hush," he announced holding up a hand. "I want a full withdrawal from this area and rendezvous with the undeployed ships by nightfall, is that clear?"

The operatives eye membrane widened in surprise. "But Commander that is just not...."

"What is your name?" Asked Pox.

"Aax, chief of Natta section," he replied.

"Well Aax I want a full withdrawal by nightfall." Pox repeated in a very light but threatening tone.

Taking the hint, Aax nodded and simply said, "Commander."

Pox turned from the screen which immediately went blank. "What to do about Lax," he said.

"I will keep his majestic Overseer content," said Dix with a smile, adding to the discussion for the first time.

"What I mean is," Pox said, "that we will still need Lax's authorising seal for this new attack."

Once again Dix grinned. "Like I said I will take care of that."

Further points were raised and discussed and all seemed relatively happy for once. The meeting had more or less ended and the first dignitaries were climbing to their feet when a huge explosion rocked the *Paraxatar*, the entire ship trembling. The screen in front of Pox lit up again but this time with a different face.

"Commander the Hooomanns are attacking on our north western perimeter," the face looked deeply worried as if it hadn't relayed all of its information.

"Is that it, what was that explosion?" barked Pox.

"Commander," continued the face, "it was the transport vessel *Sarax*; the Hooomanns have acquired some of our own assault vehicles and destroyed it with prolonged concentrated fire."

Pox flopped into the seat which automatically began moulding to his frame, already he was beginning to know exactly how Lax felt.

XL

The destruction of the *Sarax* was utterly spectacular. Lieutenant Parkin, Sergeant Doberman and his Platoon of Paratroopers had taken the Desirion's completely by surprise. Moving among the sparsely manned edge of the base they had very handily come across three of the caterpillar tracked mobile guns. Quickly and quietly dispatching the dozen or so crews so as not compromise their presence, they took over their prizes. Although unable to move the vehicles under their own power, the sappers were in possession of the knowledge of how to operate the weaponry and this they did with devastating effect. Swivelling each of the quads until twelve glowing tips were trained upon the ship at a mere five hundred yards, they simply locked the gun into position and fired.

Giving everything they had, countless red and orange thermal transfer plasma energy bolts lanced into the plastic polymer hulls one after the other. The huge Transport vessels shields, not modified to absorb their own energy weapons held for a few minutes but soon relented to allow each bolt to chip away at the outer hull until finally, they penetrated.

Continuing to strike, they ripped into the interior of the ship causing untold mayhem and carnage until with nothing left to absorb the attack, the bolts found the propulsion system deep inside the craft.

Parkin and his squad were themselves shocked by the magnitude of the explosion which reached high above the castle itself, each man rapidly vacating his vehicle in order to find cover from expected reprisals not to mention high velocity pieces of space vessel.

"Holy shit!" said Doberman to no-one in general. Had anybody been in audible range of his expletive it would have been totally wasted as each man now enjoyed the hearing level equivalent to someone who spent a good couple of hours attending a Motorhead gig.

"Holy shit!" remarked Havelock as the Marines observed the huge orange ball of flame reach toward the heavens from their concealed position."Well done Parkin," he added, the explosion Visible for all to see for miles around.

"Holy shit" said Captain Bridger.

General Fartlington turned at the exclamation. "That, Captain Bridger, is not the sort of language I expect from my staff, in particular a lady," he said not taking his eye from the fireball currently reaching skywards and illuminating the night sky a deep orange, although when he thought about it, holy shit was quite a good summing up of the spectacle.

"Captain, I want you to find out exactly what that explosion was and I want some reports back from the Patrols around Beeston."

"Sir," replied Bridger, glad to have an excuse to get away from her bumbling commanding officer. Offering a quick salute she left the ancient tower upon Chester's walls.

As the heavy wooden door shut with a hearty haunted house thud the General peered towards Rowton through his binoculars. This past week his belief in the supernatural had been turned upside down, the materialization of an entire ghost army of seventeenth century soldiers and then to cap it all King Charles himself appearing in this very room. Being the man he was, Fartlington had initially demanded that the ghostly monarch produce some identification but the sudden coldness of the room and the kings thousand yard stare had soon quietened him until as suddenly as it had appeared the apparition simply faded away.

He still stole nervous glances towards the window where Charles had appeared before forcing his concentration upon the diminishing flames over Beeston. Had there been no obstructions or contours of the ground and had it been daylight, and had his binoculars been of significantly more power, then the General would have been able to focus quite nicely upon a wild looking man with dark hair carrying an alien gun with a devilishly evil looking Ghurkha knife tucked into his belt, while around his head a bandana held an Ace of spades playing card in an almost vertical position.

XLI

"Don't thoot, don't thoot, ith me Woodth," said Woods flinging himself to the ground to find cover behind the farms wall.

Audible sighs of relief came from the Marines sheltering behind the wall and various pieces of Farm detritus unstrategically scattered around the yard. More footsteps could be heard from the same direction; again rifles were pointed in their direction.

"Ith okay, ith thir, err, Gary," Woods corrected.

On this occasion the Marines took somewhat longer to stand down, an action backed up by the open comment of, "shoot him anyway." making their feelings very clear on the matter. As expected the lumbering form of Gary emerged from the darkness. He too flung himself to the ground but instead of rolling comfortably into position he hit the ground flat and just stopped dead, jarring every bone in his body while reigniting the throbbing pain in his backside.

"Mister Woods where have you been and what the hell have you got there?" Asked Havelock, referring to the hefty looking alien rifle clutched tightly in his grubby hands.

"I thought I said you were to have a pistol..." His sentence was cut short as his vision fell upon the crawling Gary armed with a similar weapon.

"Oh no, I don't think so Mister Spam. You will hand that over to me immediately."

"It's mine, I won it," replied Gary, determined not to be pushed around anymore.

"Thir we came acroth two of the thonth oth bitcheth back in the houthe. We err dealt with them," explained Woods fingering the weapon with pride.

"Are you able to use it?" asked Havelock, his voice betraying suspicious concern.

"Sir," interjected Sergeant Hornby. "We don't have much time."

"Yes indeed Sergeant, You two keep those weapons away from us and stay where I can bloody well see you, clear?" Havelock said reasserting authority.

"Thir," said Woods and offered a salute into the bargain. Gary simply glared and nodded.

"Okay," said Havelock to his men. "When that fireball has diminished we will move, I want two groups utilising all the cover we can find, we must take those guns." Havelock pointed the weapons out as best he could in the orange tinged darkness.

The fireball had pretty much dissipated by now and the resultant glow was that of the burning transport which would surely be there for the duration.

"Let's move," ordered the Marine officer carefully raising himself above the walls parapet and steadily climbing over, closely followed by Hornby and his men with Woods and Gary bringing up the rear. The Marines scrambled, bent over, looking for cover and making sure the far flanks were visible to each other. Finding cover was easier said than done as other than the target vehicles themselves, there was virtually none between the farm and the Alien ship. Regardless, they were making good progress when just thirty yards from the nearest mobile gun a badly timed explosion from the burning transport illuminated the marines for all to see. Fortunately the majority of Desirion's who had been working in this area had either returned to the safety of the other ships or render what aid they could around the burning transport. Even so the fire that was sent towards them was heavy, bolts of energy fizzing through the black night air giving a tinge to the soldiers who had immediately gone to ground.

"Sergeant," shouted Havelock, risking raising his head to locate Hornby who was just visible in the glow. "I need covering fire, I'll try to reach that." He pointed towards the alien vehicle, so close he could almost reach out and touch it.

Without a word of confirmation, Hornby's squad opened up forcing a significant reduction in the attack. Havelock jumped up and sprinted toward the vehicle before diving at its base, coming to land against a caterpillar track. Looking up he saw two marines and two sappers following likewise, he also saw the rather unnerving sight of Alien fire flying in his direction from his own lines. Quickly he realised that it must be return fire from the bloke with the lisp and the Pratt, *Christ I hope they know what they're doing,* he thought.

Woods felt completely at home with the extra terrestrial weapon. Everything about it seemed right. To look at him holding it, it looked as though it was made just for him except maybe a trifle too small. Gary, on the other hand was not safe with his. As far as he was concerned what he held in his hands was a twenty fourth century federation issue phaser Rifle.

Once he had pulled the trigger all his fears and worries dissolved. He felt raw, he felt power, and he felt immortal as the energy bolts kicked out from the guns pointed tip with no particular accuracy. He felt like a super hero. He felt like Captain James T Kirk.

The Marines and Sappers reached the mobile gun safely and paused for the smallest of breaths, but no time. Havelock, taking a quick peek around the vehicles side came face to face with a gun toting Desirion. The Officers weapon was already pointing in its direction. Pulling the trigger, he watched the startled alien crumple to the ground with a scream. Behind the twitching body he could see the still forms of others lying silent upon the grass, there were however, plenty more upright and mobile ones still evident.

Hornby and his group of Marines and Engineers had also reached a mobile gun while those remaining, along with Gary and Woods, made for one of the tracked transports in order to use it as shelter from the re-intensified alien fire.

"Okay you know what to do," said Havelock to the two Sappers sheltering with him, "we'll give you covering fire."

Sergeant Telford looked bothered, despite this she didn't falter; climbing into the open entry hatch she was quickly followed by her colleague. The Marines opened fire immediately bringing down two more Desirion's who had dared to get too near. From within the vehicle a high pitched whistle began to build before the gun on top gently pivoted with a smooth hiss before coming to a stop with a soft click. Seconds later it too began firing.

Havelock, shooting around the corner of the animated gun saw that the engineers were clearing the field in front of them, alien after alien falling from the onslaught of this fearsome weapon. From the environs of the gun its operators could be heard shouting. "Have that yer bastard, you like it? You like it?"

Although he didn't approve, Havelock ignored the shouting. Another peek and the resistance had withered to almost nothing. To his right a second mobile gun opened up, this one discharging directly into the nearest ship. A smooth hiss and the one which he sheltered behind joined in too. To his left was another, silent, and without a Sapper it could not be operated. Quickly, scanning the scene he caught the distant faces of those sheltering behind a transport. Like a Hollywood incarnation of a World War two G.I, whose signalling ability allowed him to order a vehicle to park on a seventeen degree slant just by raising one eyebrow, Havelock received the relevant hand signal and sprinted, this time to the third gun. Arriving safely he turned to catch his breath. Marines, O'Brian and Murray were close behind him while the Sappers were just leaving the cover of the transport when the mobile gun he had just left received a direct hit from a similar weapon operated by the enemy. The vehicle rocked backwards before regaining its position, the barrel on top still firing, however three more hits in quick succession forced it to slam over onto its side. Havelock saw where the fire was coming from but was powerless to do anything about it. More bolts ripped through its shielding, penetrating deep before the gun blew itself to pieces.

Gary watched the destruction of the weapon. He had no idea who had been inside but assumed that as it had been firing upon the ship, the engineers must have still been in there. He felt sick but the hero inside him was still flying high.

"Come on thir," said Woods, "no time for that." Woods knew how Gary was feeling right now; he also knew they didn't have time to dwell upon casualties and must keep moving.

The second captured gun continued firing, not at the ship but had re targeted to fire at the mobile gun which had killed the Sappers. However this one was doomed too as another three Desirion weapons began a concentrated attack blowing it too onto its side. This time the two Engineers managed to crawl out, one appeared badly hurt, his colleague dragging him from the damaged vehicle.

Havelock knew a bad situation when he saw one and this was pretty bad. Starting with O'Brian and Murray he began a defensive withdrawal, increasing fire until he joined Hornby and the others, who looked a little bewildered. With the message finally through to everyone the whole squad retreated back towards the farm house in good order. Eventually they reached the familiar perimeter wall they had sheltered behind and rapidly sought its cover.

"Sergeant do the roll," ordered Havelock.

Thankfully the alien fire had ceased, the Desirion's orders were to defend their ground and not pursue any humans.

"Sir," reported Hornby, his muster complete. "I'm afraid Sappers Telford and Higgins are missing and Corporal Solanki needs a hospital."

"Telford and Higgins are dead Sergeant they were in the gun when it blew," said Havelock, looking for the first time, very grave.

"Sarge where are those two civvie dickheads?" asked Parvetti.

Heads turned before peering out across no man's land, searching for the absent Woods and Gary, but to no avail.

XLII

Supreme Overseer Lax lay comfortable in his reclining seat. The contours hugged so snugly that he was hardly aware his body was actually in contact with anything. His whole being felt as though it was floating upon the softest cushion of bubble filled air. If his body felt relaxed then this was nothing compared to how his mind perceived things, complete contentment, his thoughts ranging from childhood memories and happy days back on Shard with his family. Those simple days were easy and with little or no responsibility, culminating right up to the present and this current disastrous campaign. From the moment the great armada had left the home world and entered the interstellar conduit, plunging deep into what was really the unknown and then touchdown on this miserable planet with its loathsome dominant species.

Lax had never even met a human face to face and in a twisted kind of way he secretly admired the fact that unlike the vast majority of races that the Desirion's had conquered, these beings refused to lay down and give up.

Admiration or not this was bad news to Lax as his entire future depended on a successful conclusion here on this third planet known as Earth. A successful conclusion however was just about as far away as Paddington Bear becoming the next Secretary General of the United Nations.

The explosions and sounds of battle had been audible to him for the past thirty minutes and showed no signs of abating, but Lax felt no inclination to fret about it. Yes, he was aware that he was prime sentinel and complete Overseer. But the calm spreader drugs administered by Dix, his chief medic, held his mind in a comfortably stable state, somewhere between floating in a weightless serenity furnished with the soft silky pelts of the Cooty Bear. A cute cuddly creature indigenous to Shard, similar to a Guinea pig but with ridiculously long hair. And the third stage of Glook induced euphoria. An event which produces results comparable to your average drunk on Earth draping himself over a complete stranger and declaring to the whole establishment that, "this man, this bloke, this great bloke is the best mate anyone could ever, ever have ever, ever, anywhere. Hic!"

These past few minutes however, he had consciously been experiencing a nagging doubt, a feeling that he should be engaged or needed elsewhere, something connected to the loud hammering bang. A microcosm of a suggestion from his subconscious told him that he possessed an awesome responsibility.

The familiar hissing of a door panel materialising fizzed. "And how are you feeling now Lax?" asked Dix from behind his Overseer, his tone somewhat more cheerily than it had any right to.

"Ah Dix my old friend," Lax welcomed, his eyes finally swivelling to greet his old colleague. "I feel rather good." He thought for a moment. "Yes I feel good," he ended, reaffirming his previous statement.

"Good, good," said Dix, opening a carry case container to reveal an assortment of medical equipment.

The *Paraxatar* vibrated violently as another explosion rippled through the ground. Lax looked uneasy, firstly at the nearest bulkhead as it shook from the reverberations and then to Dix.

"Dix," he enquired, leaving the question hanging for a moment. "Why do I feel that I should perhaps be making a contribution to what is happening outside, after all I am the Overseer. Look, it says as much upon my robes." Lifting up his left arm gracefully adorned with the calligraphy of the Desirion language he showed it to Dix as if to prove as much to the medic.

Dix ignored the remark, his face betraying a little suspicion. *Damn,* he thought, *Lax seems to be coming out of the drugs control sooner than expected,* and went straight to the container with the calm spreaders in.

The ship suddenly shook, the result of an impact not too violent but enough to make both Dix and Lax look up and cease their respective activities, which in Lax's case was very little. Another shockwave rippled through the superstructure, quickly followed by another and another, each one growing stronger and stronger. The outside bangs were soon accompanied by the sound of the command vessels own defences opening up.

Dix proceeded toward the still glowing doorway which opened with a fizz on his approach. Hoping to find the cause of this worrying disturbance he entered the light blue lit corridor. The sound of distant alarms blaring could be heard coming from both directions.

"I think Lax," he said turning. "That we should get you out of..." Dix never finished his sentence; his body was propelled forward by an explosion causing his head to collide with a bulkhead and knocking him unconscious. Lax fared slightly better, his entire frame lifted a good three feet from the sucking comfort of his recliner before landing with a heavy thud upon the floor, temporarily forcing all of the air from him. Like a beetle upon its back he wriggled around. Quickly regaining a small amount of composure he found his feet and staggered like a drunk towards the still open exit.

Dix lay to his right, Lax checked him. His head had received a nasty knock and very dark red blood, almost black, oozed from the resulting cut. Lax however, seemed happy he would be alright. Reaching the corridor outside he finally saw the reason for the mayhem. A number of the crew were running its length, each one behaving very apprehensively around a certain point. Here, a jagged hole, approximately five feet in diameter, had been pummelled into the outer hull. Layers of polymer hull fragments curled away like orange peel to stick out, while from outside the shockwaves and bangs continued to ripple through the Desirion command vessel.

XLIII

"Thir we mutht go... Thir hurry," shouted Woods, his voice displaying clear urgency.

"Yes Woods I'm trying, I can't free this bloody thing," Gary gasped desperately fumbling with the tunic of his battledress.

When Havelock and the marines had beaten a hasty retreat, Gary and Woods had sensibly thought it prudent to do likewise. Following in the wake of Sergeant Hornby they had initially made good progress until an energy bolt slammed into the ground just a few feet in front of them and flung them both headlong. Although not injured the two were somewhat stunned. Woods being the first to regain his composure, picked himself up and went to the aid of a flailing Gary who had resumed his earlier shouting tirade of "Bastards, bastards," as he had when grappling with the alien at the farmhouse. Unfortunately he had been blown onto a piece of old rusting farm machinery left in the field from many a year ago. A large twisted piece of metal had pierced the sleeve of his tunic, impaling the flapping left side of the chest area. Luckily, and some might say by sheer fluke it had not even scratched his skin but alas he was in a hopeless, tangled mess all the same and quite unable to free himself.

Woods watched before pointing out with a shout, "ith you wath to stop punching and kicking like a demented octoputh, we might get you free."

The outburst impacted upon Gary's mind and immediately he ended his flailing allowing Woods to attempt to unravel him.

The exchange between the Marines and the Desirions had ceased, for the moment, so Woods felt relatively safe to kneel while he worked. "Thir it's no good, I can't free it, you'll have to take it off," he said, already trying to force Gary's arm from the untangled sleeve.

A familiar sound now took over the battlefield, the sound of artillery shells, a rush as each round screamed through the air with the sound of a sudden singular oncoming hurricane. Woods and Gary both looked up hoping to identify the intended location of the ordinance but saw no point of impact. Curiously they heard no explosions, just heavy thumps until the sheer intensity of bangs; rushing sounds and thuds became completely intermingled.

"AP roundth," said Woods."

"Eh" replied Gary staring at his would be rescuer with wide staring eyes.

"That thoundth like AP roundth, armour pierthing," continued Woods, his head moving from side to side searching for the tanks which would inevitably deliver such a projectile.

"Err Woods, if you don't mind," said Gary indicating the coat before adding an exaggerated cough for encouragement.

"Thorry thir," said Woods and continued to free Gary from the farm machinery. "There you go," he said some moments later having at last managed to manoeuvre his companion from the tunic in the same way a mother would undress her three month old child.

"Thank you," said Gary. He was aware that Woods was staring at him, his shirt in particular.

Gary looked down, "I know, impressive isn't it?" he said, resplendent in the yellow ochre jersey of a Starfleet captain, Kirk era. The diagonal rip across the chest area of the material obtained when he had made his exit from the Landrover visibly evident.

At that moment the form of Sergeant Hornby and Langhorne emerged from the darkness.

"Thergeant," remarked Woods, his voice raising a couple of octaves at the surprise return of the NCO.

"Saw you was in a spot of bother," said Hornby referring to Gary being tangled up. "Didn't see you come in so I thought I'd better come look, don't like to lose an old soldier." This last reference spoke volumes. The mere fact that there was no mention of the hapless Gary was no coincidence and was all that needed saying.

More alien fire opened up but not in the area occupied by Woods and Gary, what did happen in that particular part of the battlefield was the sudden movement of the majority of the alien combat vehicles, all turning in the general direction of the castle.

Thath odd, thought Woods and then cottoned on. "They're heading towards the thound of that artillery," he said largely to himself.

The nearest Desirion vehicle, a transport, probably no more than fifty feet away, slowly began to get under way, its heavy tracks digging into the soft earth creating a deep furrow before finding a grip. It had only managed thirty feet before its absence revealed a group of armed Desirions, fifteen in number who had been assembled behind it. Gary, Woods and the two marines spotted them immediately, the latter dropping to the ground and laying down a fierce fire.

Woods did likewise but Gary emphasised his total lack of any combat training by standing fully erect and somewhat bravely blaze away with his thermal transfer energy gun, held out in front in the style of a green plastic toy soldier. As he operated the weapon he made a point of trying to look into the aliens faces. The look on their faces changed from surprise to one of determination and it wasn't long before they returned fire. It also wasn't long before this latest contact descended into a classic fire fight, two groups blazing away at each other until the inevitable odds that apply to battles of attrition take over.

Miraculously, no humans had been hit, no doubt thanks to Langhorne hauling Gary to the ground and informing him through the gift of sexually suggestive metaphors that if he wanted to live he would have a better chance in a horizontal position.

The Desirion numbers swelled to more than twenty but they had taken two casualties, both being dragged away by their comrade. It was clear however, that their numbers and firepower were just too great for the four humans. As if to force the issue the now advancing extra terrestrial soldiers loosed off a couple of well aimed bolts at them. Thankfully both missed but the ground in front burst apart showering them with clods of hissing earth most of which flew straight into their faces causing an enforced ceasefire. Hornby was the first to recover something resembling normal vision. Casually looking along his rifles sight he loosed off another round knocking an advancing alien off its feet but it was quite clear that they were hopelessly outnumbered. The responsibility weighed heavy round his neck. No soldier of responsibility would ever wish to be put in this position, but he was in that position now, that of surrender.

Langhorne, Woods and to a lesser extent Gary were laying down a heavy suppressing fire but the nearest aliens were no more than twenty feet from them and their numbers had increased yet again. Hornby looked down his sight once more but instead of firing he shouted to his companions to cease fire. Even to Woods who saw himself as some kind of invincible super human, impervious to all things earthly and capable of any feat, it was a no win situation and reluctantly he rested his weapon upon the ground before raising his hands and placing them behind his head. Gary, relieved to see Woods gesture threw his own weapon out in front of him and carried out a similar arm gesture. Hornby knelt, rifle at his feet and hands in the air as he looked into the face of the Desirion's as they came near. Recognising this gesture of surrender, the Desirion's complied by ceasing their own fire and at gunpoint forced the four humans to get up and walk in front, their destination clearly a waiting transport some two hundred yards distant with its entry hatch open awaiting its passengers.

XLIV

"Got em sir," said Corporal Clarkson as he searched for his missing colleagues through his night vision binoculars. His face fell at the next sight, that of Hornby and Langhorne with their arms behind their heads and a large number of aliens pointing guns at them while being jostled towards a caterpillar tracked transport vehicle.

"Sir," continued Clarkson, his tone a touch more sombre. "They've been captured and are being forced into one of those vehicles, one of the big buggers with tracks."

The next view was of Gary followed by Woods also being prodded into the transport, "those two dickheads are with them as well," he continued.

Havelock raised a hand and held it to his forehead gently massaging his furrowing brow. "Oh Jesus," he said, followed by a deep sigh. Quickly, he snapped back into life. "Right Corporal, take over Sergeant Hornby's squad, let's go."

To say that they actually had a plan was being very generous, the only strategy was, that as the aliens attention seemed to be taken up elsewhere, namely the newly opened up armour piercing fire from some unknown source, then they should be able to regain the element of surprise. Havelock took one final look through the binoculars and saw Woods climbing into the transport. Scanning it he couldn't see any of the others assuming that they must already be inside. He also noticed that as with the vehicles the number of aliens on foot was decreasing considerably as well, probably also moved away to areas of higher activity.

"Okay lads we have to be quick, we don't have much time," said Havelock and for the second time that night they climbed the farms low wall.

*

"Okay, Okay, don't push," said Gary as his back was prodded with the barrel of a gun. The Desirion seemed to be combining a good opportunity to prod while at the same time gesturing to Gary to sit in one of the seats. Langhorne and Hornby were already sat when he was jostled into the Transport, frustration and anger etched across their faces. Gary finally sat as Woods, the last of them was pushed up and into the vehicle.

"Don't touch me you damn ugly yellow bathtard," Woods

warned.

His comments were complimented by an even more ineligible gobbledygook than his own.

"Well done Woods," said Sergeant Hornby, "but I would recommend you comply with them.

"How can we do that if we can't understand what they are saying?" Gary asked, an air of cleverness thick within his tone. Another stream of quick dialogue spewed from the alien behind, which Gary assumed meant shut up or no talking.

The whip of the bullet slamming into the plastic material of the vehicles outer casing was completely ignored by Gary, as it was by the alien it was intended for. Not by choice but because it was dead before it had time to register that its head even hurt. It emerged from the other side of its head, sending the limp body crashing into Woods.

Woods, thinking it was the alien trying to hurry him up again glanced around intending to administer a seriously destructive stare followed by a thump if need be, but instead, saw two more aliens dropping and a line of camouflaged figures running towards them. At that moment the vehicles entrance closed with a smooth hiss and they were closed in. The Desirion's inside, fearing that the humans might react to the attempted rescue coming from outside trained their guns upon their captives, at least a dozen in number while another three busied themselves, operating various pieces of equipment or apparatus. Woods looked at the Sergeant, who in turn was glaring at the alien who seemed to be giving the orders, while Gary realised that the chairs they now sat in were downgraded versions of the one he had familiarised himself with on the downed alien craft back in Tarporley. He sunk into it before the contours began to envelop his lower body.

*

A number of aliens sheltering behind a nearby transport began to open fire upon the approaching Marines but were soon outflanked by Clarkson's unseen squad and the short contact soon fizzled out as they were either killed or fled. Havelock stood under the cover of the transport that they now occupied and looked about him. Six Desirions sat at their feet, he didn't need the encumbrance of prisoners but was unwilling to dispatch them as his orders depicted.

"O'Brian, tie these bastards up and put them in there," he said indicating the transport.

While the captive aliens were demobilised he scanned the field for the transport containing his men, Woods and Gary. With horror he realised that with the exception of the vehicle they now occupied there were no more static transports on the field.

Indeed there were four he counted, currently making good distance from him in the direction of the castle and with further horror he realised that his men had to be in one of them. The few vehicles left were either disabled or combat vehicles and there were few of them, all others having departed in order to counter the threat coming from the unknown attackers on the other side of the castle.

Havelock's initial thought was to follow the transports on foot, he knew they were travelling faster than he and his men could but he would pursue it anyway.

"Okay lads let's move, follow that..." His order was cut short by the mobile gun opening fire upon them. The first bright red energy bolt slammed into the ground plumb into the middle of Corporal Clarkson's squad, dispersing them like skittles while throwing great lumps of steaming soil and grass into the air.

"Scatter," shouted Havelock as he distanced himself from the man nearest to him. Gathering his wits he ran, no time to think, he just sprinted towards the gun which had opened up on his men. It fired again but this time finding no target as the scattering Marines had drawn its fire.

A couple more men had instinctively known the Lieutenant's intentions and now also ran at full speed towards the firing gun. Havelock reached it first, the crew noticing him at the last minute, a frenzied human, speeding towards them and giving them no time to draw personal weapons. Jumping up onto the slowly moving caterpillar track Havelock reached an extended arm into the open entrance hatch. Still holding onto the SA80, he pulled the trigger. "Have that you bastards," he shouted, all order and resolve gone. The other two Marines soon joined their commanding officer. Parvetti, following a similar line to that of Havelock, leant into the crew area and loosed off round after round. Hooper, the third marine launched himself bodily at the opening, landing on his stomach with his upper body leaning into the operator's area he looked in. Bringing his rifle to bare he fired only once, the sight convincing him that those inside were no longer capable of operating any equipment ever again.

In the still dark night Havelock breathed hard and heavy. Dropping from the caterpillar track he drew a blood splattered hand towards his face before checking at the last moment and wiped it on his battledress.

"Well done Hooper, Parvetti it won't be forgotten."

The two Marines exchanged glances of differing questions. Emerging from the darkness he could see the rest of the Marines and Royal Engineers joining him. The first to greet him was Clarkson.

"Corporal Clarkson, casualty report please," said Havelock, his demeanour calm again.

Clarkson paused. "Sir, Rainsborough and McCormack were injured. I'm afraid we lost Chapman sir, I ordered Rainsborough and McCormack to retire to the farm house, they've taken poor Chapman with them," as he finished Clarkson bowed his head.

Havelock's face remained unchanged. Extending a hand, he reached out and rested it upon Clarkson's shoulder. "Okay Corporal well done." His initial thoughts rested upon the loss of three dead and four others injured, but also with the missing Sergeant and Langhorne and to a much lesser extent the two civilians. *This is not going well,* he thought as he stared into the darkness.

This part of the field was now almost silent and pretty much deserted. Havelock gazed in the direction of the departing troop transports, swallowed up by the darkness. A few lights were visible at the base of the castle to enable work to continue on preparing the still dormant ships for readiness. In these illuminations he could make out a number of shapes, silhouettes of aliens tooing and froing. A vehicle began to move away some distance from them. As it cleared their view it revealed another hitherto concealed vehicle, this one was different from any they had previously seen.

"Binoculars," snapped Havelock with a click of his fingers. The desired item was handed down. Focusing upon the new vehicle it resembled a hovercraft, a large cushion all around its base. The vehicle wasn't in fact hovering and was clearly not working as it should. The main give away being the number of aliens clambering over it, complete with an array of tools. What was clear was that this vehicle's sole intention was to cause destruction in a big way.

Unlike other Desirion vehicles, vessels or craft, this one had an obvious area where a driver or operator would sit and control the vehicle. Along each side of its structure the now familiar energy gun sat, identical to those attached to the caterpillar tracked vehicles. On top of the superstructure, a third of the way down was what looked like a huge cavernous tube pivoted at the rear end, obviously a gun and a bloody big scary one at that.

The gears of Havelock's mind had already begun to engage. Hooper's suggestion of, "maybe we could make some use of that," was as late as the wakeup call of the early warning, impending natural disaster bell ringer of ancient Atlantis. Time wasn't however, their best ally right now and the best laid plans of mice and men seldom end up anywhere but caught in a man sized mouse trap.

"Corporal, take your squad, flanking movement on that vehicle now," barked the officer already on the move. "My squad, with me. You engineers get this gun firing upon that thing."

"Sir," came the reply from Corporal Clarkson, instantaneously followed by the clatter of equipment and a number of men moving quickly with a motive.

XLV

The Challenger's of the second royal tank regiment had begun firing from a distance of just over a mile. Approaching from a south westerly direction, having arrived via the A41, they turned off road and headed towards Beeston using minor roads where possible or cross country when those roads couldn't accommodate the huge vehicles. Quickly detected by the invaders they were under fire all the time, although not very heavy as the command ship they were attacking was suffering the not uncommon defensive systems glitches.

Having identified their target the crew's loaded high velocity, armour piercing rounds. The incredible speed of each shell, tipped with depleted uranium, was something in excess of fifteen hundred metres per second. Initially they were absorbed by the *Paraxatar's* shield but thanks to their static target, the tanks were able to deliver with pin point accuracy, each shell impacting more or less in exactly the same spot as the previous one. The highly controversial weapons had recently been outlawed amid concerns of radiation contamination after being fired, but in this instance it was considered of no consequence as they were being used against nasty aggressive invading extra terrestrials who shouldn't be here in the first place.

Each shell that struck made a larger dent in the hull until the law of averages took over. Initially a small hole appeared upon the fore area of the Alien vessel. The sight of this breakthrough gave heart to the men who began to pound away with even more ferocity and vigour, causing more and more blue flashes to ripple along the outer hull of the ship as very slowly breech after breech was made upon the defensive shielding.

Inside the *Paraxatar,* Lax inched his way along the corridor until he found himself just a few feet from the impromptu opening in the hull. He stopped, frozen as another impact, devastatingly loud, almost knocked him off his feet with the vibration. *That's not good,* he thought while the pleas of passing crew members, insisting that their Overseer remove himself from danger caused his suppressed thoughts to slowly de mist. Another round slammed into the aperture widening it further, shards of plastic polymer bending back until eventually pieces snapped off or splintered, showering those in range.

Curiously Lax felt no fear, if anything his face showed jubilation. This wasn't the supreme Overseer of the Desirion exploration and occupying force, dealt with the responsibility of the vanquishment of the Human species and the colonisation of

Planet Earth. This was Lax, a spaced out alien verging on a state of barking mad and currently investigating an ever widening hole in the hull of his command ship, a situation sure to send your average sentient life form, alien or otherwise scuttling for the nearest safe, comfortable hiding place.

Steadying himself he darted forward, poking his head to the very edge of the aperture until he could just see through the jagged hole and the darkness outside. Another shot slammed into the weakening shield, igniting another blue dance of sparks. Slowed tremendously it still thudded into the hull no more than five feet from his head. He could actually see it, its momentum almost halted before clattering to the ground, adding to a growing pile of spent ordnance.

"Ooh!" he uttered before jumping back, his lack of fear still in situ but not enough to blot out his sense of caution and natural instinct. "It's those awful Hooomanns again, I must tell someone."

Those privy to Lax's actions at that particular moment would have witnessed their supreme overseer turn around and skip back down the corridor like a child towards his personal chamber. On entering he was immediately aware of a form picking itself up from the floor. The figure, dressed in the robes of a medic, a very senior one at that, with a fair amount of blood, most of it now drying, smeared over and down his head.

"Dix my old friend, are you okay? What happened to you?"

A quick glance and images of the room came flooding back to him, his mind whirled and his head began to ache. Inside he felt happy and carefree but deep down he still had the nagging suggestion that he should be aware that he was something else, someone who shouldered a burden, but what?

Rising slightly, Chief medic Dix instinctively brushed small lumps of debris from his robes. He paused before rubbing his head, drawing his hand away quickly as the pain coursed through it. "Arrgghh," he groaned. "Lax?" he began, focusing on the Overseer. "Are you okay? What's happening?"

"It's those hooomann's again Dix, they err...*Lax, my name is Lax,* he thought suddenly. *Lax, Lax, Lax, over and over again, I'm important I'm important,* and then bang it all came back. *I am Lax, Supreme Overseer.* His expression changed dramatically because he realised he was really scared.

Dix was searching through the upturned mess spread across the chambers floor. Picking up a case he set it upright and opened it. As he did so a small amount of liquid seeped out followed by the tinkling sound of broken glass, "Damn," he said.

The damage was to the last of the Relaxing calm spreader drug he had dosed Lax with, the nearest other source would be in his infirmary, a few minutes journey at the best of times.

With the current attack still battering the ship who could tell how long it would take, not to mention his reluctance to leave his overseer alone for even the smallest amount of time. He glanced at Lax whose face was currently attempting to break the galactic record for individual feature changing in any given time period. Each expression a measure of his emotion as his thoughts readjusted to reality, the effect of coming down from the maintainer drug.

"Lax are you alright? Will you be okay while I go to the infirmary for a moment?"

"Dix, I am...okay...I'm fine... I don't need any more of your drugs, your maintainers, your calm spreaders...I'm okay, okay".

Dix looked unsure. To him, Lax's words betrayed his physical expression. Another bang, louder than the previous ones echoed down the corridor and into Lax's chamber, accompanied this time by a more intense vibration.

"Dix we have to get out of here," said Lax, all hint of lunacy gone, his voice displaying only cold emotion.

Although seriously unsure of his Overseer's state of mind, Dix was in agreement, they did have to leave this place, maybe even the ship. *And where on Shard are our defences?* Dix thought as he gathered a few effects. Shortly the pair exited the Chamber and headed towards the stern of the ship and away from danger.

XLVI

The Desirion brought out a small dull black device approximately the size of a shoe box. It looked cheap, the kind of storage box available for purchase in discount shops. Setting it down upon the console panel he connected it to the transports power system and with a barely audible fizz it seemed to liven up, causing a deep distorted rumble to emit from concealed speakers.

Gary watched as those Aliens not employed with pointing guns at their heads fiddled with the box, appearing to adjust its controls. On a bulkhead panel a face appeared and a conversation began between the face and one of those fiddling with the box. Shortly, unintelligible dialect flowed through the air. Gary looked at Woods who stared directly ahead, his face appearing to be in a state of meditation again.

"Grlllhung jiuopliknot," said the alien adjusting the box, amplified throughout the vehicle by the speakers.

"Wertyng druftyltrr gggh... fuck... trehhe...ing thing, I'll fucking... ooh think that it." He concluded rather happily. "Right," he continued; or rather didn't, not directly anyway. The English emanated from the speakers while the alien continued to communicate in its own tongue.

Gary looked up confused at first and then realisation dawned upon him, "a universal translator," he said aloud, this time his words translating to Desirion.

The alien tinkering with the box turned to Gary and eyed him, "correct you are puny Human," it translated

Sergeant Hornby was watching the extra terrestrial as was Langhorne. Woods however, was unbroken, meditation still holding his mind.

"Now humans, you," the Desirion pointed towards the Sergeant aggressively. "You answer questions."

"Hornby, Andrew, Sergeant, 6123789," said the Sergeant and then sat to attention in his very comfy chair.

"What?" said the alien, looking confused.

Hornby raised his middle finger, but the gesture was lost on the extra terrestrial.

"You," why you have different attire to others?" this next question was aimed at Gary.

Gary glanced at each of his fellow Humans. Hornby stared straight back at him, his eyes wide with a pleading look upon his face.

"Tell them nothing," he snapped.

"Silence," shouted the Alien.

A long pause ensued, "why in different attire are you?" It repeated.

"It's because," said Gary struggling, "I am a Starship Captain serving with the United Federation of Planets. Gary Spam, Captain, err 9768956.

All of the Desirions and Humans, which included Woods who had re-joined the real world, stared at him. Hornby, fearing that Gary would say the wrong thing and give away too much information couldn't believe what he had actually said. This however wasn't the end of it.

"And," Gary continued, feeling considerably braver now. "Let me point out to you Mister alien that, by holding us like this in captivity you are contravening inter stellar law. Amendment six, sub section seven I think you'll find. And when my superiors are informed about this there will be very strong repercussions I can assure you," he finished with a creditable wagging of his finger.

Sergeant Hornby had covered his face with his hand. The Alien strode purposefully towards Gary and slapped him across the face.

Woods leapt up, "Get your Dirty handth off him," he shouted before being forced to sit back down by a number of guns moving closer to his head.

"I command here," Said the Alien, "and do as you are told you will."

From the panel another face appeared. The alien who had been asking the questions operated a control on the translator before taking a stride towards the face. After a brief conversation the screen went blank and he returned to his subjects and operated the translator once again.

"Our destination has arrived. Transported you will be to our ship where you will further have questions." As if to confirm this the transport slowed noticeably before coming to a halt. The entrance at the rear swished apart and Woods, Gary, Hornby and Langhorne were invited to leave their seats and vacate the transport.

From outside the sound of battle returned to their ears although now much more distant, while in the sky the first vestiges of light were just beginning to make their impression on a still very dark scene. As their eyes adjusted to their surroundings they realised they were standing upon grass, possibly a field. Directly in front, as they emerged from the transport and impossible to miss, was one of the huge and impressive chewy rubber dog toy shaped ships. It's interior illuminating the field.

Frenetic activity continued all around, the aliens pausing

momentarily from their duties in order to gain their first glimpse of a Human. Woods glared back at them suppressing the almost involuntary impulse to shout or lash out. He also sensed a certain uneasiness among them, jerking his head towards the ship it dawned that this would be their one and only chance of an escape. In front was Sergeant Hornby and with a difficult to comprehend, whispered lisp, he managed to convey his sentiments.

The sound of artillery drew closer and just seconds later a huge bang ricocheted around the area. This explosion, close to the castle caused many of the aliens, their guards included, to instinctively duck.

Hornby took his chance, "Run," he shouted firmly.

They needed no second telling and as one all four humans sprinted in the opposite direction away from their captors. As Gary was at the rear he was the first to flee. Turning he was aware of the Desirion who had slapped his face. Already in motion he pulled his foot back and kicked it directly on its backside, toppling it over and forcing it to bang its head on the ground. Speeding past the sprawling figure he shouted, "That'll teach you to mess with Captain Spam; you green blooded, yellow, inhuman..." The rest of the insult was drowned out by another explosion rocking the ground and igniting the sky behind the castle with a brilliant luminous fireball.

Gary ran. He ran as fast as he had ever run before because he knew that within seconds he would be pursued by many aliens. His predictions weren't disappointed as the first bright orange bolt split a bush apart just a few feet to his right.

The texture under his feet suddenly changed and without looking down it was clear that he was now running on loose gravel, it was then that he recognised just where he was. The visitor's car park at Beeston Castle, a small half gravel half grass area cut into a field off the country lane. In front, looming from the darkness was a mock medieval building, the castles entrance. Glancing behind he realised with horror that he was on his own, *where were the others?*

More energy bolts came his way, some dangerously close. On his own or not he consciously decided, rather wisely that he would waste no time in trying to find out. Looking to his front, Gary's heart jumped with relief at the sight of Woods, Sergeant Hornby and Langhorne, who had at that moment overtaken him and were crossing the road and making for the arched entrance to the Castle. Tearing through, the thick stone walls gained them temporary relief from the alien firepower still hard on their heels. A further thought struck Gary that there were no guarantees that the castle grounds weren't also full of aliens.

No time to be cautious, not to mention their complete lack of options, the four fugitives came up against a door upon the left side of the building. Thankfully it rested slightly open and without a further glance they made a hasty entrance. Taking the lead Hornby slowed considerably as he crossed the threshold, wary of any presence lurking within. Once inside it became apparent that they were in the shop and visitor centre. Frantically glancing from side to side he sought a suitable hiding place but the whole interior seemed to be in a bit of a mess. Not through disruption from the invaders although they certainly had been in there. Prior to the unprecedented events of late, the visitors centre had been in the process of undergoing a refurbishment. English Heritage, having closed the monument for a fortnight to allow the work to be carried out. It looked as though the decorators had left mid work, the exhibition area stripped of all of its exhibits and information boards, replaced by masses of white protective sheeting, plastic and cloth. The odd stepladder sat propped against a wall while covering the floor was a whole host of decorating tools and at least a couple of dozen large tins of emulsion, colours varying.

To their left was the shop, blocked by a torn polythene sheet hanging down, with all its merchandise still on display and covered by similar sheeting.

"This will be a good place to defend for a short while said Hornby."

Outside the sound of pursuit was audible, with that Woods slammed the iron grilled gate on the outside of the entrance before closing the inner doors with a slam. Inside, the others began dragging anything heavy they could find to bolster the door which was already being tested by the aliens.

"Check for other entrances and make them secure," Hornby said searching the room.

The Whacks upon the door hammered loud as large bookcases and other pieces of furniture were wedged against it. Through the newspaper covered glass panels daylight began to filter through and peering, Woods could see the Desirion's. Unperturbed, he was confident they would hold for now, the glass being the reinforced type with steel wire running along its length.

"Thergeant we need thomething to protect ourthelves with," stated Woods moving into the half decorated area. He returned moments later with a wide grin and three decorator's knives in his hand. "They're not big but they'll do," he said as he offered the other two to Hornby and Langhorne.

"They'll do for a start," replied the Sergeant, eyeing the would be weapons, a little happier but still anxious. "Go back in there and check for anything else useful," this suggestion he offered to both Woods and Langhorne but only Langhorne took up the challenge.

"What about these? We could use these," Said Gary holding up a small wooden sword complete with dainty little rope coils bound about the handle. In his other hand he held a shield of similar design. Waiting for the inevitable rebuke he held his breath. Silence temporarily reigned and slowly he realised that it might not actually evolve. There were no compliments or acknowledgements either but beggars can't be choosers.

Sergeant Hornby's face screwed a little, "maybe," he said. "Use this to sharpen the points", he held out the decorators knife intending it to be used to turn the innocent children's play things into lethal weapons, or as lethal as is possible. "You can do the same to those bow and arrow sets too," Hornby continued, his eyes settling on the new wooden toys stored in a box on the floor.

All sounds of forced entry from outside had ceased but it was clear that the invaders hadn't left; footsteps and alien chatter could still be made out.

"We need some more heavy furniture," It was Langhorne, bursting through from the area being decorated."There's another door and I think our ugly little friends have just found it." He shouted in warning.

Following Langhorne, Woods and Hornby dashed through the polythene sheet. On the far side, partially obscured by a ladder with sheets draped over it the concealed door opened to reveal a Desirion. Quickly, it raised its weapon. Langhorne who was nearest leapt, the decorator's knife ready for use. Hornby began to move knowing he was already half a dozen yards behind but instinct forced him on. Woods however, searched the floor immediately around him; the nearest thing was a pot of paint, light grey he noted uselessly. Picking it up he held it aloft, *it's full,* he thought, *a good heavy weight,* and threw it.

Sailing through the air it just missed Hornby, passing his head by a whisker before slamming into the door frame on the Desirion's right. The alien had its gun in a firing position but its face showed confusion and hesitation, two moving targets rapidly approaching. It decided upon the nearest one, pulled the trigger and a bright orange bolt of sizzling plasma discharged from the gun, brushing Langhorne's hip and causing a painful burn before slamming into the far wall with a small detonation, gouging out a large burnt crater.

The tin of paint hit the door frame at exactly the same time as the alien fired causing it to slew to one side in order to avoid the clumsy missile. As it hit, the lid flew off, the paint inside, most of it splashing against the wall and open door not to mention the small amount which splattered Langhorne.

The remainder covered the left side of the aliens face. Righting itself it levelled the gun again. With taught finger muscles it attempted to pull the trigger but its brain wouldn't allow it, something else far more urgent was happening. The paint began to melt into the Desirion's head and shoulder area, screaming and writhing, it convulsed in the doorway therefore blocking it and creating an obstacle, temporarily barring its colleagues who were anxiously grouped behind. Langhorne had reached the alien now and just for measure buried his knife into its neck but it felt nothing from this new attack and seconds later its thrashing ceased. Quickly, Hornby pulled it into the room before Langhorne slammed the door with a heavy bang.

Hornby, Woods and Gary who had just ventured to join the fight sought more heavy items to jam against it. Woods managed to wedge a small step ladder beneath the handle which gave them time to find other suitable items. Less than a couple of minutes later the door was tightly shut with another large bookcase resting against it along with two more ladders and somehow Woods had managed to rip up the reception desk, still complete with cash till and drag it into the area before wedging it squarely against the door.

XLVII

The large Hover vehicle had, as was suspected broken down, its crew unable to get it to move. At that particular moment, motion was rather a priority, the sudden attacks by the humans being the prime motive. Panels had been accessed to reveal smooth lines of glowing tubes, rather resembling the underground map, each one a conduit for liquid and other substances to unseen areas. One tube however was not glowing and there lay the problem.

"That's it," remarked a very jumpy Commander Tox, to one of his crew.

The two Desirion's worked together to fix the problem, nervously ceasing their toil every minute to look about for more advancing Humans. This cautiousness slowed the process considerably and despite guards present to deal with any human threat, Tox was not happy, which deepened when the rest of the vehicles began to move away.

"Try it now," came a call from another headless figure buried deep inside the vehicles inner workings.

Tox's colleague climbed into the cab and illuminated a panel. The dull and lifeless tube slowly gained colour before glowing a healthy red. Moments later the whole craft lifted from the ground, stuttering at first until it hovered smoothly to a height of around a foot.

"Excellent!" Tox exclaimed. "Right, let's get out of here," he continued, eager to leave the area.

*

Corporal Clarkson's squad closed in on the hover vehicle from the right flank. As they had a good dozen yards head start upon Havelock, they were the first to realise that the aliens had fixed it and were in the process of embarking. The dozen or so sentry's were disbanding but Clarkson knew that they must attack now if they had any chance of taking it.

Signalling a halt he stopped and knelt, the area was relatively quiet, the sound of human artillery and small arms crackling mixed with the whooshes and fizzes of not so earthly weapons in what seemed like the far distance.

At a range of just two hundred yards the Marines opened up, the cracks of the rifles instantly spoiling the calm. The Hover vehicles operator was the first to go down while Tox took a bullet to the arm as he climbed aboard. All surprise gone, the Desirion guards returned fire in a very ordered way. A line of red, orange and yellow bolts lancing through the air almost in symmetry. It was very accurate too churning up the ground with a hiss just three feet in front of Clarkson's men.

Another alien was killed before the remainder, numbering around eleven guards and three crew, took shelter behind the hovering vehicle.

"Keep this rapid fire up," shouted Clarkson above the din, "can't let them seal the vehicle or get it moving."

With the slight back footing of the aliens a number of the Marines took a few steps forward, this was met with a second volley of fire. Corporal Barnet died instantly, his body taking three bolts while Parvetti was knocked backwards as he took one in the arm. Shocked though they were the Marines had no time to show it.

"Fucking bastards!" Clarkson yelled meaning every syllable as he pumped bullets at the enemy, while Starley and Hooper dashed forward to drag the stricken Parvetti to safety.

The vehicles protective shield was now engaged, giving off blue sparkles of light with every bullet strike and keeping the Desirions safe.

Now it was Havelock's turn to exact some revenge. Closing in on the left flank the Lieutenant had no idea of Clarkson's casualties. Drawing nearer they were greeted by the sight of a dozen or so Desirion's sheltering behind the hover vehicle, completely unaware of the closing marines to their rear.

Havelock briefly had second thoughts about opening fire on such an easy target and was even contemplating seeking their surrender when another group opened up on Clarkson's squad. In that same glare he saw the still form of a body, a Human and instinctively knew it was one of his men. A controlled rage built up within and with all sympathy suitably ejected, Havelock's men opened fire. The hail of bullets took the Desirion's completely by surprise with half a dozen dropping immediately.

The survivors ran realising their situation hopeless. One flung himself onto the ground, spread eagle and face down upon the mercy of the Marines. Another two escaped into the darkness but the rest were picked off by the murderous joint fire as Clarkson's men opened up on the fleeing confused extra terrestrials.

All gunfire ceased as Havelock quickly caught up with Clarkson's men. Approaching them he was aware of a number of bodies lying on the floor. The unfortunate Parvetti, his badly injured arm was being tended to and the even more unfortunate Corporal Barnet, who would never recover from his injuries. The horror of his losses was at the forefront of Havelock's mind but they still had duties to perform, the grieving could come later.

Sappers were already at work upon the hovering vehicle, with a steady hum it sat stationary. The Crew, including Tox the commander, had surrendered on seeing the demise of the rest of their comrades.

"Take up defensive positions, I don't think we've seen the last of those bastards," said Havelock. Glancing at the still forms of the aliens he had just dispatched, he noticed their weapons spread about. "Grab hold of them," he continued pointing at the guns. "Maybe they'll be of some use."

"Sir what shall we do with these two?" asked Park, one of guards standing over some captives.

Again Havelock felt the anger rise. His base instinct was to waste them. "Bind them and leave them where they are," he replied through gritted teeth. Turning back to the vehicle he heard the distinctive sound of violence being administered to the captives, refusing to intervene he strode towards the hovercraft.

"What have we got?" asked Havelock.

The Engineers were busy in the control area, a number of schematic diagrams open upon their laps. "Well sir," replied the sapper commander, Sergeant Hadley. "This is totally different, almost a completely new technology, no relation to their other stuff but I think we may have the measure of it. You see this control here?" The sergeant pointed to a large T shaped affair similar to an aircraft control stick. "I think this is the x and y axes elevation for that bugger up there."

Following the proffered finger Havelock was drawn to a huge cavernous barrel which ran the length of the crafts roof, he then offered the Sergeant a look of utter confusion. "X, Y, Christ can you get it to fire?" he snapped.

"Well yes we think so, but we need your authority to try it out," said Hadley.

"Err yes carry on Sergeant, yes," said Havelock cursing under his breath. *Honestly can anyone make a decision round here*, he thought.

"This control here is strange," said Hadley, indicating another lever, "I think maybe it works in conjunction with this," he continued, his features betraying not for the first time, apprehension.

Havelock held up a hand, "I don't care for the controls, can you fire it?" he repeated.

Hadley looked slightly crestfallen; he enjoyed explaining things to people and had been looking forward to doing so to the Marine officer.

"Yes sir but we don't know how to position the vehicle; we can't move the bloody thing".

A pause ensued as those present stared at the machine.

"Sir I've got an idea," offered Murray.

Havelock nodded.

"Well it's a hovercraft of sort's innit? Floating on a cushion of air?"

Havelock looked deep in thought as if attempting to unravel the mystery within Murray's idea.

"Yes," jumped Hadley, of course."

Havelock's penny still hadn't dropped.

Hadley didn't wait, arranging the marines to line up around the hovercraft and then Havelock grasped it.

"Aye of course that's right, very well done Murray," he congratulated, trying to cover up somewhat for his inadequacies.

Upon the order the marines and Royal Engineers heaved the machine around on its cushion of air until it faced the now deserted but worryingly closed up Desirion ship.

XLVIII

Temporary, Supreme Overseer Pox waited for news. All previous traces of the traditional time honoured and inbred calmness associated with the general workings of a Desirion vessel, war or otherwise, had completely dissolved and with good reason.

He waited for news of the battles raging outside. The Humans, it almost brought on a headache when the name of the species was mentioned, had changed their tactics drastically. His thoughts were all over the place and to be honest he was pretty much at a loss as to where to turn next. The all out full frontal attacks had been replaced by a stealthy Guerrilla, hit and run strategy. Firstly upon personnel, then using diversions, drawing the remaining armed vehicles away by attacking the command ship, add to that their new found knowledge of operating captured Desirion equipment. However, in this ever changing and ever darkening scenario the plan had changed once again. A far cry from the previous order to up sticks, relocate and attack the country's capital city, the order for a complete evacuation from the whole planet had been passed by Pox some thirty Earth minutes previous, the situation really was that grave.

Pox, Bex and many other high ranking Desirion's had made their way to one of only three unmolested Capital ships left upon the field. Lax and chief Medic Dix were nowhere to be seen and could not be contacted despite wide ranging searches. The Supreme Overseers chief advisor, Pix had delivered a message while bravely fleeing an attack. In his own words the damage to the command ship was so severe that it was unlikely that either were still alive. Far be it for Pox to take an advisors word as gospel he took it upon himself and sought complete clarification from sources in the field. Amidst all this chaos the *Luxera's* Hub was fully crewed, each one portraying a manner far more placid than that of Pox.

He paced, tapped, groaned, sighed, not to mention a number of other functions that Desirion or indeed Human kind had no name for.

The outline of a door appeared in the wall, fizzed brightly before the two halves separated to reveal Commander Bex with an anxious looking Pix scurrying behind. The latter trailed a good half a yard looking utterly dejected. The reason for his manner being the ever more likely permanent absence of his Overseer, sad though he was over the likely death of Lax, his main concern was that for all intense and purposes he would very likely become unemployed.

"Pox," said Bex firmly, "What are we stalling for, we should leave. Have you seen the state of things out there?"

"Firstly Commander," said Pox turning angrily upon the newcomer. "I am awaiting a full report on all events. Secondly..." He paused, his double elbowed arm reaching for the top of his yellow head before inserting a long finger into one of the small holes on top of it. His face screwed a little before he inspected it just as a child would after a successful nose pick.

"Secondly, we are going nowhere until I have every Desirion aboard. I will not leave them to the mercy of these damn Humans," he shuddered.

Bex spoke up again but was interrupted by the screen behind Pox illuminating into life with a face appearing on it.

"Commander I have news," said the face.

"Yes Mex report," replied Pox, knowing he didn't really want to hear, but relented to the inevitable; as he spoke he subconsciously flicked the finger he had used to poke his head hole. A panel operator directly next to Pox looked up in response to something hitting his head from above.

"Commander we have three Capital ships, the *Nerax*, the *Axam* and our own *Luxera* ready, serviceable and awaiting the order to depart. A further three, the *Garefex and Xeboc* are damaged and the *Salax* has been destroyed, the *Paraxatar* is also badly damaged and unserviceable. All units have been given the recall but many are engaged in heavy fighting on a number of fronts with small groups of humans. All other capital ships and transports bar one have left the area and are on en route to the fourth planet. Commander..." Mex paused and lowered his head, "I have no news of the supreme Overseer."

"Thank you Mex that is all," Pox said calmly; The Hub was quiet, bar the continuous subtle sounds of operation. "So there you have it," Pox stated to a smug Bex, this time he had no answer. Striding toward the viewing area, he took one look and turned away. "Give the order to leave to begin final evacuation," he said just about audible.

XLIX

General Fartlington had finally left King Charles tower upon the walls in the centre of the city of Chester, much to the relief of the skeleton staff he had ultimately left behind. Along with Colonel Watkin and an entourage of other shirt tail grabbing, promotion seeking hopefuls, he had requested transport to take them to RAF Sealand.

A slow drive through the vehicle clogged city streets, dodging large numbers of worried looking civilians, their sense of concern deriving from the huge palls of smoke slowly drifting over Chester on the prevailing wind from Beeston. Finally they were delivered safely to the redundant crumbling air base. Once inside, Fartlington had assumed control of the entire operation, advising the newly arrived Home secretary of the latest proceedings. Whilst these briefings were taking place reports began to filter in from Beeston castle stating that the many small covert squads which had been put into the area were enjoying very considerable successes against the alien invaders. In fact it seemed they were enjoying such success that some reports stressed that the aliens were in fact evacuating.

"This is splendid news," the General announced to the Home secretary on receiving the information and then he paused. The smile slowly faded from his face as he looked at the sweating soldier who stood by him.

"Corporal, are there any reports of Seventeenth Century soldiers in the vicinity?"

The Home secretary looked up.

"Err no, none at all sir," the corporal barked in a voice loud enough for the parade ground.

"Are you sure?" He asked again.

"Yes sir quite sure," he repeated although much quieter this time.

"Very well that's all," he said.

The NCO left the room and the Generals smile returned. "Home secretary," he said, leaning across the table to pour himself a brandy. "I think it would be appropriate to mobilize operation Flusher."

The Home secretary raised an eyebrow, "I thought you said the ground forces were successful?"

"Indeed they are," replied Fartlington, "And this is the perfect time to implement it."

Operation Flusher was the mobilisation of an ever present

force of men comprising two infantry Brigades accompanied by large amounts of supporting light armour, covered from the air by a force of attack helicopters not to mention the use of attack jets if required. Included in this force was a unit of United States, light infantry tanks. Not particularly needed but requested by the Prime minister as a political move just to keep our friends across the pond happy. The thought of a major dust up occurring and them not being involved in some way, was, to them, unacceptable, even if as almost always happened it meant bombing your own people. The added forethought also contained the hope that maybe the trigger happy Yanks would possibly think twice about deliberately instigating the use of a nuclear device upon their own troops should things go wrong.

The large force of military hardware and muscle was originally intended to act as an instant defence force should the aliens descend upon Chester again, however, the top brass were sufficiently impressed with the goings on at Beeston that it was considered a prudent move to keep the momentum going by backing up the small squads with an attack en-masse, and if the unexpected did occur, in that the invaders did in fact mount another challenge upon Chester. Then an even larger number of men and hardware were already in position ready to defend it.

L

"Spam, you're going to have to do something about the clothing, you stick out in the darkness like a lollipop Lady caught in a full beam." Sergeant Hornby said referring to Gary's attire.

He had been employed with filling a large number of small clear plastic bags with paint which had been found in a small office down some stairs, behind where the reception desk used to be, until Woods generously removed it.

The rediscovery of the acidic reaction caused by paint was an additional weapon to their arsenal, while the bags had given Woods the idea of using them as paint bombs not to mention employment for the otherwise useless Gary. Pausing from his work Gary smiled at first, thinking that Sergeant Hornby was joking. When it dawned upon him that he wasn't he felt offended. Wearing the clothes synonymous with his heroes gave him a sense of greatness, almost bravado, just as a teenager feels comfortable dressed in the latest fashion, however ridiculous they should look.

Gary did look ridiculous but all the same it gave him that feeling of superiority and he didn't feel like a total dickhead at all.

"Ith very quiet out there!" exclaimed Woods, sharpening wooden arrows with the small decorator's knife. He appeared the proper little carpenter, whittling away while a small pile of wood shavings steadily grew at his feet. It wasn't however just the arrows he had transformed from innocent children's play things, equipped with a harmless sucker into that of a lethal missile. There were at least three dozen now, stowed in the little hessian quills, along with a whole host of wooden medieval weapons of death ready to employ upon an unsuspecting alien force.

Langhorne had decided to pull back a corner of the paper covering the window. As he peered through the small triangle it offered them vital information and it was very bad. "Sarge," he called, the corner of paper still resting against his nose. "Better check this out."

Gary's recent sulk had fizzled out at around the same time as he had finished filling the last of the bags with paint. With no other tasks assigned to him he took advantage of the current lull in activity and decided to explore the small area they now occupied. Passing to the far side of the shop he noticed a door which opened to reveal a large storage cupboard. "Hey look...at...this," he uttered, his eyes opening with wonder at what lay within. As usual no one took any notice. Woods was still busily engaged on shaping wooden weapons into ever more sadistic shapes while the two marines were tasked with studying the scene outside of the window.

"Guys come and have a look at this," repeated Gary, only to be met once again by silent ignorance.

The more pressing news was outside. The view obtained by Hornby and Langhorne showed that the Desirion's had manoeuvred a caterpillar tracked mobile gun into the car park across the road. It didn't appear to be aimed at them but there were no doubts about their intentions.

"We need to get out of here now," said Hornby moving away from the window and pointlessly replacing the small triangle of newspaper. "They're bringing up the heavy stuff." Then he paused. "Although they'll never be able to drive it through the gate, it's too big," he continued, "at least I hope it is. He paused again, deep in thought. "They're going to take out the outer wall," he indicated, slapping the inside face of the said wall with his hand.

"Well I'm finithed here," said Woods, "we had better equip ourthelves with thethe."

Langhorne grabbed hold of the supply of paint bombs and placed them into four plastic carrier bags, "about ten each," he said. "We could take the remaining tins with us," thinking of their possible usefulness.

Woods handed everyone a small wooden Longbow and a supply of arrows before reaching down and picking up a wooden crossbow. He waited for complaints regarding his superior weaponry but they weren't forthcoming.

"Where is Spam?" Hornby asked, his head rotating like an owl searching for prey. He always felt concern when the bumbling Gary was not in his immediate vision.

The other two returned blank looks.

"Spam, we're leaving, come on," he shouted although not too loudly.

A metallic thunk and tinkling could be heard at the far end of the shop, followed by Gary's strained and strangely distant voice. "What do you mean we are leaving?" He said sounding like someone in dire need of a lavatory.

The others looked toward the sound of the voice before confronting each other with looks of worried appeal. Hornby forcefully strode towards the cupboard from which Gary's voice was coming. "There is a mobile gun coming this way and in something like a couple of minutes this building will be a pile of smoking rubble.....oh-my-god."Hornby stopped dead in his tracks and stared aghast into the confines of the cupboard.

More metallic thunks and jangles emanated from within,

"hang on just a moment," said Gary.

"Sarge we really need to leave now," said Langhorne; the seriousness upon his face revealing all that needed to be said.

"Spam, move yourself, I'm not fucking about," said Hornby recovering his senses.

No sooner had he spoken when clangs, clinks and strained movement was heard with Gary eventually emerging.

No longer visible was the distinctive yellow ochre torn shirt. Gone were the black turned up trousers of a Starfleet Captain even though he still wore both. What stood out more was the full set of replica chain mail and steel armoured trousers, each link carefully and skilfully connected to the next to form an impenetrable shield. A similarly made tunic covered both arms as far as the elbows, right up to the full chain link balaclava tucked tightly beneath his chin, the cause of his strained voice. Within this, a flesh coloured egg glowed visibly, the oval broken only by the nose protector protruding from the steel helmet which crowned the whole outfit. A broad grin beamed out almost touching either side.

Hornby however, was far from smiling. His resolve and politeness had finally hoisted a white flag and departed upon the road of no return. "Spam," said the sergeant, his voice full of all the menace of years of enforced military aggressiveness. "What the fucking hell do you think you're doing you stupid bastard? Get that ridiculous…"

Suddenly the whole building violently shook, the front wall visibly moving.

"Shit," cursed Hornby, guessing correctly that the sudden disturbance was the result of a hit from one of the mobile guns outside. "Quick over there now," he shouted, indicating the rear of the building, the part which was in the process of being decorated.

This order didn't seem to include Gary although if truth be told, the Sergeant had discharged responsibility of the armour clad moron. All the same Gary headed in that general direction, first moving his left leg, the metal rings scraping together to make a heavy clanking sound. Surprisingly, although intensely heavy and cumbersome, movement wasn't quite as difficult as he had anticipated. The right leg soon followed and within a few seconds he had managed to master a curious motion whereby his legs didn't bend to propel him, rather a sideway sweeping motion with straight legs all the time, causing his arms to adopt a similar movement to counter the awkwardness. He resembled the tin man from the Wizard of Oz but far more exaggerated, all the same it took him steadily to the visitor centre and away from danger.

Over on the far side, the door which had been obscured and

subsequently breached by the aliens was now open again, this time by human hand, allowing the gathering daylight to flood through. Slowly and with utmost caution a heavily camouflaged figure could be seen moving almost in slow motion. In his hands a crude child's wooden long bow, loaded with a similar arrow sharpened to a point. A number of other arrows protruded from a hessian quarrel attached to his belt while also tucked into that belt was a wooden short sword and a wooden dagger, both similarly sharpened.

Behind Hornby was Woods. He was simply bristling with homemade weaponry. Foremost was the Kukri knife, held firm in his right hand, while slung over each shoulder was a wooden bow. Quarrels of arrows, sharpened wooden stabbing weapons and a plastic bag full of paint bombs hung from his belt.

"It's clear out here at the moment," said Hornby, venturing further through the heavy door.

Woods followed, who was in turn followed by Langhorne, himself similarly adorned with rudimentary weaponry. Hornby noticed Woods Kukri and wondered how the hell, or more worryingly, where the hell he'd managed to conceal it when they had been taken captive by the Desirion's. Finally, far behind all of them clanked Gary, who, although finding the art of motion somewhat easier as he walked or rather straddled, the combined knack of rapidity and motion was just that bridge too far. As he passed the table he made a grab for one of the wooden swords laid out where Woods had been working. His metal clad arm colliding with the table, sending the swords clattering to the floor, "damn," he said.

It was here that a further problem presented itself, that of bending down. Simply put, he couldn't. At that moment another strike from the mobile gun brought half the outer wall down and engulfed the building with plumes of choking dust and flying masonry. Not wishing to feel the effects of the alien weapons for a second time Gary swiped at a plastic bag which contained the paint bombs and exited the building, following the others as fast as his state would allow.

Passing through the doorway he immediately felt the effects of the early rising sun as it cast a deep red orange glow upon the hill ascending towards the castle. In front he could see Woods, Langhorne and Sergeant Hornby, sprinting for the relative safety of a nearby heavily wooded area covering the steep slope.

The first alien appeared around the corner from the partially destroyed gatehouse, amazingly, it didn't spot Gary. It did however, see the three running figures. Raising the gun it fired, the bolts discharging into a tree ahead of Hornby whose instinct was to make for the ground. Realising that the alien was intent on firing at the others Gary delved into the plastic bag full of paint bombs. The alien was quickly joined by two more of its comrades who also opened up.

The two Marines and Woods hadn't reached the tree's but fortunately had found considerable cover behind a deep contour with large bushes and young saplings spread unevenly along its crest, not brilliant but enough to partially shield them from view at least.

Incredibly the Desirion's were still taking no notice of Gary as he clanked and tinkled, armed with a paint bomb in his hand and another in reserve. Slowly the invaders began to move towards the hidden humans. As they neared they were earnestly greeted with a fearful hail of stones, heavy sticks and small wooden arrows intermixed with shouted statements informing them in which direction they could go and how they were to do it.

The arrows proved next to useless, the slight breeze deviating their course in the same way a cheap plastic football brought from beach kiosks and emblazoned with the name super striker does when given a half hearty kick.

The stones and sticks did no real damage either, dispelling on this occasion a well known saying. What they did do however was to check the advancing aliens, whose numbers had swelled to six with the promise of many more approaching from the gatehouse.

This gave Gary his opportunity. At a distance of perhaps forty feet he took careful aim at the group of Extra terrestrials, bringing his arm back as far as the metal suit would allow he let fly. As he threw, the weight of the armour almost wrenched his shoulder from its socket, but the pain was soon forgotten as he saw with joy that his bomb had scored a direct hit upon the closest alien.

Stunned at first, purely by the unexpected impact upon its torso the Desirion briefly stared at the odd looking metallic thing from which the missile had originated. Curiosity soon turned to pain and then agony as the paint burned into the unfortunate being like acid. Not expecting this counter attack, the other five aliens, fearful of their writhing companion on the floor who was on the verge of administering his death kicks, stepped back a few paces before as a one they raised their guns and aimed at the strange medieval figure on their left flank.

Sensing the inevitable, Gary let fly with the other bomb, his free arm scrabbling blindly into the plastic bag for another at the same time. Throwing as hard as he could, harder than the last, it impacted the ground five feet in front of his target, the only damage caused by splatters of paint splashing onto their legs.

This last unsuccessful salvo was in fact Gary's saviour and downfall all in one. The strength and power he had administered in the throw not only nearly dislocated his shoulder once more but the momentum caused him to overbalance, the extra weight of the suit forcing him down like a lead balloon to smash into the ground with a thudding crash. "Urrghh," he grunted as his lungs were squeezed. At that precise moment the Desirions opened fire, each bolt perfectly aimed, flying through the vacant air in the exact position of where Gary had stood just moments earlier.

The sudden change of target gave Hornby his opportunity and he took it. Without a word, for none was needed, the three figures, Hornby, Langhorne and Woods burst up and out of the small depression and through the bushes brandishing wooden weapons. As they descended upon the unsuspecting aliens they took on a far more sinister appearance.

Langhorne was the quickest; covering the small distance first he leapt upon the nearest Desirion, burying the point of the wooden sword deep into the upper body, blood soaking into the blade in great gushes. The unfortunate Alien crumbled, impacting the ground heavily and bellowing a deep guttural scream. The others attempted to scatter but had no time to even slightly evaluate the situation.

Hornby was next into the melee taking an alien down with a rugby tackle, the shocked figure being dispatched with a dagger to the throat as it fell. Woods came on in his own inimical style, the Kukri held aloft like a cleaver while screaming like a demented Banshee before descending upon the hapless alien like it's worst nightmare, which to be fair wasn't far off the mark. The wicked Ghurkha knife never found its target, the alien dodging the blade after noticing Woods at the last moment. The momentum of his attack did bring it crashing down with the raging Van driver on top of it, once sufficiently recovered the two combatants entered into a half scuffle, half fist fight.

The two remaining aliens, backed off, the sight of four of their comrades rapidly and ferociously taken out filled them with abject fear and the need to seek out security in numbers.

The words, "eat that you filthy bathtardth," echoed from Woods as he finally ended the living career of his latest adversary.

Two more Desirion's appeared from the gatehouse entrance but were swiftly met by energy bolts administered from the guns of their dead comrades, turned upon them by the humans.

Gary stared at grass and soil from a very close range as a troop of ants marched beneath his face. The last one stopped, turned as if to look at him and nipped the tip of his nose with its powerful pincers before scuttling away.

Wallowing upon his stomach like a beached Whale he was

unable to get up, unable to do much except thrash about hopelessly. He could look ahead, just, although this movement combined with the restriction of the chain mail helmet almost cut his wind pipe in two and so wisely he ceased.

Taking a laboured glance, he gained a small idea of what was going on since he had joined life in the undergrowth. Initially he had expected nothing more than the effects of a searing hot energy bolt coming into contact with him, followed, hopefully by a quick and painless death.

Obviously as his vision was still taken up with close contact grass examination the inevitable had not happened. Looking left again were the six aliens who had been firing in utter confusion before being descended upon by the others. The Gatehouse to his rear where they had sheltered not so long ago had sustained further hits from the mobile gun but rather than gain the aliens entry, all it had in fact achieved was to destroy it and block any vantage point.

Word had obviously got back that the humans had broken out and in addition to nasty sharp items; they were now armed with bolt guns, emphasised by the evident caution being displayed. This allowed a lull in activity and the next thing Gary new was that he had been grabbed around the ankles and was being dragged across the ground in a backwards motion. As he was pulled his face was dragged through all manner of flora and fauna, not to mention various other substances not altogether pleasant and he had to use all the strength he could muster in his neck to avoid substantial facial injury. Aware of a sudden lack of sunlight he assumed that he was being pulled through dense undergrowth or at least a shaded area. His mind had barely comprehended his latest journey when all movement came to a halt, whereby he was unceremoniously dumped in a tangled heap.

Still laying face down and unable to turn himself over Gary became aware of the change of terrain. Gone was the soft green grass, replaced instead with the rotting, under canopy detritus of a dense wooded area.

Feeling hands upon him once more he was crudely turned over. The first face he saw was the sweating form of Sergeant Hornby, calmer and somewhat gore splattered with Woods peering over his shoulder.

"Right Spam, get that bloody armour off," he spat before leaving Gary's field of vision.

Woods bent down and began relieving him of his cumbersome garments. "I wouldn't worry thir, he'th actually quite pleathed with you, the way you attacked them gave us a chanthe to kill them and find sathety."

Gary grinned, "Yes Woods of course," he replied, rather

surprised, *although it wouldn't have hurt him to have said so himself,* he thought.

"It was all actually under control Woods," Gary continued. "I realised you were in trouble and thought you could do with some help," he blurted, ending the sentence with a large sigh, mainly in relief as Woods tugged the heavy helmet from his very sweaty head.

Woods didn't comment, instead he stood up.

"Err Woods?" Gary called, leaving the question open, "err hello, need a little help here," he continued in a mock American accent. Moving his head round as best he could, which was still very limited, he saw the same concerned look upon the faces of Sergeant Hornby and Langhorne although by now Woods had assumed a satanic grin. The three were all concentrating their attention in the same direction, towards the gatehouse and although Gary was unable to force his head in that direction it didn't take the brains of a genius to work out just what they were looking at.

Without warning his legs were gripped again and he was dragged once more into even denser woodland further up the slope.

LI

"I'm not sure what this weapon will do sir," remarked Sergeant Hadley the Engineer attempting to operate the hovercraft.

"Sergeant," said Lieutenant Havelock with yet another sigh, "if we don't open fire, that ship, by the look of things won't be here much longer. If it blows up and kills us I will assume personal responsibility," he finished, rather tongue in cheek.

The Sergeant grinned, not because he found it funny but more to cover his own nervousness and anxiety. "Okay sir here goes."

The huge tube atop the hover vehicle boomed, in an identical fashion to that of human artillery pieces, not a major surprise really as this was essentially exactly what it was doing, firing a projectile. That however was where the comparisons ended, for what flew from the muzzle was no shell. All they saw was a bright orange ball burst from the tube and rotate towards the alien ship. The short distance was covered in no more than a couple of seconds and a miss was out of the question thanks to the point blank range.

As it hit, the glare spread, enveloping the entire vessel with a sparkling orange plasma lightning show. Intermixed with it were blue sparks as the shield battled with the hostile weapon. The diminishing blue fizz indicated that the shield might just be losing while a few moments later the orange colour from the projectile itself began to dissipate. As it disappeared, the ship, although structurally intact, looked very much the worse for wear. The red brown colour of the outer hull, visible in the early morning light had been replaced in many areas with one identifiable with heavy scorching, more akin to a vessel subjected to many months of constant battle conditions.

Havelock stared at the ship through his binoculars, its surface looked melted. Scanning fore and aft he felt a certain satisfaction. That was until the hexagon shaped structures rotated upon the large rings surrounding each sphere. With horror he quickly realised they were weapons. Rising, he shouted to the engineer Sergeant before returning his gaze once more to the ship.

"Sir," Hadley replied in response to Havelock's order to fire, "I'm not sure if it will," concern was etched across his face as he faced the officer.

"Fire the bloody gun," shouted Havelock.

Hadley pulled back the lever and rested two fingers upon the relevant area of the touch panel.

BOOM!!! It echoed but with surprisingly little recoil; a second bright orange ball of destructive energy was on its way.

The ship's crew, long since realising that it was time to bid farewell began to lift off. As it did the fore guns began to fire, a continuous stream of plasma lancing through the air, striking the ground no more than ten feet in front of the hover vehicle.

Havelock watched as the bolts crept towards them while from the corner of his eye he marked the progress of the orange ball, the couple of seconds it took to complete its journey taking a lifetime.

Crack! the huge alien ship's energy bolts had found their target, the first direct hit connecting with the front right hand corner of the hovercraft causing the superstructure in that area to buckle and melt. The impact forced the craft to jump, first downwards then up before settling again. The humans inside, some heavily bruised were buffeted about like toy soldiers. As their senses returned they realised they were moving backwards, the impact had shoved them a good twenty feet, and then the sky in front turned orange.

The second ball of rotating energy had found its target slamming into the rearmost sphere a good ten feet below the first impact point. As it struck, what remained of the defensive shield said a final so long and took a permanent holiday. As before, the entire ship was enveloped by the bright glowing orange lightning show until some seconds later the entire form could be seen to buckle. The outline bent before twisting out of shape until with an enormous explosion the vessel blew itself out of existence.

The shockwave rocketed upwards and outwards not to mention the sizable crater gouged from the ground. A red, orange inferno reached towards the heavens with alarming speed, far more impressive than when the transport happened upon a similar fate. Like a pyroclastic flow it travelled outwards reaching Beeston castle, causing considerable structural damage to the ancient building. Large chunks of the north and west wall toppled into the bailey while similar pieces of the opposite wall took the long drop, smashing into even smaller lumps and coming to rest among the trees below.

The shockwave didn't spare the hover vehicle either. Its proximity to the detonation was far too close to escape, however once again the very nature of its build was its saviour although not entirely.

Preceding the fireball was a wall of invisible kinetic energy, a shockwave which struck the hovercraft like a cricket bat hitting a ball. The craft accelerated from zero to sixty miles an hour in a second, the sudden backward propulsion slamming all those within, up against the rear bulkhead or against the seats they sat in. Those not directly involved with the craft had retreated from the area when the firing had commenced and had now reached the relative safety of the railway line behind the hills at Beeston auction site. This was the exact place where the hovercraft eventually came to rest. The momentum carried it ahead of the terrifying wall of flame which to the thankful, watching eyes of the crew, dissipated before causing any serious injury to the Marines. Alas for those inside the hovercraft, they were unable to steer or stop it and therefore open to the mercy of whatever lay in their path.

They could see the hill behind them as it approached, their speed slowing considerably but not enough to avoid the inevitable. As the hovercraft touched the slope the cushion of air accepted it as just another contour to overcome although this one proved a little too steep. With the vehicle almost vertical, alarms began to sound, lights flashed upon panels all around them. Not that Havelock and his men were noticing them much; they were doing all they could just to hold onto something and avoid being ejected. Giving in to gravity the craft eventually began a new career upon its roof.

By then the velocity was little more than a crawl, but this was still sufficient to throw its occupants to the ceiling which had now became the floor, causing Havelock to slam his head into a stanchion and sustain a nasty gash to his temple. Murray and Flynn were unfortunate too receiving a broken arm and hand respectively.

The craft came to a rest at an angle, the large gun causing it to pivot on one side. Havelock untangled himself from his own limbs and wiped a hand across the side of his head, "arrgghh," he exclaimed aloud wincing with the sudden pain, blood thick on his hand.

"Here sir let me have a look at that for you," said the welcome and somehow calming voice of Sergeant Hadley as he climbed from his seat. Hadley firmly pressed a torn piece of material to the Officers head wound, he winced once more.

"Is everybody else okay?" Havelock asked, the pain obvious behind his gritted teeth.

"Think me arms broke sir," came a pained cry from Murray as he was tended by another soldier.

Those who had escaped the short melee and sought refuge behind the hills appeared once more hurrying to their comrade's aid. Shouts of, "is everyone okay?" and, "where's the Lieutenant?" could be heard. Once all were accounted for and wounds and injuries bound they vacated the shelter of the upturned craft. Havelock stared towards a huge burnt patch of ground with a sizable crater in the centre, strewn with blackened debris where a large alien spaceship had once stood.

The farmhouse, where they had sheltered behind the low wall was now well ablaze, the whole scene apocalyptic.

Despite all of this Havelock was able to offer a grin, "got him," he muttered under his breath.

LII

The latest massive explosion had jerked Lax into some resemblance of sanity, enough to realise that his force was rapidly disintegrating around him. Bravely he attempted to get away.

Returning to the Hub of the battered *Paraxatar,* he entered an almost false scene. The ship rocked from repeated blows, but at least the command vessel was finally returning fire. It was incredible how those Desirion crew members operating consoles and panels continued as serenely and efficiently as usual, not the least trace of panic upon their faces or in their actions. The only vision of anxiety was that of Chief Medic Dix who paced, anticipating the return of Lax.

The Supreme Overseer bent over a panel, the operator moving aside to allow access. "Put out a fleet wide call. I want to know exactly who is still alive and which ships are operating," He said with authority.

"Lax we must leave here," challenged Dix, clearly frightened. "And what on Shard was that huge explosion?"

"Majestic Overseer," the operator paused," that was the *Axam.* It's been destroyed."

Lax and Dix offered hopeless glances to each other, "Poor Arx. How has it come to this? We should have been victorious, everything pointed to a glorious victory," Lax's face was almost white, most of the colour having long since drained away.

"Majestic overseer, there are currently two ships still operational, the *Luxera,* Commanders Pox and Bex are aboard. The *Nerax,* commanded by commander Zex is just three hundred and fifty Metres away," said the console operator almost as if he knew of his overseer's intentions.

Crossing to another touch panel, Lax changed the view to one showing the outside of his own ship. It was full daylight now and once the smoke cleared, provided good visibility. He flicked through the various views available until the *Nerax* came into view. Enhancing it further he changed to panoramic. Now he could see the entrance to the building the Hooomanns called Beeston castle or rather what was left of it. Two guns were entering the area beyond the ruined gatehouse with another couple waiting, accompanied by a large number of troops. Coming the other way, carried by their comrades were what appeared to be the bodies of Desirion's, at least half a dozen. Lax turned from the screen. In that split second he came to a decision, "Dix accompany me please," he said and left the Hub.

Once in the corridor Lax explained his plan to his Medic, "one of the escape vessels it's the only way," he pleaded his case.

Dix looked horrified, "Lax you can't. You can't desert your people, you're the supreme overseer."

"Dix, this fight is over, we must retreat to the fourth planet and rejoin the remainder of the fleet, we can hold out there and wait for reinforcements." Lax replied.

Although in agreement with the latter part of the plan, Dix was reviled by the thought of Lax deserting his people. "I'm sorry Lax I want no part in this, you must reconsider, we will persevere and be victorious."

Lax gave the medic a look, "For goodness sake have you seen the state of things out there? We are finished." The whole ship juddered alarmingly before slowly, very slowly it began to take on a list.

The Challenger tanks which had been pounding the command ship had come in for some punishment of their own when their target had returned fire, quickly losing a third of their force. The depleted attackers had had a rethink on tactics; a suggestion from a commander that another ship had been crippled when its stanchion had been destroyed had been taken on board. A tricky manoeuvre with such a small target but it was becoming more and more evident that it would take considerably more pounding to put this vessel out of action. With casualties rising, not to mention the ammunition reducing at a rapid rate the suggestion was carried out and with success.

Huge cheers erupted from the crews as the supporting leg not only gave way but was completely amputated. This new event also put more doubt into the mind of Dix. His own thoughts of self preservation slowly came to the forefront again and all of a sudden Lax's idea of using one of the escape vessels wasn't as immoral as it had sounded just moments ago.

Quickly the two senior Desirion's made their way along corridors, passing nervous crew members with many offering their seniors anxious and worried glances. They soon came upon the lift entrance they sought and on entering they too exchanged nervous glances before Lax spoke.

"We have no choice, we must get away." As he spoke the general order was given to abandon via a ship-wide announcement. Strangely, after a moment this it was replaced by calming sounds designed to sooth, accompanied by ever changing calming lights flooding through each room and corridor.

The lift door opened to reveal a large open area. Within were a number of escape craft, small but capable of carrying thirty occupants, maybe more in an emergency. They were identical in design to that of the reconnaissance craft and combat aircraft.

The commander in charge of this section, who had not attempted his bid for safety yet, eyed the two curiously. "Majestic Overseer," he offered, bowing.

"Which craft is ready?" asked Dix, tension overcoming him and now more eager to get away than his overseer.

"Err, any, they are all operational," he replied but his words were lost on them both as Lax and Dix were already in the process of making their way towards the nearest one. Inside, they quickly took up positions at the controls. Lax glanced behind, noticing an empty area lined with black seats waiting to be of the utmost comfort to its next occupier.

"Dix, do you think we should wait to fill the ship?"

Dix glanced behind as a look of pure guilt flashed across his already anxious face, but thoughts of self preservation soon returned as the *Paraxatar* took another alarming lurch.

Lax deftly flicked his fingers over touch panels and the propulsion unit began to power up. Lights illuminated, changing colour to indicate systems readiness and within a couple of moments the vessel was ready to depart.

"Okay," he mouthed, taking deep breaths. Many thoughts ran through his head, the bulk of which concerned the ship and crew of whom he would shortly leave behind to their own fate, not to mention how their flight would be viewed by those awaiting upon the fourth planet.

"Let's go," said Dix, his mind not as conscientious as that of his Overseer. Regardless of his new found lucidity; Lax would still be considered by many as a total fruit loop, allowing Dix to state that he couldn't allow his very sick Overseer to leave by himself.

With short hisses the small vessel sealed itself, all exits disappearing from view while the gentle hum and vibration built up. The two occupants sank into their seats which adjusted to fit their body shape. On the outer hull of the *Paraxatar* a large doorway glowed and parted to reveal, rather surprisingly to the occupants of the escape vessel, some trees, no more than forty feet in front of them.

Lax gawped at the large Earth plants, initially with confusion, then with realisation. The fact that they were looking at trees and not the open sky was caused by the ships ever increasing tilt. His mind filled with an onrush of sudden panic, *are we going to clear them*? He thought.

It was all academic really as there was no time to change his mind, the automatic launch sequence had completed and the escape ship was ejected from the command vessel with a gentle nudge. All sounds and sensation of mechanical attachment faded and at last they were powering free of the command ship. At that precise moment the list accelerated alarmingly and the edge of the exit aperture came into contact with the escape ship. Not violently but enough to cause a severe judder as it was forced downwards along with the *Paraxatar's* gradual destruction.

Panicking, Lax fought to control the ship and instinctively engaged the thrusters to maximum, giving a similar result as a car driver slamming the brakes on when skidding on ice. Vibrating wildly, it attempted to free itself from the still descending mother ship before with a jarring shudder all resistance and vibration ceased and it was free. Quickly it accelerated from a near horizontal position to one of almost instant verticality.

Dix and Lax, although used to the stresses and strains of space travel were thrown about violently, only saved by their super comfortable seats. Not only the ultimate in comfort but not too bad on the safety aspect either. They were however, literally speaking, not clear of the woods yet. The downward momentum of the command ship had forced them ever nearer to the ground. When at last they were clear of its environs they found themselves no more than eight feet from the ground. Free from restraint the escape craft shot forward at enormous speed, like a bullet from a gun. The tree's, which had initially greeted Lax and Dix when the ships doors had opened, now came into play. Almost clear, the very tip of the aft section struck a large oak. In excess of two hundred years it had stood and although it wasn't and never would be common knowledge, it grew on the actual spot where King Charles I had engaged upon frivolous activity with one of his many mistresses one night back in 1645 shortly before the ill fated original battle at Rowton Moor.

The impact upon the tree almost caused the craft to flip over, the control thrusters just about compensating before putting it back upon a correct trajectory. The tree fared less well losing a good fifteen feet from its top. Branches and greenery showered the ground below, making an old and well respected family of squirrels homeless at the same time; fortunately all were away gathering food for the forthcoming winter. Finally they began to gain altitude on a correct course but Lax and Dix were far from relieved.

"Something doesn't sound right Dix," Lax remarked.

Dix turned to face his Overseer. "Of course it's not right. If you hadn't noticed, we...You are deserting you're..."

"No," Lax interrupted. I'm talking about that." He pointed toward their feet, a reference to the strange and definitely not okay, grinding, scraping sound emanating from beneath them, the same area where the engines were situated. Dix was on the verge of recovering his wits for the umpteenth time that morning; his pale face stared at Lax. "I think we should land," he admitted with much concern.

Without a word Lax punched in a few commands and then stared at the touch panel, his mouth opening wide. Repeating it, his mouth opened wider.

"Err Dix," he said. The sinister tone causing the medic's already overanxious mind to overload and without further ceremony he quietly passed out.

"Oh superb," remarked Lax. "And you're supposed to be the medic."

The craft still gained height, its velocity increasing all the time. This was good as they were finally escaping the nightmare on the surface. The bad news was that the controls were completely unresponsive, damaged by the collisions as they left the command ship. Unable to alter the course it rose higher and higher into the sky. The height sensor, working perfectly of course, showed a height of 16,600 metres.

Outside the atmosphere was thinning as they began to leave the Troposphere and enter the Stratosphere, and then the engine became very ill. The grating sound intensified before abruptly, all sounds died away and there was silence. Momentum kept the craft climbing for a few more seconds but not for long as gravity inevitably took over. Now at its apex, the small escape craft came to a halt, levelled out slightly and began the descent, slowly at first but gathering more and more speed as it dropped.

Lax sat inside fully aware of what was happening. The worst part of it all wasn't the fact that he faced an almost certain death, that, he was fully prepared for. The main problem was that the instruments in front of him gave him an accurate reading of all the bare and grim facts in extreme detail, most depressing of all, the circular green flashing light indicating that there was a serious problem regarding the engines. He spent the next precious moments attempting to bring them back on line and hopefully rectify the ships downward plummet but to no avail. With extreme effort against the G forces he reached across into a locker by his side, extracted a large flask, opened it and begun to drink.

As he drunk the emergency Glook ration Lax was hopeful that its calming, inebriating effects would soon overcome him, he glanced at the still vacant Dix.

"Oh Dix, you Stupid Bastard," he said and put a hand upon his friends shoulder. "Oh well, at least you won't feel a thing."

LIII

One or two of the rabbits, those brave enough or just really hungry, poked their heads above the warrens entrance. They had no comprehension whatsoever that they were witnessing a full scale evacuation by an invading Alien force. All they were aware of was that it was all really rather loud and unnecessary.

"There's a weird thing," said Ergon carrotfurrow III, his big long ears ramrod straight while pointing toward the mayhem with his whiskered twitchy nose. Aronaught gardenpen wasn't interested, he'd found a large, dense, thick patch of nice green grass and was merrily munching his way through it.

Mmm, looks good, thought Ergon and promptly joined him.

The next explosion scattered the rabbits, each one scurrying back to its burrow, just in time too, as a large piece of jagged melting plastic hull landed on the spot they had occupied just moments previous.

No less than twelve small squads of infantry were operating on the fields around Beeston castle causing massive damage and confusion among the Desirions. Daylight had arrived and with it those teams had scaled back their activities, most now blending into the surroundings. This is not to say they were idle. The latest enormous explosion had been the detonation of the command ship toward the rear of the rocky outcrop, caused by a sustained and savage bombardment from the tanks. Lieutenant Parkin, along with Sergeant Doberman and their accompaniment of Paratroopers and Royal Engineers had been responsible for the destruction of no less than two of the huge transport vessels a few hours previous, not to mention smaller land based vehicles, the tally of which reached into double figures.

Time, along with a phenomenal amount of ordnance and firepower had at last convinced the Desirion high command, such as it was, that although to die an honourable death for your home world was to baste oneself in everlasting valour. The old adage of discretion being very much the better part of glory was now the more preferable option.

The evacuation and retreat, despite some very well ordered rearguard actions had quickly degraded into a full scale get the hell out of here. Just two Desirion Capital ships remained operational upon the ground. The *Luxera* contained the remainder of the high command which was shut up tight and on the verge of departure. The other was strangely in the process of deploying a large amount of firepower and personnel, bent upon the pursuit of just four humans, currently hiding out among the trees and dense undergrowth upon the slope leading to the castles summit.

"What in the name of Shard are they doing?" Gasped Pox, staring wide eyed at the viewer in front which showed the *Nerax* in the process of deploying rather than evacuating. "Has Zex not received the evacuation order?" He added, not moving from the display.

"Commander," the unidentified voice came from the row of console operatives. "The evacuation order was received by Commander Zex's and confirmed."

"Well what in Shard is he playing at? Re-issue it and ensure it's understood as an order," Pox barked, in no mood for a disobedient commander.

No sooner had he quietened down when the entire ship vibrated to the sound of repeated impacts. Those around him in the Hub began to look increasingly concerned.

"Pox," said Commander Bex. "I think it's time to go." His words were interrupted.

"Commander," said the operative. "We are under attack from human artillery believed to be the same vehicles responsible for the command vessels demise."

Pox suddenly thought of Lax. He had seen the explosion when the *Paraxatar* heeled over and had received the report that a number of escape craft had in fact got away. *Could Lax have been in one?*

"Commander," It was Bex again, interrupting his train of thought. "We need a decision, his words almost drowned out by the thunderous impacts made by the armour piercing rounds.

Pox dallied still. Those around him agitated, some on the verge of desertion. Finally the acting Commander turned to the navigation operators, "let's get out of here," he said and promptly turned back to the viewer. Those watching him saw his face contorted with rage. "Destroy those human mobile guns then head for this city of Chester before we leave. I want some payback."

The opinion on this new order was divided. Some displayed contented grins of satisfaction, completely in agreement with their senior's intentions. Others, mainly operational crew members slunk into their chairs, a blank unassuming look depicted upon their faces.

The long rubber dog toy bone shaped *Luxera* powered up. The huge rings upon the rear sphere manoeuvring before pouring out a noise similar to a gale force wind rushing past the ears. There was no bright red emission of awesome power, thrusting flames into the atmosphere and propelling the ship heavenwards. Just a slight change in the engines tone and very slowly and smoothly it lifted from the ground. The shield sparkled blue as the shells from the Challengers repeatedly struck, their chance of a second kill diminishing with each inch the ship lifted away.

Higher and higher the impressive piece of alien technology rose into the sky. Pox watched with growing concern and gathering resignation at the continued deployment from Zex's ship, still displaying no sign of evacuation.

Those Desirion's being deployed watched the *Luxera* taking off and were rapidly filled with alarm. Why was this ship leaving? A number had taken account of their surroundings and come to the conclusion that it looked considerably empty around here right now. As this realisation dawned, more and more of those not deployed as part of the attacking force around Beeston gatehouse began to display a state of extreme agitation.

Pox changed the view on the screen, his facial expression altering with it as the sight before him unfolded. Around ten of the mobile Human artillery vehicles were in the process of moving, their previous target, Pox's ship was already too high for the Challenger's guns to traverse. As a unit they moved away from their position, churning up mud and vegetation and leaving dark brown smears upon the landscape before appearing to make straight for the *Nerax* and Zex.

"Oh no you don't," Pox raged. He had been joined by Bex and Pix, the latter's features still exuded that of a lost little boy. "Target them and fire," Pox ordered with determination.

The *Luxera*, now far above the Challengers activated every gun it could bare, the menacing weapons smoothly rotating until each one was trained directly upon the tanks below. It appeared to hover rather easily, although in truth, to maintain a steady flight in a gravity atmosphere the engines were required to operate at almost maximum power. To enable it to go into attack, the last remaining reserves would be required. Never the less it was a very short time before it began to discharge sizzling red plasma bolts into them.

The very first shot found a target, converting the tanks famous Cobham armour into a congealed melted mess. The Challenger slewed to one side a little but still appeared to be operational. Further direct hits upon the hull penetrated before with a whoosh and a ball of flame it burst apart.

Pox wasn't finished. The ships systems found new targets and began to pound away causing another tank to brew up, the detonation disabling its immediate neighbour as well.

The computer suddenly latched onto a new and different target. This one was high above them in the sky and closing rapidly.

"Commander, we have locked onto..." A long pause followed.

Pox looked at the news bearer. "Yes, yes, locked onto what?"

He snapped angrily, annoyed at being disturbed from watching these damn Humans receive some punishment, punishment which should have been dished out long ago, and would have been had Lax not wasted time with risky ground attacks.

"Commander it appears to be of Desirion origin. It's transmitting a recognition signal, and it's closing on our position at extreme velocity."

Pox and Bex strode over to the operators position. The specifications on the screen and the information provided gave the ship's identity away immediately.

"It's an escape ship," said Bex somewhat puzzled.

Pox wasn't puzzled. He knew exactly what it was that was heading their way.

"Move, get us out of here, NOW!" he shouted. "Get this ship moving."

LIV

Lax stared through the window. He had consumed a huge amount of Glook in an extremely short period, enough to floor him for a week. Slowly it had begun to produce the desired effect and then quite suddenly it didn't. The reason for this unwanted lack of intoxication was the sight of a Desirion Capital ship hovering a few thousand metres below and closing very fast.

He didn't panic, he knew what was going to happen and he knew he was dead. The escape craft was totally disabled and dead in the water. He simply watched the ships close and there was absolutely nothing he could do about it.

Strangely enough, his only thought was to wonder who was commanding the ship below him, he would be aware of the approaching craft from above and how miffed he was likely to be by what was about to happen.

"Unidentified escape craft, this is Commander Pox, is that you Lax?" Pox said, the message coming over crisp and clear from the speaker.

Lax didn't move he just stared at the ship in front of them. "Oh, so it's you Pox my old friend," said Lax dejectedly with barely a whisper.

"Lax, steer away you are on a collision course. Acknowledge, acknowledge, Lax...Lax."

The form slumped in the seat to his left stirred.

"Oh Dix," said Lax, his speech showing that he was actually more affected by the Glook than he thought. "Wrong time to wake up my friend," he slurred.

Dix gradually opened his eyes, focusing slowly until he saw the un-missable form of the *Luxera* through the viewing window. He turned his head in a snapping movement towards Lax and quickly offered a darting look at his Overseer before pointing and emitting a long squeaking mew.

"It's okay Dix, everything will be..."

The *Luxera* moved, her engines drawing upon every possible ounce of power in the hope of thrusting her forward but the power required for such an immediate response was incredible. A roar coursed through the superstructure as the engines fought against an atmosphere and a force that it wasn't really designed to operate within, but sure enough it moved, but not nearly enough.

Sensing the inevitable, those upon the Hub braced for impact, Pox shouting to hold on to anything they could, and with surety it came. The escape craft struck the middle sphere. The shield handled the collision well, absorbing an incredible amount of kinetic energy, reducing the escape crafts speed from Maximum descent to just forty mph, but it just couldn't cope fully. Lax and Dix felt nothing as they died, the cessation of inertia killing them before their frames were shattered from the impact. The escape craft exploded, blowing away part of the ring system and the mounted weapons, creating an impressive fireball high up in the sky, visible for miles around. The resulting boom joined the visual display some seconds later before disintegrating into small parts which quickly rained down upon the ground below.

Forced down, the *Luxera* plummeted. Bucked and rocked violently by the impact. The aft part of the central sphere was severely damaged; the dismembered part of the ring along with the guns and a considerable amount of other equipment from the impact zone began a free fall towards the Earth, along with the burning remnants of the escape craft. Inside, the crew were thrown about violently. Initially towards the ceilings and then as their fall was rectified, ultimately connecting with the deck or a bulkhead. This caused some hideous injuries, the vast majority fractured or dislocated bones and muscles sprains but there were a couple of fatalities thrown in for good measure.

Pox shook his dazed head and rubbed a hand over a very bruised leg. His right arm wasn't in the best condition either but gathering himself he managed to stand up on two legs once more. Looking around he could see those that were capable, were returning to their stations. Despite the seriousness of the situation, no alarms rang, just a few panels flashed and the rooms lighting had changed to orange.

A hand grabbed the material of his leg covering. Looking down he saw Bex slowly regaining his composure, his head oozing blood from a deep cut while next to him lay Pix, unconscious and by the looks of his twisted form, badly injured."Get med teams up here now," roared Pox. "And I want a full status report."

It didn't need a report or evaluation of any kind to work out that the ship was in a bad way, especially the engines, you only had to listen to them. The sound reverberating and vibrating badly as the *Luxera* struggled to remain on line.

"Commander?"

It was the voice of the ever present console operator, this time somewhat racked with emotion. On hearing the shaky tones Pox came to realise that he only really heard the voice when bad news was to be had, he was also well aware that he needed to hear it right now.

"Power is reduced by sixty percent. Weapon stations three, four and six are offline, shields are non operational and off side thrusters two and five are non responsive, this is just the initial report. All other department's reports are pending." He paused for his commander's comment but none was forthcoming and so continued. "We are able to compensate but our course will be unpredictable, in fact we appear to be on a locked course with helm off line too."

"And just what is our course?" asked Pox.

"We are..." There was a pause. "Heading as per your order, straight for the Human dwelling of Chester," skilfully finishing on the one piece of good news. He was rather puzzled when he saw his commander's features drop a notch further.

"Pox?" Bex questioned.

"We have no shields, little power and cannot steer," Pox replied. "But we can still fight," he added, sudden realisation lightening his mood. "Destroy everything in our path," the commander exclaimed dramatically, his enthusiasm and anger overflowing into rabid obsession.

A few heads turned. Nothing was said, but many thoughts were raised within moral minds as to whether this was the correct course of action, not to mention the fact that to continue fighting without any protection was inviting certain death. The Desirion military mind above all, demanded unswerving, unquestioning loyalty, and even though this harshest of all orders was given it was obeyed with superb obedience. The vessel flew on in a style comparable to one in the old black and white Flash Gordon TV series, a thick smoky dark purple trail pouring from the large jagged impact mark created by the collision with the escape craft. Every now and then the stabilisers faltered before compensating and temporarily rectifying the problem only to assume the tilt once again.

As it left the area, those weapons still operational, which still numbered seven very destructive and powerful thermal transfer plasma guns, began to blaze indiscriminately at anything that appeared to be of human construction. The already heavily battle scarred Beeston castle was the first casualty as four simultaneous bolts struck the crag just a few feet below the north wall. The ancient natural rock splintering as it was blasted causing the man made structure above to cascade into the tree's and rocks below. The uncontrollable speed and direction of the ship didn't allow for it to hang around and it wasn't long before, after a few more not so destructive salvos the whole of the Beeston area was out of range.

The unfolding scenario in the air and the subsequent destruction on the ground filled the already anxious Desirion's besieging the castle's entrance gate with even more nervous apprehension. Concerns were raised at the thought of their fellow comrades departing or even abandoning them, while some thought that the sounds of battle were at last a long overdue and crushing victory for them. Either faction was given further enlightenment or thoughts of self preservation respectively as their own ship suddenly began to power up, the roaring engines discernible through the distant explosions.

Moments later all commanders in the field were issued with an immediate recall to the ship. Some, largely those whose mood aired towards the pessimistic side turned and fled, not necessarily in good order, believing a mass human attack imminent. While those with considerably more bravado turned with loaded weapons, joyful at the prospect of joining their comrades in the *Nerax* and inflicting some serious punishment of their own. Either way you looked at it they were still withdrawing from the field.

"Commander I am picking up ten... No, fourteen... No twenty two flying craft approaching from the east, Human origin. They are on an intercept course," said the bad news console operator. Pox however, wasn't listening. He was revelling in the destruction being metered out. It was almost as if he had gone the way of his recent predecessor and lost his mind.

"How long until we reach the city?" He asked with absolutely no reference to the impending fighter planes whatsoever.

"Commander, our course will not in fact take us directly over the human city, we shall skirt its southern perimeter."

Pox thought. *No matter, we can still carry out a sustained attack.* "Proceed as instructed," he confirmed.

The alien ship scorched through the sky. The purple mist had worsened to become a dense trailing smoke, however the list had finally been stabilized and as it approached the southern extremity of Chester it was met by a terrific hail of small calibre weaponry which despite the ships prone situation inflicted only minimal irritation.

The advancing aircraft were still a minute or two away but this didn't hold back bad news operator as he spoke up again.

"Commander partial control has now been regained over navigation; we also have limited direction control on all axes."

Pox grinned, "This was more like it." He stared for a moment out of the viewing port at the mass of human dwellings laid out before them. "Aim for the central area," he ordered.

The resumption of the helm introduced his mind to the possibility that they may just actually be able to carry out an attack upon the city and have a reasonable chance to attempt an escape. Pox rested his head in his hands and winced, a sudden reminder of injuries received from the recent collision.

I wonder, he thought. *I could turn this round. If I can create some sort of devastation down there then maybe if we get away, I could come away from this with some notoriety.* His thoughts wrestled with the reality of the situation, one which to most people would be hammering into their mind that they were still well and truly in the shit." Supreme Overseer Pox," he mouthed soundlessly. "I like the sound of that."

"How long till the human air craft intercept?" He asked, his tone changing for the umpteenth time in just the last couple of minutes.

"Two Earth minute's commander," came the reply.

The *Luxera* began to turn towards starboard and the city centre, albeit, slowly and cumbersomely but turn it did. The new course change prompted many more guns, including the large calibre artillery, those huge mobile guns and artillery pieces set up in the park to begin pounding away. Immediately they straddled the extra terrestrial bringer of death. Hand weapons by the thousand were loosed off, their range falling far short but mostly in the belief that to do something, anything, was better than to simply do nothing.

The painful turn and the still excessive speed had taken the Desirion's beyond the environs of the city, and as it completed the laborious manoeuvre it was positioned precisely above the Welsh border and RAF Sealand. The whole of the Chester skyline resembled London during the blitz, explosions bursting apart in the sky but very few going even close to the target. As its course straightened it opened up again, large red energy bolts slamming into the ground, not caring what it hit and blazing a trail of destruction through the residential area of Blacon before once more their luck changed.

The shell from a 105mm gun impacted upon the ships front underside, just to the rear of the front sphere. Damage itself was relatively light but thanks to the ships already perilous state it managed to ignite further power problems, ensuring the engines slowed considerably, thus making her a sitting duck.

LV

The Royal Navy patrol vessel HMS Brockenhurst was Moored upon the river Dee, upstream from the old Dee Bridge at Handbridge. As warships go it really was small, no frigate or destroyer, measuring just forty six metres from stem to stern the Brockenhurst displaced a mere eight hundred Tons.

Her commander, Lieutenant commander Toby Wolffe had kept his equally small crew at a perpetual state of heightened readiness for the last twenty four hours. Following the disabled alien ship, firstly upon radar and then with their own eyes, they had witnessed its laboured flight to the south of their position before turning some distance away. As they watched, its course changed again, turning until almost completely bows on, it headed directly for them.

Wolffe turned to a rugged and impossibly hairy officer charged with responsibility for weapons control. "Okay Mr Hardman?" he said sternly.

"Main armament closed up sir," he replied with a grin.

Wolffe scanned his command, senses tingling as he took in the bridge, the crew, and then outside on the focsle. The shape of the bow as it tapered to meet in a point at the prow and then the gun. He glanced at Hardman, sensing that he and every man and woman on board were just waiting for the moment, their moment. Those not employed upon the bridge stood by on the gunwales armed with machine guns. The ship was also equipped with a twenty millimetre cannon, two miniguns and four General purpose machine guns, a formidable armament for such a vessel of its size.

His gaze fell once more upon the main armament, a thirty millimetre cannon. He knew it wasn't much but in the best traditions of the senior service he, his crew and his ship would bloody well give them everything they had.

Scrutinising the alien ship he noticed that it was enveloped by little puffs. Each one caused by a shell as ordnance and bullets struck its surface. He also witnessed a much larger explosion strike home, followed quickly by another. At first it made little impression upon him but on closer inspection it was clear that the ship had begun to slow.

This is it, this is it, his mind screamed until without realising, his mouth opened. "Open fire, main armament," he shouted.

"Main armament, shoot," Hardman replied, as cool as a cucumber.

That felt good, he thought. It sounded even better when just a couple of seconds later the thirty millimetre gun spat fire.

The *Luxera,* now at a range of no more than eight thousand feet suffered no further damage from the Brockenhurst's first salvo, its trajectory making no impression upon Pox or his crew within.

"Adjust three degrees," said a bridge crewman observing the fall of shot, that done, the small but impressive piece of hardware belched fire again.

"Yes," shouted the crew, Wolffe with them as they found their target, but no time to rejoice as the resultant explosions bursting directly upon the front sphere were already clearing to reveal the oncoming ship.

The Desirion's were still firing with their own weapons causing untold mayhem as they came. The Brockenhurst Lay directly in its path. It seemed to Wolffe that it was best not to mention to the bridge crew that it only seemed a matter of time before the small patrol vessel became its next victim.

"Sir?" It was the communications Officer. "Reports indicate that air cover is en route, ETA one minute."

"Good, thank you Chivers," replied Wolffe with a smile, knowing that even one minute would be too late.

The gun fired again. More cheers as another shot hit home, but the spacecraft continued ploughing up mostly industrial land as it advanced.

Pox and Bex watched through the viewer. The acting overseer was defiant but with the sympathy of many others Bex attempted to persuade their commander to abandon this pointless action and rendezvous with the remainder of the invasion force. Pox however was having none of it, like his overseer before him, his mind had been absorbed. Unlike Lax, Pox was being driven insane by the personal need to cause as much destruction to these irritating, vile, damn Humans. "Who do they think they are? Do they think they can..." and then he saw it. Plumb in the centre of the large view screen. Floating upon the thin strip of water, directly in front of a crossing the small grey vessel fired its puny weapon at him. At him. "At me!" He muttered. "How dare they." A short pause followed. "Target that little err err," he paused again.

"They call it a boat," informed a voice close by.

"Target that boat. Destroy it," Pox ordered.

Bex continued to protest but eventually realised he was wasting his time. At that same moment he realised with a very real certainty that his own life could very well be approaching its end.

Despite her spectacular lack of success, HMS Brockenhurst continued firing all weapons, creating a hell of a noise. The momentum didn't falter as the first of the retargeted energy bolts from the Desirion's fizzed into the water just a few feet from the patrol crafts bow. The dissipating energy dwindling as it ploughed deeper into the brackish water, causing a small slimy crater in the silty mud on the river bed.

Oh god, thought Wolffe, fear filling him, knowing that he and his ship were now the singular target. The main armament fired again, shells bursting forth from the guns muzzle before finding clear air. Flying at an immense speed towards their target, each crew member inwardly cheered them on their way.

Pox's final moments, indeed his last vision was to observe the shells as they flew not just toward the *Luxera*, but him personally. His direct eye line was exactly that of a shell. He watched its trajectory, saw its approach, and said "bollocks," as it took out the front viewer and never said or thought anything ever again.

The projectile penetrated the ship directly through the main viewing area upon the front sphere, ploughing unabated straight into the Hub. Smashing through the transparent polymer viewing screen, it took Pox's head clean off his shoulders. Not satisfied, it continued to travel for at least another several feet before embedding itself into a maze of wiring and tubes set behind the rear most bulkhead. Those who had not been flung to one side or dived for safety as the shell tore through the outer screen ceased what they were doing and simply stared at the terrifying object. Not for long though as it exploded with an infernos roar. The explosion causing a mass of chain reactions as highly flammable substance's mixed with others of a similar nature just waiting for a spark, and they were not disappointed. One moment a huge, super technological alien Capital ship in the shape of a giant rubber dog toy hung in the sky, the next it was replaced by the largest detonation the city of Chester had ever witnessed.

LVI

Woods, Sergeant Hornby and Marine Langhorne had spread themselves out among the trees and undergrowth. Poised and ready, they were each armed with a selection of differing weaponry, ranging from captured Desirion guns to the hastily improvised, but still essential, sharpened wooden children's swords, bows and arrows. Not to mention a number of the already proven and effective paint bomb.

Cautiously they observed from their concealed position amidst the dense wooded area at the base of the slope leading up to Beeston castle. Gary lay on the ground still wearing the replica chain mail he had clamoured into inside the shop. "Woods, Sergeant, somebody, get this off me, hello anyone?" He called in as loud a whisper as he dare.

"Yeth thir, we will thoon, juth be pathient." came Woods equally whispered reply.

Close by and rapidly filling the ruined gatehouse was a couple of hundred heavily armed aliens, backed up by mobile guns. The addition of the two pieces of heavy weaponry seemed to swing things slightly in their favour.

"Odds look pretty even Sarge," Langhorne chuckled nervously, fingering his energy gun, he'd given up counting the enemy after around sixty.

Hornby grinned, "We've seen worse."

Woods voiced his agreement, although there was no sarcasm labelled to his tone, "yeh leth do the bathtardth," he spat.

Gary had managed, through a miraculous act of contortion, to turn himself over by rocking from side to side. His improved field of vision revealed a large and increasing force of Aliens assembling with the expressed intention of using him for target practice.

"Arrgghh!" Stifling a short scream he wished he hadn't exerted himself. Convulsing, he attempted to remove some of the heavy armour, his entire frame still clad with the exception of his head.

Unbeknownst to the four humans, the alien position wasn't as strong as it appeared. Sure the Desirion's outnumbered the Humans by a good fifty to one but they were very jittery and unsure, having watched their supporting ship take to the air. Their fear was exacerbated by the sound of battle nearby and then witnessing that same ship depart with all guns blazing, ultimately to leave the whole area with an eerie and foreboding silence which seemed to close in like a fog. Couple this with the fact that success wasn't a habit they had grown used to on this planet and here they were, ordered into yet another fight, one which at this moment had gone back to hiding in the trees.

Most had no idea that they were only hunting four humans, and all these facts combined to make the mass of Desirion's very apprehensive. Wary or not they were advancing towards Gary and his comrade's position.

"Right here they come again," Hornby announced through a grimace, not that he found the situation amusing. Deep intakes of breath and curses could be heard amidst tinkles and clanking as Gary continued to fumble with the chain mail. Woods watched him and took pity. Stepping towards the stricken idiot he figured he would probably just have enough time to help with at least some of the armour before he had to engage the enemy once more. *Besides another pair of hands would always be handy,* he thought.

"There you go thir," he said, as together they slipped the heavy chain shirt over his shoulders.

"Thank you Woods," sighed Gary, the removal of the garment and its subsequent weight reduction caused his shoulders and arms to feel weak. He was also aware that he felt exhausted thanks to his continuous thrashing about. That however, was about as far as he and Woods would get, there being no time to remove any more due to the alien advance.

"Okay here come the bastards, get ready," said Hornby for the fourth time in as many minutes, although to be fair the actual distance that the Desirion's were from them definitely merited an, "okay let's get ready."

Simultaneously, Hornby and Langhorne raised their energy weapons, ensuring they had a good sighting. "Steady," said the sergeant, "steeaaddy."

A bright red flash illuminated the area on the far side of the perimeter wall, followed immediately by a rush of air and a heavy explosion. The shot from the mobile gun had discharged out of sight of Woods and his companions. It was followed up by more of a smaller nature as well as the more familiar sound of small arms rifle fire. Those aliens at the front continued to advance, although noticeably slower, while it also became evident that a larger number, chiefly those towards the rear offered anxious glances in that direction in the hope of gaining an insight as to what the new confusion was.

Hornby, intuitively assuming that the aliens were under attack from the rear, gave the order to open fire. Four bright red bolts flew out of the trees, singeing the odd hanging leaf and helping it to an early autumn. Three found their target, the recipients flung to the ground never to move again. The fourth, fired by Gary, who had retrieved his own gun, shot up at an acute angle, the bolt only just missing Sergeant Hornby.

The sudden attack from the tree's combined with the sounds of battle from the rear, and their already nervous state was all it took for the Desirion's to break and run. The front runners stayed, they were the brave ones, the stalwarts, those with little or no sense of fear and similar to Woods in a way. Unlike him they were to become a forlorn hope and would soon be dead. The mass retreat was already in full flow as they fired again taking out another quartet of fleeing aliens. Even Gary scored a direct hit, although in truth it was an easy target, a large mass, scrambling to escape through the ruined gate house and possible safety.

The crescendo of noise from behind the wall reached fever pitch while to their front Hornby and his comrades took aim after aim at the routed enemy and then Woods went berserk again.

Crashing from the tree's, the demented van driver sprinted at full speed, screaming a blood curdling cry of "BATHTARDTH," before springing high into the air with the dexterity of a Panther and landing heavily upon one of the braver Desirion's who still held his ground. The sight of Woods ruined his heroic stance and the ensuing melee was equivalent to that of a Grizzly bear bearing down upon a hamster. The unfortunate alien was dead even before its brain had time to realise such, the bloodied blade of the Ghurkha knife indicating its ruthless efficiency once more.

Hornby watched with awe as the lunatic spewed from the forested area. He loosed off a couple more bolts before pulling out the wooden child's sword and sprung into the attack. The decision of those aliens who had not retreated was now called into question as more insane Humans began appearing from the woods, screaming like savages and holding aloft very sharp things. If that wasn't enough, their decision to eventually have it on their toes was swayed by the sight of a half human, half metal creature appearing, brandishing a long wooden stick.

Taking a deep breath Gary roared as he advanced. The effect completely lost as his exhausted state forced his already tired lungs to run out of air, downgrading the roar to something akin to a small girls squeal.

Two more Desirion's were killed by Hornby and Langhorne before they finally broke. Following the retreat, the Marines used their captured guns, firing indiscriminately. Gary brought up the rear, his pace reduced to slightly better than a rapid Sunday stroll. The main body of Desirion's attacking from their left flank had at last overcome their fears and were returning a good defensive fire, but as those fleeing the castle slopes poured through the remains of the visitor centre it caused a large gathering of unordered alien soldiers, who, at that moment were only able to soak up stray fire from the attacking humans.

Lieutenant Parkin and his platoon of Para's had now battled their way through to this position. Initially successful in destroying one of the large space going transport vessels by capturing and turning one of the caterpillar tracked mobile guns onto it. It was now one of these which fired at the mass of aliens swarming around the last ship on the field.

Alerted to the threat, the *Nerax* attempted to train its own weaponry upon the new attackers, the smooth hiss of the trucks as they glided along the huge encircling rings surrounding each sphere. Those heavy mobile weapons still in the possession of the Desirion's were stuck, unable to manoeuvre within the morass of fleeing soldiers at the gatehouse. So it was left to the trusty foot soldier to do the dirty work. Those who had safely fled the castle slope and the throng around the gatehouse were being ordered to gather safely behind the *Nerax*, out of range of any humans. Forming up into battle groups, they quickly made rows ready to be deployed when the time came.

"Sergeant," roared Lieutenant Parkin, his voice just about audible above the din of battle.

Sergeant Doberman appeared at his officer's side with a dive as a small explosion detonated not too far away. Parkin remained upright, unflinching, setting an example and all that. "Ah there you are Sergeant," he said, "We are going to have to push forward and break out of here."

"Isn't it a little dangerous sir?" asked Doberman, his thick West Country accent more prominent when anxious.

Just to prove the point, three bolts struck the ground between the two soldiers, each one erupting small clods of soil and showering them with a mixture of earth and flying greenery.

"It's too bloody dangerous to stay, we are committed now, "said Parkin. "They're digging in; we have to get em on the move. It seems to be clear on the opposite side of that ship," he continued pointing at the last remaining Alien vessel. "We'll move over there and get our mobile gun to concentrate fire upon the ship."

Without another word Doberman disappeared, informing his men that they were to move out while the mobile gun operators changed their target, a clear indication that Dobermans order had been relayed, the red bolts fizzing as they slammed into the ships shield. Blue sparks danced, intermixing with the red as the two energy patterns reacted. The blue colour outlasting the red but with each impact it slowly became clear that inroads were being made upon the ship's hull.

Reacting to the greater threat, the *Nerax's* weapon trucks moved again, but hesitated for fear of firing on their own.

The well rehearsed drill of moving out began. Those in the front increased their fire to a shattering rate while quickly; one by one, the Para's moved from their positions in a spearhead formation. The covering fire worked and in no time at all, every human had left their position and were rapidly taking the ground upon the opposite side of the Alien ship.

Doberman ran, his teeth clenched tight before with a shocked realisation he almost collided with the man in front who had suddenly checked his forward motion.

"What the f...?" He shouted. Looking up he immediately realised the cause.

Ahead of the decelerating Para's were solid and ordered lines of alien soldiers. Lots of them, far, far more than there were humans. The Desirion's had not been expecting the humans and now both races opposed each other in a very heavy standoff.

The Para's grouping was ragged after their surprised halt but weapons were ready and aimed, with the Desirion's at a similar state of readiness.

Parkin stood frozen, *shit, what'll I do?* He thought *if I order an attack we will be mown down, if I don't I'll...*

"Sir?" the questioning voice belonged to Doberman.

Parkin's reply never came; the sound of gunfire, both alien and human emanated from behind the neatly lined up Desirion's.

"Christ that was well timed," thought Parkin with absolute delight and relief. He witnessed the ranks disintegrate into utter confusion, the second time in just a short period these poor unfortunate beings had been panicked and they were having no more of it. Those at the rear were taking heavy casualties while those in front experienced a state of near frenzy.

"Fire," shouted Parkin, almost regretting giving the order to open up on such an easy target, but fire they did and with devastating effect.

LVII

The castle side of the gatehouse was now completely devoid of living aliens. By the time Gary reached its crumbled, smoking remains he was also the only human this side of it too. The sound of battle however, was still so close on the other side of the wall that it rebounded around the inside of his head. In dire need of a rest, not to mention the removal of the remainder of the chain mail armour he perched upon a large jagged chunk of masonry. Judging by the shape, this was the remains of one of the towers battlements. Grunting with sweating effort, he tugged and pulled at the armoured trousers until at last, with one final effort they came off. *Oh the relief,* as with when he removed the tunic. His legs felt weak and trembly at the sudden loss of weight. Looking down he noticed his black Starfleet trousers were in shreds and soaked with sweat.

Shoving the mail to one side with his foot he took a very deep breath and sat for a moment, attempting to take everything in. Cupping filthy hands together he covered his face and rubbed the palms deep into his eye sockets, massaging them for a brief second before resting his elbows upon his knees and staring at the scene of destruction around him. The line of rubble extended a few feet from his seat before it gave way to worn grass and soil and then just grass as the ground contoured sharply, finally elevating toward the slope and the castles summit.

Underneath the rubble he noticed a partially hidden yellow object a few feet to his right. Curious, he lay his gun down and unsteadily got to his feet before making his way over to examine it, making sure all the time he was sufficiently low enough, so as to avoid detection from those on the other side of the wall. With bare hands he cleared some of the smaller lumps of masonry, revealing the object to be a fire hose. The long yellow rubber coil still tightly wound around its spindle.

"Thir." Woods voice made him jump, his heart beating super fast while his senses shot up to maximum levels.

"Bloody hell Woods don't creep up on me like that," Gary barked, slowly calming down.

"Thorry thir. What have you got there?" Woods asked, eyeing Gary's find.

"It looks like a hose Woods, a fire hose!"

Woods passed Gary by, seemingly disinterested in both him and the hose. "Come on thir, leths get back in there and kill the bathtards," he said, beckoning Gary to follow, eager for more carnage.

Instead, Gary climbed onto some of the rubble from the gatehouse, once again careful not to be detected until he found a point where he could see clearly what was happening outside. The fight had moved further across the road, the car park almost empty of anything living. The majority of action appeared to be taking place in the field around the alien ship. Those closest seemed to be in total disarray. To his left he could see a number of humans kitted out in camouflage. "No it couldn't be could it?" he muttered under his breath, *it looked like Lieutenant Havelock.* To his right another body of people came into view, also in camouflage, these he didn't recognise. Directly below at the foot of the wall, concealed behind large pieces of fallen masonry were Sergeant Hornby and Langhorne. From their hidden position they were mercilessly picking off unsuspecting and confused aliens whenever they should stumble into range. To their right, obscured within the lengthy grass he noticed a dull metallic square cover, similar to a Sewer entrance lid but smaller.

"That," said Gary to himself, "is a fire hydrant." Of course he didn't recognise this by merely knowing exactly what it was by sight, fire hydrant spotting not being one of his more bizarre past times. It was the words FIRE HYDRANT in six inch high, raised lettering which gave the game away. In the adjacent field beyond the car park, the ship was beginning to embark large number of alien soldiers. *Looks like they might be going,* he thought, before his mind wandered back to the fire hydrant cover.

The sound of disturbed rubble close by caused him to nervously glance that way, it was Woods again. He opened his mouth to speak but was beaten to it by Gary.

"Woods give me a hand with this will you?" He said, jumping down and indicating the yellow fire hose.

"Thir," said Woods, his features showing bewilderment. He hadn't the slightest idea what Gary was on about.

Gary sighed. "Look, I watched a programme about fire hoses once. These are really powerful."

Woods still looked blank.

"Think of a water cannon," he suggested hopefully, plucking the thought out of the air.

Woods brain suddenly clicked into gear. "Yeth thir," he said realising that Gary could actually be onto something. Impressed with the irritating office worker, he almost saluted.

The two men bent over and began removing debris. When sufficiently clear, they took hold of it and attempted to lift it clear. It was actually much larger than they expected and both were more than surprised by the weight. Without a word they clambered down the mound of rubble, Gary stumbled a couple of times but managed to regain his balance without spilling their load.

The sound of mayhem on the other side of the wall continued, albeit more subdued but they struggled on until finally, they reached the remains of the gatehouse entrance where they set it down. Gary looked puzzled as he played nervously with the fraying edge of his yellow star fleet captain's shirt.

"How are we going to get it past that?" he said, suggesting the battle that raged on the other side of the building. Woods as usual showed no sign of concern, he did stay silent however, as though deep in thought.

Gary reached into his trouser pocket and unexpectedly retrieved a couple of the plastic bags filled with paint, surprised that they were still intact. A further inspection revealed that one had in fact split, the goo running down his fingers.

The battle dragged on as the Desirion's, sensing defeat, boarded their troops upon the *Nerax* with increasing alacrity. Not an easy feat as most were engaged either in fighting, hiding, running or dying.

Parkin's men had advanced upon the ruined lines and attacked until the whole formation broke up, fleeing in any direction they could. Sensing final victory he pursued, until from nowhere, came face to face with the familiar features of Lieutenant Havelock. The Marines, fresh from their destruction of the ship on the eastern side of Beeston had regrouped, tending to their injured before once more setting off to pursue the fight, ultimately ending up on the alien's right flank.

The combined force of Royal Marines and Para's, as well as the attached Royal Engineers along with a further four squads slowly pushed back the only large body of aliens left on the field, the vast majority of which no longer had the stomach for a fight.

Woods had finished processing his thoughts and had come up with precisely nothing. Gary also came to the same conclusion but without the pauses and contemplation, and so together they decided the easiest course of action would be to just hump the hose through the gate and towards the hydrant. Remembering the paint bombs he had found, he searched his pocket during another pause in their transporting, finding them he launched them as hard as he could into the nearest group of panicking aliens. He watched their flight and trajectory until almost lost in the mad throng.

The tiring humping and ever present danger from the aliens, no more than a stone or paint bomb throw away, was causing Gary to lose heart with his idea of using the hose. He opened his mouth to voice as much but Woods had resumed lifting and

Gary felt compelled to assist. Grabbing hold of one side the two staggered up and over rubble; thus far unscathed and undetected they eventually reached the hydrant cover. The fact that they achieved this feat not only intact, but unnoticed was a minor miracle, bearing in mind Gary stood out like a sore thumb with added extra fluorescent effect in his bright yellow star ship captains jersey, carrying a bright yellow coiled up rubber fire hose.

Rounding the corner of the base of the gatehouses they saw Sergeant Hornby and Langhorne still more or less in the same position as before. They were now in the process of firing sharpened wooden arrows from the small children's wooden bows. The effect was negligible but it kept their minds occupied since the alien weapons they were using had now completely discharged and were useless.

"Sergeant," said a sweating Gary as he and Woods deposited the hose beside the two Marines within their place of concealment.

Hornby and Langhorne stared at Woods and Gary incredulously. They then stared at the ship and the dwindling numbers of aliens before it. With equally unfathomable stares they turned their attention to the fire hose.

"What are you doing?" asked Hornby in slow deliberate tones; Gary was oblivious to his questions as he was in the process of unwinding the hose reel, with Woods firmly attached to the other end.

"Spam, what..." said Hornby before Gary cut him short.

"We're going to turn this on the aliens," Gary said.

Hornby rolled his eyes.

"Actually Sarge," said Langhorne, "that's not a bad idea. Those things are really powerful, can easily knock a man down and gotta be better than these," he finished holding aloft the pathetic flimsy wooden weapon.

Gary raised a secret smile, one of pure sweet satisfaction, even affording himself an inward chuckle. To any observer this just made him look as though he was struggling for breath.

"Right thath it," said Woods. "The connecthion point ith jutht over there," he continued, his arm hanging in the air as it loosely pointed to the other side of Hornby and Langhorne's place of concealment.

"I'll take it said Gary," still floating on the cusp of his good idea.

Hornby and Langhorne took charge of Gary and Woods discarded energy guns while the two civilians moved out into the open in order to connect the hose. The two Marines trained their newly acquired weapons towards the throng of aliens, the number of which was now much, much less, in fact the sound of battle had died down considerably.

"We'll cover you with these," said Hornby, appearing to have warmed to the idea after Langhorne's appraisal.

With a quick look to one side, then the other, Gary darted forward, breaking cover, safe in the knowledge that he was concealed when in fact his whole torso was still completely visible.

"Just move it," shouted Hornby on noticing Gary hesitate.

Once more he ran forward holding the hoses nozzle while Woods brought up the rear with the connector. The two heroic figures reached the hydrant cover. Gary, ducking down low, holding the hose while he watched Woods quickly clear away the small amount of debris covering it. Grasping at the edges he was unable at first to get a grip, however he soon resorted to his trusty Kukri, quickly prising the cover up with slow grating movements until it came free. Inside, the hydrants connector shone silver.

"A new one," he noted to himself as he faced up the two ends before screwing it on. That done he signalled to his companion. Gary gave the thumbs up and Woods reached for the stop Cock.

LVIII

Lieutenant James Havelock was at the head of his squad of men, leading by example and ever onwards toward the next fight. The main body of resistance from the aliens had virtually disintegrated, most of whom were simply running away in any direction, while the rest, those that hadn't been shot were surrendering.

Parkin's men had once more flanked the ship, this time meeting little or no resistance. In the process of deploying they had managed to manoeuvre the remaining Desirion's into the jaws of a pincer movement.

"They can't last much longer," Havelock remarked to Corporal Clarkson, who was keeping pace with his officer. "They can't number too many now either," he added.

"I seriously hope not," said Clarkson, "we're running low on ammunition."

That much was true. The prospect of picking up any number of discarded alien guns was open to them but almost to a man the Marines preferred their own nice, homely, human made rifles. Clarkson didn't look comfortable, his face showed pain, his mind focused upon controlling the fire pulsing through his arm, the result of receiving the niggling edge of an energy bolt. Cautiously, they approached the ship. All signs of resistance had completely disappeared, in fact there was very little gunfire audible from anywhere, and then out of the blue it happened.

The entire body of Desirion's began to lay down their arms. One after the other as if an order had swept through them. They simply stopped whatever they were engaged in and put their weapons on the ground.

Not trusting the situation, Havelock ordered his men to begin rounding up those visible and stockpiling their weapons, never once did he stop looking at the ship and it's silent but fearsome guns, knowing all the time that it could open fire at any moment.

To his right he heard very clearly, the words, "right you bastards cop this." A quick glance in that direction and Havelock's face took on a look of amazement, as if he'd seen a ghost. It was no ghost. It was Gary Spam holding... "What the bloody hell is he holding?" Havelock gasped.

Gary saw the Marines officer at the last moment and was almost compelled to give him a wave as if he were a long lost friend.

"Okay ith on thir," Woods shouted, "here it cometh."

Gary stood poised with the hose firmly gripped in both hands, expectant of the powerful flow. Grinning from ear to ear he looked for all intents and purposes as though he was about to give a garden a good drenching. He also noticed that the aliens were in the process of something different, never once did it register that they were actually surrendering, besides, his mind was so mixed with emotion and excitement that it probably would never have made any difference anyway.

The hose gurgled and spluttered as long trapped air was forced from its long winding coils. It spluttered some more before spectacularly, nothing happened. Gary shook it, hoping the movement would release the blockage or something. He was even tempted to take a quick peek down the nozzle. His smile returned, *huh not going to get me with that one,* he thought...

More gurgles, stronger this time, assured him that water was finally on the way, "now you ugly little..."

"NO SPAM, NO!" Havelock shouted, his plea coinciding with the force of water spewing forth from the hose, which unfortunately drowned the words out.

Gary's face showed that same determination it always displayed when he was serious about something. The same perseverance he adopted when sat around the table with Nigel and Keith as they put the universe to rights with the aid of nothing more than a number of different shaped dice, a pen and paper and some exquisitely detailed star ship models. As of then, his brow deepened with just the tip of his tongue poking through the left hand corner of his mouth.

The hose bucked in his hands once more before Gary was lifted bodily from the ground. "Arrgghh," he screamed as he crashed back down to Earth. Next he was thrown sideways as he clung desperately onto the wildly flaying hose. Water rocketed into the air soaking the already miserable aliens as well as Lieutenant's Parkin and Havelock, not to mention a good number of men.

"Wooooodddsss, heeelllppp," Gary squealed as the grounded hose dragged him from side to side, colliding with pieces of rubble. The movement created a rough snow angel effect upon the dusty ground.

Woods, grasping the enormity of the situation pounced at the writhing Gary but his cohort moved too quickly. Changing tack, he made for the bucking yellow tube, but as he made a grab it made an involuntary backward sweep and promptly slammed into him, taking his legs away.

Upon the *Nerax*, a door outline fizzed into existence and parted.

Parkin, the first officer to wrench his astonished attention from the incident, opened his mouth to issue an order but was subsequently beaten to it by his own and Havelock's men as they attentively trained rifles upon the opening. Security was made that much more complete and the atmosphere more comfortable by the arrival of a human controlled, Desirion mobile gun. Arriving under its own power suggested that the men in white coats must have at last managed to crack the propulsion system problem. Smoothly, it bumped over the not too uneven terrain before efficiently swivelling the menacing gun to cover the newly opened entrance to the ship.

From the confines inside the doorway, blue light cast shadows from at least three approaching figures. Emerging into daylight, they were dressed differently to the many soldiers, all of whom were coming to terms with yet another defeat, their attitude, a mix of dejection and elation. The flowing robes of the new comers caught the breeze and began to flap gracefully; as they did Havelock noticed the scripture running down the length of one arm. He had in fact noticed this before, but compared to those occasions, these guys had enough material for an essay. Thankfully there were no weapons in sight; all had their arms raised slightly. Regardless, the soldiers were taking no chances, as each was aware that although the aliens had appeared to surrender, they were still vastly outnumbered.

Woods had managed to grapple his way, hand over hand, along the length of the hose and was now desperately holding onto the nozzle with Gary. Even with both of them holding it, the hose bucked and kicked viciously.

"Turn it off, turn it off," shouted Woods to anyone in ear shot, which just happened to be everybody.

Commander Zex exited his ship forlornly and was immediately drawn to the bizarre goings on concerning two humans and a long yellow pipe. The thought ran through his mind as to how on Shard this armada had been beaten by this ridiculous race.

Soaking wet, Havelock and Parkin stepped forward and stood in front of the emerging alien Commander. Both had drawn their own personal side arms, but with barrel pointing at the ground for fear of reigniting the situation.

The din from the fiasco with the hose had died, Hornby having had the sense to turn the cock and switch off the supply. Gary and Woods lay next to it somewhat bruised, battered and soaked to the skin.

Zex offered a very low bow to the two officers as did the other two Desirion's behind him.

Havelock was puzzled, should he return it? Parkin offered the solution when he stood to attention and simply saluted, Havelock followed suit.

The alien stood upright again, took a step forward and held two impossibly long arms out in front. Opening its mouth, a guttural speech, quite audible and understandable said, "Hooomanns." A pause. "I la down ar arms, we fight no longar."

As if to signify, the two other Desirion's wearing robes moved to the front, flanked Zex and offered Havelock and Parkin a large metal stick and an energy gun. What they were supposed to signify was anybody's guess but they took them all the same. They were then invited aboard the battleship, however, the offer was refused until a sufficient number of reinforcements had arrived to secure the situation, not to mention an officer of high enough status to take charge of the situation and relieve the pressure from the five Lieutenant's now there.

The brigade of infantry duly arrived, as upon Rowton Moor, after the battle with the parliament army had fizzled out. Brigadier Richard Hodsworth, commanding phase one of operation Flusher, officially took over proceedings and within a matter of just an hour the whole area beneath Beeston castle was a mass of military figures of one sort or another.

Gary and Woods had dried somewhat by the time they were awaiting to be transported back to Chester.

"We are still awaiting your bus sir," said a very patient corporal armed with a clipboard, he didn't look at all comfortable with his task. "It's going to take a while to get things sorted," he continued, his mind really on other more important things.

The two had decided against an all out argument with the soldier and in the end chose to kill the time by taking the short walk to the top of Beeston castle or rather what remained of it. After traversing the steep slope they shared a few moments to reflect. There were dead Desirion's littering the floor, although they were now in the process of being lined up for removal. Woods bent down and picked one of the wooden arrows he had personally carved into a point, Gary watched him.

"My god Woods," he said. "Just a few short hours ago we were on this same spot, fighting for our very lives."

"Yeh, who would have thought we would be here and now in entirely different thircumthanceth?" Woods replied.

Crossing the steep arched bridge which miraculously still spanned the deep chasm, they entered the castles inner bailey and what a dreadful mess it was. Large chunks of the already ruined castle walls had simply gone, vanished over the side while the ground had been churned into a shocking state, thanks largely to air strikes and artillery bombardments.

"Is that really it, is it all over?" Gary asked, smoothing the tatters of his star fleet uniform.

Woods looked to the sky, "I don't know thir, thomewhere out there beyond our imaginathion are worlds..." Woods suddenly stopped, they had reached the edge. It never used to be the edge.

When the *Luxera* had left, it had taken out a large chunk of the castles northern wall and the natural rock below it. In fact very little on that side remained at all, only in the corners where it met the east and west walls. The two stepped forward and very cautiously peered over the edge. The sight was nothing short of spectacular, very disturbing and rather sad all at the same time. Far out across the field, the burnt out remains of a number of large alien space ships could be seen, still smoking heavily. The shell of a nearby farm and buildings could also be seen smouldering. Intermixed were many hundreds of human soldiers, moving around and looking very small from this height, each one busily going about their respective duty. Also visible were many abandoned alien vehicles, war machines and transports alike.

Saddest of all, and more or less everywhere you looked were the dead Desirion's.

"There must be hundreds of them," said Gary. A further jocular thought occurred that Woods was probably attributable for most of them.

In the distance far away in the direction of Chester, smoke could be seen billowing, forming very high up into a dark grey smear upon the otherwise clear sky. This, unbeknown to them at present was the damage and subsequent destruction caused by Pox's ship when it reached Cheshire's principal city, its own ruined shell contributing considerably to the cloud.

Gary stood, a tear forming in his eye. Presently he peered down into the huge vent carved from the north face when it had given way. "What's that?" He said to Woods, his eye catching something not quite right about the scene.

Woods peered into the depths, attempting to follow Gary's finger.

In the rock was a deep narrow shaft. At first it looked unordinary but on closer inspection it was evident that it was actually lined with brickwork.

"It lookth like a well," said Woods.

"It must have been revealed when the blast destroyed the cliff face," added Gary, "but what's that at the bottom?"

The channel was indeed an ancient well, opened to the elements for the first time in many hundreds of years. At the bottom, approximately fifty feet below, appeared to be what looked like a large wooden box, half covered in mud and silt. Scattered around it were a number of small shiny objects.

"I think it's a chest," said Gary excitedly, his mind plunging into a world of Pirates and buried treasure.

"I think we can get down," said Woods, equally excited and already beginning the descent. He made the passage rather easily in the end thanks to the way the rock had given way to form a very handy staircase effect. After a few moments he returned, his face a picture of enlightenment. Digging a hand deep into his trouser pocket it quickly re-emerged. Opening it revealed a palm covered in coins.

Gary grabbed Woods hand, "Jesus!" he said.

"They're really old," remarked Woods.

The coins, a mixture of gold and silver depicted impressions of various objects. Some displayed Medieval style boats, some, the head of a person, presumably a king, or so the crown on the head hinted. Around the edges were inscriptions, probably in Latin or some other ancient language. One thing was for certain, they were very old.

"Woods," said Gary carefully, his eyes glinting. "I think we've hit the jackpot."

LIX

With the Desirion surrender came jubilation. Party's on a scale not seen since the end of World war two reverberated throughout the country, particularly in Cheshire, but Along with celebration, a whole new cluster of headaches announced themselves. First and foremost was the immense task involved in the clear up operation. The vast majority of alien technology, intact or in pieces, had to be cleared from where it had been left. True, it was an unprecedented opportunity to assimilate some of the alien technology, of which Great Britain had first dibs upon. A sure fire guarantee to fill this country's enemies with a considerable amount of anxiety for many generations to come, unless of course the present and future Governments should continue to adopt its usual stance by selling to the first bidder who should come along.

The damage caused to Chester was considerable, nothing on the scale of wartime devastation but bad enough. Not so the villages of Waverton, Christleton and Rowton. They had more or less ceased to exist while the sprawling estate of Blacon had a large Alien spaceship inserted into it. Even if a grand rebuilding scheme was agreed upon, the huge problem of the dead interfaced army still lay upon Rowton Moor and its surroundings, not to mention the few who had wandered from the battlefield only to die elsewhere. The literally untouchable bodies were simply left to rot where they fell. Not a pretty site, especially in the case of Rowton Moor, many, many thousands of dead aliens slowly decomposing. At least they gave off no smell thanks to their inter-dimensional state. Just as well, although complaints from the spectral world regarding nauseating odours were already coming in thick and fast via the worlds psychic mediums.

Finally the only plan of action that was feasible was to simply bury the corpses with thousands of tons of earth, which also meant burying parts of Christleton, Waverton and Rowton.

LX

The English Heritage inspector surveyed the damage to Beeston castle. Sad at the destruction caused to such a valuable and irreplaceable example of English Historical architecture, especially as the vast majority of it had been caused by human counter attacks. Despite this, a wry smile managed to escape from her upturned mouth.

Entering the inner bailey she stopped and scanned the northern face of the structure, a considerable amount of activity was taking place. A temporary A-frame crane had been set up on the edge and as she approached another small bucket full of coins was brought to the summit. Those hauling the bucket beamed as they eyed the ancient hoard.

"That's the seventh one so far," said the crane operator as he noticed the Inspector.

On the floor beside sat a large plastic box lined with soft material. Peering in she carefully picked one up, it felt good as she grasped it. This time she broke out into a full one hundred per cent beaming smile, for in their possession they had the long lost treasure of King Richard the second.

LXI

Leo stared through the narrow gap in the partially opened door; the unseasonably warm air made the garden a very pleasant place to be.

On the verge of a bout of cleaning, he paused and stared towards the wooden shed at the far end. A brief flash of remembrance passed through his thoughts, something to do with a strange shiny, floating object some time ago. Dismissing it he began to lick his front paw. Extending the limb out straight his attention was suddenly distracted by movement from the same area he had just been focusing upon.

His still keen eyesight was alert but his ageing feline mind was now more likely to adopt the less physical option and so he reverted back to the outstretched leg and resumed licking. Another flash of movement disturbed him, down towards the back of the shed. With this in mind Leo continued with his ablutions. Changing to the other leg he began to clean with equal preciseness when the frog jumped out from the shed area and onto the concrete path. It scanned the garden with two large unblinking eyes before settling on the cat at the far end. Without a second thought, it leapt contentedly into a large puddle left over from the rain a couple of nights back.

His cleaning finished, part of Leo's mind was in favour of taking up the challenge and chasing the amphibian. Instead, he simply settled down onto the warm patio and curled up as tightly as his body would allow. With a last look he poked out his tongue and flicked it over the tip of his leg before pulling it back into his body. Closing his eyes, he was fast asleep within a matter of seconds.

32209330R00151

Printed in Great Britain
by Amazon